All It Will Take

Geoffrey Robert

First published in 2025 by Geoffrey Robert,
an imprint of Red Piano Limited.

www.geoffreyrobert.com

ISBN 978-1-0670781-0-2 (paperback)
ISBN 978-1-0670781-1-9 (hard cover)
ISBN 978-1-0670781-2-6 (ebook)

For Jasmin & Jade

Also by Geoffrey Robert

The Alo Release
Finding Fabi
The Ghost Shipment

Author's note

This story has been more than four decades in the making.

As a teenager, two books left an imprint on me that never faded: *Animal Farm*, George Orwell's brilliant allegory of the Russian Revolution, and *Watership Down*, Richard Adams' powerful tale of survival, leadership, oppression, and freedom. Somewhere in the space between those two stories, an idea began to take root.

In the early 1980s, I was a young journalist, sitting on top of Table Mountain in Cape Town, looking out across the sea to Robben Island. Nelson Mandela had spent 18 years there, imprisoned for standing against the brutality of apartheid. That was when the seed of this story was truly planted: a story that might blend allegory with emotion, politics with heart.

Mandela would remain behind bars for another decade. And yet, when he walked free, it was without bitterness. He chose peace where there could have been vengeance, offered unity where others might have sown more division. He lit a path forward, one grounded in dignity, compassion, and unshakable moral courage.

He became not just a leader, but a light in the dark standing alongside other towering figures of the last century, like Gandhi and Martin Luther King Jr.

As for me, life moved on. Career. Family. The passing of years. But the story idea never left me. It waited, quietly, for the right moment.

I believe that moment is now. We're living through a time when fear is rising, when people shout past each other instead of listening, and when difference is too often treated as a threat. In the noise and division, Mandela's voice calls us back, to something better, braver, more human. Perhaps it's fitting that a story about rabbits can remind us what humanity can look like at its best.

Rabbits, like people, live between fear and hope. They rely on community, courage, and instinct to survive. As Richard Adams once did, I found in them the ideal mirror for a story about resilience, leadership, and liberation.

Unlike *Watership Down*, which drew its name from a real hill in Hampshire, England, the world of this novel is entirely fictional. But it's rooted in a real place not far to the south: the fields and hedgerows of the River Itchen valley, near the small village of Ovington. I have fond memories of that landscape, and of a quiet pint at the Bush Inn by the river. Those places are part of the story too, in spirit if not in name.

All It Will Take is being published on International Nelson Mandela Day, a day that asks not only that we remember the great man, but that we carry his legacy forward. If this story brings one reader closer to the values he lived by, then it's done what it was meant to do.

Geoffrey Robert, Aotearoa New Zealand, 18 July 2025

PART ONE

THE AWAKENING

1. The eye of evil

IT BEGAN as it would end, with the jerk of a head. Nell reacted instantly. He knew Henry, his father, expected him to follow. What he didn't know, could not at his age even imagine, was where the following would lead. Only later, much later, would he look back on that seemingly innocent gesture as the start of a journey that would force him and every rabbit of his colour into a nightmare beyond belief.

The daystar had dipped behind the poplars as father and son crossed the field towards the top bend. Nell struggled to keep up as they moved through the warren's poorer grazing range. Rabbits in their path made way for Dom Henry*, who slowed only when he neared the trail running alongside the bank.

He rubbed his chin against a stone, motioned to the row of alders. At the end stood an ancient tree, the bottom of its trunk covered in silt built up during floods outside the memory of the warren. Nell was led along a boggy part of the trail winding through the waterside plants. He tilted his ear, winked his nose. There was no danger.

Had he been alone, he would have felt the natural anxiety of a rabbit on unfamiliar ground. Behind Henry, all doubts were cast aside, and Nell couldn't resist taking exaggerated leaps to land in the larger paw-prints of his father. He was in mid-air when the older rabbit stopped suddenly. Nell managed somehow to swivel his hindquarters and drive

---

* Dom is short for the dominant rabbit, or leader, of a warren. It is usually a buck, but not always, as we shall see.

his left foreleg downwards. He landed, like a leaf, less than a paw from his father's tail.

If the older rabbit was aware of what had gone on behind him, he didn't let on. Rising silently, he looked up at the tree. The gnarled trunk divided into three sturdy branches. Moss clung to the bark, which was almost black, and wore the weathered ridges of age. It wasn't until Nell let his eyes slide down the trunk that he noticed the claw marks etched into the ground. Fresh prints. At least two lots. Some crossed over others, so there could be as many as four. He had a hunch what animals had made them, but the slope had distorted the markings enough to put doubt in his mind.

'Come,' said Henry in a tone that confirmed Nell's guess was right. The prints belonged to rabbits.

Nell scampered up, losing his grip in the slippery soil, before joining his father on the lip of a large hollow formed at the base of the trunk. Three faces greeted them, and Nell was immediately conscious of the mud sticking to his chest. How embarrassing to be seen in such a state.

The nearest face belonged to a buck, slightly larger than the others, with a crumpled face and bald chin. His fur was a similar shade to Henry's, though heavily mottled, and it hung more loosely over his cheekbones. Not a speck of mud on it.

Sitting upright at the far end was a rabbit of perhaps thirty moons, his chin matted yellow. Powerful shoulders and neck. Pitch-black fur, the darkest Nell had seen. Wedged between the two was a lighter-coloured buck with the sort of middling, featureless face easily forgotten, but whose oversized hindquarters suggested he could race the wind. All three carried the scars of life on the brink. A whiff of digested watermint showed at least one had been eating beside the rindle flowing silently beneath the alder's stretching limbs. Mother would have been able to figure out exactly where each lived. What they ate, where they fed, where they'd been. All with one wink of her nose.

As the rabbits shuffled to make room, Nell saw this was no chance meeting. The trio had been expecting Henry, were waiting for him to speak. The dom introduced his circle of stewards to his son. Nell was relieved they were more interested in his forehead than the mess on his chest. He couldn't help thinking how strong the stewards appeared alongside his father. Yet they respected the dom in a way Nell found puzzling. Until he looked closer.

No single feature set Henry apart. There were the unhurried, yet precise movements. Relaxed shoulders. The certainty flirting with stubbornness in the subtle crinkling of the brow. The wisdom in those brown eyes that saw more than was in front of them. And the steady, confident voice now interrupting Nell's thoughts...

'As you have no doubt heard, a member of our warren was caught past the forbidden line last night. Claims he was looking for sorrel for his mother's fever, but found nothing more than the claw of the governor's son.'

All three bucks nodded. Bad news spread like dandelion seeds.

'We expect,' Henry continued, 'to be called by dayspring to explain the rule-breaking. We'd appreciate your advice.'

Nell had never heard his father say *I*. It was always *we* think, *we* believe, *we* expect. Nell had been teased about it by other kittens, until his mother explained it was something passed down from Henry's ancestors. The next kitten to tease Nell about the way the dom spoke was the last.

There were no sniggers in the alder. The oldest steward glanced at Nell.

'Ignorance of the rules is no excuse, as we've learnt to our loss many times. There's no mystery to it, no grey area of doubt. We can graze to a line from the last alder to the top of the hazel fork. The rest of that side of the field is for white rabbits. It's the rule. Black and white. Simple. Hop over the line, suffer the consequences. And unless we make an example of the buck, he or some other bonehead will do it again.'

The second buck also looked at Nell, as if seeking permission.

'None of us like these rules,' he whispered, peering up at the tree's foliage as if the leaves were ears. 'But what can we do? Without rules we'd have chaos. Perhaps that's something we have the whites to thank for. The sooner we learn to accept our place in life and get on living it, the better off we'll be. I agree an example needs to be made, not only of the buck. The mother is as much to blame for putting him up to it. If there's an example to be made here, she'd be at the top of my...'

'She's passed into the field of silence.'

Henry's blunt announcement stopped the buck in mid-sentence. A gagging stillness gripped the hollow, amplifying the trickling of the rindle into a rhythmic taunt. A cough from the third rabbit cracked the silence.

'You have to think of the whole warren here, Henry,' he said, half rising, half crouching.

'I feel for the buck, understand why he did it. Sometimes wish *I* had the spine to take on Governor Vort. But unless we make an example of the young rabbit, strong enough to satisfy Vort, we'll all suffer. Who knows what he'll do? He could extend their range further, forcing us over the rindle.'

He looked sideways at his companions, then faced Henry.

'I don't see you have any choice but to turf him out.'

Nell choked.

No-one noticed.

'Ignorance of the rules,' Dom Henry began in a measured tone, 'is not the issue here. The youngster might have been ignorant of the risks, but he knew exactly where he was, that he'd crossed the line.'

Henry paused, then faced the second steward.

'You talk of accepting our place. What though is our place? Beneath the paws of the whites, our whiskers pressed to the mud? That may be comfortable enough for some of us, but our ancestors knew a different *place*. And I'm not talking about the ground where we dig our burrows. I'm talking about a place of respect.'

Nell listened carefully. Some of what they were saying meant little, though he could tell from the grim expressions the matters were serious.

He felt the eyes of the three rabbits on him, and turned to see Henry also staring at his forehead. When the dom resumed, Nell noticed the faintest shudder in his voice.

'The dream that our warren will one day return to the rightful place of our ancestors is what, until tonight, has kept this tired heart pumping.'

Until tonight. They were more than words, and they hung in the air from some invisible web suspended between father and son. Voiced less through the mouth than the eyes, filling Nell with a mixture of awe and fright.

The moment passed. Henry rubbed a paw over his ear.

'Choices. The buck had a choice. He could have stayed home, watched his mother pass. Or he could have tried to do something about it. Might have got away with it. She might have passed anyway. He put his mother's life ahead of his own. She made the ultimate sacrifice. You now want the same outcome for her son?'

No reply was expected.

'Choices.' Henry tossed the word back into the faces of his stewards.

'Life is all about choices. We face them every night, every moon. We choose whether to feed in the rain or go hungry in the hope the next night will be dry. If it rains again we have fewer choices, and they become more painful, though most of us could survive a second night without eating. It is only when we face the likelihood of starving, we run out of choices. Once we stop making choices, we give up on life.'

'That may be so,' said the dark buck with the matted chin, puffing out his chest and stretching his ears to appear larger, more important. There was also a new harshness in his voice.

'I'll give you another *C* word. Consequence. I take it from your little speech, Henry, you're thinking of challenging the say-so of the governor. Don't forget choices have consequences.'

His companions fidgeted, neither sure whether to look at Henry or the speaker.

Both chose a nowhere point on the ground as the younger buck went on, his face still fixed on Nell.

'We've all heard the rumours about the white supremacists. Their dream of driving all black rabbits from this side of the Torrent. I see nothing but misery coming from taking on the whites.'

He spun to face Henry, spitting his challenge through gritted teeth.

'Are you prepared to put the entire warren at risk because of the foolishness of one?'

The dom never got to answer.

*****

'HENRY! Get your varlet[*] backside out here.'

That shut them up. Levi had smelt them before he heard them. Up in a tree like frightened dunnocks, as father said they'd be. The wizened face of the varlet dom appeared, dragging a grimy frame of skin and bones. Riddled with fleas, for sure.

Levi didn't want to get closer.

'The governor wants to see you.'

'Does he now?,' replied Henry.

Levi swivelled to leave. Let it follow, he thought, wondering how far a flea could jump. He started along the trail, then looked behind to check the gap.

The scrawny dom was skulking back into the tree.

Five powerful bounds and Levi was at the entrance. The pong hit him. Sweat and dirt and filth. Varlet wind, father called it.

'That was an order, not a request.'

There were four of the disgusting varlets. Four and a half, if you counted the runt. Three trembled against the wall of the rat-hole. The old dom and the runt had the nerve to stand their ground, ears flat against their backs.

'If the governor wants to see us,' said the dom, 'we're sure he'll manage to find us.'

Levi couldn't believe it. He turned his good ear to the dom, and scowled. The varlet fool didn't flinch. Levi dug his hind paws into the ground, ready to pounce.

The snivellers lowered their noses to the soil, braced for his strike. The dom, though, showed no fear.

The air became tight, sticky, as Levi fought to control himself. As he hesitated, he became aware of a slight change in the attitude of the three, who appeared to grow in size. Only a whisker, but enough to tell him he was outnumbered.

He could take two, three at a pinch. Four were too many this night.

'You'll suffer for this,' he hissed.

His eyes roved, leering at each of the varlets, before fixing on the cocky runt with its nose in the air.

---

[*] Varlet is an offensive term for a rabbit with black fur.

NELL'S EYES were being drawn towards those of the white rabbit. He was aware of the sharp, earthy scents of hazelnut, saliva, and a flawless coat shimmering in the moonlight as the intruder swaggered forward until the two youngsters were face-to-face.

Sound, time, stood still.

Though his eyes were screaming for relief, Nell refused to blink. Slowly his view was sucked into the pupil of the rabbit's right eye. As he stared deep into that place of innermost secrets, he saw… hate. And something else.

Before everything went dark.

2. A world upended

NELL HAD BEEN CONCENTRATING so intensely on the white rabbit, he hadn't noticed him scoop a pile of soil in his claw. One lightning swat sent fine grains tearing into Nell's searching eyes. When he was able to squint them open again, the rude buck had gone.

The hollow remained numb for a long while. Nell, afraid to disturb the calm, licked his paws and quietly cleaned his chest. Only a murmur of pink lingered where the daystar had fallen when Henry declared by his movement the meeting was over. He led his son down the mound.

Nell wasn't sure if he should feel proud or terrified. Last night he would happily have gone anywhere with his father. Henry was unbreakable, never-ending. All-powerful. Nell had stopped worrying about carns*, such was his faith in the dom's ability to sense trouble. Now he saw a worn-out rabbit. Once powerful hind legs stumbled, shoulders sagged. The field that had until then been the safe haven at the heart of Nell's world was suddenly a wild place. Clefts appeared in the hedgerows. The hawthorn fragrance had soured. Unseen creatures watched from the grim places untouched by light from the fattening crescent moon.

They shadowed the rindle upstream, Henry looking for food as they went. Nell's thoughts were somewhere else, with his appetite.

'Who *was* that rabbit?'

'His name's Levi.'

---

* Carns are the natural enemies of rabbits; meat-eaters such as foxes, stoats, weasels, owls and other birds of prey.

'He's enormous.'

'He'll get bigger yet. He's the same age as you and your sisters. Born the same moon.'

'Who does he think he is, talking to you like that?'

'It wasn't *him*, Nell. He was merely repeating the words of his father, our glorious governor. Levi wouldn't fart unless he was told to.'

They both laughed. Nell relaxed a little, but Henry's expression became serious again.

'What did you think of our meeting, son?'

Nell had so many questions.

'What's a supremacist?'

'It means different things to different rabbits. The supremacists they were talking about think they know everything, that their extreme view of the world is right and all others are wrong. Some of them are prepared to do anything to prove it.'

'What do they look like?'

'Like us.'

'You mean they're rabbits?'

'Afraid so.'

'What colour?'

'The ones they were talking about are white. But any rabbit can have extreme views.'

'Could *you*?'

Henry smiled, the way he often did when Nell was pestering him with questions.

'We could, but we don't. Some rabbits, though, would say your mother is a bit extreme the way she goes on about her healing plants.'

Nell couldn't imagine his mother wanting to chase rabbits of any colour from this side of the Torrent, whatever that was.

'There's nothing wrong in believing strongly about something, son. It can be a good thing.'

'Like the buck who tried to get sorrel for his mother's fever? Is he one of the supremacists?'

Henry looked back the way they'd come. Nell caught in his face a sorrow he'd never seen.

'No son. He is a world away from a supremacist. What he did was extreme. But he was thinking of his mother, not himself. And he wasn't trying to hurt anyone. The trouble with supremacists is not only their narrow minds. They have no time for rabbits who disagree with them.'

They nibbled at stems of foxtail, all the time moving upstream. Nell was digesting more words than grass.

'Those stewards. They looked at me as if *I* was the dom, not you.'

'Perhaps they're smarter than...'

'They seemed, the first two, to be waiting for me to tell them they could speak...'

'We suspect they were.'

'...the other one, the rude one, was angry at me.'

'Not angry, son. Jealous maybe. He fancies his chances of taking over the warren once we're gone. Sees you as a threat.'

'That's crazy.'

Henry dropped his voice.

'It's strange how we can live a full life, be respected by other rabbits, yet never be guided enough by the voice inside our head telling us what is right and what is wrong – our conscience. All the time, not only when it suits us. We suppose these are the things rabbits start worrying about when they near the end. The actions of that young rabbit who tried to help his mother have made us rethink… everything.'

The soft breeze had shifted more to the west as Nell and Henry got to the first willow. They nibbled at the spiky leaves on a branch that had fallen to the ground. It was Henry who stopped eating first.

'The white rabbits,' he said, 'get away with what they do because we choose to let them. We do as they say, and they take our silence as acceptance. As long as we let them, they'll keep tormenting us. Things will get worse rather than better. Perhaps we have only ourselves to blame for our *place* in life.'

The dom's voice got louder, as though he no longer cared who heard him. Nell felt he was being spoken to not as a kitten. As an equal.

'Can't you see what the white rabbits are doing? As they unite and channel their energies and strengths, they've split us up and cut us off from our neighbours. Like blocking the main passages of a burrow. And worse than the physical barriers, they've broken our spirit.'

Nell began to ask a question, but was cut short.

'You know who the real hero is here, son? The rabbit who tried to get sorrel for his mother. He showed courage. Showed us that in matters of life and passing, no action can be too extreme. That sitting quietly on your backside in the face of injustice is nothing to be proud of.'

The breeze that had been filtering through the leaves fell away as if the night was taking a breath. There was no exhaling. The air became heavy, almost stagnant. When Henry continued, the voice was drained. For the first time in Nell's life, he heard his father use the *I* word.

'I've been dom of this warren for how many moons? If you asked all the bucks, and the does, most would find good things to say about me. I deserve none of it. I see now I have failed them, failed *you*, where it matters.'

A single tear appeared at the corner of his eye.

'There are times, son, when a dom must listen to the voice inside his head and hop out in front of the warren. Lead it to a better place, even if it means he can't take the journey with them. Indeed, he must welcome the worst, because any outcome will then be satisfying.'

Henry peered up the slope in the direction of the governor's rowan.

'It's time to face a truth I've been avoiding for too long.'

*****

LEVI HOPPED through the main entrance and along the southern hall to the crossing under the trunk of the rowan. He entered the upper living chamber opposite the food storage burrow. Two days earlier, the family had shifted up from the deep living chamber used during the cooler moons. It would remain empty until leaf-fall.

Mother was alone, though Levi hardly noticed her through the heavy odour of the governor crowding the chamber. It was lighter up here, and as Levi's vision adjusted, he saw his mother was dozing.

'Where's father?'

She yawned.

'You stink. Where have you been?'

'Getting the varlet dom.'

Vort's voice rumbled through the passage.

'Bring Henry in here.'

Levi hopped uncertainly into his father's chamber.

'It's... I'm not sure, sir. It wouldn't come.'

'Why didn't you make it?'

'There were six, seven of them, sir. The dom said if you wanted it…
you'd know where to find it.'

Vort groaned and stood.

'Can I come with you, sir?'

'I suppose. You might learn something.'

Levi followed his father into the southern den. The guard bowed as
they emerged into the night. Vort cleaned the dust from his chest, then
strode off into the field. Power oozed as he glided past the top alder.
A few bounds behind, Levi tried to copy the don't-mess-with-me
confidence of his father. The alert eyes scanning. Large ears registering
every sound. The flickering nose detecting every smell.

Vort stopped beside the stump of an elm. He screwed up his nose,
then bent to scratch his chin against the bark, releasing a pungent scent
into the night. Levi tried to copy him, but his chin glands were not yet
fully developed, and nothing came out. He pissed on the stump
instead, then chased after his father.

Heart thumping, Levi guessed they were aiming for the sagging
crowns of the willows in the corner of the field. He sped up to pass his
father. A cuff on his ear sent him sprawling.

'Never move ahead of me again,' growled Vort, towering over him.

'Sorry, sir.'

Levi expected to be hit again, but Vort's face relaxed.

'You've got a lot to learn, son. Discipline. And respect. Respect for
your betters. *Knowing* your place. These varlets do. Most of them. Most
of the time. Sometimes they get cheeky, so you give them a thrashing.
They don't complain because they know it's for their own good. The
black rabbit is like a kitten. Now and then it needs to be reminded of
its place. So. Let's find Henry.'

'If its kit's there, can I remind it as well?'

'If you wish. But stay behind me.'

*****

NELL HEARD A COUGH, like the clearing of a throat, from the other side of the rindle. Then, from behind them, the unmistakable crunch of a heavy paw on fallen leaf. He glanced at his father. Henry's coat had lost its shine and was mottled with grey fur. The eyes, normally so steady and bright, were moist.

'One rabbit is all it will take, son. One rabbit to unite us again.'

The dom's voice weakened to a whisper.

'You carry our star, Nell. It's a gift, whether you realise it or not. Others do. They will look to you. Be the one.'

*****

THE SWEET FLOWERS of the campion expand at night, attracting moths that can reach the honey at the end of long narrow tubes. Clusters of the large white flowers also make a good hiding place. Fleet was confident he could not be seen.

From his vantage point in the hedgerow, he had a good view over the rindle to where Henry and his son were talking, and the air was still enough for him to hear almost every word. He could also see the two white rabbits approaching from the field. In the moonlight, the governor's coat shimmered over powerful shoulders and hindquarters suggesting strength rather than speed. He moved effortlessly. This was a rabbit aware of all, afraid of nothing. It crossed Fleet's mind he could warn Henry. A single alarm stamp would do it.

Governor Vort got to the top of the bank. Fleet saw Henry motion for his son to slip behind one of the trees. Vort started speaking from several bounds away.

'You disappoint me, Henry. Of all the varlet parasites infesting our fields, I expected you at least to have a whiff of common sense.'

He kept advancing, and Fleet cringed as the black dom rose defiantly to face the governor.

'If common sense had anything to do with it,' said Henry, 'we'd both be in our grazing patches enjoying the delights of the season, rather than standing here, arguing.'

'Ah, that's where you're wrong, you varlet fool.'

Fleet found the raising and slowing of the governor's voice

distressing. Alarming. Vort circled, his back arched, chin in the air as he sneered down his nose at Henry. The black rabbit stood his ground, claws clenching the soil, ears rotating to track his rival.

'I have every intention of enjoying the rest of the night,' the governor hissed, stepping with astonishing speed up to the face of Henry. 'And no intention of arguing.'

Vort lashed out. The black rabbit was expecting an attack, but his reactions weren't quick enough. A fully extended claw swiped his face, opening a deep slit. The power of the blow lifted Henry off the ground.

As Fleet withdrew further into his hiding place across the rindle, Vort rushed forward. Somehow Henry managed to scramble out of the way. The white rabbit charged again, this time anticipating the dodge. Henry was knocked off balance and howled as sharp teeth sunk into his shoulder.

Fleet winced as he watched Henry wrench free, losing a large chunk of fur. Vort spat it out and pounced again. The two rabbits grappled, aiming bites at each other's neck, and thrashing their hind legs. Dirt and leaves and fur were flung into the air as they rolled in a black and white blur.

They broke off, and Henry hobbled up the bank.

Fleet breathed out, then gulped as the black dom hurtled back, catching Vort off-guard. He leapt onto the governor's back, planting his teeth into the soft skin of the neck. Thick red blood from the gash on Henry's face oozed onto Vort's white fur. The black rabbit hung on as Vort reared and bolted directly at the tree. A heartbeat before impact, the enraged governor twisted violently to one side.

Fleet had to close his eyes.

*****

NELL WAS CLOSE ENOUGH to hear the crunch of bone as his father's body was crushed against the trunk. Close enough to feel the tree shiver, smell the blood, taste the sweat. So close he could see the tiny muscles at the edges of Henry's lips quiver at the beginning of a scream.

No sound came.

Henry's jaw was cracked, though it was the injury to the hind leg that left the dom unable to move and at the mercy of his attacker.

Nell looked at Vort and saw that the fight was over. The governor crouched, stretching one of his hind legs and wincing as spasms of pain shot up his body from tendons ripped in the final savage twist. His fur was speckled with blood and soil, his eyes like dark stones.

Levi, emboldened by his father's victory, blustered towards Nell, snarling and jutting out his chin in a bullying challenge.

'No, son. It won't be necessary,' said Vort, spitting bloodied fur.

'You promised.'

'Come. I'm sure the varlet fool's son has learnt an important lesson here tonight.'

Levi snorted, then fell into step behind the governor. The echo of munched hazelnut clung in the air.

Nell watched them leave, the son mimicking the limp of his father.

3. Two sides to every story

A THIN LAYER of cloud had slipped in front of the dipping moon before Nell got the courage to sidle up to his father. The body lay still, the once noble head slumped on the ground, the mouth gaping silently at the scarlet root of the willow. Ruffled fur dangled from the crippled skeleton. Nell had never felt so alone. He bent to lick at the blood drying on Henry's chin, shuddering at the vile taste.

He didn't recognise the sound at first. There it was again. A wheezing, a faint whistle from the depths of Henry's chest. The dom, his face knotted, tried to rise. Half hopping, half dragging, he lurched forward, the injured leg trailing uselessly behind.

Nell knew then he would get his father home. No matter what. His thoughts darted forwards, over each bound to the burrow. Clumps of reed and loosestrife along the rindle would give some protection, though much of the route was exposed.

At the first sign of a carn, he'd have to distract the hunter away from his injured father. He would hightail, fall over, pretend to limp. On his front leg. On that side.

The dom stumbled forward and collapsed again.

Nell's ears, nose, eyes scanned furiously while he waited for Henry to regain his breath. As soon as the old rabbit tried again, Nell was beside him, nudging, encouraging. A groan, a stagger, and the dom would collapse in a panting, drooling heap. Nell checked the ground downwind and the sky, prepared to bolt.

Luck, if little else, was on their side. They had almost reached the combe when Nell saw Maisy, his mother, hurrying to meet them.

'Cress,' she whispered, after sniffing her mate. 'Be sure to take it from running water.'

Nell had seen spikes of the white flowers near the bend. He crept down the slope to the rindle, thinking of his mother's face. How could she be so calm? By the time he returned to the burrow with a bunch of fiery leaves, Maisy had helped Henry below and onto the ledge of his meeting chamber. She thanked Nell for the cress, and asked him to check on his sisters.

All three does were asleep, so Nell crept along the main passage to his own hole. There he crouched, exhausted, concentrating on the sounds and smells from the meeting chamber.

*****

MAISY NOSED the mangled body of Henry, and the calmness she'd tried to show in front of her son dissolved. All the healing plants this side of the downs could do nothing to save her mate.

They could, however, make him more comfortable. And give her something to do rather than worry about what would happen in moons to rise. Rabbits drawn to the burrow by news of the dom's injuries, whether curious bucks or concerned does, were sent to find all manner of plants. Yarrow or shepherd's purse for the bleeding, comfrey for the broken bones, elm bark for the loosened teeth, sow thistle for the unseen injuries within. The most urgent plea was for the soothing plants – hops, sorrel, plantain. Maisy would even risk henbane or foxglove, though could tell from the startled reactions of the does, they would not be brought.

As Henry lurched closer to the field of silence, Maisy was thinking not of passing, but of life. How the dom would live on through his children. *Their* children. And though there were four, her thoughts were on the buck. Of the joy on Henry's face the first time he saw the streak of light fur on his son's forehead.

Extraordinary, was how he'd described it.

'So, you agree?' Maisy had asked.

'Yes. We couldn't name him anything else. He shall be Nell, after his grandfather.'

Henry stirred, and when his eyes opened, Maisy believed she was seeing a miracle. Through the last of the twilight filtering into the meeting chamber, she saw determination reappear on Henry's face. The glazing was gone, as was the stench. The muscles in his cheeks relaxed, and he floated away again, his heartbeat steadier. Maisy dared believe.

*****

NELL COULDN'T SLEEP. The floor of his hole was like cold stone. Throughout the night he was tormented by the groaning of his father. From time to time, the shadows of blood and sweat trickling through the passages were pricked by the musky aroma of herb robert, the fragrance of plantain root or other plants delivered to Maisy. The distracting bursts were short-lived. Gradually, the air thickened into the foul taste of decay.

Once, Nell heard the soft voice of Maisy whispering to his sisters. He caught some of what his mother was saying. There were words of encouragement. Did it mean the dom was getting better? Or were the frightened does being soothed with what they wanted to hear?

Two sides to every story, was what Henry had told Nell. It seemed an age since those words were uttered. Incredibly, it was only two nights ago.

Nell had been spending less time with his sisters or mother, and more with his father. The pair had gone above ground early, fed hard, then rested. Nell had been trusted to keep watch as Henry dozed. He took the job seriously. Being treated as an equal gave him a tingling sensation as enjoyable as the late spring warmth.

Nell scanned the horizon in all directions. The trees and hedgerows were filling out. The distant hills were soaked in the delicate late afternoon glow of the daystar, making them appear closer. He noticed Henry wasn't really sleeping. The eyes were shut, though not tightly. The ears were not fully relaxed, and the nostrils twitched at the merest hint of a wind shift. It was the forehead, though, that had grabbed and held Nell's attention. There were one or two wrinkles of age, but not a speck of light fur. He was so absorbed, his father's voice startled him.

'What's troubling you, son?'

'I was thinking of grandfather. How brave he was to show those rabbits the way here.'

'Ha. What's that mother of yours been telling you?'

Nell was surprised at his father's reaction. And curious.

'I can't remember the whole story. It goes something like this: Moons ago, our ancestors lived over the downs. I assume it was those high hills over there behind the trees.'

Henry nodded.

'Things were different then. They ate strange plants, talked funny. Primitive, I think mother said.'

'Did she now?'

'And they'd never seen a rindle, had no idea what it was. Then one day the dom had a vision. Of a magical place, water on one side, fields filled with the sweetest of grasses on the other.'

Henry smiled. Nell went on.

'All the rabbits wanted him to take them to this magical place. But he was too ancient. So grandfather Nell was chosen to take them.'

He paused, giving his father the opportunity to correct him. Henry's smile, broader now, was annoying Nell, but he was almost at the end of the story.

'They traveled, many nights, sheltering in bolt holes the old dom had also seen in his vision. When they got *here*, they found this place waiting for them. Dry burrows, plenty to eat, like in the vision. Grandfather became the new dom.'

Henry chuckled.

'Let us tell you something, son. There are two sides to every story. At least two. And the truth usually lives somewhere in the middle. Here's the story as we know it. No doubt you'll tell a different story to your kittens one day.

'Old Nell had no choice but to come here. At the time, he was second in charge of a warren that had lived behind those downs for generations. They were proud rabbits, with their own language, own customs, their own rules that kept them fed, safe and as happy as rabbits can expect to be.

'Then one day an enormous white rabbit and a pack of bruisers showed up and ordered the entire warren to up and leave. He said there were to be new rules throughout the fields. Black rabbits had to live in certain areas and all the rest was for the whites. The dom refused and was mauled on the spot, in front of his mates and kittens. Your grandfather agreed to lead the warren over the hill to prevent a massacre.'

Nell was shocked.

His father wasn't finished.

'They were hounded by the bruisers, who hustled them to keep going under the daystar and through the nights. The carns – foxes, buzzards, kestrels, owls – feasted. Half the rabbits lucky enough to survive the attacks passed into the field of silence from their injuries or plain fatigue. Some of the old ones who couldn't keep up were dragged off. Never heard of again. When they were allowed to rest, the bruisers took over burrows abandoned by other rabbits already driven out. Old Nell and the others had to take their chances above ground.'

This was unbelievable. How could mother have got it so wrong?

'Your grandfather *did* become dom. You're right about that part. You're also right to be proud of him. There was nothing here when they arrived. He organised burrowing groups, teams to search for unfamiliar food in unexplored fields. Until the burrows were dug, the entire warren was vulnerable to the carns. This was happening all over the countryside.'

Henry stopped talking. He appeared to be staring at something past the line of alders. Nell saw nothing unusual. Only a magpie landing at the top of the rowan.

'You mustn't think badly of your mother, Nell. She wasn't trying to mislead you. Nor is she the only rabbit who prefers her version of the story. Who can blame them? It's got a happier ending than ours.'

Henry's eyes hadn't left the rowan.

'That's the problem with history, son. It's like a piece of bark stripped off a tree that's been chewed by so many rabbits you can't tell what it used to taste like.

'Some rabbits have trouble accepting the taste has gone, or changed. They need reasons, explanations. So, they use their imaginations. When that happens, the bark becomes flavoured with their own desires. Perhaps it's harmless if it helps them feel better. It's also sad.'

Nell's astonishment had given way to curiosity.

'What about you?' he asked.

Henry scratched his chin, as if choosing his words carefully.

'We don't waste much time worrying about the past, son. We're more interested in a living tree than a tasteless chunk of bark. The only history we think about is the history being made as we breathe.'

His eyes went back to the rowan.

'Our family got to choose the burrow we live in today, son, because Old Nell was in charge of the warren. Though he was the dom, it wasn't the best burrow in the field. Not by a thousand bounds. That belonged to the white governor, over there under the rowan. Where his son Vort lives as we speak, still controlling our lives.'

Nell had been shocked by his father's version of the world. Now, as he sat in his hole listening for signs of life from across the passage, he understood that Henry's version was closer to the truth than his mother's.

News of the dom's fight and his injuries had travelled quickly. Throughout the night, Nell was aware of a stream of rabbits arriving at the burrow. He smelt the leaves of plantain, cress and other plants brought by the does, heard words of sympathy from the bucks. The night had been sprinkled with groans and the occasional cough from his father. There had been no sound from the chamber for too many whiles. Just the smell.

Alone in his cold hole, the walls and roof closing in, Nell became desperate for company. He didn't want to disturb Maisy, so shuffled quietly to where his sisters lay shaking. Nudging into their warm huddle, Nell licked their faces, hoping to appear stronger than he felt, hoping they wouldn't sense his guilt. There he lay through the grim whiles of early morning, until the tapping began.

The dom's injuries, Maisy told him later, were too crippling for his tired body, let alone his weary heart. The cracked jaw would allow few of Maisy's healing plants to pass. The loss of blood from the torn artery in his leg had left him weak and confused, triggering a stinking, unquenchable sweat. But it was the broken rib that finished him off. Maisy suspected splinters of bone had pierced his lung, filling it with frothy blood that eventually drowned out his breath.

When the beetle stopped tapping, Nell knew his father had passed alone into the field of silence.

*****

FLEET WOULD HAVE TO WAIT to be sure, before reporting the news. Some of the hasty seers* would have been satisfied with what they'd seen and would rush to tell the world. Fleet was careful. Accurate. Mistakes had been made by not checking, being sure. Two, three, four he was aware of. Mistakes could be embarrassing.

He'd decided Dom Henry's passing would be worth including in his next report on the South Bank. Happenings at the small Willow Warren would not normally be considered important enough. But it was the reason for Henry's passing that was interesting. Newsworthy.

Fleet went over what he'd seen from the shadows. The black dom and his son, deep in discussion. The white governor and his son approaching, stalking, full of bravado. The arrogant language becoming increasingly common this side of the Torrent. Words like *parasite* and *varlet* – rarely uttered in the North.

It was clear there was to be a confrontation. The black rabbits must have done something to annoy Vort. Stepped over a forbidden line, or broken another of the local rules, perhaps. Rules were rules, and violence necessary from time to time to prevent disorder. But did the governor have to be so brutal? He had also chinned after the fight, which was unnecessary. Outrageous that far from his rowan. Vort was a brute. A monster. Fortunately, he was only an outlying governor.

Fleet wondered again if he should have got involved. It would have been easy. He could have warned Henry. His heart told him one thing, his head another. So, he did nothing.

He was saddened at what he'd seen. As a seer, he'd witnessed many fights, though always he'd remained apart, at a distance. This one

---

* Seers are rabbits whose job is to observe happenings and report what they see and hear to other rabbits in their warren. They are similar to human journalists or bloggers.

affected him differently. He felt the pain of the strikes as if it was his body, not Henry's. And what about the efforts the young black buck took to save the dom, to nurse his father back to his burrow? Words came in a flood. Bravery. Tenacity. Determination. Devotion. And loyalty. Such loyalty. This Nell was a rabbit to keep both eyes and ears on.

A trout sliced through the surface of the rindle to snap at a mayfly. A black doe was struggling up to the burrow, carrying a stalk of shepherd's purse. Fleet had watched the comings and goings, eleven counting this one, though this doe was the first visitor for whiles. She was met at the entrance by the dom's mate, and Fleet could tell from her crumpled forehead and empty stare that Henry was in trouble. The visitor dropped the shepherd's purse and left.

Fleet crept towards the water, taking care to stay hidden. Seeing, and not being seen, was the secret to his role. Be seen and you ran the risk of becoming involved, part of the story, and therefore no longer an observer.

No-one must ever know he had seen what he had seen. In his report he would say he *heard* about the fight. Or arrived at the end. Yes, that would do it. A seer couldn't be everywhere. He edged out onto a limb overhanging the rindle. The water formed a pond, still enough to show his reflection. He saw a rabbit, white, average build, ever so slightly overweight. The face was honest. Serious. Perhaps a little too serious. He gazed into the eyes, deep into the eyes. And saw shame.

4. Like moss on a rock

MAISY COULD TELL that Nell was affected deeply by what happened to his father. The young buck had seen the fight, the terrible injuries to Henry, though Maisy realised the root of her son's pain lay deeper than what he'd witnessed. Nell was going through his first grief, always the worst. Only when a rabbit had experienced real sorrow, overcome it, and found fresh hope, was he or she hardened for setbacks in moons to rise.

Nell's behaviour showed Maisy that the anger he'd felt at the way Henry passed into the field of silence had changed to a feeling of abandonment. He withdrew into himself, moping around the burrow, hardly talking, eating only when hunger forced him. Maisy gave her son space, hoping time would heal the hurt inside.

She did her best to reassure the kittens, appearing calm in front of them, speaking with a gentle firmness that showed she had taken control of the crisis. She saw herself as a tree sheltering her family from the buffeting winds of a storm threatening to engulf them.

Ever the practical mother, Maisy also prepared the kittens for the consequences. For as well as losing a father and mate, the family would have to give up the status of a dom. She was grateful it took four nights for a new leader to be decided. When the new dom and his mate arrived to take over the burrow, Nell was showing signs, outward at least, of shaking off his gloom.

Maisy had two offers of holes. One on the poor side of the Willow Warren that had been flooded during the last storm; the other at the warren of a cousin downstream behind the alders. Keen for her offspring to have a fresh start, she chose the latter.

The three does had been dreading the change, and as the time to leave neared, their fears grew. Nell, however, appeared to welcome it.

Early in the evening, Maisy let the buck lead the family along the trail beside the rindle. She noticed how naturally he took the front. The first quarter moon was shining brightly over their shoulders as they reached the alders marking the boundary of the Willow Warren. Nell volunteered to watch for danger as Maisy stretched to pull fresh leaves from the hanging branches.

She had been aware of tawny owls calling in the wood during the last few nights, as male owls setting up boundaries liked to do in the hedge moon*. This latest call was closer. Maisy whirled to see the owl, broad rounded wings outstretched, on its silent glide. She noticed Nell also guessing the line of the carn's flight to see what it was hunting. A young black doe was grazing alone in the middle of the field, one of her ears hanging limply as if asleep. Nell was the first to react, stamping his hind paw in alarm. A heartbeat later, Maisy felt a second stamp from the hedge on the north side of the field.

The young doe's response was immediate. She leaped into the air and hit the ground hightailing. Normally any rabbit within sense would rush for cover at an alarm, but Maisy and her kittens were safe enough underneath the alders. The doe quickly hit top speed, hind paws landing in front of fore, tail in the air. The watchers willed her on, as she zigged and zagged to baffle the hunter. They could see the owl making adjustments to its speed and angle of dive.

The first surge had given the rabbit a slim advantage. The carn was closing again when a strange thing happened. The doe stopped, scanned rapidly to her left and right, then turned on the spot and charged into the line of the swooping owl. Maisy gasped.

Her concern switched to admiration when she realised the tawny had been thrown off-balance. The doe shimmied to the left and side-

---

* Rabbits mark the passing of the year by the moons, and the names they give to each relate to the natural world around them. May is the hedge moon after the blooming hawthorn and mayflower. A list of moon names, and the reasons for them, is in the glossary (Afterwords, p.xvii).

stepped her attacker. The owl wheeled in the air to attack from another angle, but the doe was gone.

A harsh *wick, wick, wick, wick* cry of frustration echoed over the field as the carn flew off to the north.

'Amazing,' said Nell. 'I would have never thought of doing that.'

'Nor did she until she noticed where she was.'

'What do you mean?'

Maisy sighed.

'That doe stopped when she realised she was about to cross into Vort's patch. She would have feared the governor's bruisers more than the owl.'

Nell looked puzzled.

'Surely the governor could see she was hightailing for her life.'

'Vort would have seen nothing. He'd rely on reports from his yes-bucks and paw-lickers. And, as your father used to say, those rabbits are as crooked as a dragonfly's legs. No son, that brave young doe stood more chance with the owl than with Vort and his rules.'

When it was time to move on, Nell hesitated. He had never been past this point. Maisy took over, guiding the family through a swarming cloud of dull-brown alder flies and along the trail that meandered through the foxtail grass. Her reluctant daughters, unnerved after the tawny attack, jumped at new sounds or smells carried on the wind that had shifted to the south and strengthened. Maisy had to backtrack constantly, reassuring them, encouraging them forward.

On the outskirts of the new warren, they were met by a twiggy buck who sniffed Maisy, and took a long look at Nell before letting them through. Other rabbits rising from holes for the night ignored Maisy as she took her family to a burrow lower down the slope.

The warren, known as the Platform because of the large flat-topped hillock at its centre, was larger than the Willow, though its rabbits were worse off. More than half the burrows were prone to flooding and there was less food for more mouths. Rabbits of little status, in which Maisy's family found themselves, were caught in a cruel spiral. Poorer grass meant poorer health and weaker bodies which left rabbits more vulnerable to carns. The warren was a popular hunting ground for tawny owls.

Maisy struggled to squeeze through the entrance to their new burrow which, compared to their previous home, was cold and cramped and smelt putrid. The bodies of the previous occupants had been taken out only that dayspring. The three does were miserable. Maisy tried to stay strong for them, but it was a struggle. The journey had been exhausting, and at times the only thing keeping her going was the prospect that the end would be pleasant. She collapsed on the cold floor, heart sick.

*****

LIKE MOST BUCKS, Nell saw a burrow as little more than a place to sleep. As his sisters brooded, he ventured out to explore his new surroundings. He tried to find the rabbit he'd seen outsmart the tawny, but was told the doe – an orphan – had left the warren. By the end of the first night, he'd identified the northern hedgerow as the most likely source of carns, learnt to pick the wind shifts and the play of the shadows from the alders now lined up to the south, and memorised the location of the warren's pitiful emergency bolt holes.

Every night at the Platform brought new experiences. Nell soaked them up like moss on a rock. Important discoveries, some that would later prove lifesaving, were made on outings with his mother. The Platform exposed Nell and his sisters to new plants, and Maisy patiently explained their uses. The bruised leaves of yarrow could be rubbed into cuts to stop bleeding, and when chewed cured anything from colds to the passing of wind. Too many, though, would give a rabbit a headache. Dried bark from branches of willows helped bring down a rabbit's body temperature, ramson leaves lowered blood pressure. Maisy had heard of two rabbits whose fractured bones healed after a strict diet of comfrey roots.

She didn't always get it right, though was quick to admit her mistakes. When Nell complained he was having difficulty sleeping, Maisy suggested he try skullcap. Instead of helping him sleep, he became giddy, and his legs twitched. She took it personally, apologising repeatedly and promising to *do more digging*. That was one of her favourite sayings, along with *you are what you eat*. Anything Maisy didn't know about a plant wasn't worth knowing. She even suggested some plants could be used to disguise a rabbit's scent.

Most of Nell's new friends were convinced she was crazy, especially when she said things like *a rabbit is only a rabbit because of other rabbits.* That saying always sent eyes skyward. But he loved his mother, and quietly stored away the seeds of wisdom he managed to extract from what others dismissed as the ranting of a doe.

Maisy was less helpful on the subject of carns, so Nell asked his friends for advice. They showed him how to recognise the cocky straight paw-prints of a fox and its inward-facing toes, the pointed prints of a stoat and how they compared to a weasel, the distinctive claw marks of a badger. Or the twisted prints of an otter, sometimes scuffed with the drag mark of its tail.

Nell immersed himself in the delights of late spring, that vibrant time of year when grass was plentiful and stomach aches more likely a sign of over-eating than hunger. There had been few willing playmates for the son of a dom at the Willow. At the Platform, Nell was treated like the other young bucks. It was a good feeling.

He was introduced to the game of Patch, which he'd watched at the Willow but never been invited to play. Rabbits would divide into teams, trying to defend patches of ground – normally small knolls. Most of his playmates relied on brute strength and speed. Nell soon worked out the advantages of teamwork, decoy runners, using bucks with certain strengths for attack and defence.

His leadership made him popular with his teammates, though also a target for jealous opponents.

Maisy stumbled on a game one night. Some of the young rabbits took Patch more seriously than others. Quick reactions and agility kept Nell out of most of the rough play. On this occasion, he'd taken a risk and become isolated from his teammates. A gawky buck, often teased by his friends as clumsy, got carried away and sent Nell flying with a kick to his stomach. He was winded, though a bigger shock came when he opened his eyes to find his mother standing over him, shaking.

'What on Earth do you think you're doing?'

She was talking not to him, but to the buck who'd lashed out. The other friends were edging closer to see what the fuss was about. Nell was beyond embarrassed, and Maisy hadn't finished.

'There's enough violence and danger in these fields without you kittens stirring up more. When will you learn to use your tongues instead of your claws?'

Nell saw the reaction on his friends' faces, and wanted the ground to gobble him up. Maisy shook her head and bounded off. The clumsy buck started to apologise.

'Forget it,' snapped Nell, shaking off the dust.

'Rabbits say *my* mother's crazy, Nell. Yours is… weird.'

'Yeah. Who's she calling a kitten?'

'She's alright,' said Nell. 'She's had a rough time. Got this thing about fighting, that's all.'

'I'd never let my mother talk to me like that.'

Nell felt he should defend Maisy, but kept quiet.

'So that's the end of the game, is it?'

Nell waited until Maisy disappeared over the rise.

'No way. Let's take the patch further up, to the forbidden line. Make it more exciting.'

*****

WHAT LEVI LIKED most about this place was that in one direction he could see past the hazel all the way to the willows and down the slope to the rindle. Twist around and he could see the trees known as The Twins in the next field. And no-one could see him.

He came to the Hide when he wanted to get away from the burrow, when his mother was ignoring him, or his father moaning, which Vort did more often since the varlet dom Henry hurt his leg. Sometimes Levi came to the Hide simply to watch, as he was doing now. Varlets were playing a game he'd seen them play before. This time he could see their faces, lit by the thinning crescent moon rising above the hazel.

He spotted the runt from the Willow Warren, the one with the smudge on its forehead. It was a lucky little turd. When it appeared the other team was winning, out of the grass something would happen to change things. Lucky turd.

'Are you in there, Levi?'

He jumped in fright, knocking his head on the branch. He hadn't heard his father approach, didn't think Vort knew about the Hide.

'What are you doing in there?'

The voice wasn't angry.

'Watching, sir.'

'Watching what?'

'Those varlets over there. Playing that game. Looks like fun.'

'Don't be fooled, son. That's not fun. It's violent, like most things the varlets do.'

Vort limped forward, chinning a branch, and blocking Levi's view.

'You must understand, son. The black rabbit is different from us. It is still a savage. Not long ago, it was roaming wild over the downs, sleeping in crannies above ground, crapping on its food, smearing all kinds of diseases. When it wasn't sending its own kind – its own blood – to the field of silence, it was mumbling in riddles or believing in absurd spirits. Many of them still do.'

Levi shuffled sideways to try to see the game.

'Are you listening to me?' growled Vort.

'Yes sir.'

'One or two of our varlets might appear peaceful, responsible, now we've shown them how to live in organised warrens. What I'm trying to say is that savagery can't be bred out in one or two generations. The most harmless-looking varlet will, at the first whisper of pressure, revert to savagery. Can't help it. It's in its blood. That's why we've got to keep it on the right path. Like a parent sometimes needs to punish a wayward kitten. For its own good. The smart ones thank us for it.'

Vort wrinkled his nose as if he'd smelt something disgusting.

'They're not like us, son. Comparing a white rabbit to a black is like comparing a fox to a dung beetle. It thinks differently because it *is* different. Lying and cheating and crapping below comes as naturally to the varlet as the daystar follows night. That's why we need rules like forbidden lines. Without them, there'd be chaos. The varlet can survive on the seed of a foxtail plant. It couldn't digest most of what we eat. It'd get sick, probably pass into the field of silence. It's happy living where it is. The smart one knows it's inferior, that if it lived up here among us it'd be constantly shown up.

'Are you grasping what I'm saying to you?'

'Yes, sir.'

'Tell me, then. What can you see down there?'

Levi hadn't been concentrating, so he guessed.

'Savages playing?'

'What are the savages really doing?'

'Practising to lie and murder and crap in their burrows?'

'Never forget it.'

5. The offer

SUMMER ARRIVED with a flair that took rabbits' breaths away and added bounce to their movements. One night, with a near-full moon glowing over the alders, Nell squeezed out of the burrow he still shared with his mother and sisters. He stood on his hind legs to scan for danger, then sat down to groom. First the face, always the face. Then the chest, the coat, and finally the ears and paws. When he was satisfied, he loped off to meet two friends who wanted to try their luck grazing up the slope.

One was a scrawny rabbit whose smell made Nell think of rain. The other wasn't much bigger, but took more pride in his appearance. Nell found them talking to a carn ranger, whose job was to patrol the northern limits of the Platform. The ranger's ears twirled constantly as he spoke.

'She's risky, risky.'

'Why's that?'

'No hiding from here to the line, even for a squeak like you. Carn knows it.'

'You seen anything tonight?' asked Nell.

'Shhh... One barn owl. Crossed a while or two ago. Too easy to see in this moon.'

'Nothing on the ground?'

'Nope. Foxes yelling three, four nights past. Nothing since.'

'That's good enough for me guys,' said Nell, eager to get going.

'I'm not sure, Nell.'

'Come on, you feather,' teased the larger buck. 'You heard the ranger. Nothing for nights, and a moon as bright as the daystar.'

'What about other carns?'

'We've got Nell. That nose could sniff a badger fart downwind of a thunderstorm.'

'Shhh...' said the ranger, struggling to keep a straight face. 'You'll attract every carn from here to the Chilling Wood.'

'He's right,' said Nell. 'Let's go.'

The soft honey balm of flag iris carried up from the rindle as they spread out in search of snacks among the foxtail already beginning to wither as the air warmed and the soil dried. Nell's companions were happy to let him take the lead, even though he was the least familiar with the terrain. Now and then, he'd have to slow down for the smaller rabbit, who never strayed far from his side.

They found little of interest that hadn't been nibbled down, so as the night deepened, they lurked ever closer to the forbidden line. Nell remained cautious, ears and nose working together and one eye always scanning. This was where the tawny attacked the doe the night he arrived. He stopped before the line, which ran from the top of the alders to a point in the hedgerow near Vort's rowan. They sank to the ground, side by side, peering into the forbidden part of the field.

'Get your bloody snout down.'

Nell was embarrassed. He'd been teased about his nose a few times since coming to the Platform. Usually it was gentle ribbing, though once he'd overheard the phrase *know-it-all*, which hurt.

'Is it true you're the son of a dom?'

'Once. No longer.'

'Does that mean we have to call you *master*?'

'Quiet. Something's moving over there.'

A white doe and three kittens were feeding about fifty bounds away. The light breeze had shifted and was now blowing from the northern branch of the combe, so their scents hadn't carried.

'How do they keep so clean?'

Nell was surprised to hear the question from the larger buck, who groomed more than any rabbit he knew.

'Why do you think they're cleaner than you?

'Their coats. They're spotless.'

One of the kittens stared in their direction, ears twirling.

'I dare you, you poncy turd,' whispered the buck, though it seemed the kitten hadn't smelt them. 'Cross that line and we'll rub your poncy face in the soil.'

Nell was shocked.

'What's that kitten ever done to deserve that?'

'He's white, isn't ...'

The faintest puff of musk brushing the tips of Nell's nostrils sent his hind paw thumping into the ground. An array of messages flashed. Large eyes allowing Nell to see forward and sideways through a wide arc detected four, possibly five dark shapes. One was slightly larger than the rest, the teeth at the end of its pointed face aimed at the little buck, its sleek body flexed for the pounce. One lightning wink of Nell's nose identified the hunters as weasels. The reek from their stink glands was sharpened with the putrid remains of their last meal. Nell's left ear felt the moist beginnings of a hiss, his paws the planting of hind legs as the large buck pushed into the air in response to the alarm thump. It was Nell's whiskers that sensed his other friend's hesitation.

All these messages fused into one as they reached Nell's brain, which also held the memory of Henry's words. A weasel will normally struggle to take a juvenile rabbit above ground. So sometimes, in the late spring or early summer, they hunt in family packs. Bitch and kittens. Young weasels copy their mother. More likely than not, she'll try to leap onto your back so she can aim her bite at the base of your neck.

The time it took Nell to receive, process and act on this information was fractionally less than it took the weasel bitch to calculate the distance to her target, extend her front claws and steady her hind legs for the pounce. A heartbeat after the first buck left the ground, Nell jumped into the path of the weasel. In mid-air he used his forepaw to flick the rump of the smaller rabbit, who hightailed. The unexpected movement caused the weasel to delay her strike, but also threw Nell off balance. He landed heavily on a front paw and rolled towards one of the weasel kits.

What saved him was his clear head, thinking of nothing but escape.

The switch from roll to hightail was so smooth, Nell sped away from his pursuers. He could see the rumps of his friends zigzagging frantically. Unsure how far the weasels would chase, he raced for home.

*****

MAISY HAD BEEN RESTING under the lone willow when she felt the first alarm stamp. Three rabbits were hurtling down the slope, Nell at the rear, closest to danger. Two more stamps increased her anxiety. The fourth, sounded at the same time she noticed the tawny, sent her heart pounding.

She imagined the enormous liquid brown eyes fixed onto the dashing rump of her son, as the silent night hunter swooped, wingbeats muted by the soft velvety tips of its flight feathers. Fifty bounds to go. Forty. Thirty. The owl altered its line to target Nell's neck. Twenty. Ten. Five. The carn raised its wings, thrust its talons forward...

*****

IT WAS NOT UNTIL he was half-way through the entrance that Nell became aware of the threat from the air. The owl slammed into the hole, hurling Nell through the narrow gap. A disappearing cry of *e-wick* told him how close his escape had been.

'We must do something about that opening,' he said to his shocked sisters. 'One more decent meal and I won't be able to fit through.'

His rump stung where it had been whacked by the owl, and although he tried not to show it, his pain must have been obvious, because one of his sisters giggled.

Soon all three were enjoying the joke.

'Seriously,' Nell said when the laughter ebbed, 'why don't you does make this place more comfortable?'

'Do you want to go and ask the governor for permission?'

Nell had been so busy disguising his embarrassment, he hadn't noticed Maisy scurry through behind him.

'What do you mean?'

'I mean this excuse for a burrow, all holes on the Platform, and the Willow Warren, belong to Vort.'

'What?'

'You heard me. It never mattered at the Willow because we had a decent burrow. But it's the truth. All black rabbits live in their holes at the pleasure of our big-hearted governor, who can turf us out whenever, for whatever reason he wants.'

Nell had never seen his mother this angry.

'Making changes to a burrow without permission,' she continued, her voice rising, 'is like crossing the forbidden line. So, unless you're prepared to go begging to the rabbit who sent your father to the field of silence, which I certainly am not, we're stuck here.'

It was the first time Henry's passing had been mentioned since they'd come to the Platform. The memory swarmed around Nell. In the darkness, he winced at the crunching of bone against bark. Gulped at the stench stretching through the passage. And the *tap tap tap* deep inside got heavier, like a weight tugging down his shoulders. It was only when his nose touched the soil that he remembered where he was, and looked up into the face of his mother. She was crying.

Nell's bottom lip quivered. Self-pity was swept aside by guilt. As Maisy and his sisters had been struggling to survive in this hovel, he'd been out having fun. Sobbing filled the burrow as his sisters followed their mother's lead. Nell felt trapped, as if the walls were pressing in on him. He had to get out.

*****

FLEET WAS LYING under the hedgerow at the northern end of the field when he saw Nell charge from the burrow. The buck, who had grown tall in two moons, stopped near the rapids and crouched, panting, close to where Fleet lay. The youngster's ears swayed in rhythm with a faint wind that brought the fruity zing of elder blossom to replace the stale odour of water lilies.

The daystar was up, taking the place of the moon which had set over the rindle. A wasp was buzzing around the bulrushes beside Nell. Fleet could see the fine pattern of green veins on a lacewing edging up

36

the stalk of one of the plants, looking for aphids. The wasp landed close to the lacewing, its bold black and yellow markings blazing menace while it sized up its meal. As it jerked downwards, the lacewing dropped off the stalk and fell to the ground, where it lay motionless. The wasp buzzed around the insect's body, then lost interest and flew away. The lacewing stirred, righted itself, gave a couple of testing flaps, and returned to the stalk.

'Clever, isn't it?' said Nell in a way that suggested he was aware of Fleet all along.

Most blacks in the South would hightail at the first sign of a stranger, particularly a white rabbit. Fleet smiled.

'Clever?'

'It did that on purpose.'

'I don't take much notice of insects. They're a bit like the rindle, or those trees over there. Part of the background. Little to do with a rabbit, unless you can swallow them.'

'Perhaps you should take more notice. It certainly fooled the wasp.'

Fleet was intrigued. 'You're giving it more intelligence than it deserves, don't you think? It's only an insect.'

Nell looked him over, nose in the air, no fear in his scent. 'You're not from round here, are you?'

'I'm Fleet. You must be Nell.'

'How did you know that?'

Since the fight, Fleet had asked around and learnt much about the buck who left such an impression on him.

'That forehead could belong only to the grandson of Old Nell.'

'How do you know about my family?'

'I knew your father. It's my job to know. And can I say how sorry I am for your loss.'

'That's a bit hollow coming from a rabbit of your colour.'

'Ha. A feisty one, eh? Spirit's not such a bad thing. Pity a few more of your high-ups don't display it more often. Though that's none of my business, is it?'

'What *is* your business?'

This was a new experience for Fleet.

Not only was it the first time he'd had a proper conversation with a young southern black rabbit, he was in the unusual position of having to answer rather than ask the questions.

'I'm known to the rabbits of my warren as a seer, though some on this side of the Torrent have been unkind enough to call me a spy. My business is to keep my eyes and ears open and report what I see and hear to Thatch.'

'Thatch?'

'The prime rabbit of all the warrens on the North Bank.'

North of what?'

'The Torrent, of course.'

Fleet could see the buck had no idea what or where the Torrent was.

'So where's the South Bank?' asked Nell.

'We're standing on it.'

'I see. If this is the South Bank and your Thatch rules the North, what are you doing here?'

'Watching and listening,' replied Fleet, enjoying the chat. More than one rabbit had mentioned that Nell was special, had some inner calmness. One doe described it as a magic aura. Fleet dismissed such talk as the quaint rambling of simple country rabbits. He had to admit, though, he was enchanted. The next question confirmed the young rabbit's intelligence, and his cheek.

'If your business is to report what you see and hear, tell me what's happening on your North Bank?'

'Nothing new. Other seers report the battle amongst the warrens to the far north and east is, thankfully, part of our history, along with the bane. Most of the warrens have recovered and life goes on.'

Nell considered this. 'Tell me about your warren. What sort of holes do your blacks have to live in?'

'They can live where they want.'

Nell squinted suspiciously.

'Rabbits on the North Bank are free to live where they want,' said Fleet. 'Eat what they want, come and go when they want, mate with who they want, be what they want, whether they are black, white or shades between. There are no forbidden lines.

'We do have rules. Warrens need rules. They're like the trunk of a tree. They hold everything up. *Our* rules are based on the customs rabbits have followed for generations. And those rules, as in all warrens except those on the South Bank, are colour-blind.'

Fleet expected Nell to take a moment to digest the information, but he was immediately bugging him with further questions.

'How did you get here? Why have I never seen you?'

'I'm the only seer working the South Bank, though a few others are showing interest. For now, I have to keep a watch on all the warrens from here to the Golden Field. I can't be in two places at once, though I sometimes think Thatch expects it.'

Fleet could see Nell was taking all this in, when they heard a voice calling. Maisy appeared and immediately crouched down, nose to the ground, in the annoying way southern blacks showed obedience to white rabbits.

'Whatever he's done master, I accept responsibility,' she said, never lifting her face from Fleet's paws.'

'It's alright mother, he's not a white. Well, he is, and he isn't. His name's Fleet, from the other side of something called a Torrent.'

Maisy looked up.

'Forgive me. I thought...'

'No offence taken,' said Fleet. 'I do however hold you and your... late mate responsible for this remarkable buck. It's moons since I've seen such intellect, such spirit, such promise in one so... young.'

He'd almost said *black*. He considered Maisy. The kind, honest, uncomplicated face of so many does from country warrens. It gave him an idea.

'No disrespect to you or your warren, mother, but it would be a waste to let such promise go to seed at the Platform. I'm sure the Patri* would find a place for Nell. I could talk to him if you wish.'

Maisy's mouth dropped, and Fleet was afraid he'd insulted the doe. He looked at the sky, as if checking the position of the daystar.

'I must be off,' he said. 'Think about the offer. Not for too long though. Life's too short. Goodbye, Nell. I look forward to asking *you* some questions next time.'

---

* The Patri is the traditional leader of the black rabbits of the South Bank.

6. This is your path

LEVI WOULD HAVE LIKED to talk to his mother about the Hide. It would be a waste of breath. She used to be talkative, they said. Then she changed, about the time Levi was born. These nights, she hardly ever went above. Thank goodness his father had explained about the savages. Levi had thought of varlets merely as dirty, foul-smelling white rabbits.

The hedgerow was flush with the aromas of mid-summer, the balsamic bluebells, the pungency of garlic mustard and other plants too strong for the varlets. The nourishment Levi got from such plants, the cow parsley and sorrel and rye grass that grew in abundance around the governor's burrow, and the hazelnuts delivered by black servants, helped explain why, though only a little over three moons, Levi was already bigger than most adult varlets.

A rabbit growing at such a rate required a lot of food, and although he was full, there was always room for one more treat to finish off. Something a little different. He burped. The warmth from the rising daystar tingled his shoulders. It was going to be a hot one. He yawned, then rolled onto his side, stretched his hind legs out behind him and let his ears flop.

He ignored the *fayee, fayee, fayee* of a goldfinch, but opened an eye when he sensed movement in the grass. A shrew was scurrying back and forth along a ditch. Levi couldn't figure out why it was ignoring a plump earthworm he could see moving only whiskers away. Suddenly the animal stopped, dropped silently to the ground. Another shrew, larger and darker, had wandered into the little animal's territory. The first shrew had gone downwind and behind a clump of grass. Like the game the varlets played. This could be fun.

The speed of the pounce was impressive. The first shrew struck not for the neck, but the tail. The intruder, a grey male probably chased out of its home by one of its own children, reacted quickly. It too aimed for the tail, clamping down hard. The shrews lurched one way then the other, legs flailing, and in a few heartbeats it was over. The grey shrew broke free. Instead of running away, it threw itself upside down, legs kicking the air, and gave a shriek of surrender. The victor, swaggering, reared up and hollered. Levi waited for the shrew to finish it off.

It was not to be. It took a few steps backwards, letting the beaten coward crawl off. Levi was appalled. *What a spineless feather.* The shrew resumed its patrol. A few moments later, it ran into Levi's paw. He swatted the stunned animal, and watched as it wriggled, exposing its dirty white stomach. A fluttering sensation swept over Levi as he considered biting it. He bent down to sniff its flanks. A coarse musk invaded his nostrils. He was so revolted he flung the shrew through the air. The little savage rolled on landing and scampered away.

Levi yawned, and ambled into the Hide. He settled down to sleep, not noticing a beetle resting on the ground. To the black rabbits of the Platform and Willow it was known as a minotaur beetle. To the white rabbits who ruled beneath the rowan, it was a dung beetle. It made no difference. Its shiny black body was crushed.

*****

NELL WAS TORN. Maisy wanted him to decide for himself about moving to Hilltop, the warren of the Patri. She talked of the advantages and disadvantages, although it was clear she thought it was too good an offer to turn down. Moving, though, would mean leaving his mother, who had no choice but to remain at the Platform looking after his three sisters until they found mates.

What sealed his decision was her comment that it would be what his father wanted. Although Henry had played a short part in his life, and Nell had become close to his mother since moving to the Platform, he felt a duty to his father. He wasn't sure what was expected of him. There had been clues, which must somehow fit together. The place of his ancestors. The colour of fur. Supremacists. Conscience. Freedom of the kind described by Fleet. And those unforgettable last words of his father: *Carry our star, be the one.*

Once he'd decided, Nell was pleased his mother agreed to accompany him to Hilltop. At dayfall, he farewelled his sisters and they started off. As they approached the hedgerow, the boundary of his known world, Nell skipped aside for Maisy.

'No son. This is your path.'

He gazed at the wall of intertwined plants. It was still, the air peaceful. He took a last look at the field of his birth, then hopped through. On the other side, he rose on his hind legs to survey the surroundings. They were in the corner of what felt like a large area rising gently to the east. Poplars blocked their view of the open part of the field. There were no signs of rabbit holes. Those trees offered the best cover, if it became necessary.

'Hilltop must be in that direction,' said Maisy, motioning to the north-east.

Nell realised only then that Maisy had never been there.

'This is the furthest I've been too, Nell. Your father visited the Patri regularly, and we often talked about his journeys.'

They padded off. The breeze had strengthened and shifted to the west, so they could not rely on their ability to pick up unfriendly scents in the field. Not knowing where to find bolt holes added to the tension. Nell skipped at unexpected sounds. The loud barks of a pair of geese taking off sent him scampering for cover, until he sensed where he was. Behind Governor Vort's burrow.

Maisy beckoned him to join her on a small rise from where, stretching to full height, they could see over the hedgerow. The first quarter moon, low to the horizon in front of them, cast a dull glimmer over the field. The top of the governor's forbidden hazel tree stood alone at the fork near the Willow Warren. Far off were the downs where his ancestors once lived. The alders hid the burrows, though Nell could see the dark tops of the willows.

He gritted his teeth at the memory.

'We'd better get going,' said Maisy. 'We're like snails without shells here.'

'Which way?'

'It's your field, son.'

Nell led her away from the rowan, then cut uphill. Hints of bindweed murmured out to meet them as they reached the edge of the field. Soon they were relaxing in the shadow of the trees.

'What did you think of Fleet?' Maisy asked.

'He was interesting, I suppose. For one of those.'

'One of what?'

'A white.'

'You think only rabbits with dark fur can be interesting?'

'Of course not. Though I wasn't sure whether to believe him or not.'

'What does your heart tell you?'

Nell's first impression of the white seer had not been good. He smelt strange, and his coat was matted and scruffy, as if he hadn't groomed in days. He was friendly though, and what he'd said about the North Bank was amusing, though hardly believable.

'He was interesting, very interesting.'

Maisy smiled.

'You should trust that heart more often. Fleet speaks in riddles to me, but your father thought highly of him. Used to tell him all sorts of things. I remember Henry coming home once, going on about how shrewd Fleet had been. How he'd had this long talk with him, told him all he knew about such and such a thing. I asked what he'd learnt from the seer, and he grinned. I can still see that grin, as if it was last night. *Nothing*, he said. *Not a petal.* That seer spoke nothing but questions. Your father always said Fleet was fair. That's good enough for me.'

Nell was about to ask about the North Bank, but decided against it. He suspected it would lead to a talking about keeping paws on the ground. He wasn't in the mood. Although tired, he insisted Maisy have the first rest. When she protested, he reminded her it was *his* field.

From where they lay, the field levelled out to give views in three directions. The rank nagging of the spindles would smother most other scents. He would have to rely on his ears to detect danger. As Maisy dozed, Nell watched squirrels playing in the branches. He was amused by the largest, which grabbed a stick and used it as an imaginary enemy, rolling and cartwheeling and scratching it with its paws. It came closer, the bushy tail arched behind. Nell flapped an ear. The squirrel froze, then edged forward again. The little animal was only a bound away when a chirp from its mother in the tree sent it darting up the trunk. Nell checked to see what had caused the squirrel sow to call. All was calm. A cinnabar moth flitted over the grass. It was only when Nell followed the line of the moth out into the field that he saw the stoat.

*****

LEVI, woken by the squirrel sow, saw the stoat the same time he saw Nell. The little varlet was standing still as a tree, nose to the stars like a stunned field vole. Levi had heard about the mesmerising powers of stoats. How exciting.

There was motion under the spindle. A varlet doe was stirring. It saw immediately what was happening, and charged. Levi stamped his paw, without thinking that the stoat would not recognise the warning. The varlet buck looked in Levi's direction at the same time the doe slammed into the stoat, sending it sprawling. The stoat recovered quickly and confronted the doe, but the doe stood its reared up. The carn scampered off.

Levi was too stunned to be disappointed. What a doe! *His* mother would never do such a thing to save him. Vort would have. Once. Before his leg was mangled. He watched the varlets speed off, the mate and son of the varlet responsible for crippling his father.

'You can hightail, smudgeface, but you can't hide,' he rasped.

*****

NELL HAD A LOT TO LEARN. He expected to be told-off by his mother for being fooled by the stoat, and assumed she would want to go in front. He was wrong.

'Are you ready?'

Nell bit his lip and made for the privet trees. He felt humiliated, ashamed he'd put his mother's life in danger. They passed tempting clumps of groundsel among the towering foxtail spikes, ignoring them in their eagerness to escape the hazards of the open. Nell disturbed a flock of goldfinches pecking at sow thistles and stopped to nose the tall plants.

'Leave them,' said Maisy. 'They'll be too tough.'

At the foot of the hedgerow was a trail wider and smoother than any Nell had seen, overlaid with the hints of many rabbits. Maisy hopped over to inspect some dog roses.

'In a moon or two this will be full of red hips. I've heard they're full of goodness. You'll have to tell me what they taste like.'

Nell wanted to keep moving. Maisy was more interested in the plants.

'You are going to be careful, aren't you son? I've heard horrid stories about what bucks do to their stomachs as soon as they leave home.'

'Yes, mother. I know. I am what I eat.'

Maisy smiled. 'What are we waiting for?'

Nell eyed the trail. It ran as far as the bottom of a steep ridge, which was covered in briar and shadow. He was tiring. Not his body. His legs were fine. Excitement had carried him this far. But he'd been invaded with so many new sights and sounds and smells, he sensed exhaustion was gaining on him.

Maisy nuzzled him forward.

'It can't be far, son.'

The trail wound its way up through a tunnel in the briar. The still air inside carried no sign of danger. Halfway up, they were confronted by a creature so strange, Nell jumped in fright. Silky black fur covered its entire body, except for the snout, which was pink. It had no ears, no neck and apparently no eyes. What it did have was teeth. Too many. Snarling.

'Have you never seen a mole?' asked Maisy.

'Don't they spend all their time in the ground?'

'Most of it. This time of year, ones like this leave their mother and go above to find new homes.'

Nell relaxed.

'We have something in common.'

The mole uttered a high-pitched squeal, which Nell took to be unfriendly. He skipped around it. They broke through the briar thicket close to the crest of the ridge, and Nell looked over what was to become his new home. The silhouette of an ancient yew tree stood at its centre, and under its canopy moved the shapes of several rabbits. Nell quickly cleaned his face, then looked over the field below. It was split by a deep combe winding down to the rindle. But it was a new flavour, which Maisy identified as honeysuckle, that was more striking than the view. He closed his eyes, sucking deeply on the soothing vapours. When he looked up, Maisy was standing in front of him.

They sniffed for what felt like an age, then Nell leaned forward to lick her nose. She licked his face. Words were unnecessary. Maisy set off down the tunnel. It was as if a part of Nell disappeared into that briar.

7. Privilege

NELL WOKE to the delightful aroma of plantain. He was lying in a dry, spacious hole. Judging from the flow of fresh air, it had to be part of a large, well-ventilated burrow with multiple entrances. As he twitched his nose, his senses were bombarded with a jumble of exotic fragrances. He had no idea where he was. Nor did he care. Surely it couldn't get better than this.

Voices swirled through the walls and floated around the chamber. Gentle, friendly voices. Beckoning. The more he listened, the more he remembered. An inner warmth flowed through his body as he recalled the previous night.

At the parting, Nell saw through Maisy's brave face and hoped she did not see through his. Part of him wanted to charge after his lone, vulnerable mother. To lick her, protect her. Tell her how much he appreciated and needed her. He couldn't. The moisture in his eyes would give away the nervousness twisting his insides, the guilt and fear of loss sticking like a thorn into his chest. As he'd stared at the briar tunnel, he vowed to do what he could to make his mother proud. To give her back the dignity and status she once enjoyed as mate of a dom.

He'd swivelled to size up the surroundings, and found he was immediately drawn to the yew at the centre of the warren, as if some giant paw was stretching out, pulling him towards the tree.

He passed rabbits nibbling rye grass. Most ignored him. Faces that looked up were friendly.

As he neared the yew, he found that the shapes he'd seen from a distance were bucks, all black, most a good deal older than Henry had been. They were sitting in a semi-circle as if waiting for someone. Nell heard the name of his father from the lips of more than one rabbit, and a whispered *Old Nell*. The idea that these important rabbits might be waiting for him quickly faded as all heads turned together.

'Hail to the Patri', chorused the high-ups in the traditional greeting to the leader of Hilltop.

Nell crouched as three black rabbits approached. Two were almost as large as Governor Vort. They could have been twins, the way their noses winked at the same time, the rumpled coats, eyes bloodshot from constant scanning. But it was the rabbit in the middle, a shorter, compact buck with an immaculate coat and noble air who stood out. An image of calm between the restless hulks of his minders.

The Patri hopped forward to touch noses with each of the high-ups. The way he dominated the semi-circle, the confidence, the wisdom in his face, the respect this black rabbit commanded, was a revelation. In that moment, Nell realised there was more to life than eating, sleeping, and playing. Or simply surviving. Here was an inviting passage to a larger world than he had known at the Willow or Platform. The Patri nosed the last rabbit in the line. Then he hopped over to Nell, who was surprised to be greeted in the same way as the high-ups.

'Welcome, Nell. Welcome to Hilltop,' said the Patri in a voice loud enough for the others to hear.

'We are honoured to welcome to our humble warren the son of Henry and grandson of Old Nell, whose deeds are remembered by all here. Such a bloodline speaks for itself. Nell also comes to us on the say-so of our white friend from over the Torrent. We are fortunate to have him among us.'

Nell scraped the soil at his paws, uncomfortable at the attention.

'Let it be known,' the Patri continued, his eyes resting on Nell's forehead, 'I accept Nell as I would my own son. My burrow is his burrow. Our warren is his warren. That is all. Go well.'

Murmurs of *'stay well'* came from the high-ups as they shuffled off for a last feed before going below.

'I was sorry to hear what happened to your father,' said the Patri.

'Henry and I were born during the same moon. Been friends since he was your age. In recent times, I'd come to value his counsel. Not only on happenings at the Willow. On matters concerning all of our warrens in these days of uncertainty. His loss was a blow to us all.'

The Patri stopped outside the largest mouth to a burrow Nell had seen.

'I also miss that quaint habit he had of saying *we* all the time. Apparently Old Nell was the same.'

Nell couldn't think what to say. Things were happening too fast, emotions yanked in too many directions to absorb. He was astonished to find the main passage even wider than the entrance. They came to a fork.

'There's someone I want you to meet,' said the Patri as he waddled down the narrower of the two passages until they arrived at a large chamber. Shifts of air on his whiskers showed Nell one wall was pocked with openings to at least eight further holes. The Patri stuck his nose into one of them, and they were soon joined by a third rabbit. The newcomer smelt scruffy. And anxious.

'Olivia, I'd like you to meet Nell, the rabbit I was telling you about from the Willow. He's probably hungry after his journey, so I'll leave you to show him around.'

The Patri disappeared along another of the passages. There was a cramped silence. The newcomer was not going to speak first.

'Impressive place you've got here, Olivia,' said Nell.

'You think so? They say it's as grand as the governor's burrow. Couldn't say for myself. Imagine the colour scheme here's more tasteful.'

The voice was as shaky as the scent, but the choice of words intriguing, suggesting a mixture of intelligence and wit Nell hadn't seen in a doe who sounded a similar age.

'Please call me Ollie,' she said. 'And speaking of taste, fancy plantain?'

'Never tried it,' said Nell. 'I've heard my mother talk about it. Supposed to be good for stomach-ache, isn't it?'

'Wouldn't know,' replied the doe, leading him to the surface, 'unless your stomach is aching from hunger. Ask me, it tastes exquisite. Prefer the roots myself. Leaves can be a touch salty. I know where to find some choice ones.'

Ollie lingered at the entrance, then crept out to groom. Nell crouched beside her. The coat over her small, lean body was flat and speckled with dirt, but she was more concerned about cleaning her whiskers. The fur around her eyes was slightly lighter than the rest of her body. Like halos around two moons. Full, popping moons. All-seeing. They made Nell think of his father.

Ollie tested the wind in all directions, then moved cautiously along a trail heavily marked by the Patri. It took them over open ground, then swung sharply and climbed onto a higher level, which Ollie said was the Patri's grazing area.

'What are we doing here?' asked Nell, peeking around to see if anyone was watching.

'The Patri's sons and daughters have special privileges,' replied Ollie. 'Here, try this.'

The plantain had large leaves not unlike the shape of rabbits' ears, and prominent veins to match. Nell found them tough and bitter rather than salty, but excellent. Ollie had gone straight for the base of the plant, scraping with her front paws then burrowing her nose to get at the roots. They released a sweet odour as she chewed. When they finished, Ollie suggested they venture down the slope to meet some of the warren's other young bucks and does. Nell felt tired, and asked if he could be shown to wherever he should sleep.

He lay there now, listening to voices in the chambers around him. One he recognised from the formal, measured tone as the Patri. Another, from a deeper chamber, was Ollie. By the amount of light seeping into the burrow, he guessed he must have slept through the day, and most of the warren was above.

*****

OLLIE COULDN'T SLEEP, though not for the usual reasons. This time, she wasn't worried about carns or the stiffness or loneliness or boredom. She couldn't sleep because she was too excited.

Excited at the possibility that maybe, if she played things right, she'd found a friend. She'd been lying awake thinking of ways to trick the new buck into liking her. Finally, she gave up and went to see if he was also awake.

The chamber was empty. All the dried grass had been pushed into a corner and there was a warm patch on the floor. How odd. There was more light up here, which was why Ollie had said *no* to the burrow when she was offered it. Too big, the only entrance too large, too close to the main passage. When she asked for something smaller, she'd been shown the burrow of a doe who had passed into the field of silence. It was ideal. Deeper. Darker. Two small ways in and out. A sanctuary from carns. Ollie's favourite place in the world.

The newcomer's scent led her to the eating chamber. Tree roots supported part of the roof. A ledge, worn smooth by the paws of many rabbits, ran around three-quarters of the wall.

'I guess this is where the Patri has his circle gatherings?' asked Nell from the other side of the chamber.

'No. He uses this for special meals, when he has guests.' Ollie replied.

'How do you rabbits get away with this, this extravagance? Why does the governor allow it?'

Ollie yawned.

'Vort doesn't bother us. His yes-rabbits and bruisers won't come through the briar. Used to, apparently. Till the Patri thought of telling them the tunnels were shadowed by the spirits of rabbits who'd passed. They say they don't believe it, but don't come through. Hasn't been a white rabbit up here for moons, I'm told. And the tunnels are too steep for the governor, after his accident.'

Nell swallowed.

'So where does the Patri have his gatherings?'

'In the yew. Never been there, myself. Heard there's space for twenty rabbits.'

Olllie could hear Nell's stomach rumbling. He had to be hungry after going to sleep so early. Here was a chance to impress the newcomer.

'I know the perfect place to eat this time of day.'

'I'll be okay until it's time to go up.'

'Nonsense. The area next to the hedgerow's usually safe approaching dayfall, depending on the wind.'

Ollie also knew they were unlikely to meet other rabbits there. Something told her the buck was going to be popular, and she had no intention of sharing him until she'd had the chance to persuade him to be her friend.

When Nell asked Ollie to lead the way, she felt like a dom. Weird, since Nell was the son of an actual dom. The daystar had dipped below the distant wood, replaced by the first-quarter moon in the sky to the south-west. The chatter of birds filled the air, and a breeze drifted over Hilltop from the field below. Ollie crouched in the entrance to check it was safe to go out. As both rabbits groomed to clear their coats of the dust that inevitably clung to fur below, Ollie noted Nell's peculiar nose-in-the-air cleaning style. He was more interested in looking good than removing soil. He was impressive, and not only physically. He had an air Ollie hoped no-one else would notice.

In the eastern corner of Hilltop, they found a half-eaten clump of cleavers, and were soon nibbling at the cold bristly leaves. A pile of pellets reminded Ollie of a joke.

'What's the difference between a white rabbit and a heap of pellets?'

Nell kept chewing, so Ollie answered for him.

'The heap.'

Nell spat out part of a leaf, appeared confused.

'The heap,' said Ollie. 'Get it?'

Nell tilted his head to the side, his nose in the air.

'I get the joke. I don't think it's funny.'

He went back to chewing. Perhaps he didn't have a sense of humour. Minor fault, thought Ollie. No big deal when you lined it up against the things to like about the newcomer. Like how relaxed he was in a new place. Ollie had been a seed pod of nerves after arriving at Hilltop, until she was shown not only where the warren's bolt holes were, but checked them all to see how deep they were. She doubted Nell broke out in sweats worrying about being stuck down a blind end with a carn.

Nell was scanning.

'Why are there no bolt holes in this part of the field, but three over there by that mound?'

'It'll be about the Patri's grazing area.'

'We're nowhere near his area.'

'Not our Patri. The one before him.'

'Isn't he in the field of silence?'

'Has been for moons.'

'So why don't they…'

'Rules are rules, I guess.'

Stomachs full, the two rabbits spent the first half of the night exploring. Nell knew so much, you'd think he'd lived a hundred moons. Like the names of stars and plants and moths and the difference between the calls of male and female owls. The buck took everything in. And the questions. What? How? When? But mostly *why*? When Ollie was able to tell him things he didn't know, it sent waves of joy tingling down her spine. Like the name of a large woody plant. Bittersweet. Or how long the blackberry fruit would take to ripen. A moon or two.

Nell was a good listener, letting Ollie finish almost all her sentences, rather than constantly interrupting like the Patri's haughty blood sons. Nell's intelligence was giving Ollie second, third, fourth thoughts about domly blood being too thick to reach the brain. He was almost too good to be true, give or take the needless grooming, and nose-in-the-air. And possible lack of humour.

Then, when Ollie casually mentioned the distant cry of a fox vixen and Nell said he hadn't heard it, and they realised Ollie's hearing in her left ear was exceptional and Nell went on about how envious he was… the inner feeling glowed. No-one had ever envied Ollie. She'd forgotten the last time a rabbit said something nice about her.

The daystar began breaking over the eastern hedgerow and the warren prepared to go below. Ollie had spent the last few whiles above and wasn't anxious in the slightest. Amazing. And though she was supposed to be showing the newcomer around, Nell was doing the leading. It felt comfortable at his side. Like she'd finally found where she belonged.

*****

OVER THE FOLLOWING NIGHTS, Nell spent whiles with Ollie and other members of the Patri's extended family. The more he saw and smelt, the further he wandered from the yew, the more Nell became aware how fortunate he was to have been taken in by the Patri.

Although other members of the warren had access to better grazing than rabbits at the Willow or Platform, their food and burrows were not up to the standard of the Patri's. Nell also noticed, because of the company he was keeping, which often included one or more of the Patri's blood sons, he was treated wherever he went with a respect he wasn't used to. Having rabbits the age of his mother move out of his way might have made the Patri's sons feel important. Nell felt uncomfortable, and found ways to avoid such encounters whenever he could. Ollie raised the matter one night when Nell suggested they take a roundabout route to bypass a fidgety doe whose grovelling manner had become annoying.

'I may be simple, Nell. I was taught the shortest distance between two places was a straightish line.'

Nell stopped to let her catch up.

'Sorry. I was trying to keep away from *her.*'

'Yeah, she's wild that one. Teeth like a…'

'You know what I mean. Don't you want to cringe at the way some of these rabbits behave when you hop towards them, the way they look at you?'

'Don't think it's me they're looking at, Nell.'

'Of course they are.'

'Not when I'm on my own, they don't. Stare through me like I'm some spider's web. Or one of those butterflies, what do you call them…?'

'Lacewings.'

Nell considered his small, scruffy friend. An example of the perils of judging a rabbit by its appearance. The fidgety doe winked her nose at him.

'I think she likes you,' quipped Ollie.

Don't be ridiculous.'

'Come on, you must have heard the talk. It's that light streak on your forehead. Some rabbits round here think it's a sign.'

'*You* don't believe that drivel, do you?'

'I believe what I see. A blotch of light fur that could resemble a star to someone with a hightailing imagination. I also believe what I know. The shortest distance between...'

'Okay, okay,' grinned Nell, noticing the doe had left.

'Perhaps she was worried you'd bump into her with that nose.'

Nell gave Ollie a light cuff. He liked her. She was fun to be around. And smart. Their conversations were fields, moons away from the Platform. Ollie was interested in talking about important things, and her level of thinking was ears higher than Nell had become used to. Rabbits at the Platform and Willow had simple, uncomplicated lives. He was only now realising how much he missed challenging discussions that forced him to think, the kind he had with Henry. Or Fleet. Nell also liked the way Ollie accepted him as an equal, rather than the son of a dom. He hoped the little doe would become his friend.

Together on outings, they played with click beetles, knocking them off blades of grass and watching them flip into the air. They took turns seeing whether they could sneak close enough to meadow browns to catch whiffs of the scent scales on their wings. And had each other giggling as they tried to imitate the way magpies jounced along the ground like kittens on their first days above. Ollie accompanied Nell most of the time, unless it was cool or wet, when she preferred to stay closer to the burrow, complaining of stiffness in her legs. The little rabbit was happiest when the two of them were alone, less talkative among strangers.

Though most of Nell's time above in his first moon at Hilltop was spent in carefree play, there were reminders of the perils of the wild. The reek of a hunting pack of stoats was picked up in one of the briar tunnels one night, though the alarm was sounded in plenty of time. Unlike the Platform and Willow, which had fewer bolt holes, carn control at Hilltop was well organised. The cluster of emergency holes was constantly being improved, though the locations of some were baffling. One dayspring, as most of the rabbits were having their last feed, Nell detected a sweet aroma wafting up the ridge on the lightest of breezes. He saw a reddish-brown coat, the dark pointed muzzle, pricked ears and brushy, white-tipped tail of a fox as it trotted less than a hundred bounds from where he sat. It was the nearest he'd been to a rabbit's most dangerous enemy.

From the direction of the wind and the way the fox was behaving, he could tell the animal wasn't hunting. Neither Nell nor the warren were in immediate danger. Other rabbits had come to the same conclusion and resumed eating. Nell was glad Ollie was safely below. The carn-obsessed little doe would have stamped in false alarm. The fox jogged into the combe and out the other side. For an instant it stared back, and Nell caught a glint in the animal's eyes before it trotted off.

On his way to the burrow, Nell stopped to admire the light from the daystar glistening on the dew-drenched web of a spider. The ever-decreasing bands of silken threads drew his gaze to its centre. The web was between him and the trunk of the yew, and he saw a withered rabbit appear out of the tree. Intrigued, he hopped over to investigate, but she'd vanished. Behind one of the ancient tree's knotted trunk stems, he discovered an opening.

When Ollie had said gatherings were held *in* the yew, Nell assumed he'd misheard her. Perhaps he hadn't. He climbed through to find a large multi-levelled chamber, lit from two cracks in the walls of the trunk. A thin shaft of daystar shone through one of the holes and onto a paw-polished root coiled like a giant adder to form a raised platform at one end. Nell could imagine twenty rabbits crouching, discussing matters of importance. He thought of his father speaking in the alder by the rindle: *The hope, the expectation our warren will one day return to the rightful place of our ancestors…*

Nell sensed he had company in the yew. He spun on his paws to see the Patri sitting on the coiled root.

'Sorry if I alarmed you. Please, feel free to look around.'

Nell nodded thanks, relieved that his face was clean. The daystar dimmed as a cloud passed overhead. The air tasted of rain.

'I imagine if these walls could talk, they would tell some interesting stories,' said Nell.

'It is indeed a special place. I wondered how long it would take you to find it. Though if it's stories you're after, I suggest you seek out Aunt

Mina. Don't believe all she tells you. She's inclined to add colour to her stories. But she's one of the best sages this side of the Torrent. Mina knows more about this tree than anyone. She should. Spends more time in it than the rest of us put together, and is in a position to see more.'

When the Patri described Aunt Mina, especially the lack of whiskers on one side of her face, Nell remembered seeing the doe once or twice since he arrived. She was almost certainly the rabbit he saw leaving the yew.

'I wonder if you could do a favour for me,' said the Patri, who hadn't left the root coil.

'A gathering is to take place here in two days. I need a reliable buck to summon the doms of the other warrens. It would be a good opportunity for you to find your paws in the field. If you feel up to it.'

'I'd be glad to,' replied Nell, wondering why *he* was being chosen instead of the Patri's blood sons.

'Excellent. Excellent. I've been receiving good reports about the way you've settled in here, Nell. Fleet was right about you. Ordinarily I would have waited a few more moons to give you such a task. But the rabbit who has been running my errands is not getting any younger, to put it politely. I've been waiting for a trustworthy replacement. It's a job that might suit a rabbit who's not afraid of a challenge.'

The Patri had been staring at Nell's forehead, but now met his eyes.

'Perhaps you could take that friend of yours, Olivia. Fleet mentioned she was particularly agile.'

8. The Patri's circle

WHEN NELL FOUND OLLIE in her burrow, she was anything but agile. The rain had arrived – a miserable, unshakeable drizzle. It was one of those days when the greyness of the sky stretched below. Ollie said she would have liked to go to the other warrens, but the dampness in the air had brought on the stiffness in her joints. The description of the yew also fascinated her, and she was eager to hear a story from Aunt Mina, if it could be arranged.

The drizzle was falling in a powdery spray, driven by wind picking up from the south-west, as Nell went above late in the afternoon. He fed hard before starting off on the first part of his journey. He wished he'd listened better when the retiring errand runner explained where to go, who to see, where to find the best cover. He'd been too excited. He was excited now.

First stop was the warren in the field behind the privets. He crawled through a dark archway and found himself ringed by busy spikes of purple flowers on stalks towering over him like bulrushes. The field was mostly flat. Black rabbits were feeding in the open. Nell squatted to clean his face. From the first doe he met, he got directions to the grazing area of the dom.

The overweight rabbit had a scratchy voice to match his bald chin and gruff face. He put Nell at ease by inviting him to try some of his hogweed roots. Getting to share the best food at different warrens, Nell discovered that night, was one of the benefits of an errand runner.

The dom arranged an escort to take him to the other warren in the field, where he enjoyed the milky stems of sow thistle.

Nell was glad of the sagging cloud and darkness as he dropped down the slope on the next leg. Moving downhill he found almost as difficult as up. He had to adjust his stride more than once or he would have fallen over. The drizzle crowded in as he ducked through the hedgerow. With sight and smell muffled, hearing became all-important. Every now and then, he stopped and stood, listening. Nothing dangerous stirred. The ground could have been asleep. At a point he judged half-way, he became swamped in a mist that huffed from the rindle to meet him like a coat of invisibility. When he recognised the outlines of the drooping trees, he cleaned his face, realising he couldn't be far from the Low Warren. By chance, the first rabbit he met was the dom, who introduced himself as William.

'Good evening, Dom, I'm...'

'I know who you are,' said William, staring at Nell's forehead. 'The Patri didn't waste time, did he?'

'I'm not sure I follow.'

'Hardly surprising. Following's not exactly in your family's nature, is it?'

'You're making no sense to me, Dom.'

'Balls too eh? Excellent. Canny judge, that Fleet. Canny.'

Nell was puzzled, and must have shown it.

'Worry not, young buck. No, no. You must be hungry. Try some of these. There's more than enough for me.'

Nell found the willow leaves bitter, but chewed out of politeness.

'You'll appreciate them when you get to the leaf-fall of your life and the joints give you grief like these do,' said William, stretching a hind leg behind him. He was one of those rabbits who was never in a hurry. His eyes were moons younger than his face, which had a forever smile. Nell told him about the gathering. William groaned.

'He won't listen to me. I've said I'll agree to whatever he decides. Anything to save me a trip up that wretched hill. Insists I go to his jaw sessions. I'm sure the Patri only wants me there to lighten the mood.'

He thanked Nell for the message, and insisted on taking him as far as the boundary of his warren.

'Keep those ears alert by the rindle. Been reports of a lone otter fishing the stretch. Could get one of my bucks to take the message to the Border Warren, if you like.'

'Thanks Dom. I'll be fine.'

'I'm not one for this *dom* nonsense, Nell. The name's William.'

'Okay William. Nice meeting you. And thanks for the willow.'

Nell set off cautiously along the trail, which soon climbed the far bank of the combe and ran parallel to the rindle. The field remained gagged in mist. Dom William's humour had been refreshing, a reminder that he was missing Ollie's company.

Light from the full moon was filtering through the murk as he was met by a ranger on the outskirts of the Border Warren, so called because it stood near a gap in the hedgerow that marked the northern boundary of the area under the control of Governor Vort. A doe was told to take Nell to the burrow of the dom, who had retired for the day. As Nell cleaned his face, he noticed differences at this frontier warren. Some of rabbits spoke strangely. There was more variety in their fur – from pitch to passed grass brown. Many were jittery, jerking like dunnocks. He understood why when the mist cleared long enough to reveal the Chilling Wood rising menacingly behind the thicket. Billowing rainclouds and the hooting of a tawny owl added to an already grim scene. Nell was astonished to see a rabbit rise out of the water close to a barrier* that crossed the rindle to join the hedgerow on the other side. The rabbit shook its coat and wandered off.

Nell found the dom nibbling on watercress. He was offered some, and enjoyed the pungent taste. He declined the offer of a burrow for the day, saying the mist should give him good cover most of the way home. The dom advised him to use the combe, and got another doe to show him the way.

The route slowed him down, but he felt hidden enough in the nooks and shadows, especially when the rain stopped, and the cloud scattered to reveal a blue summer sky. When a buzzard appeared over the field, he hid in some yarrow plants. He was tired, despite the rests. If he did this again, he'd pace himself better, now he knew the distances. Keep

---

* A wire mesh fence.

more in reserve. There were risks, but there were more advantages. Good food. Interesting company. It was lonely between warrens. It would have been nice to have Ollie to share the experience, though his friend would have hated it. The unfamiliar spaces that gave Nell such a feeling of freedom would terrify the doe.

He waited for the buzzard to disappear, then pressed on. His hind legs were sore. It was tempting to spend the day in one of the bolt holes in the side of the hill. But he was determined to finish the job and get back to Ollie. He cleaned his face and entered the briar tunnel.

*****

OLLIE WAS CONVINCED Nell had been taken by a carn, and didn't recognise him until he was a few bounds away. She was so relieved, she almost forgot to tell him about Aunt Mina. The sage had promised a story if Nell returned before the daystar was at its highest.

'Says she never sleeps until then. She's seriously odd.'

Ollie stepped aside at the entrance to the yew to let Nell in first, and got a light cuff over the ear for being *so absurd*. The ancient doe was sitting in a corner, smelling of dog rose petals, and whispering. They sensed no other rabbit in the tree, so assumed she must be mumbling to herself. When Aunt Mina raised her lids, there was no doubt she was awake. The eyes were huge and bulging, as if she was in a trance. Her head was heavily wrinkled and the claws on her forepaws stretched out like talons. There was not a single whisker on one side of her craggy face, and the silvery wisps dangling almost to the ground from the other side gave her an unbalanced appearance.

Ollie was having doubts, until Aunt Mina began talking. Her voice was too deep for a doe, though few who heard her speak mentioned the tone. The words, from the first she uttered, danced with such vigour, such passion, her audience was soon captivated. Ollie rotated her good ear so she wouldn't miss anything.

'Once in many moons, perhaps once in the lifetime of a warren, a rabbit comes along with the right character to bring about change.

'Far away over the Torrent lives a warren of rabbits unlike any you've seen. Aidins they're called. Their coats are black like ours. Their ears are small, like their bodies. Dingha was such a rabbit. Born many moons ago. Timid little kitten. So terrified of the daystar he refused to go above till it slept. But Dingha was a special one, oh yes. Had a gift. Could see into the hearts of others. His dom believed such a gift should be put to use for the good of all the Aidins. So Dingha was sent to the Oakwood to learn the ways of the judges, rabbits skilled in the settling of arguments. He watched. He listened. He learnt. Said little, for the shyness remained.

'Dingha had been close to his mother, and when he heard she was ill, he rushed home. Sadly, he got there too late. In his grief, he was asked to settle a disagreement between two Aidin bucks who both claimed the same doe. Though he could see the solution immediately, his tongue knotted like a clod in his throat. When they laughed at him, he ran away, ending up here on the South Bank, where a small number of his own kind lived in burrows by the Torrent. When they learnt of his skill, Dingha was asked to try to end a dispute between two does who had been arguing for moons over the ownership of a burrow. He solved it immediately.

'Dingha was upset at the appalling conditions the Aidins were expected to live in. Whenever the Torrent rose, their burrows flooded. He was given one of the driest holes, but couldn't rest, thinking about others being worse off. So, he began living above. He'd overcome his fear of the daystar, but was exposed to the weather, the foxes, otters that hunted along the bank, the buzzards, kestrels. Many of the Aidins thought he'd gone mad. He kept settling their arguments, though, and was generous. Played with the kittens, helped does repair burrows after floods, was always the first to offer help if a rabbit became ill. Some bucks who liked what he was doing joined him. Soon, half the Aidins were living like him.

'One day, Dingha was attacked by three white rabbits. For the simple reason he looked different. After surviving countless attacks from foxes and buzzards and the like, he couldn't understand why other rabbits could act so roughly.'

Nell groaned, and Ollie could smell her friend was angry.

'From that day, Dingha vowed he would never give in to violence from another rabbit, or ever use violence himself to make a point. A moon or so later, he was beaten unconscious and had one ear torn when he strayed into a white area to retrieve a lost kitten. Dingha did nothing to defend himself. Took a long time to get over his injuries, and soon the bank was bitten by the worst winter in memory. Food became scarce, even for the whites on the Upland. They changed all the grazing zones. The blacks were pushed further out towards the Torrent, and the Aidins left virtually nothing. Dingha was outraged.

It is better to pass into the field of silence than to give in to such injustice, he said. His supporters agreed, and followed him to where some white does were eating. He'd chosen an interesting moment to challenge the rules. The head rabbit was hosting high-ups from the Oakwood Warren. They were watching from the Upland as the white rabbits charged at the little Aidins. Dingha calmly lay down, ears relaxed, as if he were asleep. Others did the same. On and on the white rabbits came. Dingha held his nerve. His supporters watched in terror. Most expected to pass into the field of silence. The temptation to hightail must have been tremendous. But they kept still. The whites charged to within a whisker of the Aidins... until they were stopped suddenly by a signal thump from the Upland. They withdrew, and Dingha and his friends were left alone.'

Nell started raining questions. Aunt Mina raised a paw to silence him.

'My duty is to tell the stories as they've been told to me, not to answer questions. You are free to take what you want from them. And if you two are as smart as the Patri tells me, you'll do just that.'

Ollie chewed over Aunt Mina's first words: *once in the lifetime of a warren a rabbit comes along with the right character to bring about change*. The sage had been staring at Nell. Her eyes were now closed, and the two friends took the hint that it was time to leave.

*****

NELL AND OLLIE spent many mornings captivated by Aunt Mina and her tales of black heroes from moons past. The story of Dingha was their favourite, and they tried to prise more information from the sage about the fate of the Aidins. All she would tell them was that

Dingha returned to the warren where he was born. Many of his supporters were captured, sent to an island, never seen again.

Nell kept running errands for the Patri, and Ollie went along on some of the shorter trips on warm nights. Nell grew in confidence. He discovered and memorised bolt holes and other hiding places along the way, and learnt to tell from a quick scan where the most likely sites of shelter would be. His long legs and lean body were ideally suited to covering distances, and his stamina was building. He learnt when and where to snack and rest to ensure he always had energy for emergencies.

Lessons learnt when he was a kitten came in useful, helping him pick the tracks and scents of carns, and to use stars for directions. Much of what Nell heard and saw, he passed on to Ollie.

Summer was running out of breath when Nell was sent to invite the doms to a special gathering to discuss a request from the head rabbit of the Golden Field for several of the strongest young bucks from outlying warrens.

The daystar was peeping over the eastern hedgerow as Nell and Dom William emerged from the briar tunnel onto Hilltop. Ollie slipped alongside as they got to the entrance of the tree, where the Patri was waiting. All the warren doms, and some other high-ups, were inside.

'I'm getting too rickety for these rushed requests,' panted William. 'When you've got intelligent youngsters around you like Nell here, I don't know why you bother bringing us old farts to some of these gatherings.'

'Come now,' said the Patri. 'The exercise will do you good. And you underestimate the value of your experience, William. You might have a point, though, about the youngsters. It wouldn't hurt them to sit in on this gathering, since it concerns an issue they will have to confront themselves sooner or later. Come Nell. You might learn a thing or two from us *old farts.*'

The Patri hopped through the opening. Nell hesitated, sniffing Ollie's anxiety.

'No way,' she said, shaking.

'What's the matter?'

'I don't belong in there. You heard the Patri. He said *Come Nell*. Not *Come Ollie*.'

'Nonsense. He said young*sters*. Not young*ster*. That it wouldn't do *them* harm to sit in.'

'I don't belong, Nell. He was only saying that to be polite.'

'If you won't go, I won't.'

'Now who's talking nonsense? *You* have to go.'

'We both do.'

'I've got things to do.'

'Like what?'

'I've, I've…

'If you don't, I don't'.

Ollie frowned.

'Relax,' said Nell. 'We'll sit in the back. They won't know we're there.'

There was little room for the two youngsters inside the yew. A large number of rabbits were waiting in a circle around the outside of the chamber. All the outlying warrens were represented. There was also a visiting dom from a warren to the north. Nell got winks of recognition, and a jab in the ribs from Ollie to get his nose down.

'Thank you all for coming at such short notice,' said the Patri, rising. 'I have invited two of the warren's newer members to sit in on this circle. Nell of the Willow, who I think most of you have met. And Ollie of the Platform. I have a hunch we might be seeing and hearing more of these two in moons to rise. Time will tell. For now, we have an important matter to discuss. The head rabbit of the Golden Field has asked for ten of our strongest bucks to be sent to him by the next moon. He didn't say what tasks he had in mind for them. My sources tell me, however, the whites are expecting a bumper hazel crop this season and want new workers trained before the nuts ripen. This is the first such request we've had for some time. We need two decisions. First, do we agree to the request? And if so, which bucks do we send?'

Having begun the discussion, the Patri crouched down on his coil and, as was the custom, took no further part until the gathering was almost over.

First to speak was the Row dom, at forty-two moons the youngest of the warren leaders present.

'If you ask me, the head rabbit's doing us a favour offering to take bucks off our paws. My warren for one is getting crowded. By winter, there'll be scarcely enough food to go around. I say those who want to leave should be encouraged to go. Some will find their own way to the Golden Field, be better off for it. All those exotic plants. Friends, action. More than we can ever offer them at the Row.'

The dom of the High Warren agreed. Like the Row, his warren escaped the ravages of the peacock moon flood and was becoming overcrowded.

'Some of my bucks will have to leave soon regardless, or I'll spend the entire leaf-fall and winter breaking up fights.'

Other doms sympathised with him, one or two nominating troublesome youngsters they'd like to see gone. The Platform dom disagreed.

'It's plain what the whites are up to. Why?,' he asked, scanning the circle, and settling on no rabbit in particular, 'why do they want only our strongest? Any rabbit can carry a hazelnut. Aunt Mina could do it. I say it's a deliberate ploy by the whites to weaken the bloodlines of the black warrens. Remove the strongest. Divide and rule. Oldest trick in the field. We fall for it every time. It's pathetic.'

His comments raised eyebrows and at least one groan, which told Nell the argument was neither new to the circle, nor widely accepted. Other rabbits had their say. Differences in the way they talked intrigued Nell. Some used stirring words or flamboyant motions. Others stuck to the facts, hoping they would speak for themselves. William of the Low Warren used humour. His speech got plenty of laughs and eased the tension inside the yew, but when the chuckling stopped the circle was no closer to decisions.

It was the speech from the Border dom, Gibson, that had the most impact on Nell. He was a wanderer, prancing around the empty space in the centre, eyeing individuals as he spoke in his unusual accent.

'If anything o'anyone be pathetic round 'ere it be us. Sitting 'ere posturing an' preening like overweight stock doves pretending, *pretending* we 'av the power tae change things. We 'av nae power. We black rabbits o'the South Bank are crushed beneath the paws o'a monster that 'av nae intention a'yielding one bit o'his power. Not a single claw.'

The dom strutted in front of the Patri.

'Yae sit there, suggesting in yae igh-up tone we can decide whether o'nae these bucks be sent. As if it make nae difference tae the whites either way. If yer believe that, yer bum's oot the burrow.'

The Patri winked his nose, apparently unruffled.

'We 'av nae say,' said Gibson, saliva dribbling over his bald chin. 'We 'av nae rights. Nae power. We be captives, nae, slaves in our own fields.'

He looked at Nell and Ollie.

'There sit the pride o'the South Bank. Leaders o'our warrens in moons tae rise. But will they one day take their rightful place in the circles o'the Willow, the Platform, the Border? Will they have any real power, other than the power tae run o'hide o'pass wind?'

Nell could almost taste the spicy tang of watercress on the dom's breath as he spat out the words.

'Nae,' Gibson answered himself, swaggering back to face the Patri.

'They, and others like 'em, will be bullied tae do the white rabbits' dirty work, in 'is warrens, when 'e wants, 'ow 'e wants. Forced tae live in damp 'oles full o'disease and depression and dark passages intae fields o'silence. If they be lucky, if they be strong enough tae survive, they'll 'av the privilege o'serving in the white rabbits' fields and burrows, risking their lives so some over-stuffed white doe can satisfy 'er addiction fae exotic nuts and nae 'av tae leave the safety and warmth o'er fancy 'ome.'

The voice dropped, but not the heat in the words.

'Let's nae fool ourselves intae thinking we face *two* decisions. The decision the bucks be sent 'as been made already. By the 'ed rabbit. We need waste nae further time o'that. The only decision we 'av in our limited power is which unfortunate rabbits tae send.'

Nell had never heard someone speak so angrily to the Patri. He could tell from the Patri's calm expression that, whether or not he was concerned about the issues raised, he was relaxed about the way the Border dom was speaking. At these circles, any rabbit who wanted to talk was listened to, though not all views were given equal respect.

Since arriving at Hilltop, Nell had heard whispered talk of a Golden Field. Most of it he'd dismissed as bragging.

The Patri signaled a break. Six does came into the yew carrying an assortment of plants. Strong-smelling leaves of white dead nettle, long leaves of mugwort, and a few early season haws. Nell and Ollie weren't sure what to do, until William indicated they were welcome to join in. Most of the doms ate in silence, although a few were mumbling between mouthfuls. Nell strained his ears, expecting them to be talking about what Dom Gibson had said. They were discussing the weather.

William approached.

'What do you think of it so far?'

Ollie surprised Nell by answering first.

'The Border dom talked... impressively.'

'He can talk, all right. It's sometimes hard to stop him when he gets going.'

'Do you agree with what he said?' asked Nell.

'Because a rabbit uses words cleverly, doesn't mean the words always make sense.'

William peeked over his shoulder, then dropped his voice.

'Gibson's the Patri's half-brother. He expected to become Patri, but missed out. I find it always makes sense to look behind a speaker to see why they think the way they do. Then you can decide how much notice to take of what they say.'

When the circle resumed, it was the turn of the lesser-ranked rabbits to speak. A deputy from the Row wondered what all the fuss was about. There was nothing new in strong bucks leaving a warren to try their luck elsewhere. They'd been doing it for many a while, before the white rabbits showed up. It was perfectly natural. Some of those who ended up being sent would probably choose to go anyway.

That, according to Gibson's deputy, was exactly the point. 'They should be free tae choose, as we are free tae speak 'ere.'

By midday, all the high-ups had spoken. It was time for the Patri to bring the discussion to an end.

'I thank you all for your... opinions. This is a matter on which there are many views. I find myself in agreement with those of you who suggest the head rabbit's interest in our bucks is more a demand than a request. And, as we have come to expect, my brother from the Border has provided a spirited and uncomfortably accurate summary of our problem.

'It would have been interesting to hear his thoughts on a *solution*,' he said. 'I'm sure there will be other opportunities. I also hear what others, especially those from higher ground untouched in the flood, are saying. That letting go of some rabbits could help your cramped warrens.

'Therefore, to sum up. Although the idea of being ordered to surrender our bucks is troubling to many of us, it is important to choose our battles. I'm sure no-one here needs reminding what happened to the last dom who questioned the authority of a governor.'

Some of the high-ups twitched their noses kindly in Nell's direction.

'It appears we have arrived at a decision. The head rabbit wants ten. The Row and High Warrens have bucks to spare. I say they should be given up, and we should leave it to the doms of those warrens to determine which ones will be sent.'

The decision seemed to be accepted. Nell noticed even the Border dom was nodding, though less enthusiastically than the others. The Patri thanked the circle again for coming.

'That is all. Go well.'

Nell and Ollie sat still as the older rabbits hopped out of the tree. The Patri noticed them and came over.

'Hope us old farts didn't bore you two to sleep,' he said.

'Far from it,' replied Nell. 'It was fascinating.'

'There's one thing I don't get, though,' said Ollie. 'Why did you let the Border dom speak to you like that?'

'Why not? He had a fair point, and every right to tell us. Sometimes a leader,' continued the Patri as they hopped out of the yew, 'has to be like a mother with kittens on their first days above. You sit back and let them explore for themselves, trying new plants, playing new games, flexing their muscles, searching out new ground. Some will be more adventurous than others. With gentle guidance, they'll all end up sharing the important experiences and believing they've discovered things for themselves. It's the same with a circle of high-ups. If they feel they've had their say, they'll feel they own part of whatever decision is made. That way they'll be more likely to accept it.'

The Patri yawned, and Nell found himself doing the same, as rabbits do.

'If you'll excuse me, I've got some sleep to catch up on. You smell like you have too, Nell.

'Go well,' they heard him say from further inside the tree.

If Nell hadn't been so distracted by the ideas swirling in his head, he might have wondered why the Patri had gone into the yew instead of his burrow. That image of him vanishing into the tree would return at a later, more critical time in his life.

Before going below, Nell's thoughts flickered down to the rindle and the Chilling Wood behind. He'd never thought about where the water flowed. As he turned to face north, he imagined two twigs carried on the current, passing through the hedgerow beside the Border Warren, then gathering speed as they were carried downstream.

9. Aim for the sky

THE WEB MOON rolled into the berry, and all around Hilltop Ollie saw signs of the coming leaf-fall. The temperature cooled and the sou-easterlies became more consistent, pulling coats of grey cloud over the fields. There were, however, still nights clinging to the passing summer. Behind the yew, the honeysuckle found a second wind, and flung its wonderful fragrance over the entire Hilltop as Ollie and Nell went above early one evening. They'd been invited to join a raid on the Patri's prized blackberries.

The daystar had set behind the hedgerow, and over the rindle the fattening crescent moon was half-covered by cloud. Nell had been reluctant at first, knowing that at this moon the berries were off-limits. But the Patri's blood son assured them his father had left for an important meeting near the Border Warren.

Watchers were positioned around the dell in case the Patri got back early, and to alert them to other dangers. Ollie felt wonderfully relaxed, and when Nell started saying he was uneasy about the raid, she stopped him mid-sentence.

'We'll be doing the Patri a favour. He'd become ill if he tried to eat all those berries himself. They'll rot, or be gobbled by aphids. And get that nose out of the stars.'

They arrived to hear the end of a joke about why white rabbits kept their ears to the sky.

'To catch as much as they can that's over their heads.'

Ollie instinctively joined in the laughter. A groan at her side told her that Nell wasn't amused.

'What's the matter, Nell?' the Patri's son asked. 'That one a bit over *your* head too, is it?'

Nell frowned.

'How many white rabbits have you talked to, had a conversation with?'

'One would be one too many,' replied the Patri's son, to more laughter. Not as enthusiastic, though enough for the buck to try another joke.

'What's a white rabbit doing when he puts his paws over his ears?'

Ollie cringed, fearing Nell's attitude was about to lose them a blackberry or ten. The Patri's son misinterpreted the quiet to mean he should answer his own question.

'Trying to hold onto an idea. Get it?'

No-one laughed. In the silence, Ollie considered how serious Nell was on matters of fur colour, how strong he was to not go along with the crowd, and how that strength was influencing the other rabbits, shaming them. How different he was to the Patri's son, a large though not particularly bright rabbit who changed the subject to the kitten-bearing potential of some of the warren's does. Two had promised to become his mates.

To Ollie's relief, Nell's interruption was quickly forgotten. During the early part of the night, as the moon sunk lower over the rindle, the young rabbits feasted on the berries, fossicking through the prickly stems and hairy leaves to find the darkest, most succulent fruit. Ollie had finished a massive berry she'd chosen to devour herself rather than share, when she noticed an even bigger one, out of reach. Suddenly the branch dangled almost to the ground. Nell had stepped on it, which merely added to Ollie's guilt.

The discussion changed to run-ins with carns. The Patri's son gave what all the rabbits assumed was an exaggerated account of evading a pair of owls. When no-one took him seriously, he challenged the others to do better. Emboldened by the comradery and with Nell at her side, Ollie rose on her hind legs.

'Tawny owls can be formidable, specially if you're unlucky enough to strike a hungry one outside the range of cover. But because they're fast doesn't mean they're smart, as I found one night.'

The others were so shocked to hear Ollie speak in a group, they pretended they were interested.

'I was grazing in the field up from the Platform. Thought I was alone, though can't have been, because there was an alarm stamp. Two. Then over my shoulder, I saw the outline of this huge owl gliding down at me.'

'What did you do?' asked one of the does.

'Hightailed of course,' said Ollie, a reply that raised some nervous laughs. 'Ran as fast as I could, weaving as we're taught. Sensed the owl closing. Couldn't shake it. And I was getting further and further from cover. It was only a matter of time.'

'What happened?'

So unused to being noticed, in a good way, Ollie felt like she was hopping on clouds. The other rabbits, including the bucks, had stopped eating to listen. All except the Patri's son, whose voice dripped with derision.

'Is that the best you can do, runt?'

Ollie's bravado evaporated like a cloud of spores from a puffball.

'I'll tell you what happened,' said Nell. 'Ollie swung around to face her attacker.'

Some of the rabbits gasped. None were as stunned as Ollie.

'How did you know?'

'I was there, watching from the alders.'

'You were the one who gave the alarm? You saved my life.'

'Oh no. I stamped only once. You said there were two stamps. It wouldn't have mattered if there were twenty-two. What you did next saved your life. I wouldn't have believed a rabbit could do such a thing if I hadn't seen it myself.'

'What happened?' yelled the Patri's son, interested now Nell was talking.

Nell looked at Ollie as if to say, it's your story... but Ollie desperately wanted her friend to continue. He did.

'The tawny was about to strike. Ollie here stopped, whirled on a blade of grass, and charged directly into the line of the carn.'

'A field of silence wish, surely,' said the Patri's son.

'Not at all,' said Nell. 'Ollie was cunning. And perhaps a little crazy. Though, as you can see with our friend here amongst us tonight, it worked. She'd waited until the last possible moment to react. The owl had thrust its feet forward for the strike. It timed its glide, though, to hit Ollie as she was running *away*, not *towards* it. The carn couldn't react fast enough to Ollie's switch. She managed to sneak past the talons.'

Ollie saw from the faces of the other rabbits that they were impressed, even the Patri's son. But before anyone had a chance to speak, a hideous face broke into the clearing.

*****

NELL WAS THE FIRST to bolt. The others, still tense from the story of the owl, scattered in terror. The Patri's son, who recognised the uninvited guest as Old Chief, the harmless former dom of the Border Warren, called his friends back.

Chief had retired to live out his last breaths at Hilltop. That had been more than thirty moons ago. No-one was sure how many moons he'd seen, including himself. Nell guessed at least eighty. One of his front teeth had grown outwards like the tusk of a giant earwig. Rabbits normally passed into the field of silence when that happened, because they couldn't eat properly. But as a revered hero, he had special privileges at Hilltop, where he was given food he could easily digest. He was the only other rabbit the Patri allowed near his blackberries.

Old Chief crouched in the dell, purple juice dripping from his tusk, as the young rabbits returned to form a circle around him. Nell felt Ollie trembling – reduced from daring to fearing in the flick of a tail. A fly was sucking on juice staining the old buck's chin. He ignored it. The deformed tooth twisted one side of his face into a grotesque scowl that made him look even more scary. Nell and the others waited for the old rabbit to tell them off for the raid. That, apparently, was the last thing on his mind.

'Listen tae yae'selves. Smell yae'selves.'

The accent might have been comical if the words weren't so cutting.

'Pride o'the warren, 'ope o'the South. Cringin in the brambles.

Frightened oot yer skins by a sac o'bones. And all yer 'av tae brag aboot is yer fancy legwork o'the number o'does yer want tae mate. No wonder we be slaves in our own fields.'

Nell felt ashamed. He wanted to look away, like the others, to hide from the eyes glowing like crazed moons. He forced himself to face the ancient rabbit.

'So yer should be ashamed. When I was yer age me an' m'comrades talked o'nothin but riddin' the South o'the whites. Regainin' control o'oor bank. Restorin' oor dignity. We looked oot for each other. *A rabbit be only a rabbit because o'other rabbits.* That meant somethin in moons past.

'All this time yer young'ins skulk round 'ere, the whites be extendin' their filthy grip. They've divided us, kicked us off oor land, now they're poisonin' oos with their *me, me, me* selfishness. And the most courageous act yer can think o'is raidin' the Patri's fruit, betrayin' 'is trust.'

Paws shuffled. Chief's voice softened.

'Yer won't be findin what yer seekin in the soil. The sky's where yer should be aiming.'

Nell looked up. A ragged crack in the cloud framed a single yellow light. The North Star.

'Please, please,' begged Chief, 'don't waste the most fertile moons o'yer lives betrayin' yer birthright, yer ancestors. I would 'ightail through the night and all o'tomorrow and the next day and the next for the chance tae spit in the face o'the white 'ed rabbit. It's too late for me. Too late for the Patri and 'is spineless 'igh-ups. Seduced, all o'them, into thinking they're dark-coloured whites. It's not too late fae yer. Yer oor only 'ope.'

Nell assumed the words were meant for the Patri's son. When he lowered his gaze from the star, the eyes of the ancient rabbit were staring directly at *him*.

*****

FLEET WAS INTRIGUED to learn that, of the two rabbits he'd recommended to the Patri, Nell ended up an errand-runner. Not that he thought him incapable of the job. The lengths he'd gone to save Henry after that terrible fight hinted at a strength of body and character. It had been the intelligence, though, the thirst for answers in the conversation by the rindle, that most impressed the seer.

Then there was Ollie, the one he sent to the Patri for her speed and agility. If any rabbit was destined to be an errand-runner, Ollie was that rabbit. When Fleet saw her dodge the tawny that night near the Platform, he had no idea she suffered from the stiffness. She'd shown nothing but flexibility, speed and sharp wits, when responding to Fleet's alarm stamp. And the Patri was probably too old-moon in his thinking to give a doe the important job of running messages.

The seer was sitting under the hedgerow not far from the Border Warren, nibbling on dead nettles, listening to the Patri praise the two youngsters.

'Don't get me wrong. They're both bright,' the Patri was saying. 'There's more to them, though, than simple intelligence. Particularly Nell. I've got other bucks, and does, who are clever. But it's been moons since I've met a youngster with such… focus. You should have seen his face in the circle, Fleet. Most rabbits his age would have dozed off. I'm convinced William sleeps through most of the gatherings, though somehow manages to keep his eyes open enough to fool us into believing he's listening. Nell, and Olivia, not only stayed awake to the end. You could tell from their faces, they were taking in every word.

'I'm not saying they're perfect,' the Patri continued. 'Little Olivia can be too flippant for her own good, and I sometimes wonder if she's faking her stiffness to get out of work. Nell can be stubborn, and eager to see the good in a rabbit. But there's something special about him, no doubt about it. Between you, me, and the stars, I'm thinking of Nell as a high-up in moons to rise, possibly a successor.'

Fleet was pleased. He might have been wrong about their respective abilities, though it appeared both rabbits had settled in well.

'I'm glad you approve of my choices. If what I'm picking up from my observations proves true, I'm afraid your warren, and other black warrens on the South Bank, could do with a few more rabbits like those two.'

'What are you seeing?'

'Not so much what I'm seeing,' said Fleet. 'More what I'm hearing. Rumours of growing anger and restlessness among the more extreme whites on this side of the Torrent. Not from anyone with the ear of the head rabbit. If anything, the head's one of the main targets of the anger. Some, believe it or not, say he's too soft on you blacks.'

'Soft! What a nerve. Tell that to Henry. Still, such rumours are nothing new. Nor do they have teeth or claws. Surely the whites have it too good to risk upsetting things.'

Fleet sighed.

'I hope you're right, Patri, though I'm not so sure. These rumours are coming from too many mouths to ignore. Makes me wonder whether Henry's… passing was as isolated as some might think.'

'It's not like you to get all dramatic, Fleet. Vort's become quite harmless, thanks in no small part to Henry. Haven't seen him since the fight. I'm told his leg's getting worse, rather than better.'

'I wouldn't underestimate Vort. His body might have slowed down. His thinking and tongue are as sharp as ever. The limp has made him worse. He might no longer have the claws to threaten your warrens, but he can influence others who do. And there are plenty of them on the South Bank.'

The Patri found a haw amongst the thorns, and Fleet was nibbling on a leaf of mugwort.

'As I was saying, if things do get tougher round here, rabbits like Nell and Ollie could come in handy. Two clever heads will be worth a hundred claws.'

Fleet could hear the Patri chewing on the haw, but could only faintly see his silhouette in the darkness. He envied the dark-coloured rabbits their invisibility on nights like this. It must be such an advantage to black seers in the North. How different their lives were. No-one called them *varlets*. They were simply seers. Like Fleet, they had the best jobs of all. Wind in their faces. Responsibility. Respect. It was a good life, and Fleet couldn't imagine doing anything else. The Patri was still chewing on the haw, so Fleet went on.

'If those two are as spirited as you say, you might struggle to keep them at Hilltop. They may be destined for bigger things.'

The Patri gave an uncharacteristic snigger. Fleet could have sworn he saw him do a little leap in the air. His face, now visible in the starlight, broke into a smile, as if he'd made an important decision.

'We'll see. We'll see,' he said, rubbing his chin on a stone. 'I must be off, Fleet. There's someone else I need to see on my way home. Thanks for your time, and your information. You must come and see us soon. My blackberries will be at their best any night now. I'll save you some of the tip fruit. They're always the sweetest.'

Fleet watched as the Patri, flanked by his oversized minders, skirted the thicket. The guard came out from his post beside the tunnel to meet him, and the two discussed something, the Patri pointing his nose from time to time in the direction of Hilltop. The guard bowed, and the Patri skipped off.

10. The taunting of Vort

NELL AND OLLIE became virtually inseparable after the raid on the blackberry patch. Old Chief's talk had a big impact on them, as had the words spoken at the circle. They sought out the old rabbit, who shared stories about the heroes of his youth. Through the ancient rabbit's memories, and the colourful stories of Aunt Mina, the friends heard for the first time of legendary rabbits like Haska, who had united the warrens surrounding Hilltop, and his half-brother, Gandeni, who took over as Patri a few moons before Nell's father was born.

According to Chief, white drifters encouraged by an evil buck named Erfeti, decided to start a warren under a rowan tree in a field to the north. They chased away families of black rabbits who'd lived there many moons. But Gandeni was generous. He decided to let the whites burrow down, as long as they were peaceful and respected the customs of Hilltop. He was also shrewd. He waited until the white rabbits had dug their first level of burrows, then invited them to share a meal.

Gandeni expected Erfeti to come alone and have a friendly chat. When the white leader arrived with a pack of terrifying bucks, who trampled through his grazing patch then circled the yew in an aggressive display of strength, Gandeni became suspicious. He suggested they celebrate the newcomers' arrival in the customary way, with a feast. It was early winter, and the food included haws and privet berries, and hazels from the tree near the Willow Warren. Then the cunning Gandeni asked his mates to bring out the climax – dried hops from the Patri's private supply. The whites had never tasted such a delicacy. They ate greedily, and became drowsy. Some fell asleep. It was a dark night. Erfeti didn't notice the large numbers of Gandeni's strongest bucks closing in on them. At Gandeni's signal, his rabbits attacked. Erfeti and his followers were easily overwhelmed by Hilltop bucks. Gandeni then told his rabbits to attack the half-completed warren in the next field, which they did, driving the whites out, chasing them all the way to the Chilling Wood.

Nell and Ollie soaked up story after story. They were like two petals stretching to absorb the fading light from the daystar. In their burrows, they talked and talked of history, of bravery, of victory. Of right and wrong. Also of pride. Pride at being part of something far larger than they had experienced. Pride in the colour of their fur. Their imaginations were fired, though Nell's was tempered by the Patri's earlier warning that Aunt Mina tended to exaggerate, and his father's advice that history was like a piece of chewed bark.

'What did you think of Old Chief's comments about the Patri and the other doms becoming dark-coloured whites?', Nell asked one night when the pair were out feeding.

'I took it to mean they're more interested in looking after themselves than their warrens. Like the whites. That stuff about *me, me, me*. Instead, they should be thinking about *all of us, all of us, all of us.*'

Nell pondered this. Yes. That probably was what Chief meant.

If their shared interest in the history of black rabbits was not enough to seal the bonds of friendship, the discovery that Nell had witnessed the tawny attack was. He learnt that Ollie had been orphaned when only a few days old, and was taken in by a foster mother at the Platform. Nell had started to ask his friend about her parents, but she shook her head uncomfortably, so he dug no further. Ollie had been sent to Hilltop the day after the tawny attack, though did not realise at the time it had been on Fleet's recommendation. She had not met the white seer.

They became so close that when Nell was sent on an errand run to the Low Warren, he missed his friend's company. As he watched Dom William chewing on willow leaves, he wondered if they would help ease the stiffness in Ollie's joints. He carried a mouthful to Hilltop, but when he got to the burrow, the leaves were so limp they were as useless as they were tasteless. One of the Patri's mates suggested he try the bark instead, which might hold its healing juices longer. Nell returned to get as big a piece as he could carry. The result was promising. Although it didn't remove the stiffness, particularly now the weather was getting cooler and damper, it eased the pain and helped Ollie get around more freely. She began ranging further from the burrow, with Nell as her guide.

As the berry moon yielded to the ivy, and leaves bound all summer to the embrace of their parents let go in riotous twirls of defiance, a late spell of warmth caressed Hilltop. Invigorated by the success of the willow bark, and the unseasonable weather, the two friends decided to go on an adventure to the Platform to visit Maisy. Nell felt sure she would recommend a variety of healing plants for Ollie's stiffness.

The night they chose was almost balmy. The moon, close to first quarter, was perched above the rowan with Jupiter tucked beside it, like a yellow kitten sucking at the teat of its mother. They cut across the corner of the field to the spindles, stopping to sniff some of the berries that had fallen to the ground. A pair of quarrelling squirrels sent a shower of unusual blossom to the ground from a tall vine. Ollie went over to investigate, and was soon nibbling away at the garlicy clusters.

The two rabbits sidled along the hedgerow. In the upper branches, a bird was feasting on bunches of berries. A flash of white grabbed Nell's attention. He quickly herded Ollie, who hadn't seen it, into the thicket. Through the leaves they saw three large white rabbits moving away to the east. In front was Levi, who had grown to an unbelievable size. Nell had been eating well and gaining weight at Hilltop, but Levi was something else. His coat gleamed in the moonlight. All muscle, and in a hurry to get wherever he was going. Since it was in the opposite direction to where Nell and Ollie were heading, they relaxed. Ollie suggested they pretend to be black heroes on an important mission to rid a warren of its white rulers.

'I'll be Haska. You can be Gandeni.'

Nell was so pleased with Ollie's uncharacteristic bravado, he couldn't object. Most other bucks and all the does at Hilltop would have waited for Nell to choose first, as if he had some special right.

As they continued down the hill, he imagined how different Haska would probably have been in real life from Ollie. Not scruffy. Not small. Would he, though, have been as smart, or as good a companion? When Nell suggested they change direction to forage near the rindle, Ollie laughed, and stumbled off on the same course. Nell found this odd. And the little rabbit's speech had become slurred. She was so relaxed, she hadn't mentioned carns for whiles.

The brave freedom fighters were still giggling as they entered the Platform field. The view reminded Nell how much fun he'd had as a youngster. Life had become more complicated at Hilltop. He was excited about seeing Maisy again. He imagined her delving amongst her beloved plants, that super-sensitive nose picking up his scent long before she could see him.

Two smells stopped him. One, the aroma of a plant he hadn't tasted since he left the Platform. The other was unpleasant, and he couldn't place it. He found the plant. Watermint.

'Over here, Ollie. Try this.'

'Don't you dare.'

Nell recognised the booming voice of Vort. He resisted the temptation to clean his face. The governor did not appear very lively. It was as if his body had shrunk, leaving the fur hanging in folds. His coat had lost its shine and Nell could tell from his face and limp that movement was awkward. The second smell was from Vort's chin glands.

Ollie ignored the white rabbit and nibbled at the plant.

'This is delicious, Gandeni,' she said.

This was so unlike Ollie. Vort scowled.

'I said leave it alone and scarper, you insolent varlet.'

Ollie kept munching. Loudly.

'Do you have any idea who I am?'

Ollie swayed, a faraway look in her eyes. Nell couldn't believe what his friend said next.

'Course, a'course. Can see right through ya.'

'What's that supposed to mean?'

Nell detected a note of uncertainty in the governor's voice, and wondered if Ollie had also noticed.

'Ya be one of them whites extendin' ya filthy grip, poisonin' oos with ya *me, me, me* selfishness,' she said.

Vort glared at Nell. Was that recognition? Nell couldn't be sure. It was as if the governor was looking at him but not seeing him. Nell sensed that in his condition, the white rabbit was powerless. And alone. Ollie, still acting out the fantasy of Haska, was enjoying herself.

'But I can see,' she said, lifting her tail, 'you're in need of a little nourishment.'

She sent a spray of urine over the remains of the watermint.

'So, you're welcome to it.'

A puff of steam floated into the air.

'You'll answer for this,' thundered Vort.

In a twinkling, the two friends hightailed.

*****

OLLIE FELT EXHILERATED. As if her new-found mobility, the inspiring stories from Old Chief and Aunt Mina, and the mood they were in as they pretended to be black heroes, had freed her, given her a new zest for life. She was also weirdly light-headed. She suspected the strange plants* she'd nibbled were to blame.

She hadn't recognised Vort at first. He was a shadow of the all-powerful governor of her kitten days. There was also something familiar about the governor's scent. She wondered, as they stopped to catch their breath, if it would have made a difference.

Ollie had become someone else, if only for a moment. Not a small insignificant doe, but a brave, confident freedom fighter. She looked at Nell, expecting to see a face full of the same excitement. Instead, she saw sadness. They nibbled at stems of foxtail, past their best. Nell was the first to speak.

'You certainly put him in his place.'

Ollie took these words as support.

'Still can't believe I did it. Felt good, didn't it?'

---

* Ollie had eaten hops, a plant humans use to make beer. Rabbits can become sleepy, light-headed, even drunk after eating it.

'It certainly was a new experience,' said Nell.

'Let's hope it won't be the last. Shows we don't have to put up with this nonsense from the whites night after day after night.'

Nell's mouth curled into a smile. Ollie saw something else in his eyes.

'Then what's troubling you?'

'I was thinking about my mother.'

'Ah, Maisy, of course. Let's go tell her what happened. She can join our celebration.'

'That's the problem,' said Nell, his brows drawn together. 'I'm sure Vort recognised me. If I'm right, my mother's burrow will be the first place they'll look for us.'

Ollie felt as small as a mouse. Smaller. She knew how excited Nell was to see his mother, and her foolish display meant the reunion was impossible. Worse, it would have put Maisy in danger.

'I'm so sorry, Nell. I wasn't thinking.'

'You don't need to apologise. Vort had it coming.'

Nell grinned.

'Still can't believe you pissed on that plant.'

He was smiling, though Ollie could tell it was for her benefit.

'What do you think Vort will do?'

'My guess is he'll limp to his rowan, rouse a few bruisers, and send them after us.'

Ollie sunk lower to the ground, and whispered.

'What do you suggest?'

Nell sniffed in the direction of the rowan, then up into the sky. The moon was about to set, but there was plenty of light from the stars.

'Vort will think we were going to the Platform. That might help us. It'll take him whiles to reach his rowan. We've got a bit of time. Problem is, we'll be like voles for the taking if we stay in the open in this light.'

A prospect that would normally terrify Ollie, if she wasn't with Nell. So calm in a crisis. Always thinking two, three, four bounds ahead.

'We'll have to find somewhere to hole up,' said Nell, using his front paw to clean mud from his ears.

'How can you think of grooming at a time like this? Who's going to see you? We're supposed to be hiding.'

Nell flapped one ear, then the other.

'I know a place. We'll have to go quickly, though, in case Vort has the hedgerow watched.'

They kept off the main trail, travelling parallel to it among the bushy plants by the rindle. Ollie was soon struggling, her legs tightening, though she didn't complain. After causing such trouble, the last thing she wanted was to add another burden. They arrived at the place where the rindle disappeared into the thicket, but found the twisted branches too thick to get through. Nell raised his ears, then set off. How different Ollie felt now than she did earlier. Then she had been Haska the hero, untouchable. Her encounter with Vort was already a distant memory as they approached the gap, hoping it was still unguarded.

They were in luck, and darted quickly through into the field on the other side. Nell followed a narrow channel through the grass, aiming for a line of willows beside the rindle. The tips of the trees' branches drooped into the water. Nell explained that the trail went between the trees and the water, and eventually passed the Low Warren.

'Is that where we're going?'

'No, it's too far. There's a hole in the third tree I found once, when I had to hide from a buzzard. You'll have to put up with the stench of weasels, I'm afraid. It's not fresh. At least two moons by now. Hopefully still strong enough to frighten searching rabbits.'

It was clear that Nell had changed his plan for Ollie's benefit. She was too tired and terrified to resist. As they made the first tree, the daystar was appearing over their right shoulders, revealing flat-bottomed thunder clouds forming over the downs. The wind, though, would carry any bad weather south, not towards them. Nell stopped long enough for Ollie to chew off a loose piece of bark at the base of the trunk. She noticed the odour of weasels as they approached the hiding tree. Thin black droppings, twisted at the ends and full of fur and feathers, littered the ground.

Nell offered to keep watch as Ollie rested. Sleep took a long while, as her head zigzagged from the awareness that she'd crossed a forbidden line with Vort and would be an outcast forever, to tingling thoughts of the remarkable rabbit watching over her.

VARLET SERVANTS were packing soil over the mouth to the eastern passage in readiness for winter, so Levi went to the hole at the top of the northern. It was the least used of the four entrances, kept clear in case the governor's burrows were attacked. The other reason it was little used by Vort's extended family was because it was for servants. Known as the Black Hole, it stunk like varlet wind. Not only because of the servants. It was also the place varlets had to wait if they wanted to see the governor.

Lightning flashed over the downs, followed by a deep rumble. Levi shuddered at the memory of the first sound to reach his ears, as he'd huddled in a nest underneath an alder tree seven moons earlier. The distant boom, which preceded the flooding of the rindle, had terrified the new-born kitten, whose eyes had not yet opened. He'd nestled closer to the shaking, but warm body beside him, as the storm raged outside.

His mother had been coming to the nest once a day to suckle them. She stayed less than a while, never said a word. Levi was left to take his own meaning from the roaring anger above. One night, he heard soil being scraped away from the entrance, then a voice. A deep, snarling voice. A thud, a wail, a splash. The scraping began again, rougher this time. Less careful. He crawled towards the noise, squinting. Cold air gushed into the nest and something wet struck his face. Sharp teeth grasped his neck, and he was lifted. Wet drops pounded his body as he thrashed his hind legs in the emptiness. Then the sensation of fast shaking that went on and on until all was quiet.

When he woke, he was alone in another nest. Warmer, dry, larger. Smells he would later recognise as thistle and hazelnut filled the air. A doe came to offer her teats. The milk was warm and soothing, so he sucked eagerly. When his eyes opened the next day he went searching for his mother. Helga was trying to decide whether to finish her meal with dandelion or nettles. She told the nanny to take the kitten to its chamber.

Levi had spent most of his first moon in the care of the black nanny, including his first outings above. His mother had all the plants she needed brought to her, and spent most of her time below. Because the nanny was black, and could only go to certain parts of the field, Levi's early adventures were limited. There were no playmates. The Hide was the furthest he strayed from the rowan.

After the fight between Vort and the varlet dom, Henry, Levi's mood had swung from elation to bewilderment. Until Vort found him watching the varlets playing Patch, and decided then and there to take over the education of his son. Time lost was soon found. Levi accompanied the governor on his rounds, where he learnt the proper places of white and black rabbits. Whites were born to rule over blacks. It was a given, as day followed night. Plain in every action, every sound, on every rise, in every burrow. Whites were more intelligent, stronger, faster, more honest, cleaner, simply superior in every way. It was part of the natural way of life. The birds lorded it over the flies. The moles lorded it over the worms. The owls lorded it over the mice or other small mammals dim-witted enough to get caught. And white rabbits lorded it over the stupid, thieving, dirty varlets.

Though Levi didn't understand it at the time, the injury to his father's leg changed things. Vort had become frustrated by his limp, but showed no interest in punishing the varlets again because the rabbit who caused the injury had passed into the field of silence. Levi, though, wanted revenge for himself, and the target of his hatred was Nell, the rabbit whose unblinking eyes had given him nightmares many times since.

A lone buck was crouched by the Black Hole as Levi entered. He didn't recognise William, and if someone pointed out to him that the rabbit was a respected dom, it would have meant nothing. If they mentioned that William had been waiting all night, it would have meant even less. The outraged voice of the governor could be heard through the burrow's walls. Levi hurried to the living chamber. He could feel the venom on Vort's breath.

'…then it had the insolence to lift its leg and piss on it.'

Father never swore in front of mother.

'Calm down,' said Helga, 'you'll do yourself another injury.'

'What's happened?' asked Levi.

'Your father has had a… disagreement with some… rabbits of colour, who took advantage of his bad leg.'

'What happened?'

'They insulted me, the varlets.'

Levi had never seen his father so furious.

'Who did this?'

'It doesn't matter,' butted in Helga.

'Of course it matters,' roared Vort. 'If the varlets think they can get away with this, they'll all be laughing in our faces.'

'Did you recognise any of them, father?'

'No. I don't think they were from round here.'

'What did they look like?'

'Like varlets. All the same to me.'

Levi was disappointed.

'There was something unusual about the buck though. Smudge of light fur on its head.'

Levi felt as if it was *he* who had been violated.

'I know that little turd. Its father was the varlet that did your leg in.'

'Henry?' said Vort, calming down. As he said the name, he screwed up his nose as if smelling something rotten.

'Nell. That's its smudge-faced son,' said Levi. 'You should have let me toss it into the field of silence when I had the chance.'

'Don't talk like that,' said Helga. 'Why does everything have to be so violent?'

'It's the only thing they understand,' snorted Vort. 'So that was Nell. I've been hearing about a Nell. Some of the loonier varlet does talk about a Nell as if it has some sort of magic powers. Madder than adders, they are.'

Vort clenched his jaw.

'Nell. Nell. Where else have I heard that name? Ah yes. A Nell was sent to live at the warren of the old git the varlets call Patri. On the say-so of Fleet, the seer from the North. The buck is apparently being talked about. We better keep an eye on this Nell.'

The varlet's moons are numbered, Levi thought, as he slipped out into the passage.

11. Choose your battles

WHEN OLLIE WOKE, it was well after midday. A piece of fresh bark lay in front of her. Nell was sprawled in a clump of grass, ears resting flat, though Ollie could tell from his nose that he was alert. He reported that white rabbits had come along the trail soon after Ollie dozed off. They returned to the field, making directly for the rowan. No other rabbits had come near.

'Your turn to rest,' she said. 'I'll wake you at dayfall or if anything happens.'

Nell started to refuse, then gave in.

The afternoon passed anxiously, but quietly. The only hint of danger came from a lone fox that appeared from the direction of the combe. Ollie watched as the carn, a juvenile that had probably left its parents to look for a territory of its own, stretched on its hind legs to snatch blackberries from branches in the hedgerow. It had not been necessary to wake Nell. The fox was too preoccupied with the fruit to look in the rabbits' direction.

A pair of chiffchaffs resting on a nearby branch took exception to a starling mimicking the *twit* notes of their song. The little birds became surprisingly aggressive, harassing the starling until it changed its tune. Nell slept through the raucous argument, but was woken soon after by the tapping of a woodpecker.

They chose two pieces of bark to take to Hilltop. Few other rabbits were above, as they skirted the Low Warren and took what Nell said was a short cut. Fog that had been closing in as they left the rindle thickened.

Ollie began tiring, and it didn't help to see her friend cruising up the hill. The lure of her warm, dry, safe burrow nudged her on. The trip had been an adventure alright, though from now on she would leave the adventuring to Nell. Hilltop would do fine, thank you very much. A great place to grow old.

They were met at the top of the briar by the Patri's son. Father wanted to see them both at the blackberry dell. Ollie's first thought was how to avoid the confrontation. She could cry exhaustion. Wouldn't have to pretend. Had news of their run-in with Vort reached the Patri? Or had he learned of the raid on his berries? Either way, they were in trouble, were sure to get kicked out of the Patri's burrow – lose their privileged status. She looked to Nell for support. He was cleaning his forehead. How could any rabbit groom at a time like this? They dropped their pieces of bark and moped off to meet their doom.

The Patri was snoring in the dell. Purple juice stained his chin and chest. The two friends crouched, awaiting their fate, unsure whether to wake him. Ollie was afraid it would make things worse. But when the Patri opened his eyes, he greeted them like long-lost friends.

'Ah, welcome back. Both of you. So grown up and mature. You must be hungry. Please,' he said, motioning to the brambles around him, 'help yourself to some of the fruit. They're at their best this moon.'

Ollie couldn't believe it. They weren't going to be kicked out after all. Her place at Hilltop was secure for moons to rise. The berries tasted better than she remembered.

The fog thickened. At one point, as they fossicked on the far side of the dell, they lost sight of the Patri, but could hear him raving about the virtues of blackberries.

'Some say they're good for fevers, though I've never had to test it.'

It was not like the Patri to bother with small talk. He was normally so direct. He came into view, still rambling.

'They're good for all manner of things. Sore throats. Bleeding gums. Blistered paws. Had a doe tell me once that they could cure the runs. Can you believe that?'

Ollie was willing to believe anything right now.

'They've helped keep me in reasonable condition, I suppose. Though there's one thing they can't do, and that's stop a rabbit ageing. I'm not getting any younger.'

Ollie and Nell exchanged *what-is-he-on-about?* looks.

'Therefore, I feel it is my duty to ensure my favourite son and daughter are properly… taken care of. I have chosen fine mates for you both. Let us announce the arrangements to the warren. Come.'

The Patri disappeared into the fog. Ollie looked at Nell, who was choking on a berry.

*****

LEVI HAD WAITED long enough and was almost to the bend of the western passage, when the voice of his mother stopped him.

'Where do you think you're going?'

He resented her meddling.

'Out. Somewhere. Haven't decided.' It wasn't a lie. He had no idea where he'd find the varlet.

'Don't do something stupid, Levi.'

Helga shuffled off to her chamber. She didn't understand. How could a doe be expected to? He barged through the chamber of Vort's second mate into the narrower passages. Karl, a half-brother who'd been hanging around him lately, was asleep in an outer burrow. Levi kicked him awake.

'Get the others and meet me at the Black Hole.'

Levi crept into the food storage chamber, hoping he wouldn't be seen by Helga.

He grabbed a hazelnut and munched it as he squeezed through the opening at the rear of the store that backed onto the guard post beside the Black Hole. The guard jumped in fright, then bowed when he recognised the governor's son.

Levi hopped into a thickening fog. As he waited for the kins, he noticed a varlet cowering by the hedgerow.

'What are you doing here?'

'Governor asked to see me, master.'

'Well don't eat anything. Or crap around here. And stay further away. You stink.'

'Yes master.'

Karl and two hefty bucks – dimwitted but strong – piled out of the hole, frowning at the fog.

'Come,' growled Levi.

*****

NELL PANICKED and bolted, spitting pips and juice as he went. He could tell, with some relief, that Ollie was close behind as he charged through the brambles in the opposite direction to the Patri, ignoring tangly thorns trying to restrain him.

The initial hightail was impulsive, to get away from the Patri. The drifting fog engulfed the two rabbits as they broke free of the brambles. Nell was thinking bounds in advance, a skill he'd learnt on his errands. He wondered if the Patri would have anticipated their reaction, what he might do to make them return. The main trail was too risky. The obvious place to post guards.

The briar enclosed the entire ridge beneath Hilltop. Almost all movement up and down was via the two main tunnels – to the combe and to the trail hugging the thicket on the eastern side. Nell had heard of one other route, a little-used tunnel called the chute, which ended in a depression ringed by elder bushes. The fog thickened into a dreary cloud. Nell took Ollie through wet chest-high grass to where he guessed the tunnel would enter the briar. Ollie flinched when she saw the steepness of the chute, but followed him down. After a few tumbles, they emerged into the lower field, scratched and sore.

They hadn't got far when Ollie asked to stop for a rest. Nell knew that, as his friend tired, she wouldn't think straight, becoming more vulnerable. The fog had gathered around them, colouring the night dark as pitch. There was little chance they could be seen in this murk, either by pursuing rabbits or carns. Smell, sharpened by the moisture in the air, would be almost as important as hearing. Nell listened hard. The only noise was the panting of Ollie.

'What are we going to do?'

'I can't mate the doe the Patri has chosen. Even if she hadn't promised herself to his blood son. I've never spoken to her.'

Ollie nodded.

'Same here. I'm sure I'm the last doe he would choose.'

'Problem is,' said Nell, 'the Patri has decided for us, which is the way these things are done here.'

'I was worried something like this might happen,' said Ollie. 'You'd think he'd know which doe his own son had his nose on.'

Nell wasn't surprised the Patri was unaware of his son's yearnings. It was not something a buck discussed with his father. Nell also realised the decision of the Patri was final. To question it would be to challenge his authority, which was not an option. He glanced at his friend, who was breathing normally again, though tensing her hind leg in the damp air.

'I can no longer stay here, Ollie. I couldn't insult the Patri like that and expect life to go on as it was. It wouldn't be fair. I must leave Hilltop. That's *my* choice. You must decide for yourself.'

The distant cry of a fox penetrated the gloom. Ollie crept closer.

'I can't believe you'd think for a heartbeat that I'd come to a different conclusion. I'll miss that place, but you're right. No choice.'

'I feel bad though, running away like this, after all he's done for us.'

'From memory,' said Ollie, 'it was the Patri who said it's important to choose your battles.'

Nell smiled. His friend didn't miss much. It was also a smile of relief. The journey in front of them would be more bearable with Ollie's company. The fog cleared briefly, allowing slithers of moonlight to penetrate. As they chewed on foxtail roots, bitter after the rye they'd become used to at Hilltop, Nell felt strangely liberated. As if he'd been stuck in a burrow for days waiting for the rain to stop. He stared at the spot where Ollie had been crouching. Her prints were unmistakable in the soaking grass.

12. Flight to the border

TERROR. That's what Levi wanted to see most of all. Terror in those varlet eyes.

Damn this fog. He could not see far, and the wetness swamped his nostrils. He stopped to listen through his good ear. Nothing. Where were those dozy dunnocks? He hollered. Answers came in grunts as white shapes appeared from the mist, like wingless, panting barn owls.

All three bucks were, like Levi, fathered by Vort. Because they were mothered by the governor's second and third-ranked mates, they had less status, and were known simply as kins. Levi was always getting the two dimwitted ones mixed up. That was *their* problem. They were a few moons older than Levi, almost as big, and liked to fight. Karl, the smaller of the three, smelt like garlic. He was smarter than the other two put together. Not that they were here for their brains.

'Come,' grunted Levi.

'Isn't it over that way?'

It was Karl.

'Shut it and do as I say.' Levi sauntered off, though had no idea where they were. Before he'd stopped, he was sure they'd been aiming for Hilltop. Changing direction to wait for the kins had confused him. Damn this fog. He hurried on in a straight line, to remind them who was in charge, then veered in the direction Karl had indicated. They reached the combe and Levi chinned against a rock. He hadn't been in this field often enough to be sure how far they were from Hilltop. The fog wasn't so thick at the bottom, and Karl said he recognised a bluff on the far side.

'If I'm right, we're one hundred, maybe ninety bounds from the bottom of the hill.'

'More like eighty,' snapped Levi.

The fog thickened again as he led them on, until a change in the density of the air warned him of a sudden rise. A faint whiff of varlet wind slowed him down, and probably stopped him tumbling into the black guard crouched beside the mouth to the briar tunnel. The varlet rose on its hind legs, then hobbled backwards when it recognised the governor's son. Levi scowled at the pathetic excuse for a rabbit, shaking like a kitten. Why didn't they put these cripples out of their misery?

'We're after the varlet, Nell. Where is it?'

'They all up top, master.'

Levi was about to enter the tunnel when he heard voices echoing from the briar. They were getting louder. He stepped closer and listened.

'... seen him so miffed.'

'Where d'ya reckon they've gone?'

'The old one saw...'

'Hey. Did you smell that?'

'What?'

'Like bark, sort of tangy.'

'It's the mist. Mixes things up.'

'I guess.'

Levi backed off quietly and waited. Two varlets seeped out of the tunnel and got the fright of their lives. Levi was annoyed that neither of them had a smudge on its head.

'Where's Nell?'

'Dunno master.'

Levi swaggered nearer, itching to strike.

'We been sent to find him too, master,' squealed the other flea-sac. 'Nell run away. Ollie too.'

'You're lying. Why would it run away?'

'Patri said he had to mate a doe, master.'

Levi snorted. *Running away from a doe.*

'I've heard the varlet doms do that,' said Karl. 'Choose mates for you, I mean.'

Levi pretended to ignore him.

'What's the *old one?*'

'Master?'

'One of you varlets was talking about an old one seeing something. What is it?'

The blacks eyed each other nervously. Levi swung his right paw, sending one of them crashing into the briar. He raised his paw at the other.

'Aunt Mina, master. The sage. She saw Nell and Ollie heading for the chute.'

'What's that?'

'Another tunnel, master. Secret one. Down the briar. Over there. Master.'

*****

'STAY ALERT,' said Nell, brushing past Ollie.'

As he suspected, their two sets of prints led up the slope.

Were those voices away to the east? He couldn't be sure. He placed his paws onto one lot of prints, then hightailed. After thirty or so bounds, he veered up the slope and went in a wide arc until he met the original prints. He crossed them and kept going in a large circle on the other side until he returned to Ollie.

'What in Gandeni's name are you doing?' she asked.

'Covering our tracks.'

'Clever.'

'We'll see if it works.'

'Did you hear something out there?'

Frightening Ollie would not help.

'Not a squeak. How about that good ear of yours?'

'You mean other than the Patri's son sobbing when he found out I'd done a runner?'

'Dreamer. We better get going though, if you feel up to it.'

'Lead the way.'

They didn't discuss where they were going.

There was no need.

It was plain from recent conversations their destiny lay in the fields to the north.

The fog deepened again. Nell was aiming for The Twins, two look-alike willows upstream from the Border Warren. There they could rest, Ollie could feed on the bark, and they could consider what to do next. The only sound was the swish of their bodies through the wet grass. Gradually the trickling of water flowing over stones became louder.

A shift in the light breeze told them they'd got to the trees. As they fed, Nell explained that the hedgerow had become so overgrown at its base, no rabbit could get through. The Border dom was responsible for keeping a single tunnel open.

'Best to aim for that. There'll almost certainly be a guard on the tunnel. We'll worry about that when we get to it. We'll have to keep off the main trail. Too many of the dom's rabbits would recognise me.'

The sound of bucks approaching brought the meal to an end. The part of the conversation they overheard suggested that the rabbits, whites from their voices, were looking for something other than two runaways.

'Reckon they're gonna show tonight?'

'Yep. This fog's not as thick as it was when we left. Give it a while or two, and I'd say it's all on.'

Nell and Ollie slunk towards the plants growing at the water's edge. Thankful for the cover of the remaining fog, they made their way carefully along the bank, stopping now and then when they heard or smelt rabbits.

They came to the point where the rindle flowed under the strange barrier.

It looked like a giant spider's web, with silver strands thicker than rabbits' claws going up and across in unnaturally straight lines.

After watching a twig hit the barrier, bobble, then reappear on the far side, Nell led Ollie up a trail by the hedgerow. In places, it had become so overgrown it hung over their path, and more than once the rabbits hopped through real spiders' webs.

Nell was thinking they'd missed the tunnel, when he heard a rabbit snoring. Perhaps they'd be in luck.

*****

THE BOTTOM of the chute was hidden by a ring of elder bushes, but Levi couldn't miss the prints. The four white rabbits followed the tracks until they came to a place where the varlet prints divided. Levi was about to suggest they split up, when Karl chuckled.

'It's a trick. The two lots of prints start again down there, going towards the rindle.

'Or the border tunnel,' said Levi, rushing past him.

13. Alone on the other side

NELL AND OLLIE might have got through the tunnel if it wasn't for a brittle leaf crackling under Ollie's paw. The sound stirred the black guard, who jumped up, blocking the opening.

'Och what we 'av 'ere then?' he said, yawning and peering through bleary eyes at the two friends.

Nell could feel his chin was still stained with blackberry juice. It was too late to do anything about it. He remembered some high-ups talking about a warren somewhere to the north called Oakwood. There was nothing to lose.

'We're going to our home at Oakwood. Sir.'

'That so? And when exactly dae y'spect tae get hame, eh?'

The accent was similar to other rabbits from the Border, and Nell sensed from the way he said *hame* that a trap was being laid. He tried to bluff his way out.

'Depends whether we decide to stop for a snack on the way. I'd expect we'll be in our burrows by dayspring.'

Nell could tell from the guard's reaction that he'd guessed wrong.

'Nice try, Nell, is it? And ye must be Olivia. Been 'specting ye. I've been ordered by ye father not tae let ye through. Ye tae return immediately tae Hilltop. Refuse and I'm tae arrange an escort.'

Nell sighed at the word *father*.

'That won't be necessary, sir. To tell you the truth, I'm glad we're not going through there. I've heard awful tales about beasts that come out of the Chilling Wood. We were unsure, weren't we Ollie, whether to go or stay? You've helped us decide.'

Nell hoped the guard wouldn't see the confusion in his friend's eyes.

'Canny choice,' said the buck. 'If the Patri's description of ye chosen mate's half-correct, I'd be willingly swappin' places w'ye. Still, I'll be havin' tae tell 'im ye were 'ere. He 'spect ye'd try tae leave the field. So maybe 'e'll go easy on ye when ye get hame.'

'I'm sure you're right,' said Nell, encouraging Ollie away. 'The Patri is very… forgiving. We're sorry to have woken you. Stay well.'

As they retreated, they heard the guard sniggering to himself: 'Oakwood by dayspring. Noo I've 'erd everythin'.'

*****

OLLIE WAS TRAPPED between depression and elation. She'd agreed to Nell's plan to head north without question, or thinking about what they might find there. Mention of beasts coming out the Chilling Wood reminded her of tales she'd heard as a kitten.

Giving up a life of comfort, safety, and privilege for a shot at danger, hunger and discomfort didn't sound like her idea of fun. Unlike Nell, she wasn't used to bounding into unknown surroundings. The more she thought about what lay behind the hedgerow, the more pleased she was to stay on this side.

If the decision had been hers alone, she would have hummed, then hummed some more, then stayed. It would have been the wrong decision, but the easiest. Safest. It seemed, though, from Nell's behaviour, that rejection at the tunnel was no more than a minor obstacle. You had to admire that about him. There was always a back-up plan.

As soon as they were out of range of the guard, Nell cut back to the rindle. The fog remained, though it was thinning quickly as they reached the water for the second time that night.

Nell dipped one of his front paws in. He withdrew it immediately, wincing. He studied the barrier straddling the rindle. An ominous feeling came over Ollie.

'We'll have to swim,' said Nell.

'Yeah,' she giggled uncertainly. 'Better still, we could flap our ears and fly over.'

'Seriously. I saw a rabbit swim under that *thing* once from the other side. He was coming against the current, so it shouldn't be too hard for us to go downstream.'

Ollie gaped at the water.

'It's cold,' Nell added. 'If we take a deep breath, jump in, and sink to the bottom, the current should carry us through. Then we float to the surface on the other side. Shouldn't be in the water long. What do you say?'

'I say you're out of your mind.'

'You got a better idea?'

Ollie felt like saying *yes*. Let's bite ourselves and wake up.

And if we find we're not in some crazy nightmare, that this is really happening, let's go home, apologise to the Patri, burrow-down with his choice of mates and live happily ever after.

Or we could go to the Platform and apologise to Vort, say we mistook him for someone else, some idiotic rabbit who was trying to convince us blacks were no different to whites, and how crazy is that?

*****

THE TRACKS of the varlets became lost in a muddle of prints. Levi stomped up to the guard and chinned against a branch.

'I'm after two runaway varlets.'

'Aye master. Yer not alone.'

Why did these pellet-heads always speak in riddles?

'Have you seen them?'

'I 'av master. Just now.'

'You better not have let them through.'

'Och nae master. 'Ad my 'structions.'

'Whose instructions?'

'Patri, master. Asked me tae send 'em back.'

'And?'

'I dae as I be told, master.'

'We've come from that direction varlet. You're lying.'

'What was that noise?,' whispered Karl.

Levi hadn't heard anything.

He'd been directing his good ear at the varlet.

'It was like a splash.'

'Probably a water vole, master,' said the guard, eager to please. 'Plenty round 'ere.'

'Shut it,' hissed Levi, trying to keep his voice down.

'Something might have frightened it,' said Karl.

Levi grunted. He told the kins to search along the trail by the rindle.

'If you see the one with the smudge on its head, grab it. Go as far as the Twins. If you see nothing, meet us here. And I want the varlet alive.'

The kins snarled, and charged off.

'Karl, come. Let's see what caused that splash.'

*****

NELL WATCHED as bubbles floated to the surface where Ollie had jumped as soon as she heard the voice of the governor's son. The barrier swayed a little as, Nell assumed, Ollie passed under it. Then he heard more splashes and gasps from the other side.

He flinched. A breeze rustled the leaves on the spindles, bringing an unwelcome scent. Digested hazelnut. His vulnerable little friend was alone on the other side. He squeezed his eyes shut, filled his lungs, and slipped into the rindle.

Nothing he had experienced prepared him for the shock. He'd been soaked through with rain many times, though nothing like this. Biting, penetrating cold stung to the heart of his bones so unexpectedly, he yelled. Or tried to yell. Instead of making a sound, his throat and soon his lungs were flooded. He felt his body lurch upwards as it became trapped by the barrier. The pressure of the current dragged him down, where he swallowed another mouthful of water. Terror gripped him. He was hooked. The crushing feeling in his chest became unbearable. Images raced through his head.

A puff of steam.

A fly crawling over blackberry juice.
The seductive smile of a stoat.
The crunch of bone against tree.
The cold, black heart of an eye.
He was hovering now.
As if his mind was parting from his body.
It was so cold.
And still.
Very still.
A field of silence.
No.
Up there.
A face.
A worried face.
Mother!
He tried to shout out to her.
She couldn't hear.
Then everything went dark.

14. Black is my favourite colour

OLLIE KNEW something was wrong as soon as she heard Nell plop into the water. Casting aside her fear of otters and pikes and eels and whatever other carns lurked in wait beneath the surface, she slid back down the bank and paddled furiously upstream.

She could see her friend struggling against the barrier, getting nowhere. Nell went down again, and stayed under for a long time before bobbing up, gasping. Ollie's body was screaming for her to give up.

The fear of being parted from Nell drove her to one last effort. She thrust her hind legs down and struck a submerged log. It gave her something to grip. She scrambled desperately along it, fighting the rindle. Nell's head had disappeared again and this time when he came up, he was still. The pain in Ollie's legs was excruciating as she wriggled under the barrier, bit into Nell's flank, and yanked downwards.

*****

NELL THOUGHT something might be tugging at his fur. Then he felt light, drifting, free at last.

The field of silence wasn't so painful after all.

No, there it was again, this time at the base of his ear. Now he was being dragged. Then pushed from behind. His paw touched something slimy. He coughed up water.

His chest felt like it had been crushed by a tree. His shoulders were aching, his ear throbbing, his heart hightailing. But he was alive.

Ollie was standing over him. Soaked fur clinging to her body made her appear incredibly small and frail.

'Sorry about the ear. You were floating away. Was the only part I could grab.'

'What happened in there?'

'You got stuck on the barrier.'

'How come you didn't?'

'Luck, I suppose. Or perhaps it was that nose of yours got stuck up.'

Nell tried to laugh, and coughed up more frothy water.

'I owe you one, Ollie.'

'One? That rescue has to be worth at least ten,' she said, grinning.

They'd come out of the rindle onto a small beach of soil and pebbles. Clumps of hawkweed flowers growing on the bank curved over them, providing some cover. Sleep came easily. When Nell woke, the fog had lifted, and the sky was a dazzling blue. Leaves on the trees overhanging the far side of rindle were yellowing. In the bright light, the wood appeared neither dark nor particularly chilling.

'How are *you* feeling?' asked Ollie, arriving with a clump of watercress and a worried expression.

'Grateful,' said Nell, between mouthfuls.

'Forget it. You'd have done the same for me. I was asking about the state of your body rather than your brain.'

Nell's ear was stinging.

'Better thanks. Where are we? Can't see a lot from here.'

Ollie explained that they were about fifty bounds downstream from the border.

'I saw a black rabbit going up that way. You think he would have come from Hilltop?'

'Doubt it,' said Nell, his head clearing. 'The Patri will be annoyed we've left. It wouldn't be his style, though, to pursue us this far. I'm more worried about those white rabbits we heard at The Twins. That hedgerow is the limit of Vort's range, so if he obeys his own rules he can't touch us over here. But if his bruisers or Levi are looking for us,

I doubt they'll worry about range boundaries. The further north we get, the more difficult it will become for them.'

He pulled himself up, feeling slightly better after the cress.

'How are you feeling?' he asked, noticing Ollie flexing her hind leg. 'That icy water can't have been good for your stiffness. Any sign of willows?'

'Hard to tell from here. If there are, they're likely to be by the rindle.'

'So that's the direction we should take.'

They moved cautiously, disturbing a coot feeding among reeds. It grunted and squawked so loudly they felt sure it would attract every carn for fields. Nothing stirred. After a while, the plants thinned and they were in the open. They looked for cover. The closest was where the rindle disappeared into the wood.

Nell saw the strange animal first, nosing around a stump. He motioned for Ollie to lie flat.

'What is it?'

'Not sure. Black and white striped face. Bristly tail. Larger than a fox.'

'Sounds like a badger. What's it doing?'

'Slurping. Worms.'

'We've got to get out of here.'

'Maisy told me once about badgers. They often send kittens to the field of silence, occasionally sick adult rabbits if they can sneak up on them. They're not quick enough to catch alert, healthy rabbits.'

'I'm not feeling remotely healthy right now,' said Ollie.

'Relax. There's no breeze to carry our scent to him. And *seeing* is not one of a badger's strong points.'

Nell watched as the animal strolled in deliberate circuits round the stump, its thick coat swinging loosely. It soon lost interest and padded off into the wood. The two rabbits crept forward to see what the badger had been doing. Around the base of the stump, they found a perfect ring of droppings. Rabbit droppings.

'At least twelve bucks,' said Nell, nosing the ground. 'All white, by the smell.'

'What do you reckon *this* is?' whispered Ollie, who was sniffing at strange markings on the stump.

A ring had been etched out of the bark. Inside the ring were four raised diamond-shaped knobs arranged in a square.

'Never seen anything like it,' said Nell. 'You think it was done by rabbits?'

'Could have been,' said Ollie. 'A large rabbit could have used his front claws to scrape the ring and outline those knobs, then his teeth to chew away the bark. Must have taken whiles.'

'It certainly wasn't done last night. Those marks have been there for moons.'

A long-tailed tit fluttered around the stump as if trying to scare the rabbits off.

'This place gives me the shivers,' said Ollie.

Nell was looking up the slope.

'There *are* rabbits up there.'

Two black rabbits, standing tall under the daystar, were staring down at them.

'Perhaps there's a warren. What do you say, Ollie? Might be worth checking out.'

'Sounds like a better idea than staying here. And black's my favourite colour.'

The trek up took longer than Nell expected. The swim had drained Ollie of energy, and there was little goodness left in the foxtail. Nell looked for thistles. Pick-me-ups, Maisy called them. He saw none. A ragwort leaf revived Ollie briefly, but she was soon lagging behind. The breeze swirled, carrying sweet earthy fragrances from the wood and disturbing piles of leaves that rustled around them, chattering, overcrowding senses. Nell turned to urge the little rabbit on, and his heart sank.

*****

OLLIE FELT the alarm stamp. Her head and heart told her instantly to bolt, but her body stuped, too exhausted to react. In a flash, Nell was coming straight for her. He skidded into her chest, knocking the wind out of her, and sending them both rolling.

Ollie was aware of the carn's talons hitting the ground in a shower of feathers and dust where she'd crouched. Probably not an owl, in full daystar, though that hardly mattered. What she'd heard about kestrels and buzzards was more frightening. The carn recovered quickly and circled back. It let out a chilling *pee-yu, pee-yu* as it dived again.

'Split up,' shrieked Nell.

The parting of prey distracted the buzzard, and probably saved them. Ollie found extra reserves of strength and speed she didn't know she had. And though the buzzard had quickly singled her out as the weakest of the two rabbits, she zigged and zagged and shimmied, managing to stay out of the carn's claws.

She felt a signal stamp, and saw Nell at the entrance to a hole. She dodged once in the opposite direction to throw off her pursuer, then tore in a direct line for the hole, scrambling inside and collapsing in a heap on the floor.

'Nice paw-work.'

Nell was standing over her, smiling. Her saviour. Her friend. Grooming as if nothing had happened.

'I guess we're even,' said Ollie, once she stopped panting.

Nell's eyebrows waggled.

'A rabbit is only a rabbit because of other rabbits.'

15. Ripped ear, one eye

NELL AND OLLIE had stumbled into one of the outer burrows of a warren called the Point. The rabbit in charge was Dom Bini, who Nell recalled from one of the Patri's circle gatherings. The does they found resting in the burrow were afraid at first, then merely suspicious. When the visitors stretched the truth by saying they were friends of Bini, one of the does agreed to take them to him.

Although Nell had seen a few rabbits of mixed colour, known as crossers, the doe was the first he'd met face-to-face. Her fur was a blotchy grey, and three paws were black. As she led the way cautiously out of the burrow, Nell was pleased to see the buzzard had gone. The doe stopped to lick her paws, which he took as a signal to groom. Once he'd cleaned his face he noticed she was in the same position, still waiting.

'This way please,' said the doe.

'After you.'

The doe shivered.

'Please, I must not go in front.'

'That's ridiculous,' said Nell. 'How can you show us the way if you're behind us.'

The doe started shaking.

'You're frightening her, Nell. Let's do as she says.'

The friends hopped off, the doe giving them directions from behind. They stopped outside a larger hole.

'This way please,' said the doe, jumping past them.

Nell and Ollie exchanged shrugs, and followed her below. She took them through a series of passages until they came to the dom's private chamber. The drafty spaces reminded Nell of his father's burrow at the Willow, although this was larger.

Bini greeted them cheerfully, which suggested to Nell he was not aware of the reason for their rushed departure from Hilltop. So far, so good.

The dom was, however, curious what would bring two of the Patri's young rabbits to the Point under the daystar, so an explanation was necessary.

Nell tried to be vague, having learnt a lesson at the border.

'I'm taking a message from the Patri to the Golden Field. Ollie here kindly agreed to accompany me.'

'Indeed,' said Bini, rubbing his chin with his hind leg. The Patri must have a lot of confidence in you to send someone so young on such an errand.'

He was considering Nell with more curiosity than suspicion.

'Still, the Patri's always been a good judge of character.'

Nell gulped.

'So,' Bini went on, 'I suppose he told you to come and see me so I could help you get through the east gate, eh?'

Nell had no idea what the dom was talking about. Nothing in his voice suggested a trap. He decided to play along.

'The Patri did say we might find it easier if we came to you.'

'Quite right, quite right. Governor Crown's a reasonable rabbit, if a bit of a stickler for the rules. Nothing like that Vort down your way. I'd be happy to take you to the rowan and introduce you to Crown. But you must be tired after your journey. Rest here a few whiles, and I'll take you up when the daystar fades.'

Nell was eager to put distance between them and Vort and Levi, though he could tell from Ollie's scent and drooping right ear that his friend needed the rest.

He gave her the best part of the sleeping hole and went above to pass pellets. Squinting in the glaze of the daystar, he saw two rabbits chatting. The buck had a torn ear and one eye almost closed over. He recognised the doe as the crosser who showed him to Dom Bini's quarters. She looked away as he went below.

*****

LEVI ADMIRED the technique, though knew he wouldn't have the patience. From his Hide he'd been watching a kestrel hovering over the field. By keeping its wings forward and spreading its tail feathers, the bird was using the wind to lift and hold. The result was that it stayed in the same place, watching, waiting. It had been there for whiles, a black shape in the blue sky, and Levi was getting bored. A varlet stumbled out from the thicket behind the rowan and snaked over to the Black Hole. Varlets weren't allowed to come that way. They were supposed to use the tunnel by the rindle.

The varlet was crouching by the hole, panting, when Levi got there. Its left ear had been ripped, presumably in a fight some time ago, because the rough tips had healed and there was no blood.

'What do you think you're doing using that tunnel?'

'Governor tells me come through there, master.'

Levi was about to thump the varlet for lying, but checked himself.

'Better be telling the truth, or you'll get a hiding. And move away. You stink.'

Levi went below. Father would be resting this time of day, so he would ask him about the varlet later. He ignored the guards at their posts, and hopped past empty burrows and servant holes until he came to the crossing. He was nearing his burrow off the southern passage when he heard voices in the living chamber, and smelt strangers. Levi tilted his good ear.

'...came across a white doe, no more than a kitten really, living in the burrow of one of those runty Aidins.'

'How vile.'

'One of Raul's mates gets below and finds two varlets inside, helping themselves to her thistle.'

'Never.'

'And you know what those scum did? Crapped on the plants and spat in her face.'

'Bloody savages. Hope Raul got them.'

'Poor rabbit's getting too old for the rough stuff. And in the dark, his mate wasn't sure who the varlets were. One of Raul's sons lined up a mob and gave them a good thrashing.'

'It's getting out of control. As we feared.' It was Vort, speaking for the first time.

Levi stretched his ear until it brushed the wall. The conversation stopped. Sensing he'd be in trouble, he coughed and hopped into the entrance.

'Not now, Levi.'

'I caught a varlet using our tunnel.'

'I'm busy. Go to your burrow.'

'Yes, father.'

'Wait a moment. What did the varlet look like?'

'Ripped ear, one eye.'

'Where is it?'

'By the Black Hole.'

'Tell it to come here, will you.'

'Down here? It's a varlet.'

'Do what I ask, Levi. Then get lost.'

The varlet jumped straight into the hole when Levi gave it the message. It knew its way around, all the way into the living chamber. Levi crouched outside to listen.

'What have you got for us?' asked Vort.

The varlet spoke so quietly, Levi heard only a couple of words. *Nell* and *Point*.

So, Nell *had* got through to the Point Warren. That lying guard.

Vort was speaking again.

'One less shadow in the grass, I say. It's some other rabbit's problem now.'

'I've heard my varlets talk of this Nell,' said one of the visitors. 'Where does it come from?'

'Forget it,' said Vort. 'A cheeky runt some pellet-heads think is possessed by a plant spirit.'

The governor's guests laughed heartily.

'I trust that's not all the news you've brought me,' Vort resumed.

Again, Levi couldn't hear the varlet's reply, only the word *Cluster*, which meant nothing. He'd heard what he needed to hear.

'You know better than to listen in on your father like that.'

His mother blocked the passage.

'I see what's going on, Levi. I'm not stupid. You shouldn't go meddling in matters that don't concern you.'

'Mother?'

'Forget about those two rabbits of colour. If they've crossed into the next field, they're Governor Crown's responsibility now. Finally. They're outside your father's range, you understand?'

Levi didn't. Why was she so keen to protect a couple of lying savages?

Helga huffed, and lurched off. Levi rushed above. He scanned the field for Karl and the kins. They'd be impressed when he told them he'd forced the one-eyed varlet to confess where the runaways were hiding.

*****

NELL FLOATED in and out of sleep until he was woken by one of Bini's mates. Ollie was snoring, on the bed of dried grass Nell insisted she use. She smelt relaxed, and Nell was tempted to let her sleep on. Time, though, was one of their enemies. He nuzzled her awake.

'Better get going.'

Ollie yawned.

'Where?'

'The east gate.'

The little rabbit flexed her hind legs.

'Explain to me again why we must go through this… thing. Why don't we find another way?'

'There is no other way. Border hedgerows are patrolled. I've heard you've only got to sniff at them in a certain way and you're for it.'

The daystar was fading in the sky behind them as they made for the rowan at the top of the field, its orange leaves sparkling in what was left of the light. They crossed a pellet line, which Bini said marked the boundary of The Point.

'Like a forbidden line?' asked Ollie, revolving her good ear nervously.

'Yes. This part of the field is reserved for whites only. You'll be alright as long as you're with me. Don't stray off this trail.'

Governor Crown was as Bini described him. The friendly face was more like Fleet than Vort. At first, Crown was surprised such young rabbits had been sent so far on an errand, but was content to accept the word of Dom Bini that their journey was necessary.

'When I was your age,' said the governor, 'I spent all my time chasing does. I've got two sons I imagine will be doing that right now. Hope they're as fortunate in their choice of mates as I was. Enough about me though. I'm sure you two will be keen to get on your way, if you want to make the Golden Field by dayspring.'

Governor Crown took them to the east gate, which they could see was a barrier in the hedgerow similar to the one across the rindle, but made of straight branches and overgrown with hawthorn, privet and blackthorn. On both sides of a gap between two of the vertical branches, crouched burly white rabbits. The governor motioned for the guards to let Nell and Ollie through.

'I'd advise you to stick to the thicket all the way to Chest Tree Corner. A barn owl has been hunting over the Common these last few nights. Must be feeding a brood.'

Nell and Ollie thanked him for the advice, and farewelled Dom Bini. A few more heartbeats and they would have got away.

16. A white lie

'STOP THOSE LYING VARLETS, they're trying to escape.'

The gate guards jumped immediately to block their way. Ollie watched in horror as Levi bounded up, flanked by three equally fierce white bucks. She wanted to hightail. Nell, though, appeared calm. He was cleaning his forehead.

'What is the meaning of this?,' the governor demanded as the bucks came to a stop in front of them.

Levi was frothing from the mouth, and showing the beginnings of matting on his chin.

'These varlets are runaways. They came into this field against the orders of the Patri, they lied to the varlet guard at the tunnel, and… they insulted my father.'

'And who might your father be?' inquired Crown.

'Governor Vort.'

'I might have guessed. You must be Levi. I've heard about you.'

'That's right. I, we, are here to take these varlets for the punishment they deserve.'

Levi stomped forward. Ollie shuffled behind Nell, who stood his ground.

'Wait,' said Crown. 'I want to hear what the buck and doe have to say.'

'They've told enough lies,' Levi snapped, continuing his advance.

'I said stop!'

Levi turned and frowned at the governor. His bruisers snarled.

'You may not have noticed,' said Crown, apparently unconcerned by the threat, 'you too have crossed into *my* field. Your father has no authority here. You have less. *I* decide what goes on in this field, and *I* said I want to hear what they have to say.'

Ollie could not imagine a worse situation. Levi's scent – an arrogant mixture of nuts and sweat – was overpowering. Two of the bruisers were extending and contracting their claws. This was all her fault, for pissing on Vort's plant. She glanced skywards, hoping a flock of carns would swoop and finish it all. Nell hopped forward.

'I apologise if we misled you, Governor Crown. And you, Dom Bini. It is true we left Hilltop against the wishes of the Patri...'

'There,' snarled Levi. 'They admit it. Now let's stop this nonsense and give these varlet...'

'Shut it!' thundered Crown.

Levi's jaw hung in bewilderment. Ollie couldn't understand what was stopping him and his bruisers tearing them to pieces. They outnumbered and out-sized Crown and the two guards. The governor turned to Nell.

'Go on.'

'We had no choice, sir. The Patri demanded that we take mates we hardly know, and who have no interest in us. The last thing we wanted to do was offend the Patri, who has been like a father to me. To both of us. Some of his ideas are a little... past-mooned. We didn't feel in our hearts we could live with this one. Nor did we think it fair, having made our decision, to keep living under the Patri's guidance.'

Governor Crown's lips stretched slightly. An almost-smile. From Ollie's vantage point, she considered the differences between Nell and Levi. Until now she'd always that believed size and strength mattered the most. All of which Levi had in abundance. Yet the white rabbit was less frightening, less imposing alongside Nell. Remarkably, Crown was showing more respect for Nell than Levi. Having spent so much time in Nell's company these past moons, Ollie had forgotten the affect her friend had on others. One of the bruisers – the buck who seemed to have the most between the ears – was ogling Nell with something resembling awe, until their eyes met, and his face changed.

Nell continued: 'What would your sons say, Governor, if you made them mate does they had no interest in?'

Levi exploded. 'How dare it speak to us like that.'

'I said shut it,' yelled Crown, who had lost patience.

'This is my decision. The black buck and doe have lied not only to me. They deliberately misled Dom Bini.'

Levi screwed his hind legs into the grass, preparing to strike.

'However. I can see why they fled. Faced the same choice, I would have been tempted to hightail myself. Lying, though, is inexcusable and deserves punishment...'

'At last, we hear some sense,' butted in Levi.

Crown hissed.

'I have been as unimpressed by the arrogance and language of you, young buck, as I have been of these two. It is also obvious that whatever punishment you and your father have planned will be harsher than they deserve. Therefore, I will not pass them over to you and your... friends.'

'What about the way they insulted my father?'

'Enough,' said Crown. 'Your father has the thickest fur and head of any rabbit this side of the Torrent. He'll get over it. Take your tail-waggers, Levi, and get lost – the way you came.'

Crown turned to Nell.

'You two, go through that gate and out of my field.'

Ollie sensed Nell nodding, so nodded too, then joined him on the other side of the gate. Levi's insults faded away as they scampered north.

*****

NELL DIDN'T TRUST Levi to obey Governor Crown. It soon became apparent, however, that speed would be impossible. Although Ollie said nothing, it was clear she hadn't recovered from the dramas piled on her since the run-in with Vort. Nell stopped. Ollie panicked.

'What's wrong? Who's coming? Where are they?'

'Calm down. Nothing's wrong. I'm looking for somewhere to rest.'

He could see no safe hiding place. Nor did he have a clue how far it was to the Golden Field. Crown had advised them to stick to the thicket, so they scurried along a trail ambling beside the hedgerow. After a while, Nell stopped again.

'They're coming, aren't they? Gotta get down, down,' blurted Ollie.

Her fear was on the wind for any rabbit or carn to smell. It gave Nell an idea. He closed his eyes, laid his ears flat and concentrated on the odours moving in the air around them. Fifty or so bounds into the field he smelt what he was seeking. A patch of wild strawberries. The fruit had been eaten, but the passing leaves let off a musky hum that would cloud them from rabbits moving along the trail. They burrowed into the leaves, and Nell kept watch as Ollie slept.

As the little rabbit twitched, Nell considered how dependent on him Ollie had become. It was not healthy, with their lives about to get more, rather than less, dangerous. He felt guilty for dragging Ollie into this. He had to get her to a safe place where she could settle down and make other friends.

It must have been some whiles after midnight when he was woken by the sound of rabbits moving in the field. Nell didn't want to risk being caught in the open, so he quietly roused Ollie. They returned to the trail. Ollie smelt like strawberry leaves and Nell assumed he must too. He hoped he'd get the chance to groom before meeting anyone.

Ollie was moving – and talking – more freely.

'Interesting, wasn't it?'

'Which bit?'

'At the gate. The way Governor Crown dealt to Levi.'

'Fascinating.'

'And the shock on Levi's face when Crown shut him up.'

'Yeah. Sticklers for rules, some of these white rabbits, eh?'

'When it suits them.'

Nell found a thistle and let Ollie have first go at the spiny leaves. She bit off a stem, sending a mass of seeds into the air.

'That was smart to think of hiding in those strawberry leaves.'

'Maisy taught me that one.'

Ollie grinned.

'What's so funny?'

'I was thinking about what we did. Stretching the truth.'

'I'm not proud of that, Ollie. It's no joke.'

'No. I wasn't smiling at *that*. I was thinking about the saying *white lie*. That's all we did. Told a white lie.'

It was good to have the real Ollie back. Nell started off along the trail, the fattening moon lighting their way. Ollie managed a steadier pace, though spun her good ear furiously and tensed at strange sounds. They noticed other rabbits, mostly white, grazing out in the field, so kept to themselves.

Leaves plucked by the breeze fluttered to the soil around them – replenishing offerings of new life from the old. Here and there they came across a different type of grass growing among the rye. The stems and smooth, hairless leaves were coarse and tasty, and the seed heads delicious – so different to the bitter foxtail of the flats with its dangerous barbs. They became aware of the rising crown of a large tree, and a second overgrown hedgerow jutting out to the east. Ollie had stopped under the outer limbs, nosing at something on the ground. She pushed it, and quickly backed away.

'What is it?'

'It bites, whatever it is.'

Nell studied the strange creature. Its skin was thick and covered in spikes. Its head was flat and smooth and had a single white eye. It kept still. The two rabbits watched for a while, and it didn't move.

'Perhaps it's sleeping,' said Ollie.

Nell wasn't so sure. He nosed closer. Still nothing. He went right up to it and pushed it. It rolled onto its side and the head came off. He grinned.

'It's a nut, you idiot.'

Ollie kept her distance. Nell licked it. Then took a bite.

'A little bitter.'

He chewed some more.

'But tasty.'

'Must be a chestnut,' said Ollie, looking up. 'This has to be Chest Tree Corner.'

The daystar was tickling the top of the hedgerow far to the east as they crept along to another overgrown barrier. This one was unguarded. They peered through. If Nell wasn't seeing it with his own eyes, he would never have believed what he was looking at. The field before them was indeed golden.

*****

THE SIGHT in front of Maisy was so revolting, so unnatural, her whole body shuddered.

The night had begun well. She'd farewelled the last of her three daughters, who had departed for the burrow of a buck of little promise but a kind heart. In the moons since Nell had gone to Hilltop, the other two daughters had mated local bucks. The third, a timid and rather simple doe, was always going to have more trouble finding a partner. Maisy had been patient and supportive, and now the waiting was over. There had been no tears at the parting. The young doe could manage only one lot of emotions at a time, which she showered on her new mate, leaving her mother to contemplate life on her own for the first time in moons.

Instead of feeling sad, Maisy felt a contented relief as she went to her burrow. She believed she had done alright as a mother, though she had no wish for more kittens. The idea of a new life alone as the respected widow of a former dom held certain appeal. She could concentrate on her other passion – digging into the healing uses of plants.

The foulness hit her near the entrance. She listened carefully, heard nothing, so entered. Illuminated in a shaft of early morning light was the headless body of a shrew.

17. The Golden Field

IN CERTAIN LIGHTS and at certain moons, the field over which Nell and Ollie gazed could appear golden. The colours they saw were the petals of countless ragwort and groundsel plants covering the Upland and the myriad shades and tints of yellow and lemon and saffron of the blackthorn, the rowan and hawthorn. And in the distance, behind a wide stretch of fast-moving water, the golden tops of poplars.

'That must be the Torrent,' said Nell.

'Unbelievable. Where have we been all our lives?'

Nell didn't answer. Something wasn't right. Beneath the chestnut tree, black rabbits were forming into a line behind two over-weight white bucks deep in discussion, facing the other way. Nell shot through the long grass to join the centre of the line, Ollie right behind him. The blacks, they soon learnt, had spent the night working around the tree, harassed by the two *clips* to collect chestnuts that fell to the ground. Clips were officers of the eclipo – intimidating bucks chosen by the head rabbit to enforce his rules. The black rabbits had been too busy to clean themselves. Their fur was rumpled, and they smelt exhausted. Their work shift had finished, and they were on their way home. Nell asked why they weren't stopping to munch on the delicious grass.

'Tim* and all the other food up here is reserved for the whites,' the

---

* Tim is short for timothy grass, the most nutritious for rabbits. It is high in fibre and coarse, which helps keep a rabbit's teeth in good condition.

buck in front of him replied.

'What about the chestnuts?'

'Same. Any black caught breaking the surface of any nut would be in deep turd.'

'What about ones that fall on the other side, in the other field?'

'Doesn't matter where they fall. All nuts are for whites only.'

'I see,' said Nell, hoping his breath wouldn't betray him.

Behind the hedgerow drifting away to their left lay the Chilling Wood. To the right, the Upland appeared to be bisected by a wide dale, and beyond that was a massive rowan tree sheltering the tidy openings to many burrows.

'Toria,' said the buck, following Nell's eyes. 'The warren of the whites.'

In single file, they hopped past indecently healthy white rabbits munching on plants lush for the ivy moon. They stopped to make way for a larger line of black rabbits moving along another trail that hugged the dale floor. Most were carrying oval brown nuts, and every head was bowed. Bringing up the rear were three white clips. Nell noticed the rabbits at the front lower their noses to the ground as the whites passed.

Then their line was off again. The group of workers entered a hole in the side of the hill. Nell and Ollie's line went down to the flats. The rabbit behind Ollie explained that the hole led to a burrow used for storing nuts. The workers would have dropped their hoard in the burrow. From there, the nuts would be taken by other black workers, of higher rank, to either the main storage chamber in the head rabbit's burrow or to a trade storage chamber, from where they would be carried to the North Bank.

At the bottom of the trail, Nell got a better view of the flats, which were swarming with black rabbits. Compared to the over-abundance of good food on the Upland, the flats had been over-grazed. The grass – foxtail to Nell's disappointment – was gone in places, leaving large patches of bare soil.

The workers were dismissed, and fanned out in search of nourishment. Nell and Ollie went with the talkative buck to forage. They passed other rabbits, and Nell was struck by their poor condition.

The daystar was getting higher as their new friend invited them to his burrow for the day, and explained where it was.

'Nothing special, I'm afraid. Least it stays dry. Most of the time.'

They accepted gladly, and were about to follow him when Nell was stopped by the voice of a white rabbit.

'You. Smudgeface. Get your skinny black backside over here.'

Nell didn't think for a moment of disobeying.

A white rabbit with menacing, impatient eyes jostled him across the flats towards a waterway twice as wide as the rindle, close to where it emptied out of the Chilling Wood. Nell joined nine other black rabbits filing over a log crossing the waterway, which was known as the bourne. His last experience in water was still fresh in his memory, and he hesitated. It was a mistake.

'Ah, little daisy don't wanna get 'er paws wet,' taunted one of the blacks behind him.

'Shut it,' barked the clip. 'It'll get more than its paws wet if it doesn't hightail over that log.'

Nell skipped across, his heart thumping. A clip at the other side was counting them off as they crossed. He stared at Nell, as if committing the face to memory. Although Nell didn't appreciate it at the time, he was standing on the most important piece of ground on the South Bank. To white rabbits, at least. It was called the Diamond, but was more a triangle. The reason for its importance, and the special clip presence at the log, were the sprawling juniper bushes lined up along the hedgerow. Nell smelt them before he saw them.

The spindly black rabbit in charge showed Nell how to crawl and climb through the prickly branches to get the blue-black berries, which ones to pull off, which to ignore. And most importantly, how to get the berries down without leaving a tooth mark. The hardest part for Nell was resisting the temptation to chew one of the bitter-sweet berries. He was left in no doubt what would happen if he was caught eating one.

'It'll be the last thing you ever taste.'

Once a berry had been picked, it was the supervisor's job to decide, based on its colour and firmness, if it should be taken to the pile for trade with the Oakwood or set aside for the head rabbit and his circle of white high-ups at Toria. Nell held his first one up for inspection.

'Second hole.'

Nell dropped the berry, so he could speak.

'Never drop them,' hissed the supervisor.

Nell picked it up. Carefully.

'Take it to the second hole. Over there.'

The smell of junipers gushed up to meet him. Inside, he found a scrawny rabbit, almost as ancient as Old Chief. The hole was shallow, letting in plenty of light from the daystar. The rabbit had only one eye, and that was glazed over. The hollow where the other eye had been resembled the knot on a tree. His head swung from side to side.

'On the pile sonny, pile sonny.'

Nell placed the berry carefully alongside others at the rabbit's paws.

'Know that star, that star,' rasped the rabbit.

Nell was about to ask what he meant, when another buck arrived, holding a berry. There was room for only one in the passage, so he hopped out.

'Don't take any notice of that old git,' said the supervisor. 'Your brain'd be as snarled up as his if you'd been breathing juniper fumes as long as he has. And in all that time, swears he's never broken the skin of a single berry.'

'How do you resist? They smell delicious.'

'Think of them as poisoned. Break the skin, and you'll fall into the field of silence.'

He rotated his ears, checking for clips, then continued in a whisper.

'Some of the berries you take down there end up in the stomach of the head rabbit or his high-ups, which I figure means one less white rabbit.'

Nell didn't see the old rabbit again that day. He saw a kestrel hovering over the flats. He and the other workers were safe in the junipers. As he watched the bird dive behind a row of trees on the far side of the bourne, he worried about Ollie, hoping his friend was below. By mid-afternoon, he was exhausted, so was relieved when the clips made them line up to cross the log. As they waited, the others cleaned the dust from their coats. Nell did the same, and noticed one particularly grubby buck wasn't bothering.

'What's with him?' he asked the supervisor.

'Thinks the lighter his fur, the more intelligent he'll be.'

The line was moving. Nell kept his eyes on the far end of the log as he crossed and was dismissed at the other side. Using the directions he'd been given earlier, he found the burrow and was soon sleeping beside his friend.

18. The vow

OLLIE HAD BEEN DREADING leaf-fall sliding into winter. The reeds finished flowering, the temperature dropped daily, and the only brightness descending from the Upland to the flats were the scarlet and orange leaves of the rowan.

Settling into the Golden Field had been stressful. There were twenty, thirty times more rabbits here than at Hilltop, and a complex web of rules about where you could eat, drop pellets, hop, fart – all to be learnt from the bottom branch in the pecking order. Not to mention the constant slurping and gushing of the Torrent and unfamiliar wind patterns caused by the Upland messing up her hearing. There were even right and wrong ways of *looking* at a white rabbit. If it wasn't for Nell, Ollie would have gone crazy. The friends quickly worked out the safest places and times for Ollie to feed, based on the likely direction of threats and the location of the few bolt holes available to blacks.

Work details mostly passed Ollie by. Blacks tended to be chosen at random, though a lucky or shrewd rabbit could go for several nights without doing work. It helped being scarce around the changeover times, or acting like a weakling who would struggle to carry a juniper berry, let alone a hazelnut. The record for avoiding work was twenty-seven days, and it was said the buck would have lasted longer if he wasn't betrayed by a black informer. Ollie was confident of setting a new record, though smart enough to keep that goal to herself.

When she was unlucky to be chosen, Nell sometimes offered to take her place. It didn't always help, because in those early days, Ollie spent the time alone in the burrow worrying if Nell was safe, imagining carn attack after attack. When they were reunited, she would be wearier from worrying than Nell was from working.

There were willow trees on the flats, though the leaves were past their best by the time the pair arrived, and the lack of nourishing plants meant Ollie had competition. So much bark had been stripped around the bases of some trunks, the trees were passing. The culprits knew ringbarking could destroy a tree. Ollie couldn't bring herself to do it, so had to settle for simply licking the bark, which gave her little relief.

Lexa, the name given to the sprawl of black burrows dominating the flats, could be lively and dull, sometimes both at once. Nights could be full of drama for rabbits from country warrens with responsibility for no-one but themselves. Ollie and Nell had held status as adopted *son and daughter* of the Patri. At Lexa, they were nobodies and had to live by the twitch of their whiskers. There were many times, particularly in those first moons, when Ollie wished she was back at Hilltop.

Large parts of Lexa were controlled by marauding packs of black bucks who would fight for food. Or for the fun of it. Ollie had a recurring nightmare in which she was found alone by Levi, who tore her to pieces and tossed her into the Torrent. The attack always happened in the same place, under a willow. She often used humour to get out of dangerous situations, particularly if she was by herself. Alongside Nell, she was a different rabbit, saying things she wouldn't dream of in a crowd of strangers.

Some black does unlucky or not smart enough to escape work duty were made to look after the kittens of the whites. Most were happy to do it, because they couldn't have families of their own. There wasn't enough for all the black rabbits to eat properly, and starving does rarely had kittens. For a small doe like Ollie, this was not an issue. What concerned her more was that Nell would find a mate, ending their friendship. She mentioned it one night, as they were looking at the star known as The Follower. It was shining bright red, close to the moon, like a kitten with its mother. Nell gave Ollie a stern chin-wagging about the state of life for black kittens, and vowed not to bring any into the field until they were free. Ollie had agreed. Readily.

Winter crept into the fur, stinging nostrils and the tips of ears. Frost and fog loitered, grinding down spirits. As the white kittening season finished and the demand for nannies slackened, some of the does were transferred to burrow duty, extending holes of the whites at Toria and digging new ones where necessary, or simply desired. At the end of their shifts making large burrows larger, the does trudged down to Lexa, where living conditions were impossibly cramped.

Ollie and Nell had been sharing a burrow with the family of the rabbit they'd met on their first day in the Golden Field. So, when Nell was offered a hole in another part of Lexa, their hosts were relieved. The new burrow, though smaller, they had to themselves. It was also a little deeper, therefore darker, which suited Ollie, who was uncomfortable in large spaces below. And although it had only one entrance, there was a small cavity at the far end into which a rabbit Ollie's size could squeeze. The space was too small for Nell and would therefore also be too small for a white rabbit, a bully, a fox or badger. It became the little rabbit's sanctuary.

Through the cold moons, the two friends often went hungry. It wasn't such a big deal for Ollie, who was used to the pain of hunger. Given the choice, she would usually opt to go without food over confrontation or danger. She joked that she was so small she needed only a little. It didn't stop Nell bringing her treats, like a dandelion or – once – a slither of forbidden chestnut. Nell had mentioned how difficult it was to have a chestnut in your mouth and not be able to chew it. On this occasion, he'd found two together and managed to tuck one in his gum without the clips or his fellow workers noticing.

Ollie and Nell were, though, better off than most blacks. They were still relatively healthy and strong from country living, compared to rabbits who'd been at Lexa for moons and whose bodies, and spirits, had been ground down. Cold and damp and poor diets resulted in many blacks passing into the field of silence.

Then in the depths of the sleeping moon came a glazed frost. Ground frozen hard was pummelled by rain that turned solid on contact. Leaves cackled like geese on trees hunched to submission. Scores of dunnocks and chaffinches and wagtails died, their tiny feet frozen to branches as they roosted, preventing them from eating. Some never got to their roosts, passing in mid-air when their wings froze. Rabbits caught above ground passed away, cocooned in ice. The weaker of the ones sensible enough to stay below passed from starvation, unable to survive four days without nourishment.

After the glaze, desperation for food made normally sensible rabbits take foolish risks, grazing in places watched by carns, ignoring alarm stamps. Competition for what little nourishment there was caused fights, and more passing. Life became worth less, and the ruffians more aggressive.

*****

NELL HAD TO GET ABOVE. They'd been stuck in their burrow for days, huddled together to keep warm, as rain drenched the flats outside. The hunger pains were bearable. He'd become used to them. The walls of the small burrow closing in and Ollie's pessimism, though, were dragging him down.

'Okay, okay,' snapped Ollie finally. 'Anything to shut you up.'

A bitter wind and horizontal rain from the north stung their faces, but Nell was not going back below. They found nothing edible near the log to the Diamond, and almost stumbled into a family of dozing otters. The rabbits retreated quietly, and tried their luck towards the fork where the bourne met the Torrent.

The wind eased, the trees stopped groaning, and the rain relaxed to a thick drizzle. When Ollie stumbled on a rare delicacy – a wood blewitt mushroom – they were so excited, they sat there staring at the smooth pale-tan cap.

'You first,' said Ollie.

'No, you found it.'

'There's enough for both of us. I'll go this side.'

Ollie had taken her first bite when three black rabbits loomed from the darkness. Rough-smelling bucks, as tall as Nell and heavier. They were from one of the packs, though he wasn't sure which one. It didn't matter. Their coats were soaked, and water dripped from the chin of the largest as he spoke.

'Run along daisies. You don't belong here.'

Nell could outrun them all. Ollie had no chance. It was so unfair. For the first time in his life, Nell had a violent thought. If they attacked, he would fight. He'd kick at the leader's throat first, then spin round to lash the gangly one on the flank.

'This isn't as good as those ones by the tree,' said Ollie, as if they were still alone. 'Let's go and finish the others.'

'What you talking about?' demanded the leader.

Ollie grimaced, as if she'd said something she shouldn't have.

'Nothing,' she whispered.

'Tell us, you snivelling pellet-head, or I'll toss you into the Torrent.'

'We saw four, five of these mushrooms, bigger than this one, at the last willow by the log bridge. But we smelt a badger coming, so decided it was too risky.'

Nell now understood what his friend was doing. He fought to keep a straight face, as he remembered the strawberry patch. A *white lie*.

'Ha,' mocked the leader. 'Frightened of badgers. Suppose you'd have run if you'd seen a mole.'

'Or a shrew,' chortled one of his companions.

'Come,' said the leader. 'Let's leave these pathetic pellet-heads to jump at their shadows.'

The three bucks tramped off, and Nell and Ollie feasted on the mushroom.

*****

IN THE NIGHTS after the brush with the ruffians, Ollie noticed they were getting stares from strangers. They'd talked to no-one about the encounter. Others must have, and news of their little victory was riding the wind. Ollie also heard murmurs – a challenge and a warning – about whether they would have been so lucky if the ruffians had been white. The two friends were cautious, expecting the bucks to seek revenge.

The owl moon drifted into the snow, and nothing happened. Ollie dared to believe they'd not only escaped the ruffians, but survived the worst of winter, thanks largely to Nell's ability to find tasty morsels or detect danger, and his endless optimism. Many black rabbits expected each moon to be their last. Nell seemed to be driven by a powerful will to live, as if guided by some higher purpose.

If leaf-fall was a time when the daystar, the leaves and spirits dropped earthwards, spring was a time when the mood of the natural world rose with the daystar in anticipation. Within days, the fields were so frenzied that memories of winter had faded. Squirrels and long-tailed tits were building nests in sheltered crannies in the hazels. Primroses and anemones coated the ground in shades of yellow and white, and from high above the trees came the excited *peewit peewit* cries of the lapwings cartwheeling and diving in mating displays.

On the Upland, white kittens were being born. The population of Lexa wormed up again – more from rabbits sent from country warrens than from births. With the coming of the blue moon, the bounce and dash of new life sent heads spinning. Ollie watched the playful antics of recently arrived swifts darting over the Torrent. It got her thinking about how the young rabbits of Lexa were missing out on the carefree moons she and Nell enjoyed at the Platform. Whenever she gazed up at the forbidden Upland, she imagined white kittens playing under the late afternoon daystar, cocooned by the aromas of plants that lost most of their tang before they strayed down to the flats.

Because of the abundance of summer food for the whites, the rules about where blacks could eat were traditionally relaxed this time of year. Occasionally, blacks were permitted through to the open area behind the Upland, known as the Common. White sages told anyone who would listen that the head rabbit was being generous and fair, and some believed this. The real reason was that the rye and tim grass were losing their vitality, and they wanted it nibbled down to prepare for the second burst of growth expected in leaf-fall. The whites also wanted to build up the strength of workers for the coming harvest. Many rabbits gorged until they became ill. Ollie heard of one buck who passed into the field of silence from over-eating.

The Common had always been available for white rabbits – and some went there for valerian. Roots of the plant had a strange effect, turning some nervous rabbits calm and sensible rabbits loopy. Black rabbits were only allowed into the field when most of the valerian was past its best. Few whites were prepared to share a feeding ground with blacks. Those who did tended to be loud-mouths itching to push blacks around.

Ollie and Nell were there late one afternoon when a series of alarm stamps turned the Common into a field of chaos. Rabbits scattered, the whites directly to bolt holes, the blacks wildly in all directions. Ollie caught a glimpse over her shoulder of a barn owl swooping, as Nell appeared alongside her. A stamp drew them towards a large hole, and Ollie was shocked to see a white rabbit beckoning them. They tumbled through the entrance and immediately spun to face the new threat.

There was no aggression in the scent.

'Thanks,' said Nell, starting to groom.

'My pleasure,' said the white rabbit. 'I'm Joseph.'

'I'm Nell. And this is Ollie.'

'Haven't been round here long, have you?'

'Long enough,' replied Nell. 'Why do you ask?'

'Not many of your kind would have accepted my invitation.'

Ollie sniffed uncertainly at the white rabbit. He was the first of *their* kind – other than Governor Crown and Fleet – who had not shown hostility to her. A new experience.

While Nell and Joseph chatted about plants and the weather, as rabbits of the same colour do naturally, Ollie nosed around the bolt hole. It was four times the size of their burrow at Lexa, and had a freshly dug rear exit. An all-clear signal came, and they went above, Nell and Joseph still deep in conversation. The white rabbit was telling Nell where the carns hunted, which types were most likely this time of year, the location of the best bolt holes. Most of the whites who came to this field, he said disapprovingly, were hop-heads after valerian. Ollie remained on high alert, particularly when Joseph offered advice on how to evade a barn owl.

'Best thing to do, if you see they're aiming for another rabbit, is sit absolutely still, because they see only motion.'

Raised voices pricked the air. Ollie wanted to hightail in the other direction, but Nell was curious, so they moved closer. There was an argument between two large black bucks and two younger – and smaller – whites. The rancid smell of valerian root was strong. The arguing stopped when the rabbits saw a clip approaching.

'Okay, okay, what's going on here?'

Ollie was surprised that one of the black rabbits – a confident buck with long tufts of fur hanging from his chin – was the first to speak.

'We were eating quietly by ourselves, sir, when these hopheads came over and tried to take the food.'

'It's a liar,' said one of the whites, slurring his words so much the last one came out like *lar*. 'My friend and I were here first,' he said, struggling to stay upright, 'and, we, er, were here first, and that's, that's, all there is to it.'

'This could be interesting,' whispered Joseph. 'One of this officer's sons was taken by a fox after getting as high as a buzzard on this stuff.'

The officer looked to be weighing up what to do next. More rabbits, black and white, hopped over to see what was going on.

'And anyway,' blabbered the other white, whose eyes were as glazed as his friend's, 'who let these varlets up here in the first place?'

'It was your head rabbit,' said Nell.

Ollie wished not for the first time that the ground would swallow her. Nell blundered on.

'It's clear who is telling the truth here, officer. There is also no dispute that all rabbits, whatever their colour, can graze here. And by the look of these two,' he said, motioning to the whites, 'my friends are doing them a favour removing these roots. Probably saving their lives.'

Ollie noticed the clip, and even the unsteady whites, reacting differently to Nell.

'He's got a point,' said Joseph, grinning.

The clip sat still, jaw hanging, until he realised everyone was waiting for his response. He ordered all four bucks to leave the valerian and *sod off*, then frowned at Nell. Without a word, he urinated on the valerian and stalked off.

'Nice going,' said Joseph when the clip was out of earshot.

*****

NELL WAS THINKING of his parents, as he and Ollie went through the Narrows, a strip of low ground between Chest Tree Corner and the Chilling Wood. Maisy had never mentioned valerian at the Willow or Platform. Perhaps there was none there. If there had been, he was sure she would have warned him of its dangers.

He wondered if Ollie was thinking of *her* parents too. She never talked about them. He was about to ask her, when he noticed a lone white rabbit nosing at a plant nearby. It was Fleet, the Oakwood seer. Nell rotated his ears and looked around for clips. The only thing out of the ordinary was a line of shrews, a mother and four babies clinging to the tail of the one in front.

'Can I ask a favour?' Nell whispered to Fleet.

'Depends what it is.'

'If you visit the Platform, could you check on my mother. I'd like to know she's okay.'

Eating within twenty bounds of a white rabbit was risky enough in this field. Talking to one was almost certain to arouse suspicion, so Nell backed away.

'I'll see what I can do,' promised Fleet.

Nell watched as a white doe and several kittens ambled past. They had probably been for an outing to see the Torrent. The clip escorting them ensured all the black rabbits hurried out of their way. Two of the kittens were strutting behind the clip, mimicking his hops. The other three were giggling. Nell had forgotten what happiness sounded like.

19. Kittens that never laugh

TEN MOONS had passed since Ollie and Nell's arrival at the Golden Field. They sometimes visited the rabbit they met that first day, and were at his burrow one morning when his daughter arrived home, shaking.

Dima was a similar age to Ollie, and had a ragged crescent-shaped hole in her left ear where she'd had a narrow escape with a badger when she was a kitten. In the natural way, she would be expected to have a family of her own. The fact she didn't was so common at Lexa, it was rarely discussed.*

Between sobbing, Dima shared her story.

She had gone to work the previous day as the nanny and servant in the burrow of a high-up white family in Toria. Her first job every day was to clean all the chambers of the burrow. There were more than twenty. Then she had to take plants from the store and put them in particular places for particular members of the family who had particular tastes. All of this was to prepare for the return of the white mother and her four kittens – three does and a buck.

Dima talked about the kittens as *my dear this, my dear that,* and mentioned a bewildering variety of nuts and plants Ollie had never heard of. The family scene Dima described, the food, the comfort, the

---

* At times of stress or lack of food, female rabbits can control whether or not they give birth. The practice, known as resorption, was unheard of in the white burrows of Toria.

safety, the choices, were outside the imaginations of most black rabbits.

Ollie had gone through periods of depression, thinking she could be living like a white, if only they'd stayed at Hilltop. She saw now that she had no idea how white rabbits lived. She assumed it was like the Patri, but he lived in poverty compared to what the nanny was describing.

A faint vibration could be felt through the walls of the burrow. Nell asked Dima to continue. Ollie could smell that her friend was seething.

The white masters had arrived home and the kittens were left in Dima's care while the parents went off to their chambers. All was fine until Dima told the kittens it was time for sleep. The three does obeyed, but the buck reacted violently and attacked her. She was trying to defend herself when the mother appeared and immediately assumed Dima was at fault. She was chased from the burrow and told to never come back.

From what Ollie had heard, such a banning was like a direct passage to the field of silence. One of the advantages of does working as servants was that they got scraps left by the whites which, in the case of the nanny's masters, were not to be sniffed at. It was the reason some black does went to work at Toria so readily. Ollie noticed one of Nell's ears turn to face the noise of the growing crowd outside. The other stayed on the distraught Dima.

'If I cannot be a nanny to my dear ones,' she sobbed, 'I don't want to live'.

*****

'FLEET, MY FRIEND. Good to see you. Excellent timing, as always. Or did you know about this stunt by our darkies?'

The speaker was a pudgy steward to the head rabbit of the Golden Field. Fleet had arrived from the Oakwood, and had no idea what the buck was talking about.

'Stunt?'

'Haven't heard, eh? Come. Should be fun.'

Fleet didn't particularly like the buck, a haughty rabbit with odd ideas. He was supposedly the head rabbit's advisor on the black warrens, though Fleet doubted he'd ever laid paw on the flats of Lexa, let alone in the burrow of a black rabbit. Not that Fleet had been inside one in Lexa himself, something he must rectify. The buck, though, had the ear of the head rabbit and was therefore a useful source of information.

The climbing daystar was slowly drawing light away from the moon. Up ahead, Fleet could see high-up white rabbits gathering beneath the chestnut tree in the corner of the field, overlooking the Narrows. Although the flats were obscured from view, a rumbling sensation through Fleet's paws confirmed what his ears were telling him: a large number of excited rabbits on the move. At least fifty, if he was asked to guess. And fifty rabbits in one place were fifty-times more likely to attract carns. Add the ten or so white bucks at the chestnut tree, and that increased the chances to sixty. A quick check with the ears and nose showed Fleet there was no danger at present. Thirty bounds to the bolt holes between the spindles. Forty to the blackthorn burrow. A similar distance to the Brambleleaf burrows.

'What was that about Brambleleaf?'

'Nothing,' said Fleet, realising he must have been talking aloud – and how tired he was. How many days had it been since he'd had a decent sleep? Two at least.

'How's Thatch?' asked the steward. 'We hear she's not getting out like she used to?'

'I'm not really in a position to know where she goes.'

'Come now, Fleet, you're being too modest. What I'm hearing is that you have the ear of the Oakwood prime rabbit, she asks for you to brief her personally, and other seers must report through stewards.'

He was right. Fleet had become a favourite of Thatch, though he suspected it had more to do with the prime's addiction to juniper than anything personal. She was often more interested in news of trade than other matters. Fleet changed the subject.

'Tell me about this *stunt*.'

'Ah, you've got to feel a little sorry for the darkies. Most of them. Your common-burrow black rabbit is not remotely interested in stunts like we're about to see. All they worry about are full stomachs and dry burrows. The trouble being so simple is they're easily misled.'

The buck stopped, and tilted his head in the superior way Fleet found annoying.

'It is wrong to think, as most outsiders do, that the South Bank darkie is merely a white rabbit in black fur. That the way it thinks will be the same as that of a... civilised rabbit. Our darkies are as different from us as the barn owl is from the tawny, and the way they react to things going on around them is also… different.'

Fleet grimaced. *Here we go again.* It amazed him how white rabbits on this side of the Torrent behaved and thought the same as those in the North on all matters except one. Fur colour. They had a fixation with it. For a heartbeat, he considered telling the buck about his recent meeting with the sages. Three rabbits of various colours, each as intelligent as the other.* It was not his place, though, to interfere. And he could guess what the southern buck would say. He'd tell him he was an *outsider*, so couldn't possibly understand.

Thunder clouds billowed. The buck was pointing out that the white bucks assembled by the chestnut tree, most peering down at the Narrows, were the head rabbit's inner circle of stewards.

'All except one. The harvest steward, who is giving the head a late briefing. They'll both be along shortly to observe the stunt.'

*****

NELL HAD BEEN SHOCKED by Dima's story. He'd heard rumours of life in the white burrows, mostly from black rabbits who had never been inside one. He assumed it was exaggerated jealousy. This was appalling. He'd been at Lexa all this time and had no idea.

How could he be so ignorant? And selfish. Although Lexa wasn't perfect, until then it had seemed to him a *happening* place. A place of excitement, if not opportunity, particularly for rabbits rebelling against the traditional ways of life in parts of the countryside. Rabbits had fun together, didn't they? There were rabbits from different warrens, who

---

* An account of Fleet's discussion with the three sages, *The History Lesson*, is in the Afterwords (p.i).

had different ideas, ways of doing things. Friendships like the one he shared with Ollie were being formed all over the place, weren't they? And weren't there exotic plants, if you knew where to find them?

Sure, Lexa had been created by white rabbits to ensure there were always enough blacks to collect the nuts and berries and dig the whites' burrows. But the flats in front of the Torrent had become so unenticing to whites, few ventured there unless they had to.

Lexa wasn't perfect. What warren was? At certain times, like the coldest moon of winter when the grass stopped growing and pressure on food became intense, things got grim. At other times, when the foxtail was growing and more plants were available, simple common sense and respect for the lives of other rabbits kept the ruffians in line.

I'm okay. I'm here. I'm alive.

Dima was still sobbing.

Nell shut his eyes. Listen to yourself. *Me. Me. Me.* What about *her*? What about Maisy? What about all the other black does who would never enjoy the sensation of kittens suckling at their teats? Their own kittens. Black kittens. Kittens that never laugh.

Dima's sobs were soon drowned by the vibration of paws on the ground outside. The head rabbit had the previous night declared that blacks could no longer feed in the Common. Some had decided to challenge the ban.

20. Safety in numbers

WINTER HAD PASSED, and by spring, when Levi was twelve moons, he had still gone no further than the Point Warren. His life was about to change dramatically. The head rabbit of the Golden Field had summoned all his regional governors to Toria. Vort had taken his son with him.

The gathering was, in Vort's words, a pointless talkfest on carn detection. It became apparent to Levi that his father was unique among those who held positions of power. None of the others, including the daisy-head governor Crown and all the members of the head rabbit's circle, shared Vort's contempt for the blacks, though they were happy to use them for their own needs, particularly the harvesting of nuts and berries or as burrow servants.

As Levi would discover later, his father's interest in attending the gathering had nothing to do with carns. Bored by the endless talk, Levi wandered off to explore the burrow system.

The size and organisation of Toria was staggering, overwhelming at first for a rabbit from the country. His home burrow near the rindle had two levels. Toria had seven. The home warren had six entrances, including the two used only by the families of Vort's second and third mates. The head rabbit's burrow at Toria had more than thirty, and others were constantly being added. Some passages were as wide as the living chamber at home. Levi got lost once and had to ask a doe to show him the way to Vort's burrow.

A wing, they called it, kept vacant for guests of the head rabbit. It had four warm, dry, well-aired and well-lit chambers for meals, meeting or resting. Varlet servants kept the wing tidy, and stocked with nuts, berries, leaves, roots, and herbs. Two days passed like a dream. When Vort announced he was leaving and had arranged for Levi to trial as an eclipo officer in one of the head rabbit's protection teams, he was delighted. On his way to the Golden Field, Levi had fantasised about tracking down Nell and Ollie and doing what should have been done moons before.

But he was soon so busy in his new role, the two varlets were forgotten.

Through the late spring and early summer, Levi spent most of his time either guarding the head rabbit when he went above, or as he rested on the terrace – a flat-topped rock outside the main entrance to Toria that had become the symbol of power on the South Bank. The head didn't go far from the burrow, so Levi rarely got to see the sprawling flats where the varlets lived. He was happy at first. So was Vort, who, on a short visit, encouraged him in his work, fussing over his importance as a member of an elite squad, and questioning him about the layout of the warren and the routines and habits of the head.

Living at Toria also opened Levi's eyes to the differences between the two branches of white rabbits living on the South Bank – Oakers and Mistles. The head rabbit and his entire circle of high-ups and stewards were Oakers, descended from rabbits who had moved to the South Bank from the Oakwood. Most treated varlets like lost kittens needing to be shown the way home. Some even refused to call varlets black, preferring *our cousins*. Or *rabbits of colour*, like Helga sometimes described them. It was sickening.

Levi and Vort were Mistles, proud descendants of rabbits from a warren far to the east who had been forced out because of their belief in the sacredness of mistletoe plants, and who knew that every lying, stinking varlet was one heartbeat from savagery.

By mid-summer, Levi had become bored and restless. He was tired of being stuck below during the best moons of the year, told what to do by the head and his varlet-loving stewards, and ordered to restrain himself when dealing with *rabbits of colour*. Worst of all was the way

Oakers sniggered down their noses at Levi and other Mistle whites. Although nothing was said, it was clear that some Oakers saw little difference between a Mistle and a varlet. One night, Levi was on duty outside a nut storage burrow when a Mistle asked the eclipo officer in charge if there were any jobs going. *I'm afraid not,* the visitor was told. Later the same night, an Oaker asked for a job and was given one immediately.

When Mistle bucks who had befriended the tough son of Governor Vort boasted about the life in roving eclipo squads, of their freedom to keep the varlets in line, and have their choice of does in outlying burrows, Levi liked what he heard and asked to join. The request raised a few brows. Levi was the first member of the head's guard to ask for such a change, which was considered a hop backwards. There was no shortage of officers wanting to replace him in the guard, though, so the request was granted.

Levi's first job with his new squad was guarding the Narrows on the night the varlet protestors came through.

*****

NELL AND OLLIE had been aware of the Cluster since they arrived at Lexa, though hadn't taken it seriously. It had been around for moons, and according to some was full on talk and empty on results.

One good thing about white rabbits' reluctance to spend time in Lexa was that it allowed certain freedoms. A rabbit had to be careful. There were informers who would rat on rabbits for the promise of a favour from the whites. But a rabbit could generally say what he or she wanted to friends or in the privacy of their own burrow. Some time ago, a small number of black rabbits, unhappy about the way whites treated them, had formed a loose grouping called the Cluster. In recent moons, with white supremacy getting worse, demands for action from some in the Cluster had become louder, to the point where something had to happen.

As the mass of rabbits moved from Lexa towards the Narrows, they were joined by others. Many had popped out of holes more from curiosity than thoughts of becoming involved in a protest. They were quickly gathered up in the black tide, experiencing for the first time the feeling of safety in numbers. Nell and Ollie had come out of the burrow to watch, and were also swept up in the stream of excitement. As the current drove them on, Nell became aware that he was being prodded forward. It was an exhilarating feeling, as rabbits swarmed around him, beneath the glare of the third quarter moon, shouting abuse at unseen whites.

Nell found himself near the head of the crowd as they approached the Narrows and the air became still. A line of clips was blocking their way. Front and centre was the sneering face of Levi.

21. Warnings

LEVI CONSIDERED membership of the eclipo an excuse for violence. His squad had been told to form a barrier and wait for instructions from the head rabbit, who was on his way to personally oversee the protest. Levi snarled at the varlet rabble in front of him, and felt the pride that comes from being part of a disciplined force. The eclipo understood the meaning of orders. They would advance as one. Finally, Levi would get to taste varlet blood. It was only a matter of time.

The mob stopped, close enough to smell their vile wind. Most were shuffling, jittery, hiding faces in their chests, hoping they wouldn't be recognised, or scanning desperately for support that wasn't there and wasn't coming. After some jostling, a buck spilled from the throng to stand at the front of the line.

Levi almost wet himself with excitement. As the largest eclipo officer, his instructions were to take out the leader of the varlets. And there was Nell, nose in the air, leading the mob. This time there would be no interruptions. He scraped aggressively at the ground, then stared at the throat of Nell, imagining sinking his teeth in.

Panicky faces of the varlets nudged his gaze up to where the head rabbit was talking to the Oakwood seer, Fleet. Great. Not only would Levi get revenge for what the varlet's father did to Vort, he'd also impress some high-ups. The head rose, and every pair of eyes looked at him. Except two. Levi, poised to leap as soon as the order came, glared at Nell. The smudgeface had the nerve to stare straight back. It had balls, if nothing else.

'Let them through.'

The line of officers broke up. Levi, who assumed he'd misheard the head's growled instruction, stayed where he was. Fear on the faces of the other varlets softened into smiles, almost smirks. Levi felt humiliated.

The mob came forward. He stood his ground, and they had to brush past him. His eyes remained fixed on Nell, whose expression hadn't changed. There was no smile. No fear. No gloating. Nothing. Without a word, the varlet backed off and disappeared through the marchers.

*****

NELL HAD LEFT his host's burrow merely to see what all the noise was, and now worried that it had been rude to disappear. So as Ollie and the other protestors went through the Narrows to celebrate their victory and feed in the Common, Nell went back to explain where he'd been. He was excited as he entered the burrow, where he found a second rabbit.

'Ah, here he is. Have you met Nell?'

'No,' replied the visitor, 'though I've heard a lot about him.'

Nell nodded a greeting.

'Do tell us, what was all that noise?'

Nell could hardly restrain himself.

'There was a protest against the closing of the Narrows. I'm sorry, I got carried away. It was amazing. There must have been a hundred of us.'

The two older rabbits' heads shook as one. Nell went on.

'The Narrows were blocked by a line of clips. There was a stand-off, until the head rabbit arrived and could see we were too strong. He ordered the clips to let us through. It was a wonderful victory. You should have been there. Ollie and the rest of them are up there feasting on rye grass as we speak.'

His host frowned.

'I wouldn't get too carried away with talk of victory, Nell. Things are not always how they appear. My friend here tells me the head rabbit received a report this morning that the juniper and hazel crops are likely to be particularly good this season. We suspect his decision to let your friends through was less big-hearted than you think. He'll want his workers to build up strength for the harvest. Last thing he'd want right now is to lose half his workers in a fight.'

He looked grimly at Nell.

'I might be getting on in the moons, and my eyes might be failing, but I'm not blind yet. I saw your face earlier when Dima was talking about her… problems. I've seen that expression before. You were outraged, which is a natural enough reaction. And you want to change the world, which is not.

'If you want my advice, you'll forget about protesting and meddling in the affairs of circles. Find yourself a mate, Nell. Burrow down. Have a family. A brain like yours, you could live a comfortable life. Don't take *my* word for it, though. Listen to my friend here.'

The visitor had seen his share of fights. Both ears had been torn and his face and flanks showed the scars of previous encounters. His voice, however, was strong.

'I've been where you are today, Nell. I was a little older perhaps. I became so incensed about the unfairness of the whites, I joined the Cluster. They called us varlets then, as they do today. Listen to a couple of white rabbits talking and that word jumps out at you from all the rest. Always has. Always will. Cuts you inside.

'But I'll tell you this. If you compare the conditions we lived under moons ago to what you must put up with today, we didn't realise how lucky we were. Weren't so many rabbits on the South Bank back then, so we could feed pretty much where we wanted. There were a few rules, though nothing like what we have now. If we'd accepted our place, got on with our lives, I doubt we'd be having this discussion today. When we complained about some new rule, they'd extend it then dream up another one, to keep us in our place.

'And that wasn't the end of it. Some of us suffered more than others. Far more. Not one of the scars you see on my body came from a fox or stoat or tawny. When I was your age, there wasn't a single natural enemy of a rabbit could touch me.

'No, Nell. All the marks you see came from the clips. And every one was punishment for sticking my nose up to question the say-so of the whites. And I can tell you they hurt like crazy. There'd usually be two or three clips at a time. They'd always wait until I was on my own. After the beatings, I'd put a brave face on it, showing my wounds like scars of honour. A body can only take so much. I would have been in the field of silence, like your father, if I hadn't woken up and seen what was going on.'

'What *was* going on?'.

'Time after time, I'd stagger back to Lexa, to be treated by the leaders of the Cluster as a hero. When I recovered, I'd go and report to those same leaders in their comfortable burrows surrounded by their loving families, and they'd send me and my friends off on some other crazy protest. Next day, I'd see those same black leaders yes-ing up to the whites, joking with them, as if life was a bunch of dandelions. It was all a game to them.'

He pointed his nose at his friend.

'If I'd had someone like your host giving me advice when I was in your position, I might have enjoyed the best moons of my life instead of letting myself be *used* by those pretenders in the Cluster. Meddling in the affairs of circles is a blind-end Nell, like a bolt hole so tight your tail's left hanging in the breeze. Mark my words, rubbing noses with those stirrers in the Cluster is the fastest way to rile up the clips, who'll have your backside for first feed, your ears for a snack, and your guts for last feed. If you don't starve into the field of silence first. You'll lose all your friends, and I'm talking about real friends, not the here-tonight-gone-by-dayspring ones you'll find at the Cluster. You can lick your family goodbye, because they'll be too scared to be seen in the same warren as you. If that's not enough, your thoughts'll become so infected by filth and lies, you might as well chomp on a bunch of foxgloves and save yourself all the torment.'

Nell was shaken by the bluntness of the message. There was more, this time from his host.

'There's another reason to think carefully whether this is a good time to become involved in the affairs of circles, Nell. If what I'm hearing is half correct, our masters are about to get tougher. There are those among the whites who think the head rabbit's going soft in his late moons. Whatever his reasons for letting the marchers through the Narrows this morning, you can be sure it will be seen by the supremacists as another sign of his weakness.'

Nell was confused, but saved from having to respond by the arrival of Ollie. He was glad to escape the clammy air of the burrow for the fresh air above. There was no time for discussing what he'd been told. They'd both been invited to a secret gathering.

*****

THERE WERE SEVEN BUCKS and three does at the gathering, all junior members of the Cluster. No-one took any notice of Ollie when she went in first, though the rabbits went silent when they saw Nell. They waited for him to speak, but he padded to the rear and sat quietly. The talk – of the triumph of the morning and what it would mean in moons to rise – resumed. There was a lot of grinning and mimicking of the faces of the clips when the head rabbit ordered them to retreat.

'Let's rise up and take over the white burrows,' said one buck.

'And feast on the junipers and acorns,' said a doe.

'Take over the eclipo and tell the whites where they can eat or fart,' said another rabbit, to more laughter.

Ollie didn't join in. Nell had explained to her about the harvest report. She noticed one other buck not smiling. It was Stephen, the rabbit with fur hanging from his chin they'd met on the Common. He had also stayed out of the discussion, but now hopped forward.

'It was a memorable morning, comrades. Let's not get carried away, though, by a single victory. And let's not forget that burrow walls have ears.'

He lowered his voice further.

'I too would like to see the backs of the white rabbits, though I have no interest in copying their evil ways. If all you care about is getting sick on juniper berries and acorns and tim grass, and ordering other rabbits around, go and become an informer to the whites. I have no yearning to be white. My fur is black, my son Matthan's fur is black, his kittens' fur will be black, and it is beautiful. Like the soil beneath our paws and the night sky over us. If we can't accept what we are, be proud of what we are, how can we expect to control our destiny?'

Ollie was impressed. Until recently, she'd wondered what it would be like to be white, to have what they had. Perhaps Stephen and Nell were right to think otherwise.

22. The voice inside your head

NELL LAY in his burrow, thinking. When he finally nodded off, his dreams lurched from the freedom and exhilaration of wind in his face running errands, to the fight between Henry and Vort and the agonising whiles waiting for his father to pass into the field of silence. Always in the background were the eyes of Levi, and the chilling vision deep within.

He was woken at dayfall with the news that he had two visitors. He barely had time to clean his face before a strong scent overrode all else. It could belong only to the Patri. Nell was unsure how the old rabbit would greet him. The last time he saw him was before he and Ollie fled Hilltop to avoid the arranged matings. He would know of their deceit at the Point Warren. The Patri, though, put him at ease immediately.

'Nell, Nell, how good to see you again.'

'Hail to the…'

'Oh, no, no, no, no no. I don't expect that nonsense from you.'

The emphasis on the *you* was unmistakable. The Patri motioned for him to sit. The old rabbit's face was the same, the coat still gleaming, though he looked smaller, as if he had shrunk.

'I'm sorry about leaving the way I did.'

'Perfectly understandable. No apology necessary.'

'I still feel bad about it, though, after all you did for us.'

'We're all guilty of mistakes, Nell. Even a Patri.'

The older rabbit scratched his ear.

'I've been hearing a lot about you, Nell. I realise you're busy, have a lot to think about. I won't zigzag around the briar. I want you to come home and take your place in my circle.'

'You flatter…'

'I don't expect a decision now, Nell. Matters of such importance must not be taken lightly.'

Nell wasn't sure how to respond.

'I won't deny that I've always considered you a leader in moons to rise, Nell, perhaps a Patri. I didn't send you on those errands because you were the fastest or the most reliable. I was preparing you, Nell. You belong at Hilltop, among your own.'

'You're very kind.'

'You'll think about it?'

'Of course.'

The Patri appeared relieved.

'Thank you. Go well,' he said, bringing the meeting to an end.

'Stay well, Patri.'

Nell was about to leave when he remembered there were supposed to be two visitors.

'Of course,' said the Patri. 'How could I forget? Wait here, I'll summon your other… guest.'

*****

MAISY NOSED into the burrow.

Mother and son licked for some time, neither speaking. Words again were unnecessary.

'Did Fleet get to you with my message?,' Nell asked finally.

'He did. I've been waiting for an opportunity to visit. It's such a long way. When I heard the Patri was coming, I asked if I could join him.'

'How long can you stay?'

'I must go back tonight. I came simply to see you, to check you were alright.'

Nell began to protest. Maisy stopped him.

'I don't belong here, Nell. My home is at the Platform. This place is too big, too complicated for a simple doe like me.'

'There are so many things to talk about. I need your advice on...'

She stopped him again.

'Nell, my son. The advice of a country doe would be no use to you. I am, however, not totally ignorant. I've heard reports of what you've been up to. You've impressed a good many rabbits. I'm glad. You face important decisions. I shall therefore give you one piece of advice. Listen to the voice inside your head, Nell. Knowing that wherever your conscience leads, you have the support and love of your mother. And, I believe, your father.'

*****

THE ROWAN above the Willow Warren was a world away from the rowan of Toria – in pace of life and attitude. Levi returned to the rindle after the embarrassment at the Narrows. He felt betrayed by the head rabbit, and frustrated he could do nothing about it. He needed to see the one rabbit who would never desert him. His father.

Too ashamed to speak to anyone, he took a winding route through the Common to a tunnel in the eastern hedgerow, along the verge, then skirted the disorganised cluster of hovels the varlets called the High Warren. He was tiring when he spotted the crosser. It was the most hideous creature imaginable. Its body was white, and the left side of its face and one ear were black, as well as the bottom of both front legs. The rabbit, if that's what it was, sat there, in Levi's path, staring through him.

It was the wide-eyed twisted-mouth smirk of a dimwit that unleashed the fury. Levi's first swipe was so violent it almost knocked the crosser's head off. It might also have saved its life. Levi put so much effort into the swing, he lost balance and fell heavily on his shoulder. The crosser recovered and darted for a hole. Levi got to the entrance first. The crosser collapsed in a moaning heap. Levi pounced. It spidered sideways.

Somehow the crosser squirmed to the rim of the hole and collapsed inside. Levi dived in after it, grabbing a mouthful of stinking fur and yanking viciously. It yelped, and scrambled into a side passage.

Levi lunged and felt the walls of the hovel tighten around his shoulders. In a rage, he planted his hind legs into the floor and heaved forward once more. The walls became tighter. The crosser was right there, whimpering in terror, at least three kins snivelling behind it. Levi reached out to claw their faces. His leg wouldn't respond. He was wedged.

'You stinking varlets!' he croaked. He tried to cough, but his chest was too cramped. He tried once more to lunge forward, sucking another shower of dust into his throat. The stench of piss and shit and sweat was horrendous. Levi could make out the shapes of the varlets, not their faces, though knew they were laughing.

Fear gripped him. The crosser had lured him into this trap. Others would be coming. He could sense them approaching, to tear him apart, leg by leg. An insect landed on his nose and crawled inside his nostril. He grimaced as its paw-falls deposited a hideous varlet pox into his blood that would devour him from the inside.

He flinched in horror. The tightness eased. He pulled again. His legs loosened. Backwards, he had to go backwards. Desperately, he wriggled and squirmed until he was free. Varlet filth clung to his coat. He licked it off, then imagined the fleas and maggots, and spat in disgust.

Water. The rindle. He scampered down the slope and through the hedgerow, past his old Hide, and on down the hill, toppling over several times in this haste. The water stung his eyes, but he stayed under as long as he could as the tingling moisture soaked through his coat. When his face broke the surface, he sucked in a lungful of air, paddled to the side, and dragged himself up the bank. After checking no-one could see him, he shook vigorously and scurried through the bushes. A moorhen rushed at him, screeching, and flapping its wings.

'Piss off,' he yelled, as if it could understand. He swung his paw in the air, missing the bird by a whisker. His other paw crunched into something soft and sticky.

'Stinking varlet birds! What a daft place to put a nest.'

23. All will be yours

IT WAS KNOWN throughout Lexa as the flower of silence, and whenever the foulness pricked Nell's nostrils, it appeared stronger than the previous time. It was the only edible plant on the flats that few rabbits would touch.

Maisy wasn't aware of this until Nell explained why. She approved. In midsummer, clusters of the deep yellow flowers were left at the base of the thicket behind the privets. Whenever a lone doe was seen snailing towards these plants, and biting through one of the blood-red stems, other rabbits stopped what they were doing and bowed. For the tansy was the marker of passing, to be rubbed on a corpse to keep away the flies and worms. Some rabbits refused to go past the privets, no matter how hungry they were, because the merciless cry of the blossom unearthed too many memories.

Nell and Maisy were able to spend the early evening together, grazing under a brilliant sky led by the white giant Venus dipping towards the horizon over the juniper diamond, and yellow Jupiter soaring above the Golden Field. Although Maisy had lost weight in the moons since Nell last saw her, the warmth of her face was unchanged.

She was interested in Ollie, where the doe came from, who her parents were and, of course, what she ate. Nell was vague with some of the answers, though told her that he and Ollie had become good friends. Maisy seemed on the verge of saying something, but didn't. Instead, she offered advice on a range of plants that might help ease the stiffness in the little rabbit's joints. She was pleased to hear Ollie was using willow.

'If she can't get that, she could try meadowsweet or comfrey, or a plant called juniper I've heard is helpful. Never tried it myself.'

Nell saw no point telling her juniper was off-limits to black rabbits.

'I've also heard stories,' she said, 'of rabbits suffering from the stiffness getting their friends to brush them with the stems of nettles. The seeds of the henbane plant are also supposed to help, though they can have a funny effect on the brain, so I wouldn't try them if I were you.'

Her eyes narrowed, as they often did when she was thinking.

'Perhaps they might help the governor's son.'

'What?'

Maisy told him about the body of the shrew left in her burrow. Nell was shocked. He'd heard about Levi's violent temper, but this was outrageous.

'It's not *his* fault, Nell. A rabbit who would do such a thing must have a sickness of the head. You mustn't be annoyed at someone who is ill. A change of diet, that's what he needs. I'll have to dig into that one a bit more.'

Maisy was clearly not upset, so Nell let the matter rest.

The Patri came to them around midnight and said they should get going. As Maisy left, she promised to do more digging, to find out more about plants that might help Ollie.

*****

'I DIDN'T KNOW it was raining above,' said Vort as Levi entered the living chamber.

'It's not father. I… slipped beside the rindle.'

Helga hopped over to him, sniffing suspiciously.

'You've been with a varlet.'

'It's my job, mother.'

'Do you always wash in water after being with them?'

'Of course not.'

'It was a doe, wasn't it? You've been with a varlet doe.'

'Don't be absurd, Helga.'

Levi was thankful for his father's support. He didn't want to explain where he'd been.

'I'd never forgive you if you'd been with a varlet doe.'

Vort cleared his throat.

'What brings you home, son?'

Levi explained what happened at the Narrows.

'It was pathetic. We had a chance to finally put those varlets in their place. Then the head rabbit and his stewards got cold paws and made us pull back, like foxes running from a vole. Then to have the vole howl in our faces. I felt ashamed to be a rabbit.'

'Why do you suppose the head did that?'

'He's a coward. Losing his grip. Worse than that, he's letting the varlets get away with everything. They're getting so mouthy. Today it's the Common. Tomorrow they'll overrun the Golden Field. Then there'll be disgusting crosser kittens crapping all over the South Bank.'

Helga huffed and left the chamber.

'And it won't be by accident,' rasped Vort, when they were alone.

'The varlet has an intolerant mind, Levi. When it talks about equality, it really means domination, being in charge. Those among the varlets who have been taught by the Oakers to count have worked out that if you put all the blacks of the South Bank together, they outnumber the whites five or six to one. Have you ever heard the phrase *a rabbit is only a rabbit because of other rabbits*?'

'No, father.'

'It's a queer varlet saying. Most white rabbits dismiss it as gibberish. The varlet will tell you it's innocent, all about helping each other. But it's a code. The varlet, you see, is driven by a thirst to rid the South Bank of whites. By itself, that would be impossible. With help, who knows? So, it has entered into an arrangement, a dirty deal with those among the Oakers who share it's loathing of the Mistle. And how will the black rabbit achieve this domination?'

Levi had no idea. Vort answered himself.

'By using its filthy seed. The varlet understands it is inferior to the white rabbit in all ways except one. Numbers. By pumping its seed into our does it will create more and more crossers which, because of the overwhelming numbers, will in time become one colour. Black. It would never have worked this out for itself. Its mind has been poisoned by the interfering Oakers who want to sacrifice our does to the varlets.'

Vort chewed an acorn. Levi felt he should speak.

'That interfering Oakwood seer Fleet was talking to the head rabbit when he halted the attack on the varlet mob.'

Vort's groan was more in frustration than anger.

'These outsiders simply don't understand the South Bank, Levi. If they lived here, they'd see that our varlets are content. They're happy left to themselves, undisturbed by the hankering and lust for a way of life they've never known. Foreign ideas about equality are bad for the varlet. They blow like a wind through one ear and out the other, fanning the savagery lying a whisker from the surface.

'The simple blacks of the Platform or the Willow, Hilltop, are not to blame, son. You could almost feel sorry for them. The problem is the varlets who've been uprooted from their primitive lifestyles and thrust into the civilised surroundings of the Golden Field. Seeing the way the white rabbit lives, fooled into believing they can do the same. Be what they're not. Will never be.'

Levi pounced at the next pause.

'Guess what some of the eclipo officers were talking about the other night?'

'What?'

'Brain sizes. Apparently there's this theory on the North Bank that there's no difference in the size of a varlet brain and the brain of a white rabbit.'

'How absurd.'

'Not all the officers thought it was a joke.'

'Unbelievable.'

'And the way the head rabbit acted at the Narrows, you'd think he believed it too.'

'Sounds like it's time we got rid of him. Replaced him.'

'With who? His high-ups are even weaker.'

Vort rubbed his ear.

'I was afraid it would come to this. I hoped we'd have more time.

Come, son,' he said, limping out of the chamber, 'there's something you need to know.'

Levi followed Vort out into the summer night, keeping to the left of his father so he wouldn't miss a word.

'What have you heard of the Erfeti?,' Vort asked between mouthfuls of sow thistle.

Levi had heard snatches of information about the secret brotherhood, exclusive to Mistle whites. Until then, he'd been considered too young to be trusted with details. He suspected his father belonged. Conversations he'd overheard had intrigued him.

'Some of the eclipo officers talk about it. I'd like to know more.'

'You shall son, you shall.'

Vort chinned, then scanned to check they weren't being overheard.

'This is neither the time nor place to introduce you to the ways of the Erfeti. I will arrange for you to receive a proper welcome at the stump. For now, I will tell you this, if you swear not to repeat it to anyone.'

'I swear,' said Levi, struggling to hide his excitement.

'Until recently, I was the Grand Master of the Erfeti,' Vort began. 'It had been decided I was to take over the leadership of Toria and the Golden Field. We were in the final stages of our planning to overthrow the head rabbit when I had my unfortunate mishap with the varlet Henry.

'I was of course replaced as Grand Master, and fully expected to be sent to the field of silence, as is tradition. It avoids clashes or complications for the new leader. I was lucky. Because of the damage to this leg, it was decided I posed no threat to the new Grand Master.

'The plot against the head rabbit was put off. Since I had been so involved in planning, the brotherhood agreed I should stay on in that role. That was why I went to the head's talkfest, to examine his protection system, how Toria's sentinels* operate. Arranging a place for you on the head's guard was a bonus, and your information has been helpful.'

---

* Sentinels are rabbits responsible for protecting a warren from carns and attacks from outsiders.

'What are we waiting for?'

'Not so fast. My plan is almost in place.'

Vort lowered his voice further.

'There is an issue still to resolve. We will get one opportunity, of that I am convinced. We must wait for the right moment, and,' he whispered, pausing for effect, 'the *right* leader'.

'Who is he, this Grand Master?'

'I'd rather not say. Such matters are not to be discussed outside the brotherhood. You'll find out soon enough.'

'You said we must wait for the *right* leader. What did you mean?'

'I'm afraid our new Grand Master isn't up to it. We must find another. One with the strongest bloodline. The brotherhood will accept only a rabbit they believe to be descended from Erfeti himself.'

'Who?'

Vort glanced around yet again, then continued in a whisper.

'You.'

Levi closed his eyes and imagined himself in the head rabbit's burrow. An endless supply of hazels and acorns and junipers and chestnuts. The choice of any doe in the South Bank. Control over every eclipo officer, every guard, every passage, every chamber, every warren south of the Torrent. Every rabbit. White and black and crosser.

'I could take out the head tonight.'

'Patience Levi, patience. Trust me, and all will be yours.'

*****

MAISY'S VISIT had distracted Nell from the choices he faced. Now she had gone, he needed time and space to think alone. He drifted in the direction of the Torrent. Rabbits, worn and wrinkled before their time, roved in search of food beneath the thinning crescent moon. A swan was guiding a cygnet that had floated too far from a nest on the skerry, a small reef of rock in midstream.

Nell couldn't help thinking it would easier if he didn't have so many choices. Most rabbits at Lexa had none. They were stuck in pitiful ruts. Does who couldn't have kittens. Bucks made to work. No choice about what or where they could eat. Nell felt like an imposter. What was so special about him? Should he take the advice of his host and his friend and burrow down at Lexa, have a family and a comfortable life?

Should he take the Patri's advice, go to Hilltop and sit in the circle with the other old farts and reminisce about moons past? What about the Platform, the Willow? Or simply leave the south, attempt to cross the Torrent to the North Bank and try his luck over there.

Me, me, me.

A rabbit is only a rabbit because of other rabbits.

Nell became aware of two black kittens playing among the reeds. They were such a rarity, he watched them for a while. They were incredibly timid, jumping at the slightest sounds.

'Okay. This time I'll be a clip, you can be the varlet,' said one.

Nell sighed. Black rabbits on the South Bank, whether they realised it or not, were poisoned about colour from birth. Those kittens could play only in certain places. Probably hardly saw their mother, who could be working in the white burrows, or their father working on the harvest. When they grew up, they were told where they could live. Even if they were born in the countryside, as he was, they could not improve their burrow without the permission of a white governor. The fear they showed now would be with them their entire life. Not a natural fear of carns, but a constant fear that they could be stopped by the clips. Everything about their lives was governed by rules that stunted their growth, reduced their potential and, heartbeat by heartbeat, snuffed out hope of something better.

Thanks to his parents and friends, Nell had learnt all a rabbit needed to know about plants and wind and carns. At Lexa, kittens had to find things out for themselves, often with disastrous consequences. They understood nothing about plants and everything about lying and cheating. Nothing about carns. Everything about evading the claws of a white rabbit.

Nell saw now that his had been a privileged upbringing. As the son of a dom. Then the moons at the Platform, which had been carefree, nourished by the loving support of Maisy. At Hilltop, the privilege reached a point where it became irritating. He remembered the words, particularly of Old Chief and Aunt Mina, that inspired him at the time. But they had been words in an empty passage, like a kitten listening to a yarn, imagining playing the part of the hero and never expecting it to happen in real life. The circle gatherings, which he once believed were the centre of everything that mattered, were little more than old rabbits looking back at their early moons and mourning their passing as if they had some power to change things. The Patri and his high-ups were tolerated by the whites and left to themselves because they were seen as harmless.

Old Farts. William.

Look over the shoulder of a speaker for their motives.

Nell had moved on. Coming to the Golden Field had changed not only his status, but the way he saw and thought about things. This was real. Real hunger. Real suffering. Real brutality.

The Patri used the phrase *amongst your own.* Who were Nell's own? A privileged member of the Hilltop circle? At the Willow or Platform with Maisy and her plants? Settling down at Lexa to have a family? Or was Stephen right, accepting what he was, proud to be black?

The daystar was waking, sending its beams to snuff out what was left of the moon and bully the remaining stars from the sky. Nell had wandered downstream to a point opposite the skerry. He watched the family of swans. Father, mother and two cygnets. A happy scene.

Without warning, the father plunged into the Torrent and paddled furiously upstream. Its massive white wings were curved high, and hisses of pure hostility spewed from its jutting orange bill. Nell saw that another swan had landed on the Torrent, a challenge to its territory. The intruder was closing in fast on the current, and its extra speed gave it the early advantage when the two giant birds met.

The water erupted into a snorting, trumpeting whirlpool of feathers and spray as each swan tried to grab the other's neck and hold it under the water. At one point, the intruder got the better, and Nell was sure the father would drown. He resurfaced, saw his mate and children watching from the skerry, and rejoined the fray. The fight went on and on and Nell became aware of other rabbits stopping what they were doing to stare.

Suddenly, the combatants pulled back and the intruder dashed for the far bank, chased by the father. The intruder flapped out of the water and lay panting on the ground, its long neck wrapped over its body. For a while, the victor stood over the vanquished, carefully rearranging feathers disturbed in the fight. When he'd finished, he arched his long neck in some signal Nell couldn't understand. The intruder got to his feet, jumped into the water, flapped heavily into the air, and flew away downstream.

The swan had stood up for its rights. Risked all to protect its family, and at one stage looked certain to lose everything. He'd stuck at it and eventually overcome.

If we're true to our conscience, we'll do what's right all the time, not only when it suits us.

You carry our star.

They will look to you.

Be the one.

Nell knew what he had to do.

PART TWO

THE PARTING

24. Nose in a wasps' nest

A MAGPIE was anting near the stone bridge. It had found a line of the insects, collected a beak-full, and was raising its wing to rub them onto its feathers, when Fleet approached. The seer hopped onto the grass beside the rutted path, so the bird could finish what it was doing, then followed the trail to a gap in the hedgerow on the edge of the Oakwood. He was about to duck through when he noticed two black rabbits coming along the verge. From their voices and scents, he recognised them as his fellow seers, Donald and Richard, who were responsible for keeping ears and eyes on warrens in the fields to the north and east. They sped up when they saw him.

'How goes it, Fleet?' asked the smaller of the two.

'Fine, and you?'

'Quiet in our patch. What about yours?'

'If you'd asked me a moon ago, I'd have said the same,' replied Fleet. 'One or two minor incidents, a few interesting rumours not worth troubling Thatch over. Then something happened the other night that could... change things.'

The three rabbits crawled through the hedgerow into the field. Neither of the other seers had been to the South Bank, so Fleet explained as briefly as he could the restrictions on the blacks, and how they had been allowed to pass through the Narrows to feed in the Common.

'Then the head rabbit decided to block off access to the field. Some of the blacks objected, decided to protest. I've been covering the South for many moons. There's always been talk of challenging the colour rules. This, though, was the first serious attempt since Dingha, and that was against a softer foe.'

'Good for them,' said Richard.

'What happened?' asked Donald.

'The decision to protest was remarkable in itself. I was expecting trouble, and for moments feared there'd be some. Then the head arrived and let the black rabbits through the Narrows.'

'Sounds like they're coming to their senses at last.'

'Perhaps,' said Fleet. 'I have a feeling there's more to it. Whatever reasons the head had for changing his mind, he's stuck his nose in a wasps' nest. This has given the blacks a whiff of power, and there are some strong and determined rabbits in the South who won't like that.'

The two seers pestered Fleet with questions. When they asked him about the quality of black leaders, he found himself unable to answer.

'What's the matter? A seer's the last rabbit I'd expect to be tongue-tied.'

Fleet recovered.

'It's a subject that's been troubling me. There are none among the current black high-ups capable of stemming what I fear will be a vicious kick-back from the white supremacists. Whenever a buck of colour sticks his nose up to challenge the say-so of the whites, he's beaten down.'

Fleet told them of the fight he witnessed between Vort and Henry.

'I saw it all from the other side of the rindle, have agonised about it ever since. I could have done something to stop it. I saw what was coming. Henry was as decent a rabbit as you'll find. He could be alive today if I hadn't sat there and watched it happen.'

'You did the right thing,' said Donald. 'A seer's role is to watch and report what he sees. If you become involved, you lose your perspective, your fairness.'

'I'm not sure I agree,' said Richard. 'We're all actors in life, whether we're a prime rabbit or a mother or a seer. If a rabbit sees a wrong being done, and can do something about it, he or she should go in on the side of right.'

'Not if you have respect for your role as a seer,' said Donald.

Richard shook his head.

'Are you telling me that if you saw a rabbit attacking one of your kittens because her fur was the wrong shade, you'd sit and watch it happen, watch her pass into the field of silence, so you could report it… fairly?'

'That's different,' said Donald. 'If a rabbit attacked my kittens it would involve me directly. I'd already be part of it. Fleet here is talking about something that didn't happen in his own warren. Who are we to judge what is right and wrong in other rabbits' fields? Meddling in the affairs of others is not only wrong, it is dangerous. How would we like it if this Governor Vort or the head rabbit of the Golden Field made us change our diets?'

'You'd probably do as he said and munch rats' turd for the rest of your life,' grinned Richard. 'You need to lighten up, Donald. You're taking yourself too seriously.'

They'd come to the glade that ran off into the heart of the Oakwood. The two black seers were going to other warrens nearer the Torrent.

'This South Bank of yours sounds interesting,' said Donald. 'I'd like to come and see it some moon.'

'I'd be glad to show you around,' said Fleet. 'Gets lonely over there at times. There are some promising young rabbits I'd like you to meet.'

They farewelled, and Fleet set off along the glade, wondering whether three rabbits in particular – Nell, Ollie, and Stephen – would ever reach their potential.

*****

UP THE SLOPE to the east of Lexa was an area overlooking the Torrent, cut off from the Upland by a gully. Black rabbits could go through to graze, and many of those living in the eastern burrows of Lexa jumped at the opportunity. The food on offer was little better than the flats, and the gully was sometimes blocked off to let carriers taking nuts, berries and acorns pass between the high ground and the trade storage burrows of Toria. Scroungers, though, couldn't be choosy, and there was always the chance of finding an overlooked blade or seed head of tim grass among the foxtail and rye.

Along the western rim of the gully grew a thick tangle of briar, which had become a favourite gathering place of rabbits belonging to the Cluster, who had dug out a number of chambers, entrances, and false burrows. It was to the briar one dayfall that Nell and Ollie went for their first Cluster gathering. They knew little about the group, other than that it claimed to oppose the colour rules and welcomed black rabbits from any of the warrens of the South Bank.

The weather had been uncomfortably hot early in the web moon. Scents from the honeysuckle and white campion were strong, though clouds gathering from the south-west hinted of a change to cooler, wetter weather. Rabbits who doubted the clouds need only sniff the drooping petals of the herb roberts to know rain was on its way.

Nell and Ollie were met by a rabbit who escorted them through the various passages and tunnels, bypassing blind-ends, below and up again, brushing through countless spiders' webs, until they were disoriented. They eventually entered a chamber to find rabbits of various ages discussing burrow workers. They recognised only one other, Stephen, so sat beside him.

A buck Nell had never seen was speaking.

'... then forced, against their will, to mate with their masters.'

Mutters of disapproval greeted this remark. The buck went on.

'Then once these lusty white rabbits have had their way, they use their brains instead of their seed. They worry what their friends will think if their nanny has a litter of black and white kittens. The does, if they're lucky, are banished to the countryside. Unlucky ones disappear. Either way, we never see nor smell them again, so we assume they've been taken by a fox or owl. Or caught some mysterious disease and passed into the field of silence. Or love their work so much they don't want to come back.'

Exaggerated chuckles echoed round the chamber. Alfred, leader of the Cluster, rose to speak.

'A colourful description, I'm sure. Do you know this for a fact? It is one thing to accuse a rabbit. Another to prove what you say.'

'I have heard similar stories,' said another buck, who Stephen identified as Mark. 'But listen, friends, does it matter if we have absolute proof? We don't need to see it to know that our does are shut up all night in the burrows of Toria, forced to dig and dig and dig until their shoulders ache, their noses and eyes sting. They're constantly watched, and if they slow down, they're beaten. Then they're herded into small out-chambers where they have to sleep five, sometimes ten to a burrow, watched over by the very brutes our friend has been telling us about. They can't talk to one another, let alone organise resistance. Unless we do something for them, their lives will go from bad to worse to...'

His voice trailed off.

Alfred huffed.

'We're doing what we can. I meet regularly with the head rabbit's stewards, at least once a moon. I can assure you those discussions are frank and meaningful. And, I might add, the stewards assure me our concerns are being taken seriously.'

Stephen fidgeted. 'He's starting to sound like the whites.'

'I heard that,' snapped Alfred. 'You and your friends should keep your mouths shut and ears open. You might learn something.'

Mark rose.

'We believe it's time to take more direct action. Our success at the Narrows showed what can be achieved when we work together. I say we put our new strength to the test. Organise a work stoppage by the does.'

There was uproar. Shouts of *yes, yes* were soon overcome with louder accusations of *insanity, lunacy*.

'Mark's proposal is... novel,' said Alfred, when he had quiet. 'He assumes all the does are unhappy, which I doubt. Perhaps we should let *them* decide, since they have the most to lose.'

'Sounds reasonable to me,' said Mark.

'Very well,' concluded Alfred,' smiling in expected triumph. 'The proposal is for Mark to organise a gathering of as many does as he can convince, to ask them what they think of his... stopping work idea. I'm sure Mark, being the fair rabbit he is, will take the trouble to tell them the likely consequences of such a ludi... novel proposal.'

'Of course,' replied Mark. 'And *I* take it, if they agree to stop work, you will let them do it?'

Alfred winked his nose in mock disgust.

'Naturally.'

Some of the older rabbits laughed. Alfred motioned for quiet.

'Mark will need help to approach all the working does. I'm sure Stephen and his two new friends will be happy to assist.'

As soon as the meeting ended, Mark outlined his plan to the others. He'd expected the decision. The gathering of the does was to be held before dayspring at a mound between Lexa and the Torrent. Nell, Ollie, and Stephen were given different parts of the warren to visit to spread the message. As they left and squinted through drizzle, Nell saw Ollie was struggling with the stiffness. He arranged to swap some of the more distant parts of the warren to make it easier for her.

Nell visited many burrows. In every one, the living space was damper, colder or smaller than the hovel he and Ollie shared. Not all the does could be found. As he'd heard at the gathering, some lived most of the time in the burrows of their masters. Although there were doubters, several agreed to attend the gathering when Nell assured them nothing had been decided about the work stoppage. It would be up to them.

*****

WHEN LEVI RETURNED to the Golden Field and his job as an officer of the eclipo, he was surprised how many members of Erfeti had wormed their way into middle positions at Toria. It was all part of Vort's plan, and nothing was suspected by the head rabbit and his stewards, because none of the Mistle whites showed interest in advancing to the inner circle of power. They sprung up as deputies in trade storage burrows, as carriers, messengers in the head's burrow, work supervisors. Some managed the web of black informers, so were aware of the planned work stoppage. No rabbits in the head's circle expected the timid servant does to have anything to do with the protest. Levi hoped otherwise.

Erfeti bucks controlled the eclipo squads responsible for keeping the varlets in order. There were four squads, each led by one of the *brothers*, as they referred to themselves. Levi's strength and aggressive streak turned heads and ears, so when the leader of his squad was injured fleeing a fox, Levi was the obvious choice to replace him.

THE MORNING was cloudy and dark. The fresh murmur of watermint shrouded the gathering of more than forty does. Nell crouched behind Mark as the buck explained the plan.

'This is what we must decide. Do you agree to stop working in the white rabbits' burrows until the head rabbit accepts our demands? I'm sure you realise you may be putting yourself at risk of punishment from the clips. What do you say? Yes or no?'

Paws shuffled uncertainly. Then a doe hopped forward, and Nell recognised the nanny, Dima.

'We who work in the burrows of Toria have no lives of our own. There is nothing the white rabbits can do to humiliate us more than they have.'

Nell could see that Dima's words had an effect on the does around her. Mumbles of *yes* flowed outwards like a rippling wave until most were nodding.

'Congratulations on the crowd, Nell, you did an excellent job,' said Mark, as they watched the does split up to feed.

'Stephen and Ollie deserve more thanks than me. They're the persuasive ones.'

Mark showed little interest in Nell's attempt to praise his friends. He was looking over his shoulder.

'I need a rabbit I can trust to stay close to me during the stoppage, Nell. To observe what's going on, watch my back. We must expect the clips will target those of us who have stuck out our necks.'

'I'd be happy to.'

25. A dark shape lying still

THE FIRST TWO DAYS of the work stoppage passed peacefully. Most of the does stayed in their burrows at Lexa, though it drizzled continuously, so the clips were reluctant to come out to harass them. The white rabbits had received enough warning of the protest to get in extra supplies of food, so most suffered little. Nell went with Mark from burrow to burrow, giving encouragement where needed. The worries of the first night eased, and by the second, most of the does were breathing normally again.

On the third, rumours spread that food and patience were running out in Toria, and tempers sharpening. Four jittery does couldn't handle the tension, and hightailed back to their masters. It took plenty of reassuring to keep the rest from caving in.

The clouds cleared on the fourth night, flushing the flats with light from a fattening moon on a low arc between the bright giants, Mars and Saturn. Nell and Mark were talking near the bourne when Ollie bounded up, panting. Does on their way home from feeding had been surrounded and hustled back to work at Toria.

'They refused and were threatened, then chased *into* their burrows.'

The three rabbits hurried off to investigate, and were climbing up towards the blackthorn when they saw an attack on other does near the privets. Six were cowering in front of clips twice their size. Some managed to evade the ring, but three of the clips were holding one of the does on the ground.

Nell was about to run to help, when further cries came from the direction of Toria. A line of terrified black does came streaming down, chased by white rabbits. One of the does broke free. Nell recognised her, and beckoned her over. She was shaking.

'It's okay,' said Nell. 'You're safe for now. Tell us what happened.'

'We were marched into a burrow up there. We had no choice. The clips were so aggressive and threatening. They expected us to do as we were told, because they left us in a chamber and went to round up more of our sisters. When the white does came to get us for work, we refused and lay down. We were left alone for whiles, until a band of clips arrived and attacked us. We managed to get to the surface. As you can see, they chased us.'

Nell watched as the other does gave in and were prodded up to Toria. The field went quiet. He looked towards the base of the privets and saw a dark shape lying motionless, flashing a memory of his father beside the willow at the rindle. He rushed over. On the ground was the still warm body of a doe with a distinctive crescent-shaped hole in her left ear. Dima's neck had been almost bitten off.

*****

THE DIFFERENCE in confidence and gestures of the two rabbits was striking, thought Ollie. A night after the brutal end to the work stoppage, Mark was on the mound, speaking to a smaller gathering of does. Nell was sitting to one side.

Ollie knew that Nell felt terrible about Dima, but could see determination in his eyes. Mark's face and twitching movements, in contrast, showed deep personal fear, knowing that the doe who had spoken up at the first gathering – on this very spot a few mornings earlier – was now in the field of silence. For daring to defy the whites, as Mark was doing now. Something else was different. The fur on the top of Nell's head was ruffled and there were specks of dried mud on his shoulder. For the first time Ollie could remember, his friend hadn't cleaned himself before facing other rabbits.

After Dima's passing, Ollie and Nell had been sent to persuade as many does as they could to come to this next gathering, organised by

Mark in an effort to regain control. There had been understandable reluctance. If it hadn't been for the heavy cloud hiding a moon two nights from full, few would have risked it. Only ten ventured out. From the safety of the reeds, Ollie watched as a pike slid silently through the water. Mark had just begun talking, when clips moved out from the shadows to form a semi-circle around the does.

*****

IT HAD BEEN LEVI'S SQUAD that attacked the protesting does beneath the privets, and he who sent the loud-mouth varlet Dima to the field of silence. He'd wanted to charge straight into Lexa on a rampage. Older heads, worried it might cause a stir at a delicate time for the Erfeti planners, talked him out of it. Levi's chance came when he was sent to break up the second gathering. He shoved his way through the terrified varlets and sauntered up to Mark, chinning, before barking at the does.

'You have until the count of ten to order them back to work or… else.'

*****

THE WAY HE SAID *else* was so chilling, it sent Ollie's heart racing.
'One, two, three…'
Mark sunk to the ground, trembling, his ears flat against his back. The does stuped*. There was no Dima to speak up this time. The clips were sneering, eager for a fight.
'Four, five, six...'
Ollie had a bad feeling about this.
'Seven, eight...'
She sensed that Nell was about to argue, which was the wrong thing to do. There would be a massacre. She sprung in front of the does.
'Sisters, sisters. You heard the officer. Let's go, let's go.'

---

* A rabbit stupes when it becomes so frightened, its muscles *freeze* and it is unable to move.

One of the does dashed off. The others remained rooted to the ground. Levi had stopped counting, appeared confused. Nell hopped over to Ollie and the two of them nudged the does away. When they'd guided the last pair through the line of clips, they saw Mark being taken away by Levi. Nell wanted to go and help him, but two snarling bucks blocked his way. Ollie noticed the fur on her friend's back quiver, so she tugged him away.

'Don't even think about it,' she said. 'Remember, we must choose our battles.'

Mark and Levi disappeared from view. It was the last time the brave black rabbit was seen alive.

26. The ritual at the stump

A BULGE in the Chilling Wood jutting into the field north of the Point had been home to a badger sett far longer than the memory of its current occupant, an ill-mannered boar who'd lived there more than thirty moons.

Fleet was hopping along the trail hugging the rindle, when he smelt the badger surfacing for the evening. He crouched to watch, as the carn ambled over to a dung pit, then padded to a raised ledge outside the sett. The seer waited patiently until the badger finished grooming and wandered off into the wood. A light westerly brought the powerful aroma of watermint from the rindle, and as Fleet got to the edge of the field, the wood canopy opened to reveal a brilliant starlit sky.

The thinning crescent moon cast long shadows from the trees to the stump, which was the reason for Fleet's visit. He'd heard that a secret ritual would take place that night and would be worth observing. If his information was correct, the performers would be arriving soon, so he chose a hiding place downwind among elder bushes, and crouched to wait. He shivered at a sudden nip in the air, a reminder winter was coming.

The rabbits arrived in pairs and threes. All bucks. All large. All prancing with self-importance. And all white. Some carried early-season mistletoe berries. They greeted, touching raised noses, and took their places in a ring around the stump. The breeze stirred again, carrying their scents to Fleet. Helpful. Timely. Lucky. As long as the wind held, and he kept still, he was confident he wouldn't be noticed.

Heads swivelled as Vort approached from upstream, limping. He climbed awkwardly onto the stump, a move that seemed to annoy the others. Grumblings hushed quickly as the southern governor cleared his throat.

'Brothers. I know it is customary for only the Grand Master to stand on the sacred stump of Erfeti. But I have news. Dramatic news.'

That got their attention.

'The Grand Master has passed to the field of silence. He met his end a short while ago on the banks of the rindle flowing behind me.'

Gasps and comments of *surely not*, and *I don't believe it* were quickly snuffed out.

'There is no question, brothers. I saw his body. And that is not the end of my news. Tragic though his passing is, we must act quickly. For we face momentous times. A new era for all of us who have waited long for the time of cleansing. A new era for which we need new leadership. A bold leader with the ruthless determination to seize what is rightfully ours, in honour of Erfeti.'

'Hail Erfeti' they cried as one, stamping their paws.

'Therefore brothers, I freely stand aside for our new Grand Master.'

All eyes, including Fleet's, had been on Vort. None had noticed the lone rabbit who now burst into the circle and leapt onto the stump.

'Erfeti, Erfeti, Erfeti,' shouted Vort, and the chant was taken up by the others. Uncertainly at first, eventually with gusto.

Levi let the chanting go on for some time, then raised his paw.

'Thank you, brothers. I am honoured to stand here on such a night.'

He looked up at the sky, and the others did the same. Fleet noticed Levi's coat was wet, as if he had been caught in a downpour. The new Grand Master appeared uncertain.

'I… now ask brother Vort to give the devotion.'

The governor winked his nose.

'Brothers, we stand at the Stump of Erfeti, under the four stars* representing the corners of his land, *our* land. Let us never forget how our ancestor, the great Erfeti, was driven from the warrens of the

---

* The four stars of Erfeti are known to humans as the Great Square of Pegasus.

North. How he brought his family and friends to this place. How he came to live here in peace, but was betrayed by the varlet dom, Gandeni, and passed into the field of silence. How his son, who mercifully escaped the slaughter, promised to avenge him. How he returned to this place, only to be encircled once more by the enemy. How he looked to the four stars we see now, and vowed that if he achieved victory over the hordes of blackness, those stars would forever be recognised as a symbol of thanksgiving. Brothers, let us never forget how Erfeti's son, his blood offspring, courageously led his comrades into battle, against overwhelming numbers, how they fought and fought and refused to stop until the rindle behind us flowed red with the blood of the enemy.'

Vort raised his face again to the sky.

'We see you, oh great one. From the four corners of your land, we have gathered at this place, your place, to honour you, to seek strength from your inspiration, to renew the vow. All here pledge that if you protect us, deliver the enemy to us, we will observe this occasion moon by moon, as a time of thanksgiving. We will instruct our offspring to join us for all the coming generations, and the glory of the victory shall be yours.'

The governor's brows snapped together, and his voice rose.

'The time for revenge is near, brothers. You know what is expected of each of you. Keep your noses to the ground, ears to the wind, and, most importantly, eyes to the sky.'

'Hail Erfeti!' shouted Levi.

'Erfeti, Erfeti, Erfeti,' they echoed.

Levi jumped to the ground, then whirled round to face the stump. He stretched out with his paw to touch the four raised diamonds. The ritual was then repeated by the other rabbits. Fleet noticed Levi talking to a buck from one of the southern warrens, and overheard the words *take care of her.*

The rabbits strutted off. Once Fleet was sure they were out of sight, smell, and hearing, he crept from his hiding place over to the stump. He felt the same uncertainty he had many moons before at another part of the rindle. Should he remain an observer? Or should he tell someone what was about to happen? What, though, was going to happen? And who should he warn? Vort's message about revenge was muddied, as was Levi's remark about *taking care of her.*

The seer saw a large object floating down the rindle. It was the body of a plump white buck. He watched as it bumped into an overhanging branch, rotated, then bobbed away on the current. Its head had been almost severed from its body.

*****

HAZELNUTS BEGIN LIFE as tiny crimson tufts appearing on twigs in the moons of the owl and snow. Fertile female flowers grow into bunches of whitish-green nuts that ripen in leaf-fall, providing a vital food source for animals such as squirrels, bank voles, wood mice.

Squirrels forage through leaves at the tips of branches, often hanging upside down by their hind-paws to grab the nuts. Then, holding them in their front paws, they roll them to check weevils haven't devoured the kernels. If the nuts are intact and to be eaten, holes are bitten in the tops and fang teeth are used to prise the shells neatly apart. If, however, the nuts are to be stored for another time, the squirrels carry them to suitable burial sites, dig shallow holes with their front paws, push the nuts inside and scrape soil over the top.

It was this habit of storing the nuts that most interested the white rabbits of Toria. Nell and Ollie were chosen at dayfall, and ordered to join a work gang in the hazel copse. It was the job of the night shift to watch and listen for squirrels hiding nuts, retrieve them and take them to a collection point. Nell thought the squirrels would have worked out what the rabbits were up to. They hadn't, which made him wonder if they remembered where they'd hidden the nuts in the first place.

He, Ollie and six other black rabbits took over from the daystar shift. They overheard the clips saying it had been quiet because of the lack of wind. Most of the nuts were found to be falsies – infested with weevil. The new arrivals groaned at this news, for a quiet day usually meant they would be harassed to work harder during the night. This had been the case for the first part of the evening, especially when the breeze picked up and the clips pushed them to chase everything that fell, even when they could tell from the sound that it was a falsie.

It was a warm evening for the ivy moon which, although fattening, was only two nights old so little more than a slither. Through breaks in the copse's canopy, thunder clouds could be seen massing. Nell heard a squirrel running down a trunk carrying a nut. He waited until it was buried, then retrieved it and took it to the collection point. Two clips sat behind the pile, munching on blackberries, chatting between mouthfuls. Nell heard the phrase *work stoppage*, so swivelled his ear to catch more of the conversation. The guards were boasting about what a failure the protest had been, how vole-hearted the varlets were, how the doe who passed into the field of silence ran into a tree.

Nell felt insulted. Though the protest was brutally stamped out, it had not been a waste of time. It had stirred something, created a lot of talk, and gatherings of the Cluster had become livelier. It attracted more members, instead of *leavings* as the white rabbits were claiming. Nell was particularly annoyed by the suggestion that Dima had run into a tree. He would have liked to argue with the clips, but was learning when to talk and when to keep quiet. One of the white rabbits noticed him lingering.

'Hey, darkie. Get your varlet backside to work.'

Nell bowed and rejoined the others, as a crack of lightning flashed over the field.

*****

MAISY DIDN'T NEED LIGHTNING to know the weather was changing. The ring around the moon just before it had set – red on its inner margins fading outwards to a dirty yellow – convinced her. Observant rabbits understood that such a moon signaled a storm.

She had ranged close to the forbidden line, when she picked up the acrid undertone of groundsel. Finally. She'd been looking for the plant for days, ever since one of the governor's mates asked her for a remedy for crusted wounds. Maisy knew groundsel contained iron, had heard it could draw out and clean old wounds. As she tracked the plant, she also felt whispers of moisture in the air.

'Bother,' she said out loud, ignoring the clouds towering overhead like giant clusters of angelica. She'd searched for so long, she decided to take the risk and stay above another while. The air around her became still, and for a heartbeat she lost the smell of the groundsel. She sensed a subtle greening of the grass, stiffness in her joints.

The wind stirred again, stronger this time, bringing back the pungency of groundsel and sending showers of leaves twitching and quivering to the ground. Maisy found a single flower on a stunted stem. As she stretched to break it off, the wind surged, almost knocking her over. The temperature plummeted, and she turned for home.

*****

LEVI WAS WOKEN with the news that the storm was moments away. A doe alerted him to the halo moon, and he had given his instructions and gone above to prepare.

Now he waited. From where he crouched in the shadow of the Golden Field rowan, he could make out the main entrance to the head rabbit's burrow in the bursts of lightning. Behind him crouched Vort and eight carefully selected eclipo officers, all members of the brotherhood. Levi was thinking about what lay ahead, and wondering how Erfeti's son felt all those moons ago when he faced down the hordes of varlets at the stump.

*****

NELL, OLLIE, and the other workers were ordered to carry the nuts to the blackthorn. This was no surprise. Although the clips would have been happy for the black rabbits to keep working through a storm, they did not trust them to work unsupervised, and the whites had no interest in getting soaked.

The rain began as the line moved along the trail beside the hedgerow, keeping clear of a badger raiding a wasp nest. Nell drooled at the untouchable plants in the whites-only field – the dead nettle, the hogweeds, mugwort and plantain, the tim grass still in its second flush. Two black does were scampering for cover, carrying marsh thistles destined for drying in the burrows of their masters. The rain strengthened as they got to the dale, and the trail became slippery. Nell dropped his nut and was clouted by one of the clips. He recovered it quickly and rejoined the line. After delivering their harvest to the storage burrow, Nell and Ollie hurried through the gathering storm to Lexa, where they were due at a gathering of young members of the Cluster.

*****

LEVI WATCHED as eclipo officers came above from the head rabbit's burrow and trudged off. They had been told that a varlet was harassing white does in the Common, and Levi grinned at how easily the fools had fallen for the trick. If other information was correct, it would leave no more than four bucks below, guarding the head rabbit.

The temperature tumbled further, and another thunder boom belched over the field. Vort nodded. It was time. Levi and his squad were allowed to pass through the outer post of Toria, guarded by a single rabbit who suspected nothing unusual from members of the eclipo wanting shelter.

*****

ALL AROUND MAISY, creatures dashed or flew for cover. The sensible thing to do would be to drop the groundsel and find shelter immediately, but she decided to go for her burrow. She hopped, stopped, detected a lull, then rushed on, aware that the area she was crossing had no bolt holes. On Vort's orders.

She was half-way home when the hailstorm began. Chunks of ice the size of hazelnuts pounded the ground around her.

*****

NELL AND OLLIE made the shelter of the meeting burrow, pleased to find that Stephen and the three other rabbits had brought snacks. One of them was talking excitedly about a discussion he'd had with a white rabbit who pitied the blacks.

'He lives not far from the hole of one of the head's stewards. Next time he sees him, he's going to ask him to go easier on us.'

'I'm sure stewards don't describe their burrows, their spacious, dry, comfortable homes as *holes*,' said a second.

Stephen was frowning.

'You're both missing the point. I've also spoken to white rabbits who *talk* about how unfair things are for blacks. Answer me this? Have any of them spent a day in a hole like this? Been forced to forage above all day because they're so hungry they've lost their fear of carns? No. White rabbits cannot speak for us, because they cannot put themselves in our place. It is simply impossible for a white rabbit to understand what it is like to be a black rabbit. We need to speak up for our...'

He was drowned out by the frenzy of the hailstorm. As they waited for the noise to subside, Nell considered what Stephen was saying. Rather than waiting for the whites to change the rules, *their* rules, black rabbits had to take control of their own destiny. And accept responsibility for letting the whites trample over them.

*****

THREE TIMES Maisy was knocked over. Each time, she dragged herself up. The outline of the Platform appeared through the squall, and she hustled forward, pushing herself to cover the final few bounds.

The hail was unrelenting, the icy onslaught deafening. She got to the burrow and recoiled in shock. The entrance had been covered over. She squatted there, as the hail pummelled her body. She flattened herself to the ground, ready to give up, until she tasted the groundsel stalk still in her mouth. With one last effort, she dragged herself over to a neighbour's hole and toppled inside.

27. We know where we stand

LEVI BUSTLED his officers down a series of passages, their progress disguised by the ferocity of the storm above, until they came to the guard point outside the head rabbit's private chambers.

'I need to see the head,' he snapped at the guard.

'He's eating. You'll have to wait.'

'This is urgent, you fool.'

The guard smelt the size and mood of the eclipo officers lined up behind Levi, and backed off. The inviting scent of acorns and juniper berries gripped Levi as he entered the spacious burrow, its roof supported by sprawling roots of the rowan. At the far end sat the head rabbit, nosing a pyramid of nuts.

'Your time's up, varlet-lover,' shouted Levi, chinning deliberately in defiance of the rules, then rising to his full height.

The head, who had seen off numerous challenges when he was younger and stronger, showed little emotion. His minders appeared less confident.

The hailstorm could be plainly felt pounding the ground above them. Levi was sizing up the head rabbit's throat, when his father limped past.

'I'm afraid he's right,' said Vort, calmly. 'It's time for a change.'

'Change to what?' asked the head, the first hint of doubt in his voice.

Vort chinned on a rock.

'You've had your chance. And wasted it. The entire South Bank is about to fall round your ears, and you and your spineless circle can't smell it.'

'What nonsense is this?'

'You know what I'm talking about. You've given the varlets a hop. Now they want a bound. Tomorrow the whole field. It's time to put them in their place.'

'What are you afraid of, Vort?'

'The trouble is that you and your Oaker paw-lickers have no idea what you are. No sense of destiny. Either you're the master, an equal, or you're inferior. I... we know what we are. What we want. And we're here to take it.'

'You've lost your mind.'

'And you have two choices. Either hightail through that hole, now, keep going and don't stop until you cross the Torrent. Or I'll sit down and enjoy some of those acorns while Levi and his friends here decide the leadership the past-moon way.'

The head puffed himself up, and Levi was certain he'd get the fight he'd been hoping for. Then the shoulders wilted, as the defeated rabbit accepted the inevitable.

The hailstorm eased as the head left. His minders were immediately replaced with two squads of Erfeti bucks who'd been waiting outside to secure the burrow. Levi went above and jumped onto the head rabbit's terrace. Beneath him the ground was covered in white.

*****

'WHERE DID this Levi come from?,' Stephen asked when a messenger brought news of the overthrow at Toria. 'Do we know anything about him?'

Nell stiffened.

'Levi's the son of Vort, a Mistle governor from down south who will be the brains behind this. Levi is strong, and mean, but I've never considered him bright. Vort's something different altogether. He and my father had a... disagreement moons ago. Vort sent him to the field of silence.'

Ollie sensed her friend was about to be showered with sympathy, which he wouldn't want, so she butted in.

'Vort didn't come out of it unscathed. Ever since then, he's had a limp. Levi is the one who does his dirty work. Dangerous combination. And if those two are now in charge, we can expect things to get nasty very quickly.'

'We need to act quickly ourselves,' said one of the bucks, 'before this Levi gets settled in'.

'I'm sure our esteemed leader Alfred has already *acted*,' said Stephen. 'He'd have been up there in a heartbeat to nuzzle up to the new head rabbit, have a frank and meaningful discussion.'

His mocking voice eased the nervous tension in the burrow.

'No, my friends, Stephen continued, 'the Cluster's become a joke. It's run by worn-out rabbits with worn-out ideas who are more interested in keeping their comfortable lifestyles than lifting a paw to improve the lot the rest of us.'

'What do you suggest?' asked Ollie.

'How about starting our own group, as part of the Cluster, to stir things up?' said Stephen.

Nell was nodding.

'I agree. Though in fairness to Alfred, Ollie and I will tell him what we're thinking. It will be easier if we have his support.'

*****

THEY PICKED THEIR WAY through a landscape shattered by the hailstorm. Balls of ice, broken branches and battered bodies speckled the flats. Most animals had seen and smelt the signs and taken shelter as best they could. Many, though, were caught out, or risked their lives for a last bite.

Chiffchaffs taking off to join a flock passing through from the north were knocked out of the air. A massed murmuring of starlings was wiped out. The elegant neck of a swan was snapped by a hailstone as big as a chestnut. Small creatures with nowhere to hide were pulverised. The crushed bodies of dunnocks and wrens, of once beautiful peacock and tortoiseshell butterflies, of shield bugs whose defences of olive and mauve offered no protection, speckled the ground.

Alfred's burrow was on a rise, higher than those of most other black rabbits. The mouth had been altered so that the most depressing parts of Lexa could not be seen from inside. The two friends were shown into an outer chamber, where Nell smelt a trace of juniper. As they waited, he noticed Ollie looking at him strangely, her head cocked to one side.

'Is something wrong?'

'Not wrong. Just different. You've stopped worrying about how you look.'

Nell smiled. The little rabbit didn't miss much.

'I think we've both realised, Ollie, there's more important things to concern ourselves with than grooming simply for appearance.'

'You're not wrong there, my friend. And think how much time you'll save. It'll add moons to your life.'

The haughty face of Alfred poked into the chamber from an inner passage.

'Friends, please join me.'

The overweight leader of the Cluster lumbered ahead, puffing, his scent an odd mixture of foxtail from the flats and tim grass from the Upland. Nell told Alfred of Levi's take-over, and the older buck made out he already knew.

'There will be a few new stewards for us to deal with. We'll simply have to adapt.'

'Have you ever met Levi or his father?' asked Nell.

'Not in the fur, no. I've heard Governor Vort is rather… efficient.'

'He's a murderer and a supremacist,' said Ollie.

'You youngsters are always jumping to conclusions. This Levi's been head rabbit less than a day and you've already judged him. You need to learn patience. More tolerance. Let's wait and see what happens.'

'We've seen how far patience has got us,' said Nell. 'I know this Levi. And his father. They're ruthless. They won't wait around to *see what happens.*'

Alfred arched an eyebrow.

'What do you suggest? Hop up to Toria and tell them there's been a mistake? Could they please go back where they came from?'

'Sounds like what the Cluster's been doing for moons,' Ollie whispered to Nell.

'I heard that,' said Alfred. 'You two have much to learn. Until you know what you're talking about, I suggest you keep your thoughts to yourself.'

The meeting wasn't going how Nell hoped.

'Nevertheless, some of us younger rabbits would like to form our own group, as part of the Cluster of course.'

'What on Earth for? What do you think a few seedling bucks and does can achieve that the combined wisdom and experience of the high-ups of the flats cannot?'

Ollie butted in: 'We could encourage rabbits, large numbers of them, to work together to challenge the whites. Like Dingha did.'

'The impulsiveness of you young rabbits astounds me. Have you heard nothing I've been saying?'

Alfred started to groom. His patience, and the meeting, was over.

'Tell your friends to forget about their little group, and this ridiculous talk of Dingha. Take a good look around you on the way to your burrows. Those rabbits out there have no interest, nor stomach, for fur-brained uprisings. Even if they did, they'd be too disorganised. You couldn't pull off a simple protest by the burrowing does. Dingha would meet the same fate as your friend Mark if he were here today.'

A black servant interrupted them to say a white messenger was approaching. Alfred herded the two friends out a side entrance, with a haste Nell found indecent.

*****

FLEET HEARD of Levi's take-over during a visit to the Point Warren. The news was important enough for him to set off immediately for the North Bank to inform Thatch. The seer wanted to avoid Toria and the Golden Field. Once over the Torrent, he found that the worst devastation from the storm had been confined to the South Bank.

He was shown into Thatch's chamber, where the scent of the prime rabbit overpowered the assortment of acorns, hazelnuts, chestnuts, juniper berries and various herbs arranged in piles beside her. As always, Thatch wasted no time on small talk.

'You've seen this Levi. What's he like?'

'Tough. Uncomplicated.'

'Are you saying he's a bird-brain, Fleet?'

'Not really. It's more his view of the world that's simple. Sees everything in black and white. In more ways than one.'

'It's not like you to speak in riddles. What are you suggesting?'

'Levi is a white supremacist, a rather extreme case.'

'You've talked to him?'

'Not yet. I saw a peculiar ritual the other night, though. Levi was there, and his father and several other bucks. All white.'

'His father's Vort, correct?'

'Yes.'

'He's been over here a few times,' said Thatch, nosing a dandelion leaf. 'Sensible buck. One of us, don't you think?'

Fleet wasn't sure how to answer.

'What of this ritual you saw?'

'The ritual, yes. It was a sort of secret brotherhood. They all sat around this stump and talked about the stars.'

Fleet realised he was babbling. He couldn't help it.

'And a blood offspring who fought and fought and refused to…'

Thatch stopped him.

'And you took it from this that the new head rabbit is a supremacist?'

Fleet looked at Thatch, who began chewing the dandelion. How foolish he must have sounded.

'Er… yes. From the way they talked. Words like *hordes of darkness. The rindle flowing red with the blood of the enemy.* I did get that impression, yes.'

Thatch chose a juniper berry and bit into the soft centre. Juice spilled over her chin, and a balsamic odour wafted into the air.

'I guess we've all got our little secrets, eh Fleet?' she said, then changed the subject.

'What of the juniper harvest? The hazels and chestnuts? This change at Toria won't affect our trade, will it?'

'I can't see why it would.'

'Good news. Good news,' said Thatch, motioning for one of her assistants to show Fleet out.

'Thank you for coming over. Keep your ears and nose open, there's a good seer.'

28. To the brink

OLLIE'S FEARS about what might happen now that Levi and Vort were in charge were soon realised. She got an idea of Vort's intentions when she met a doe who had finished her shift at Toria working in the burrow of a white sage. The doe had spent the previous few nights extending her master's meeting chamber, and overheard him arguing with another sage.

'*Parting* is what Vort's calling his master plan,' the doe said. 'He wants to keep black and white apart. Separation, according to Vort, is in all rabbits' interests. Clear boundaries make happy neighbours, he says. There's talk of rules about where black rabbits will be allowed to drop pellets.'

'You must be joking,' said Ollie.

'Wish I was.'

The news explained a rush of other rules imposed since Levi's take-over. Black rabbits were banned from more areas. Movement through the gully to the east of Lexa was restricted. Blacks could now only pass through if the daystar was in the sky, when they were at the mercy of carns. It was the moon when adolescent foxes left home to mark out their own territories. Rabbits weakened through poor eating and sickness were also taken by buzzards that in normal circumstances would have difficulty handling healthy full-grown rabbits.

Ollie knew the restrictions had little to do with food. The whites had more nuts, berries, dead nettles, and stores of dried thistles than they could possibly swallow, and seasonal delicacies like the sweet wood blewit mushrooms growing in the hazel copse.

In the moons before Levi's take-over, black and white rabbits often chatted to each other when their paths crossed. White kittens played with the kittens of their black servant does. Not anymore. Under the Parting, almost all forms of contact were banned, unless it was a white telling a black what to do. Black does could still nanny white kittens, or work in the white burrows, but the subjects they could talk about were severely limited.

Ollie had heard of rabbits living in holes too close to white burrows being kicked out, and the does ordered to cover up the entrances. Ousted rabbits had few places to go. No new black burrows could be dug, nor existing ones expanded. More clip squads were formed to ensure the new rules were obeyed. So stronger blacks chased weaker ones out of their holes, forcing black against black.

Rabbits driven from burrows they'd lived in for moons crowded in with others, and the weakest had to live above, where they were preyed on relentlessly. Otters attacked rabbits grazing too close to the Torrent. Ollie heard of one doe who was snatched by a pike, which was unheard of. Weakened rabbits were also caught by stoats, and barn owls which at that moon hunted during the day. Kestrels also became a nuisance. At night, frail rabbits were taken by badgers stalking from the Chilling Wood. Some black rabbits became so hungry they were easily persuaded to become spies for the clips in exchange for special treatment.

The doe's description of the Parting also explained what had happened to the crossers – rabbits of mixed colour. In past moons, they'd lived mostly amongst blacks. Now they'd been chased out to live in the Row Warren away to the south-east. Any rabbit the clips suspected had mixed parents was sent there. Blacks living at the Row were hunted out. Bucks and does who had been loyal mates for countless moons were split up because of the shade of their fur. First-moon kittens were dragged from the teats of their mothers.

'My master has the ear of Vort,' said the doe, 'and is a high-up in the Erfeti'.

Ollie had heard of the strange brotherhood of the Mistles, but dismissed it as a fringe pack of in-bred extremists.

'Surely rabbits belonging to this Erfeti rabble will be outnumbered and over-ruled by whites with at least some common sense.'

'Wish you were right, Ollie, but that's not what I'm seeing. New recruits to the Erfeti come to see my master for *lessons*. We used to get one, maybe two recruits a moon. The reason I'm making the meeting chamber bigger is because my master's now getting two or three a *day*. Including rabbits from the North Bank who have crossed the Torrent to live in what sounds to them like a white paradise.'

Ollie felt sorry for the doe – an intelligent rabbit who wasted her days cleaning and digging burrows for whites because her fur was a different colour. The doe sniffed, then continued.

'Levi, on Vort's say-so, has promoted Erfeti bucks into all the important positions on the South Bank. They've taken over the running of work gangs, trade storage burrows, clip squads, the prime's personal guard.'

'Prime?'

'Haven't you heard? Levi's declared himself prime rabbit of the South Bank. Sees himself as Thatch's equal.'

'Now I've heard everything,' said Ollie.

The doe was yawning.

'I've got to go below, get some rest. I start work again at dayspring.'

'Oh course. One final question. You said your master and another buck were arguing. What about?'

'A new rule for sages. Most of the ones working for the previous head were honourable rabbits who took their roles seriously, passing on the lessons of their experiences honestly and without favouritism. They've been told to stop teaching anything other than the Erfeti version of history and the virtues of the Parting. Some refused, and have been replaced by bucks with little between their ears and even narrower minds. Vort wants to send white sages into black warrens. There simply aren't enough to go around. In the meantime, it's now against the rules for an adult black rabbit to talk to a kitten about history, including his or her own kins.'

Ollie was thinking of the *lessons* she and Nell got from Aunt Mina and Old Chief at Hilltop, as the doe went on.

'The buck my master was arguing with – one of the most knowledgeable sages on the South Bank – objected to this, and was dismissed instantly.'

*****

EASTERLIES COMMON early in the owl moon had been buffeting the Golden Field for days. During the previous night, the wind swung fiercely to the north, dragging ice-laden air from some distant, unseen body of water. The result was a layer of chilling fog so thick, it shrouded the Upland for most of the day.

Levi slept through the worst of it, but wisps remained as he and his personal guards went above just before dayfall. The formidable bucks loped along the trail to the blackthorn, then descended into the dale. Levi's good ear pricked up when he heard a black buck talking to kittens.

'Bring that varlet to the brink,' he grunted.

Levi had discovered the ledge the day after the take-over. As Vort immersed himself in meeting after boring meeting, Levi explored the vast web of passages. *All mine*, he thought as he scampered like a hyperactive kitten through chambers and halls and storage burrows. Like a kitten, he'd became disoriented, then lost, until he noticed a faint light.

It was coming from a chamber that hadn't been used by rabbits for some time, judging from the stench of bird droppings. The daystar had been shining through a small hole two-thirds up one wall. Intrigued, Levi scraped at the floor until he'd built up a pile of soil to stand on. He found that the hole opened on the other side near the top of the cliff overlooking the flats. He told no-one other than his guards of the discovery, and got a servant to enlarge the hole and widen the ledge – which he called the brink – until he was satisfied.

Levi sat there now, gazing out over Lexa under the first quarter moon, listening to the cries of protest from the varlet as it was pushed along passages to the chamber. Since the take-over, Levi had been kept so busy carrying out the instructions of his father, he scarcely had time to think about individual varlets. Tonight, Vort was away.

It was time for a little sport.

The buck, a cocky varlet with tufts of fur hanging ridiculously from its chin, stumbled through the entrance.

'What on Earth is going on here?' demanded the varlet, who the guard identified as Stephen.

'Do you know who I am? asked Levi.

'Vort's paw-licker.'

'You insolent varlet,' Levi hissed, then winked his nose at one of the guards. Stephen didn't see the kick coming. The powerful hind-leg struck it in the chest, lifting it off the ground and into the wall.

The guard moved in to finish it off. Levi held up his paw.

'Bring it over here.'

The buck roared as the guard bit into its ear and dragged it across the ground.

'Have you heard of the varlet, Nell?' demanded Levi.

The varlet stared dumbly ahead.

'The prime rabbit asked you a question,' the guard yelled, before sending the varlet crashing again into the wall. It was almost unconscious as it was dragged back by the ear.

'Well?' asked Levi.

The varlet nodded, keeping its eyes shut.

'That's more like it,' said Levi, doing his best to sound friendly.

'Here's what you're going to do. When you're feeling better, you're going to hop along to the eclipo post and tell them you saw this Nell mounting a white doe.'

'Never,' spat Stephen.

The guard raised his leg to strike. Levi had a better idea.

'I think our varlet friend here needs another sort of persuasion. I'm in no hurry. It can stay here until it sees sense. Make it stand on its hind legs. If its front paws touch the ground, send it to the field of silence.'

*****

THE WONDERFULLY LIGHT BALM of winter heliotrope delighted Maisy so much, she gave a skip. She found a delicate bunch of pale lilac spikes flowering in a fold in the bank of the rindle, and was about to push her nose against the leaves when she was buzzed by a large fly. It was not unusual to see bees around heliotrope during the sleeping and owl moons when butterflies were hibernating. Not flies. She slanted her nose to the wind and picked up the smell of dread.

Beyond the heliotropes were the rotting remains of four kittens. From what was left of the fur, she saw they all had white bodies and black paws. Maisy had heard gossip at the Platform about new rules forbidding mating between rabbits with different coloured fur. It was said a high-up white buck had been caught mounting his nanny. The black doe was torn to pieces and the white buck given a good talking to.

There were also rumours of mixed-colour kittens being abandoned by terrified mothers, but Maisy had dismissed the talk as nonsense. Mating between white and black rabbits, though not common, had been going on for moons, particularly in frontier warrens. Here, sadly, was proof.

*****

OLLIE WASN'T SURPRISED to hear rabbits describe the winter as the worst ever. It was as if the hailstones that descended on the day of the take-over had been sent to punish the earth. The balls of destruction had long melted, but a suffocating gloom still crowded the flats. The moon and the daystar were too frightened to show their faces. Some feared they'd gone for good.

Old rabbits fell first into the field of silence. It was freezing for nights and days, though Ollie blamed the gloom. They'd simply lost their will to live. Young rabbits were the next to go, passing in their dreams if they were fortunate, or snatched by buzzards or owls as they bunched for shelter in the lee of rocks or prowled the desolate flats for anything worth eating.

The appalling weather coincided with Vort and Levi's crackdown, and the twin evils squashed the spirit of even strong rabbits. For Ollie, the hunger for resistance was lost in the daily struggle to find food, to keep warm, stay alive. It was also a testing time for the friendship. Ollie could see that although Nell was losing weight and condition, he never lost focus. He became more determined. He could be so stubborn.

If anything was needed to sharpen the focus of Ollie, it was news of what happened to Stephen.

*****

NELL HEARD IT from a black doe who had been widening passages in the upper levels of the prime rabbit's burrow. Stephen lasted four agonising days. Not a morsel nor drop passed his lips, nor a single word of betrayal. When his front paws finally touched the ground, sending him to the field of silence was unnecessary. Levi told the guards to toss the body off the cliff and leave it where it would be seen from the flats. As an example.

*****

OLLIE WAS NUMB. She nosed at the spot where Stephen normally sat during their gatherings. His scent was still there. Until now, Ollie assumed that she, Nell and Stephen possessed some kitten-like immortality. Life was somehow a game. Like the one Nell and she played the day they pretended to be black heroes. She had been living in a field of stories.

The empty feeling sunk into sadness. Sadness for Stephen, who had been so full of life. Had so much to offer. Ollie closed her eyes and mouthed Stephen's words. *My fur is black, and it is beautiful. Like the earth beneath my paws and the night over my head.* She didn't agree with all Stephen said, but admired him for his intelligence, his passion, his heart.

Nell took charge.

'That settles it. We form our group. With or without Alfred's support.'

Taking courage from her friend's decisiveness, Ollie offered to go with him for one last attempt to persuade the Cluster leader.

'Sorry for being so glum lately,' she said when they got above. 'I haven't been myself.'

'Forget it, Ollie. It's been hard for all of us. I've never doubted your support. It's not about you and me, though. It's about *them.*'

She followed his gaze to a pair of skin-and-bone rabbits nosing among the bulrushes. Ollie looked up at the full moon and a tiny blue-white star crouching beside it like a speck refusing to be over-awed by a colossus.

'Surely Alfred will think differently now,' she said, 'after what happened to Stephen'.

*****

BY THE TIME they reached Alfred's burrow, Nell's thoughts about what happened to Stephen had festered into exasperation. Being asked to wait to see the Cluster leader didn't help. When they finally got below, Alfred said he was disappointed about the restrictions imposed by the new prime, but powerless to stop them.

'How many more black rabbits have to pass before the Cluster will do something?'

Alfred yawned.

'The cause of Stephen's passing is… unclear. There were no marks on his body. Perhaps he got a disease. Or passed from hunger. A lot have succumbed this winter, black rabbits and white.'

Nell couldn't believe what he was hearing.

'Stephen was strong, healthier than all of us, and was seen being forced into Levi's burrow. I've spoken to a doe who heard clips boasting that Stephen was made to stand on his hind legs until he passed.'

'Even if what you say is true, we are powerless to…'

'I'll tell you exactly what needs to happen, Alfred. Domination by white rabbits must end. The unnatural bans on grazing and burrow-digging must end. All rules based on the colour of a rabbit's fur must go, including the ones that mean only blacks can dig or clean burrows or take care of kittens, and only whites get to be clips, work supervisors, carriers, use the safest bolt holes. And black sages must be able to teach black kittens...'

Alfred snorted.

'And tell me, how are you and your little friend going to achieve all this?'

Nell had heard enough.

'The time has come for serious action, involving as many rabbits as possible, like Dingha's non-violent protests. All of us, you and the other Cluster high-ups included, must stand up to these unfair rules, and, if necessary, face the consequences...'

Nell was about to add *as my father did*, when Alfred interrupted.

'Some of my friends told me you were a sensible rabbit. Nell, they said, he's one to watch. Leader in moons to rise, they reckoned. What you are suggesting is not only absurd. It's dangerous. Reckless. It would give the new prime rabbit the excuse to crush the Cluster.'

The stern face softened.

'The type of protest you talk of, Nell, may happen on the South Bank in moons to rise. Right now, we have a new prime we haven't had time to get to know, to soften. Such action would be fatal. As your friend found out.'

The mention of Stephen shook Nell. Was Alfred right? Was he being too hasty? The answer became clear when a black servant asked Alfred where she should put the juniper berries that had been delivered. The Cluster leader and the whites had such a cosy relationship, there was no way Alfred was going to support anything that would jeopardise his privileged position.

'We didn't come here to argue,' said Nell. 'We hoped what happened to Stephen would stir the Cluster into doing more than having frank and meaningful discussions with murdering supremacists like Levi and Vort. Some of us are going to do what must be done. Either support us, or we'll move against you.'

Alfred sneered.

'How dare you come here with your crude, juvenile threats, disrespect for your high-ups. Get out. Leave.'

29. An unfortunate passing

LEVI AND VORT were stretched out on the floor of the large chamber for meeting guests, enjoying some particularly tasty acorns from the Oakwood. They ate noisily, chewing the kernels and spitting out the husks, to be cleaned up later by black servants.

Vort had been over the Torrent for the last few days, so this was the first opportunity Levi had to tell him about the varlet Stephen's passing. He expected his father to be impressed, so was annoyed when a guard announced a visitor from the North Bank.

'Whoever it is, tell him we're busy. I'll see him if and when I decide.'

The guard glanced uncertainly at Vort, who stopped chewing.

'Who is the visitor?'

'The seer, Fleet.'

'I wouldn't leave *that* rabbit waiting too long if I were you,' said Vort.

Levi was furious. The praise he'd been seeking from his father, was sure he was about to get because of the way he dealt with the varlet troublemaker, was seeping away like mist on the downs.

'You are *not* me, father. I am the prime and I'll keep him waiting as long as *I* want.'

Vort looked back sternly. He was the only rabbit who didn't cower for Levi. The varlet Nell didn't count.

'Why do you keep cosying up to these daisy-heads from the North, father? We've got what we want. We don't need them.'

Vort scratched his ear.

'Enjoying those acorns, are you?'

'What's that got…?'

'Trade is a two-way arrangement, Levi. We give the North junipers and hazels; the Oakwood gives us acorns. You don't want enemies in the North. Fleet, whether you like him or not, has the ear of Thatch. I'd show him some respect if I was fond of acorns.'

The flowery, overweight, varlet-loving seer was shown in, and after introductions and customary sharing of food, got to the point of his visit.

'The warrens of the North Bank are watching developments in the South. Some close to Thatch are disturbed by what they've heard about the passing of a rabbit of colour called Stephen.'

Levi was incensed.

'The varlet broke the rules and…'

'Its passing was most unfortunate,' interrupted Vort. 'The buck, spirited from what I've heard, was having a discussion about the new rules, when it got excited and jumped out the hole. I'm sure it had no idea it was so high up the cliff. Eclipo officers tried to revive it, but the fall was too great, I'm afraid. Most unfortunate.'

Levi couldn't understand why his father was using the same puffy language as the seer, why he was so keen to impress the northerner.

'As I was saying,' continued Fleet, 'Thatch has asked me to keep an eye on developments this side of the Torrent. And report what I see.'

Levi chinned, then sized up the seer's neck. Vort hobbled between them.

'And tell me, Fleet. Did you *see* this Stephen pass into the field of silence?'

'No.'

'I'm sure you're far too experienced a seer to report what you don't see.'

'I've got ears.'

'Indeed, you have. And you've just been told what happened.'

The daisy-head opened his mouth to speak. Nothing came out.

'So good of you to come and see us, Fleet,' said Vort, guiding him out of the chamber. 'It is important Thatch is kept informed about what's *actually* happening over here. I'm sure she doesn't base decisions on wild rumours.'

As soon as the seer had gone, Levi spun to face his father.

'I could have sent him to the field of silence there and then. And any other rabbit that stands in my way.'

'Don't be such a fool. Have you heard nothing I've been saying? Look at Fleet and imagine you're looking at Thatch. Sending Fleet to the field of silence would be as good as asking Thatch to invade the South Bank.'

'Let them come. I'll toss them all...'

'There will be no more of that,' shouted Vort with a sudden authority that rattled Levi. 'If the North decided to invade, they would have more than enough rabbits to overrun us. I doubt they will, certainly not with Thatch ruling the Oakwood. I believe Fleet was speaking for himself more than Thatch when he talked about what you did to that varlet. He said *some* rabbits were disturbed, not the prime herself. Nevertheless, we would be foolish to provoke the North.'

Levi bit into another acorn.

'Trust me son, sending varlets like this Stephen to the field of silence might be fun, but it could also turn them into heroes. That could help unite the rest of the varlets, and I don't need to remind you there are far more of them than us. If they all end up in the field of silence, who's going to do your dirty work? How will you attract the stronger varlet bucks from the country warrens to harvest the junipers and nuts we trade for those acorns?'

Levi remembered the defiance on Stephen's face, the insulting way it described him as Vort's *paw-licker*.

'We can't let them break the rules father, laugh in our faces. They need to be punished.'

'I agree. There is, though, another way. Keep the troublemakers in secure holes. Have guards to ensure they don't escape. Give them just enough food to stay alive. Keep them there for days, moons, depending how irritating they are — as long it takes to learn their lesson. They do it on the North Bank to particularly difficult rabbits. Only ever one or two at a time, and not for long. I can't think why it wouldn't work with larger numbers, if necessary. They're only varlets, after all.'

Vort spat out a husk, and passed wind.

'The worst varlets, Levi, the ones stirring up the trouble, could stay in the keep forever. That's what these holes are called in the North. Keeps. No rabbit likes being cooped up for long. It could be worse than passing, which they'd be pleading for eventually. The North couldn't accuse us of sending them to the field of silence. And we'd say we got the idea from them. All we need do is find the right place to dig enough of these holes for the number of varlets likely to need them.'

Although Levi wasn't convinced, he knew the ideal place.

*****

IT DIDN'T TAKE LONG for the news to reach Nell, from one of the black does ordered to dig the holes behind the top of the cliff. She became so ill from overwork, she was chased away. Nell asked if she'd be prepared to describe what she'd seen to a gathering of the high-ups of the Cluster, which he'd heard was taking place before dayspring.

As Nell approached Alfred's burrow, with Ollie and the doe, he smelt the presence of several rabbits. A black guard was squatting outside the hole.

'They're waiting for you,' he said.

'You mean they're waiting for the doe?'

'No. They're waiting for *you*, Nell. They want to hear from her, but Alfred says the gathering will not start until you arrive.'

As they went below, Nell felt all the ears and noses on him, sizing him up.

All except Alfred, who was sniffing the ground.

The gathering was waiting for Nell to speak, so he introduced the doe, and squatted beside her to give her confidence.

She explained how the keep holes were dug underneath the prime rabbit's brink, high on the cliff.

Each doe was responsible for a number of holes, arranged in the shape of a badger's paw print with five small cavities leading off a slightly larger exercise area. The clusters of holes, to be called pads, were linked by a single passage extending from a central guard post.

'How many of these pit-holes are being dug?' asked one of the high-ups.

'I was one of twelve does.'

'That could mean sixty rabbits at a time. This is outrageous.'

Alfred held up his paw. His eyes darted anxiously to the entrance.

'These measures are indeed outrageous. Forcing rabbits to stay below for days and nights on end, cut off from their families and friends, in a space less than a quarter the size of this burrow, defies belief. But I'm afraid this new keep's not the only bad news.'

He looked up again, as if expecting unwelcome visitors.

'I have learned of a new rule. Gatherings like this – of more than four black rabbits – are now forbidden, unless they are work gangs supervised by clips.'

There were whispers of *how dare they?* and *they've gone too far this time*, though Nell noticed they were uttered softly enough to remain below.

'Nell here is right,' said Alfred. 'Our past-moon ways of dealing with the whites have got us nowhere. Drastic measures are needed. Fresh ideas. Bold action. New leadership. I am therefore hopping down as leader of the Cluster, and name Nell my successor.'

*****

THE RABBIT least surprised by Nell's rise to the leadership of the Cluster was Ollie. Bucks were said to be at their physical peak sometime around their twenty-fourth moon. At twenty-two, Nell was fully developed. Ollie realised, however, more than physical presence would be required to take on the whites who, though less numerous, rabbit-for-rabbit were far stronger. To have any chance of success, the blacks had to be led by a rabbit who used the brain and heart rather than claws and teeth.

Nor was Ollie surprised how quickly her friend took control. It was as if he knew he would one day run the Cluster and had been planning for moons. Nell's first act was to convert the home of Alfred into a headquarters and safe burrow for rabbits on the run from clips.

Alfred was persuaded to retire to his birth warren. His confused scent was still strong as Nell and Ollie hopped through the passages, suggesting uses for various chambers. Nell took one of the smallest holes for himself. The spacious chamber Alfred had slept in was to be used for meetings, and other spaces Alfred used for his servants were left free for rabbits on the run.

'How about keeping a pile of soil nearby in case we need to seal off that entrance in a hurry?' Ollie suggested.

'Good thinking.'

'And we could ask the rabbits in one of the adjoining burrows if we could extend the back passage to within a few whiskers of their hole, to give us an emergency exit.'

'Excellent idea. Let me talk to them.'

Ollie offered to find off-duty does willing to risk making the alterations.

If she was impressed with Nell's sense of urgency, she was astonished by his energy. As the new leader of the Cluster, he spent the following nights roaming the fields, spreading news of the keep and his plan for challenging the new rules. He called it the Resistance.

It had been Ollie's idea to have a mass gathering on the eve of the protest. She'd heard that although plans for the size of the keep were vast and new pads were being added, there would be space for no more than eighty rabbits. Ollie convinced Nell that if a gathering enticed more than a hundred, they couldn't all be put away. And if they were, it would cause massive disruption to work shifts. Nell wanted the first action of his leadership to be bold, so decided the gathering should be above ground. He was prepared to go to the keep, but insisted that Ollie stay out of sight, so if he was taken away, she could keep the Resistance going.

The crowd grew steadily through the early part of the evening, and was an impressive size when Nell was due to arrive. From her position, Ollie listened through her good ear to snatches of conversation, from outrage about the keep and questions about the new leader of the Cluster, to the usual discussions about where to find food.

The rabbits went quiet as clips moved into position on both sides of the gathering. There was no hiding, with the fattening moon only one night from full.

Hundreds of paws shuffled uneasily. The air grew thick.

Murmurs sprouted among rabbits nearest the trees, growing to a hum and prodding eyes up to the ridge. Fleet had arrived to observe. Ollie was intrigued at the affect the North Bank seer's presence had on the clips. They began talking and joking among themselves, appearing less threatening, and the hum of the crowd returned, though weaker. Nell appeared, looking uncertain, until he also noticed Fleet. He relaxed, and climbed confidently onto the mound.

'Friends. Thank you for coming here tonight. I'd also like to welcome the officers from the eclipo. What we are here to discuss concerns all rabbits of the South Bank. Black, white and shades between. To those of you who do not know me, I am Nell, son of Henry, grandson of Old Nell. It is my honour to stand with you as the new leader of the Cluster.

'Most of you have heard of the Cluster, how it has tried for moons to get a fair deal for the black rabbits of the South. How despite those efforts, our noses have been pushed further and further into the soil of this land. Our land.

'First, they told us where we had to live. We complained, then did as we were ordered. We were told where and what we could eat, which bolt holes we could use. Again, we complained. Same result. Even that wasn't enough for some of the whites, including the buck now calling himself the prime rabbit and his father who is prime in all but name.'

Ollie noticed that the clips had resumed their menacing stances.

'Our pitiful grazing areas have been reduced further, as have the places we can live, what we can say, who we can say it to, which version of history our kittens will be taught. If all that were not enough, we now learn those those of us who complain will be tossed into a keep being created up there.'

A few brave rabbits glanced up to where his nose was pointing. Most kept their heads down, afraid to be recognised.

'We don't ask for much,' Nell said. 'All most of us here want is simply to live in peace in a field where every rabbit – irrespective of colour – is treated equally. The problem my friends is this: The buck who sits under the rowan and the rabbits around him who stand to benefit most from his unjust rules, have no interest in living alongside us in peace. Whenever we meekly accept a new restriction on our freedom, they stamp us with another. And it will go on and on and on. Until we challenge them.'

The clips Ollie could see moved in closer. Nell appeared unconcerned.

'So, challenge them we will. Selected bucks and does will deliberately resist rules based on colour. I don't want to pretend that volunteering will be easy. I'm sure Levi is eager to try out his new keep, and those of us who resist the rules will get to spend time in its bowels. I urge you, though, to act peacefully at all times. If our peaceful actions are met with violence, we must not retaliate.'

Nell looked up at Fleet.

'Discipline, my friends, is all-important. The eyes and ears of rabbits everywhere will be on us.'

Ollie was relieved when, as the gathering ended and the rabbits dispersed, the clips retreated up to Toria. She wondered how long it would take for Nell to smell the inside of Levi's keep.

30. A mouthful of nonsense

FLEET WAS SURPRISED at the restraint shown by the eclipo. It didn't occur to the seer that it was his presence preventing the officers breaking up the forbidden gathering and taking Nell away. He was also impressed at the way Nell spoke, and felt a twinge of pride at the part he'd played in the buck's rise.

The first nights of the Resistance went without drama. Fleet watched as brave rabbits remained past the gully after the dayfall curfew. They were marched up to the keep to the cheers of their friends and families. The next night, a group including the ancient buck Chief, who'd made a rare trip from Hilltop, brazenly crossed the log bridge to the juniper diamond. There was a standoff, the eclipo officers unsure how to handle the wizened and wild-eyed buck who tottered among the resisters spitting words of encouragement. They were eventually led away.

Fleet noticed Nell observing both incidents. The seer was intrigued how the black buck was organising the protests, even arranging for the eclipo to be told in advance of each act of resistance.

On the fourth night, things changed. Fleet heard from one of Levi's stewards of a protest at the Border Warren. He arrived to find black bucks attacking a pair of eclipo officers. The outnumbered whites fled through the hedgerow to the east. Fleet was told by a passing white doe that a black buck had been caught carrying a forbidden hazelnut, and when the officers questioned it, they were mobbed by the *varlets*.

The seer then met a different white doe, who appeared to be waiting for him. He thought nothing of it at the time, as he was told of another incident near the Point. Eclipo officers had been watching a *mob of varlets* crossing the forbidden line when two bucks, *high as the sky on valerian,* called them names. The officers tried to take them away, and were attacked by the varlets' friends.

Fortunately, eclipo reinforcements were not far away, and order was restored. One of the varlets passed into the field of silence.

Fleet found it odd that both incidents happened about the same time in different fields. He also noticed the similarity in the way the two does described what they'd seen. He was pondering whether to believe them, when he noticed a black buck hopping in a wide arc to avoid them. The white doe beckoned him over.

'Old Pys is from the Point. Ask him what happened.'

Though the buck could see out of only one eye, and one of his ears was badly disfigured, he was surprisingly confident in the presence of the two white rabbits. He confirmed the doe's account of what happened. Fleet asked him if he knew Nell or Ollie, or had seen them. Pys scowled.

'Yes I know them. Scoundrels both. Living the high life while the rabbits they claim to be representing are being dragged away to rot in the prime's new keep.'

*****

IT WAS OBVIOUS to Nell that many of the new rules were intended more to annoy blacks than achieve any real purpose. One of the more bizarre was the rule that no black rabbit could drop pellets within fifty bounds of a white burrow. In most places in the Golden Field this would not have been an issue, for blacks were not allowed on the Upland unless they were working. Even the workers had to drop in marked areas, which were cleaned by black servants. What infuriated the blacks was that the no-pellet zone included fifty bounds from the base of the slope, far away from white burrows.

The protest organised for the fifth night of the Resistance was for black rabbits to go through the gully and drop pellets in the forbidden zone. Nell was tailing the protestors, when he noticed Fleet gesturing to him from the shadow of the briar thicket. The seer was on his way back to the Oakwood. He told Nell about the attacks by black bucks at the Border and Point Warrens.

'Are you sure?'

'I've heard about it from three separate sources.'

'What colour?'

'What do you mean?'

'Were your sources all white rabbits?'

'Two white, one black.'

Nell was disappointed.

'I suppose you're going to report this to Thatch?'

'It's my job to report what happens, Nell. I also need to tell you I've been hearing murmurings from black rabbits about you and Ollie. How the two of you are living in luxury in Alfred's burrow while others are being dragged off to this new keep.'

'You don't believe that, do you?'

'Why shouldn't I?'

'Because you're being fed a mouthful of nonsense.'

'You think so?'

'I know so. That's not the point, though. If black rabbits are tricked into believing fake stories like that, if Ollie and I are seen as out of hop with ordinary rabbits, it could be disastrous.'

They parted, Fleet advising him to be careful. Nell continued through the gully to see the last of the resisters being taken away. He was hungry, so decided to make for the flats.

'Where do you think you're going, varlet?'

Nell was caught unprepared. He almost told the clip that he was simply organising the Resistance, and it was not his turn to protest and be detained until the following night. That would sound ridiculous. The line of resisters had stopped. Eyes and ears were turning in his direction. Given Fleet's warning, this was the wrong time to appear out of hop. He joined the line.

The rabbits were hustled up the slope, then through the middle of the field. It was the first time many had been in the whites-only area. The resisters drew curious stares from white does feeding on long pointed leaves of sorrel, and kittens taunted the *filthy stinking varlets*. The black rabbits didn't care. The mood was light, and they joked among themselves as they were taken to a side entrance to Toria. One buck shouted, '*Hey Levi, show us to your keep, we want to try it out.*'

The first section of the burrow was vast compared to anything Nell had seen. They were soon taken through a new opening and the smell hit them – a mixture of urine and sweat and the aggressive reek of clips. He sniffed around at the other resisters welcoming their comrades like brothers and sisters, boasting about their bravery. Sounds of celebration carried through the walls from other parts of the keep.

During the day, another buck – with one eye and a torn ear – was brought in. Nell recognised him from his first visit to the Point. The poor rabbit was limping and being harassed by the clips. Nell complained and got a swipe to the face for his trouble. The injured buck moaned all day, and Nell sensed the morale of the captives thinning. There was talk about them being left there to pass into the field of silence.

'No-one's going to pass in here,' said Nell. 'There's no room for anyone else. We've only got to wait for another bunch of resisters to be brought in and we'll be released. We need to stick together through this. Can't you see the whites are afraid of what we can achieve if we join together? They didn't expect us to be so organised. They're used to being in control, and for the first time we are.'

Cheers of agreement echoed round the walls.

'Then what's the plan from here?' someone asked.

'We need to keep them guessing,' said Nell. 'I'm sure Vort will dream up more unfair rules, so we'll have to come up with more effective ways of protesting.'

'Like what?'

His reply was drowned by excited shouts: *Crap on their sorrel, refuse to work, eat all the juniper, occupy the white burrows*. When someone suggested sending Levi to the field of silence, Nell decided it was time to calm things down.

'You're right to be excited, friends,' he said. 'Our lives have been controlled by a bunch of white bullies. Freedom, though, is close. Can't you smell it? And when it comes, I'm sure fairness will prevail.'

Several rabbits spoke at once.

'The field of silence is too good for them all, I say.'

'Chase them into the Torrent.'

Nell's head flashed a warning, to caution against such words and thoughts. His heart, though, yearned to share in the raw emotion of the moment.

'You may be right that the time for direct action is near. I too am thinking the past-moon forms of protest, the work stoppage, this Resistance, will not change the rules. The whites are determined to cling to power, whatever it takes. Sooner or later, we must be prepared to meet claw with claw.'

Another round of cheers was cut short by the appearance of one more captive, who was welcomed like a hero. Nell insisted the newcomer take the place of the injured one-eyed buck.

31. Over our silent bodies

THE DAYSTAR filled the sky with a burning anger that blinded Nell as he was released from the keep two days later to make way for more resisters coming in.

He hadn't expected to be released, after what he'd said in the keep. *Walls have ears*, he recalled Stephen warning. Yet Nell's words hadn't sprung from a void. They had roots in something deeper. He could see Vort's rules were leading to even darker places in moons to rise, if that was possible. During his last whiles in the keep, he'd remembered the story of Dingha, and wondered if the little rabbit's passive resistance would have worked if the likes of Levi and Vort were in charge back then. Non-violence might work only against an enemy who believed in the same rules. If peaceful resistance was answered with savage violence, the chance of bringing about change was virtually nil.

Nell had some serious thinking to do. He considered going to see Ollie, but didn't want to put his friend in danger, so after following the other released captives to Lexa, he hopped on alone in the direction of the gully. He was starving.

He got unexpected pleasure from the simple feeling of fresh air on his whiskers and nostrils. He revolved his ears to concentrate on the sounds around him. There was a loud chorus of birds from the rowan tree – a song thrush, dunnock, chaffinch, and a reed bunting.

As he became accustomed to the brightness, he watched a little owl struggling to regurgitate the undigestible part of a meal. The bird was jumping from one foot to the other on a branch. It choked, shook all over, then spat out a ball of bones and feathers.

Early signs of spring lifted his spirits – the unexpected scent of an early oxeye daisy, a pair of long-tailed tits using feathers and moss to build a nest. If he hadn't been watching a mole drag the remains of a passed bird below, he might have noticed the four clips closing on him from behind, downwind.

'Good of you to save us the trip down your varlet stink-hole, Nell,' said the sergeant, gloating.

The clips appeared amused rather than aggressive, so Nell relaxed.

'Always my pleasure to help out members of the eclipo, officer.'

The sergeant chuckled.

'The pleasure's all mine, Nell. The pleasure of telling you that you are the lucky first varlet to be punished with the new rule of Mute. It means you cannot talk to another rabbit, or go further than ten bounds of your hole. Any rabbit caught talking to you will get the same punishment.'

'For how long?'

The sergeant's mood darkened. He swivelled and kicked Nell in the stomach, winding him.

'You will listen, not talk, you insolent varlet, until the prime rabbit decides you've learnt your lesson. And that's not all. Any gatherings the prime considers a threat to the peace of other rabbits are now banned.'

Although Nell's ribs hurt from the kick, and storm clouds were forming as he was led to Lexa, he felt… satisfied. He'd stood up for what he believed in. Could hold his head high, a rabbit who challenged the overwhelming might of the whites – and lived. For now.

*****

FLEET WAS INTRIGUED that when he gave an almost identical report of events in the South to rabbits in poorer areas of the Oakwood, he got a different reaction to that of Thatch. When he suggested that if things got worse in the South, juniper berries might stop being brought across, the blank stares and wandering eyes of rabbits who had never tasted such delicacies showed they couldn't have cared less. What got them excited, however, was the seer's account of Nell, who they saw as a champion of the ordinary rabbit. They asked Fleet so many questions about the young black leader, he wondered if he'd exaggerated Nell's qualities.

In the comfort of his burrow, Fleet considered what all this meant. The poorer rabbits of the Oakwood lived in inferior burrows to Thatch, and the food available to them was nothing like the range enjoyed by the Oakwood prime and her inner circle. They had nothing to lose from a disruption to trade. Thatch and her high-ups, on the other paw, had become so accustomed to juniper and hazel, they didn't want to do anything to upset the South that might threaten the supply.

Fleet was friends with white rabbits who, although careful not to say it too loudly, considered themselves better than rabbits of other colours. The sort of rabbits who said one thing and meant another. They were more concerned about reports of rule-breaking than complaints of supremacy.

*****

THE SNOW MOON softened into the peacock, and signs of spring were everywhere. Even the air seemed charged with a fresh energy. Hawthorn leaves were unfolding on the hedgerows, providing a change in diet for some of the luckier black rabbits in the South. The first willow warblers arrived from their winter migration, and countless white does were celebrating the birth of litters. Black kittens were born too, though in shrinking numbers.

What was growing, reflected Ollie as she grazed opposite the juniper diamond, was interest in the Cluster and the reputation of her friend. Ollie had not expected the Resistance to end the colour rules. At best, she and Nell hoped it would simply show that the Cluster was capable of action as well as talk. It did more than that, and despite restrictions, Ollie was being sought out by eager rabbits roused by the protests. Some gatherings had to be dispersed, because numbers grew so large there was a fear they would be detected.

The Resistance had also thrust Nell into the starlight, which had its good points and bad. Levi had been so busy stamping his authority over Toria, he had not taken a personal part in bullying the blacks, nor shown interest in Nell. Ollie always knew it wouldn't last.

The number of rabbits prepared to resist the colour rules rattled the whites. The keep Levi had ordered burrowed out of the cliff was too small. There were so many rabbits waiting their turn to be put away, the time they had to spend in the keep became almost tolerable. Dreamers expected Levi to admit he was wrong, fill in the keep, perhaps end the colour rules. Not a chance, thought Ollie. Within days, it was announced that more keeps were to be dug throughout the South Bank, beginning directly below the first one.

The area was known to black rabbits as Poshia. Stretching the imagination, it could be said its inhabitants lived on the same hill as the whites. In reality, the holes were just as small, damp and exposed as black holes all over the Bank. What made Poshia different was its *attitude*. It was said that a Poshia rabbit was bigger and braver. The kind of place that appealed to rabbits like Stephen, who had lived there, and a few black rabbits from the North Bank tempted south by Poshia's reputation for bold living. No more. Black rabbits in holes in the base of the cliff were given three days to clear out. Ollie had heard that was how long Vort reckoned it would take servant does to break through from the main keep above.

With excited rabbits volunteering to watch for danger, Ollie and Nell met four bucks from Poshia to discuss how the Cluster should react. It was agreed that black rabbits should gather outside Poshia when the three days were up, and refuse to leave until the removals stopped. Because of Nell's Mute restriction, Ollie was given the role of spreading the message – that Poshia would be wiped out *over our silent bodies*.

As the dayspring deadline neared, rabbits from all over the flats edged to the base of the cliff. A pair of hot-headed bucks yelled *Over our silent bodies, Over our silent bodies*. The cry was taken up by rabbits around them and soon blossomed into a mass chant.

'We have to call it off.'

It was Nell, who had hopped up behind Ollie, panting.

The distinctive mark on his forehead was hidden under a layer of mud. He had to shout to be heard.

'I've been talking to one of Levi's servant does. He's going to use the protest as an excuse for a rampage. The clips, they've been given instructions to *toss the varlets into the field of silence*. We must call it off.'

'They're not going to like it, Nell. Listen to them.'

'I know.'

'There's so many of us. They can't do all of us in.'

'That's not the worst of it, Ollie. The doe saw a squad of clips being shown how to lure foxes here.'

The mention of carns was enough for Ollie. She passed the message on, and was amazed how quickly the chanting stopped.

Alarm stamps sounded. Rabbits hightailed in all directions, thumping into others stuped with fear and the terrifying smell of foxes. The stamping became frenzied, even from the Upland. Hysterical cries rained over the mayhem, as black rabbits charged from the holes of Poshia, chased into the open by white clips gushing from the new passages.

32. A scene of utter madness

FLEET COULD TELL from Donald's eyes that the black seer wasn't convinced. Fleet wasn't sure whether to believe the rumours himself. They were heading to the South Bank along the trail through the Chilling Wood, and reports of the attack at Poshia had overshadowed their conversation.

'I've heard there were six foxes, and each took at least two rabbits. Tawny owls took another three. Add to that the nine apparently sent to the field of silence by eclipo officers, and we could be talking more than twenty.'

'I find it hard to believe, Fleet. What does the prime rabbit say?'

'Haven't had a chance to ask Levi yet. His stewards claim the number is a wild exaggeration, that the rabbits stirring up the trouble were given repeated warnings to disperse, so the blacks have themselves to blame, and it is fantasy to suggest the eclipo attacked the protesters. At least one officer was apparently injured trying to save a black doe from a fox.'

'Pity you weren't there, Fleet. The truth must be somewhere in the middle.'

They crossed the log over the rindle where it narrowed next to the badger sett, then continued along the bank until they reached the tree stump with the strange markings. Fleet was telling Donald about the bizarre ritual he witnessed there seven moons earlier, when they heard a shrill wail from up the rise in the direction of the Point Warren.

ONE OF MAISY'S DAUGHTERS had persuaded her to move to the Point after being caught out in the hailstorm. The discovery of a supply of comfrey – a good plant to ease bruising – confirmed that the decision was right.

Maisy divided her time between foraging for healing plants and looking after the kittens of her daughter. She was particularly fond of one of them, a buck with a streak of pale fur over one eye, similar to his uncle Nell. That wasn't the only similarity. The youngster was adventurous and inquisitive, like Nell at that age. She'd have to watch him closely, so he didn't get into trouble.

She had offered to take the kitten above to enjoy the late afternoon warmth, and was watching him chasing an orange tip butterfly. It was a delightful day, washed with the starchy aroma of the bluebells and the sweet murmur of primroses. The songs of nesting dunnocks and goldfinches hummed from the wood and thickets. As she relaxed, a light breeze tingled the fur on her flanks. It carried the distant aniseed murmurs of hawthorn that forever reminded Maisy of the day they had to leave Henry's burrow at the Willow. The wind strengthened and she detected the arrogant odour of a white buck.

She was on her paws instantly, thinking of her little grandson. He'd disappeared.

*****

THE FRAGRANCE of hawthorn and bluebells and primroses went entirely unnoticed by Levi, as he dozed thankfully upwind of The Point, wallowing in his good fortune, and watched over by guards who would alert him to danger.

Before coming on this visit to inspect the new keep being dug beside Governor Crown's rowan, Vort had reported to Levi on a favourable meeting with Thatch over the Torrent. Vort told the Oakwood prime how appalled he was at the passings during the Poshia *incident*, which had unfortunately become necessary because of growing unrest from a small number of troublesome rabbits. Vort assured Thatch that the blacks had plenty of time to get out of their burrows, and the eclipo officers who encouraged them politely to leave couldn't possibly have known from below that foxes were nearby. Vort had also guaranteed the supply of junipers and hazels, and had been promised a steady supply of acorns in return.

Levi had arrived at the rowan to find the limp-pawed governor, Crown, stuttering with fear and the keep completed. After a good feed, Levi had been dozing happily. His guards ignored the varlet kitten chasing a butterfly. Their only concern was carns. The orange tip landed on a stone not far from the sleeping Levi. The kitten crept closer, using the outstretched body of the white rabbit to conceal its approach. When the insect took to the air, the kitten pounced, misjudging the distance, and landing clumsily on the foreleg of the white rabbit.

Levi leaped up in fright, flinging the kitten into the air. One of the guards laughed. Levi's embarrassment quickened when he saw what caused the disturbance. The kitten was still chasing the butterfly, which was fluttering towards him. He noticed the spot of light fur above its eye, and was about to swat the insolent nipple-sucker when an eclipo officer arrived to report a large mob of varlets gathering at the Point rowan to protest against the new keep.

'Attack,' growled Levi. 'Let's give them a teaching they'll never forget.'

*****

THE WAIL heard by Fleet and Donald was the first of many that afternoon as white rabbits ruthlessly attacked the protesting blacks. Some passed instantly into the field of silence, others as they fled to what they assumed would be the safety of their burrows, only to be chased below and cornered. Dom Bini, alone in his chamber and taking no part in the protest, was felled by a savage kick to his flank.

At the sound of the screams, Fleet and the black seer hightailed for The Point. The scene in front of them was one of utter madness. Eclipo officers, their white faces stained red, were chasing bucks, does, kittens — any rabbit they could catch. They appeared totally out of control. A pair of weasels were tearing at the body of a rabbit that had passed, and further up the hill, the seers were stunned to see a wounded doe, her leg broken, being attacked by a bank vole less than quarter her size.

Fleet stared in disbelief, scanning the chaos, settling on the still figure of Levi, watching calmly from a small hill. A shimmer of black yanked the seer's eyes to a doe zigzagging frantically. It was Maisy. Carrying a kitten. Behind her, gaining fast, was one of the blood-crazed white bucks.

Fleet stuped. Should he intervene? It was like a snail-pace repeat of Henry's fight with Vort. He willed Maisy on, though could see she was tiring and the buck almost on her. Maisy looked up and their eyes met. Fleet's heart pleaded for him to do something. His head, his training as an observer who didn't become involved, pressured him to stay where he was.

33. The biggest thorn of all

NELL COULD SEE where the discussion was leading. He'd listened to the views of the other Cluster bucks about what had gone wrong at the Poshia protest. It was time to bring the gathering to a conclusion.

'Our biggest mistake, friends, was to say that Poshia would be wiped out *over our silent bodies*. Although they were only words, they got too many rabbits excited, making them think they'd give their lives for the struggle. Which wasn't the plan at all. We're not ready to tackle the whites head-on.'

'Then what are we here for?'

The question came from a large buck with patches of exposed skin on his shoulder where clumps of fur had been torn off by a clip.

'A fair question,' said Nell. 'We've tried every peaceful method we can think of to make the white rabbits see sense. We've tried words, threats, stopping work, refusing to collect their hazels and junipers. We've marched peacefully. We've lined up to volunteer to spend time in their keeps. Whatever we've tried has resulted in harsher rules, more violence. Our peaceful path has got us nowhere. Worse than that, we're going backwards.'

Nell scanned the ditch, noticing the ripped ears, the nervous twitching, the brooding faces.

'I fear the time is coming when we need to consider using the white rabbit's methods against them. To fight claw with claw.'

Further discussion was halted abruptly when one of the watchers came to say that a white buck was approaching. The rabbits scattered, and Nell and Ollie dived into the pre-arranged hiding place inside a clump of heavily scented flag iris. Through the broad leaves, Nell watched two rabbits approach. One was a large black buck he'd never seen. He was favouring his left hind leg and having troubling keeping pace with his white companion, who Nell now recognised as Fleet. He hopped out to greet them.

After introductions, the white seer described the massacre at the Point. Nell was immediately concerned for his mother. Fleet, who appeared less confident than usual, reassured him that Maisy was safe, for now.

'Thanks to Donald, here. The eclipo officer was about to overrun your mother when Donald charged out and tackled him. Maisy and the kitten escaped.'

'I can't thank you enough, Donald.'

'I'm honoured to meet the rabbit we've been hearing so much about.'

The seer had the same Oakwood accent as Fleet. It seemed strange coming from the mouth of a black rabbit.

'Now I've seen for myself what you rabbits of the South are up against,' said Donald. 'Must admit I found Fleet's reports hardly believable until today. I'll do what I can to let rabbits in my patch in the North know what's going on, put pressure on the Oakwood high-ups to do something about it.'

'We'd appreciate that Donald.'

'What would help, Nell, is for you to visit the Oakwood, talk to Thatch directly.'

'He's right, Nell,' said Fleet. 'And after what we saw at The Point, you and Ollie are going to be hunted rabbits.'

Nell swallowed hard.

'I appreciate your concern. Don't get me wrong. But this horror at the Point convinces me it's time to meet claw with claw. Levi and Vort have left us no choice. My place is on the South Bank, side by side with my friends.'

'What about Ollie?'

'My place is beside Nell.'

He looked at his little friend, trembling and wide-eyed, her ears flapping like a reed in a whirlwind.

'Thanks for the support, Ollie. Fleet and Donald, though, are right. You understand better than anyone what's going on over here. You could give the Oakwooders a burrow-born account.'

Ollie's mouth opened, but no sound came out.

'There's another good reason,' said Nell. 'I've been wondering what would become of the Cluster if something happened to me, if it became impossible to keep up the struggle on the South Bank. We need a rabbit who could keep things going from the other side of the Torrent. Someone who has the respect of the Cluster, could speak on its behalf.'

Ollie was still lost for words. She stretched her hind legs, one after the other, as she often did when her joints stiffened. Nell asked Fleet if there were willows on the North Bank?'

'Not at the Oakwood, I'm afraid.'

'There are some in my patch past the bend in the Torrent,' said Donald.

That settled it, and Ollie agreed that if she was going north, there was no point delaying. After farewell licks, Nell watched the trio leave, with Ollie and Donald taking up the positions of *servants*, a few bounds behind Fleet.

It was an emotional parting, and Nell retreated to the sanctuary of the flag iris to arrange his thoughts. A snail was rasping on one of the stiff leaves higher up the plant. As he watched, a thrush swooped, and the snail retracted into the safety of its shell before it was snatched. The bird flew to a rock jutting into the Torrent, and smashed the shell to get at the flesh.

Nell shivered. He was going to miss Ollie and her calm advice. And wit. He wondered how long it would be until he saw his friend again.

*****

LEVI WAS ON A HIGH after watching his eclipo give the varlets a thrashing at the Point. He hadn't become prime to brown-nose to anyone, whether it be his father or Thatch.

Vort had been busy telling rabbits throughout the white warrens that the passings were an unfortunate though necessary reaction to stamp out an uprising. Messengers were also sent to the Oakwood to ensure that Thatch received the correct version of events.

Let them play their games, thought Levi. He had no time for it. And as for the responsibility of leadership his father went on and on about, Levi felt responsible to two rabbits only. Himself and the memory of Erfeti. Yes, the Point lesson was deeply satisfying. Now the rebellious varlets knew what they were dealing with. And the feather-head whites on the North Bank. He, Levi, was a prime rabbit to be respected. Feared. He yelled for a servant to bring another acorn.

'Karl is waiting outside to see you, master,' said the doe after dropping the nut at Levi's paws.

'Send him in.'

The smallest and most foxy of Levi's kins was becoming an excellent, and trusted, extra pair of eyes and ears. He slipped into the chamber.

'What do you want?' growled Levi.

'Right. Two things really. This talk about a varlet uprising is frightening some rabbits. The does particularly. Two families left during the night for the Oakwood.'

'No scents I'll miss.'

'Right. Others are asking if you can spare officers from the eclipo to provide protection around their burrows.'

'Protection from what?'

'The uprising, I suppose.'

'That's ridiculous. There is no uprising. And if there were, the eclipo would be needed elsewhere.'

'Right.'

'Is that all? I'm busting for a crap.'

'Right. Remember that scrawny doe, used to hop around with Nell? Ollie, I think its name is.'

'I know the filthy varlet, alright. It was the one that pissed in my father's face.'

'Right. One of our black informers swears this Ollie has got over to the Oakwood.'

One less weasel to deal with, thought Levi.

'What about Nell? What's that varlet up to?'

'Right. According to Pys, it's gone into hiding.'

The only blight on the clean-up at the Point was the escape of that Nell look-alike kitten and the doe, who Levi assumed was the varlet's mother. It was time to deal to the biggest thorn of all. On his way to the surface, Levi passed the burrow of his other kins, the ones he used for special tasks. He kicked them awake.

'Find the varlet, Nell.'

'Can we send it to the field of silence?'

'No. Bring it to me. I want to look into its eyes as it passes.'

*****

AFTER THE HORROR at the Point, the remaining leaders of the Cluster agreed it was too risky for Nell to stay in his burrow, even if it meant breaking the Mute rule. The challenge was that he needed to be invisible to the clips, but highly visible to the black rabbits who saw him as the face of the resistance.

Nell came up with the solution. From now on, he would go from warren to warren, staying in different burrows, constantly changing his appearance and scent, and popping up unexpectedly – out of disguise – to show that the Cluster was still fighting.

'That would be far too dangerous...'

'You won't know what carns live in what fields...'

'Or where the bolt holes are...'

'...where to find food...'

'And you'll be away from all your friends. On your own...'

They were right. But when a rabbit could not live the life he wanted, he had to survive as best he could in the shadows. And becoming a drifter wasn't as hard for Nell as it might be for others. Memories of his days as an errand runner were still fresh, and part of him longed for the freedom of roaming alone.

It would be foolish to move about Lexa under the daystar, so he spent the rest of the day in a safe hole. After dayfall, he rubbed soil over his forehead and went above. He rolled in mud, letting it cake into the coat of a drifter, then set off for the lone spindle tree at the fork where the bourne spilled into the Torrent. Stretching on his hind legs and taking care not to break the surface of the poisonous bark, he snapped off a twig covered in small oval leaves and four-petalled white flowers. He rolled over it, releasing a fetid smell as it bruised.

Nell spent the early part of the night on the flats. Whenever he saw a rabbit who knew him, he tested his disguise. No-one recognised him. He got to the Narrows about midnight, as two bucks were arriving to relieve the clips on duty. Crouched in the shadows, Nell overheard them talking about orders to double the number of guard posts. As they were distracted, Nell crept past them.

Clouds of tangy cow parsley out of reach along the hedgerow lit up the night. He wanted to check on survivors of the attack at the Point Warren, test their mood and appetite for further resistance. And see his mother.

Nell wondered how he'd be greeted. Would they see him as the rabbit responsible for their misery, or thank him for keeping resistance alive?

From Fleet's report, Maisy could have passed into the field of silence in the attack. An attack that almost certainly would not have happened if he had chosen the easy life in the Patri's circle.

Rabbits up the slope from the Point moved away as he approached, not because they recognised him, because they were on edge. Many had fur missing or injured legs.

Nell was unchallenged until he arrived at the entrance to Dom Bini's burrow. The passage was blocked by a lanky buck, a festering wound on his shoulder.

'Since when has Bini needed a guard?'

The buck stared at him through bloodshot eyes.

'Piss off.'

'I'm here to see the dom.'

'Doesn't talk to strangers.'

Nell smelt a doe coming from behind, before she spoke.

'I know that voice. Is that you, Nell?'

It was one of the dom's mates he and Ollie met on their last visit. She turned to the guard.

'This is no way to treat such a distinguished rabbit. Come Nell. I'll take you to the dom.'

The guard was confused, but let them through. In side chambers, Nell saw and heard rabbits groaning from a variety of injuries, the sweat of their gloom almost overpowering the odour of healing plants – plantain roots for the bites, yarrow leaves to stem bleeding, comfrey for damaged bones.

'Is Maisy here?'

The doe stopped outside the dom's chamber.

'She left soon after the attacks. Terrible fright it was for her, Nell. She stayed long enough to advise us on the best treatments, though we could tell she wanted to leave. Brave rabbit, that mother of yours. If only some of our bucks had half her courage.'

'Did she say anything… about me?'

'Now you mention it, yes. Wanted you to know she was returning to the Willow Warren, and not to follow her there because she was likely to be *watched*.'

Nell wondered what that meant. Did Maisy not want to see him? Did she blame him for what happened?

Bini welcomed him warmly enough.

'One or two of my circle didn't expect to see you again, Nell. Doubted you'd have the balls to show your forehead after what happened.'

'What about you, Dom?'

'Never doubted you'd come. You'll always be welcome here.'

'Thanks. But how about you? I heard you were injured.'

'Winded is all. It'll take more than the hind-leg of a white supremacist to knock me off my perch.'

After a snack, Nell cleaned the mud from his face and was taken up to the meeting chamber, where four of Bini's circle who survived the attack were gathered. There were three empty places.

Nell listened to survivors' accounts of what happened, his agitation growing. Two blamed him for the massacre and had no interest in further resistance. The other two insisted on revenge, or the passings would be in vain.

'What are your thoughts, Dom?'

Bini's shoulders were hunched and his coat dull. He shrugged.

'I'm getting too feeble for this nonsense, Nell. What do *you* think we should do?'

'No words from me will bring back your friends and mates. My advice is do nothing to provoke the whites until I check the mood of the other warrens. Until then, stay safe. Be kind to each other. Regain your strength.'

On his way to the surface, Nell stopped to talk to a buck he recognised from an earlier visit. The left side of his face was badly bruised, and a doe was gently rubbing a leaf of wood anemone over the wound. Nell asked him how he felt.

'Better now you're here. I'd heard you'd gone to the field of silence. That would have been the end. Long as you're around, there's hope.'

Nell thanked him.

'My mother always said celandine was good for the eyes. Think you use juice from the stems. You could also try meadowsweet, which should be showing soon.'

'Thanks Nell. You show those bastards.'

Nell asked Bini to wait for a few whiles, then tell the clips he'd visited.

'Say I left in the direction of the Golden Field.'

34. Nothing else matters

MAISY WAS SHAKEN AWAKE by the smell of digested hazelnut and teeth closing around her hind leg, dragging her from the hole.

'Where is it?' a white buck demanded.

She tried to concentrate. Her leg stung. She'd have to find plantain leaves to crush and rub on it. Rabbits were rising from holes to see what the fuss was about. They ducked back down when they saw the white rabbit.

'I'm sorry. Where is *what*?'

'Your varlet son.'

'I haven't seen Nell for moons.'

The buck stuck his head into the hole, then backed out, twitching his nose frantically. He stomped up to Maisy's face, his foul breath reeking of decay. She tried to tell him dandelion leaves were good for toothache, and was knocked to the ground.

'If I find the varlet's been here and you don't tell us it's here, you're passed meat.'

The buck spat on her and left.

*****

IN HER FIRST NIGHTS at the Oakwood, Ollie was introduced by Fleet to rabbits of all shades. A few were interested in what was happening in the South. Fleet had been busy. Four elderly white bucks, including a former prime rabbit of the Oakwood who was missing most of his teeth, and two former doms from warrens to the west and east, were outraged, and vowed to cross the Torrent to *kick up a storm.*

When it was time for Fleet to go to the South, he arranged a comfortable burrow for Ollie not far from the large complex of passages and chambers of the Oakwood prime, Thatch. Fleet had warned Ollie that although interest in the plight of black rabbits on the South Bank was growing, and it was good that the four respected high-ups were crossing the Torrent, it would take longer to convince the current high-ups to do anything about it. Fleet's parting words were to *be patient.*

Ollie was amazed what she could do at the Oakwood, what she could eat, where she could go. Rabbits of all colours were free to graze in any part of the clearing, except a high patch near the lake reserved for Thatch, her family and circle. One of the prime's mates and two of her stewards were black.

The daystar was touching the tops of the oaks behind the lake when Ollie went above. The growing light was washing out two tiny blue stars that had been holding the thinning moon in the sky over the glade like two points of a spider's web. A white doe moved aside to let her pass. Surely Fleet was being too gloomy. The seer was probably right that the old high-ups would achieve little on their visit. But it seemed that Thatch was a highly intelligent rabbit, and when she heard the true story of what was going on, she would surely use her influence to make things right.

Ollie decided then and there to go and see the prime. She got as far as the outer entrance to Thatch's maze of burrows.

'Can I help you?' asked the guard relaxing beside the hole.

'I'd like to see the prime rabbit. If that's alright.'

'Why?'

'To explain to her what's really happening on the South Bank.'

The guard was the size of Levi, though there was nothing threatening in his voice.

'And you are?'

'Ollie. From Lexa. Actually, from Hilltop. And before that the Platform.'

The guard raised an eyebrow, as if these warrens meant as much to him as the moon.

'I come from the South Bank. Me and Nell…'

'Nell?' You know Nell? Should have said so. Down there to the right.'

The passage was wide enough for four rabbits. Strange high-up voices rumbled through walls as smooth as ice, and Ollie realised how unprepared she was to meet the most important rabbit in existence. She entered a chamber to find at least ten other rabbits waiting to see Thatch. As she listened to conversations around her, about buck rivalries, burrowing techniques, plant reports, carn threats, circle gatherings, weather forecasts, her hopes of getting the prime to help out in the South dimmed.

One or two had heard of the attacks at The Point, and said Thatch would be able to help. Ollie was alarmed to hear some bucks describe their prime as a tyrant who would act only if it was in her best interests or suited the Oakwood circle. Others had not heard of problems in the South. Nor did they care. One overweight buck stinking of juniper sneered down his nose at Ollie, disgusted at the *cheek* to think of bothering Thatch with such trivia from over the Torrent, when there were so many pressing problems in the Oakwood. After waiting half the day, one of the prime's assistants entered the chamber and asked for Ollie.

'Over here.'

'I regret to inform you that the prime will not see you because she does not talk to outcasts.'

*****

LEVI WAS IN A SOUR MOOD. It was bad enough that Nell had slithered under the noses of his eclipo. Then Levi had to sit through a meeting with four relics from over the Torrent who had the nerve to tell him how to run the South. The creaky bucks didn't come only to him. They spewed their poisonous message to other white rabbits they met on their way home.

Two more Toria families were crossing the Torrent, afraid the

South was about to be overrun by the varlets.

Karl appeared.

'You wanted to see me?'

'What I want is Nell caught. What else can we do to snare the slimy varlet?'

'How 'bout a new rule that varlet burrows can have only one entrance? That'll stop them moving from one hole to another below. Drive Nell to the surface, where we can see it.'

'Do it.'

Vort appeared unannounced from a side entrance to the prime's private chamber, something Levi was finding annoying. Karl showed more respect for Vort than him. Levi chinned to remind his kin who was in charge.

'And tell the eclipo I want more roving patrols searching for the varlet. All over the South Bank. And more random raids on their burrows. Hit them when they least expect it.'

Karl glanced at Vort, then Levi.

'We'll need more bucks for the eclipo.'

'Get them.'

'Where from? The most suitable bucks are already officers.'

'Can I make a suggestion?'

It was Vort. Levi screwed up his nose.

'If you must.'

'We should recruit and train varlet bucks for the eclipo.'

'Good idea,' said Karl. Too quickly.

'That's insane.'

'Why?'

'They can't be trusted. You were the one who told me that lying and cheating comes as naturally to varlets as night after day. And they stink.'

'That's true. I'm not suggesting we invite them to live here amongst us. Think of this: who understands best what a varlet thinks, where it goes, where it hides? Another varlet. And there's more of them than us. If we choose bucks carefully, train them properly, they could become useful.'

'Why would any stinking varlet want to join the eclipo?'

'Privileges. Give them better burrows. Better food. We've got more than enough. A rabbit with a full stomach doesn't join protests, doesn't refuse to work, or volunteer to spend time in a keep.'

Levi wasn't convinced, though it was worth a try if it meant catching Nell. He puffed himself up to full height.

'Here's my decision. No varlet burrow to have more than one opening. Eclipo patrols to range all over the South Bank, raiding burrows at any and all times of the day and night. Varlets to be trialed in the eclipo. My father here will personally choose them and supervise the training.'

'It shall be done,' said Karl.

'One more thing. Catching Nell is the highest priority. Nothing else matters.'

35. Creature of the shadows

NELL BECAME A CREATURE of the shadows, keeping to his hiding places as the daystar was in the sky, or the moon bright, and moving above in darkness. He spent most of his time near Lexa, only travelling further when necessary. He slept in deserted burrows, in the reeds, in ditches, wherever he could be alone and unnoticed.

He changed his appearance so often that his friends in the Cluster had trouble recognising him. One night, he'd be scruffier than a kitten that spent all day rolling in soil, the next he'd be spotlessly groomed – except for his forehead which he kept coated in charcoal from the remains of a tree struck by lightning. His posture jerked from erect to slouched, his manner from cocky to cringing, his movements from limp to swagger. When he found their droppings, he borrowed hints of moles or squirrels or field voles, otherwise his scent jumped from flag iris to corn mint to garlic mustard to bluebell. Rolling in urine enhanced the disguise of a drifter. He took on the acorn-flavour of a black guard after hiding for three days in the burrow of Joseph, following a narrow escape from a suspicious clip.

Renewing his friendship with Joseph was fruitful in a surprising way. The white rabbit had a distant relative in a warren north of the Oakwood, who had been involved in a successful uprising against a dom. Although the rebellion was over burrowing restrictions rather than unfair colour rules, the relative might have useful advice for the Cluster. Joseph offered to get a message to him.

The more Nell roamed, the more he appreciated the importance of his upbringing. Maisy's insistence on teaching him how to find plants to sustain him or relieve illness, how rain disguised scent, and the experience, awareness, and stamina he soaked up as an errand runner, prepared him well for the life he was now forced to live. It was his memory of a tree, however, that saved his fur when he visited the Patri.

Early in the elder moon, Nell arrived at Hilltop after a roundabout journey that took him to the Point, the strawberry patch in the Common to the east, and via the Row and High Warrens. The first rabbit he saw was the doe who would have been his mate if he'd stayed there. When she realised it was Nell, she was hesitant, unsure if it was safe to be seen with him.

'Is the Patri in his burrow?'

She looked up at the sky. The daystar was midway between the hedgerow and its peak, and the first-quarter moon was rising over the rowan in the field below.

'Sure to be.'

'What about Maisy? Have you heard where she's living now?'

'No. Though I've heard she often visits the place where your father passed.'

Nell wondered if that meant the willows where Henry and Vort fought, or his former burrow at the warren. He thanked the doe and asked her not to tell anyone he was here. He kept away from other rabbits. At the mouth of the Patri's burrow, he licked his paw, wiped the charcoal from his head. The guard gave a bow and let him through.

The Patri was alone, dozing. The two rabbits touched noses. Nell answered all the old buck's questions about the Golden Field, the Point, the creeping ravages of Levi's colour rules.

'It's horrendous,' said the Patri. 'We've been given two moons to block off all entrances except one in every burrow in the entire Hilltop field. Bini has only one moon. How's he coping?'

'I saw him four nights ago,' replied Nell. 'He's not doing too good. Blames himself. Thinks he should have been better prepared for the attack.'

'No-one could have predicted how vicious they would be.'

'*I* should have.'

'Nonsense. Levi and Vort are worse than a skulk of foxes.'

The Patri didn't seem much different to the last time Nell saw him, unlike Bini, who had withered since the attack.

'How are you coping here, Patri?'

'Strangely enough, we're doing better than most. Sure, these stupid new rules are a nuisance. Vort and Levi, though, are now spending their time at Toria, so most things are more relaxed around here.'

They were interrupted by one of the Patri's minders. A clip patrol was approaching.

'Where's the closest bolt hole up above?'

'Not enough time, Nell. They'll get to the entrance ahead of you.'

Nell scanned the chamber, panicking. Loud voices swirled down the main passage.

'Quick,' said the Patri. You'll have to use my private tunnel. Over there, behind that mound.'

On the other side was a cleft invisible from the rest of the chamber. Nell crawled through. It opened into a passage laden with the Patri's scent. He remembered seeing the buck disappear *into* the yew for a sleep after a circle gathering. The passage must stretch between the Patri's burrow and the tree. From the harsh voices of the clips, they had been well-informed. They went straight to the Patri's burrow, and although the old buck managed to stall them by saying the yew was sacred, and powerful spirits would punish rabbits that showed disrespect, it didn't take them long to discover the passage to the tree.

Nell made it to a section where the roots of the yew spiralled in a tangled knot. He picked up the faint sweet aroma of dog rose petals, stirring memories of Aunt Mina. The main passage went all the way to the Patri's meeting chamber, but Nell trailed the smell and found the start of a tunnel behind the knot. He crawled through. Echoes of the sage's scent swirled around him. He peered up and noticed another slit, chewed out of the root. He climbed through and twisted round the gnarly wood to find a tighter tunnel winding up the inside of the trunk.

Nell stuped when he heard clips talking in the passage beneath him. An underling was reporting to the clip sergeant.

'Officers have been sent to block access to the yew chamber, sir, so the varlet will be trapped.'

'Good,' the sergeant replied. 'Let's finish this.'

Nell heard them go in the direction of the meeting chamber. He sat still and waited. A shaft of daystar glinted further up, highlighting a strange object like a fly agaric mushroom that had lost its colour and had unnatural markings around its stem*. There were some dried rose hips tucked into a crevice in the wood. Nell pulled one out and chewed it, then used his front paws to rub the paste over his face and chest to further muddle the air. When the clips returned, the bravado was gone from their voices. They muttered instead, of tree spirits and *magic disappearing powers.*

Once they'd left, Nell twisted further up the spiral. He found a cavity that must have been Aunt Mina's burrow. The daystar was shining through narrow openings in the scaly brown bark. He peeked through. To the east, the view was over the thicket to the field of the Row and High Warrens, and to the west he could see as far as the Border and Low. He thought of the Patri's words moons earlier: *Mina knows more about this tree than anyone… and is in a position to see more.* From high in the yew, Nell watched the bucks of the clip squad meet up and head down the briar chute, dispirited.

He climbed back to the main passage, and out through the meeting chamber to the sacred ground beneath the leafy branches of the ancient tree. Rabbits huddled around him, smiling, congratulating him on his escape. Like the greeting the Patri received when Nell and his mother arrived at Hilltop for the first time. He thought of Maisy, how much he missed her and wanted to see her.

*****

LEVI HAD BEEN FEEDING near the Stump of Erfeti with a promising new recruit – a tough buck named Thaden – when he heard that Nell had eluded the eclipo at Hilltop.

The sergeant who dared blame their failure on varlet spirits had his

---

* The object Nell saw was a champagne cork. To learn how it became wedged inside the yew, and why the owner of the farm left the fields to the animals, see *Joy's Legacy* in the Afterwords (p.xiii).

tongue ripped out, and Thaden was appointed in his place.

In a rage, Levi charged to Hilltop, where he barked at the Patri to assemble all his high-ups and guards. Once the varlets were lined up, Levi demanded to know where Nell was. An annoying quiet engulfed the field. Levi hustled along the row, staring down at each varlet, repeating the question: 'Where. Is. It?'

No one answered. Next in line after the Patri and his circle bucks was a grotesque ancient, one of his front teeth growing outwards.

'Go mount yourself, pellet-brain,' it lisped. Then made a *hoiking* sound and spat at his paws.

Levi was so shocked, he took a hop backwards. He wanted to thrash the monster for its insolence, but was more worried about catching a vile varlet disease. He eye-balled the next buck in line, larger than the rest and with the build of a fighter. One of the Patri's minders, no doubt.

'Where. Is. Nell? Tell me now, or I'll get my buck Thaden here to pummel it out of you.'

Thaden leaned closer, baring this teeth. The varlet wet itself. Thaden clawed the ground.

'Ne… Nell talked about visiting Ma… Maisy, his mo.. mother.'

'Where?' roared Levi.

'The Willow Warren. She's gone back there.'

*****

PRETENDING TO BE SOMEONE other than himself required little change for a black rabbit on the South Bank used to zigzagging between colour rules and common sense, living in the mist between forbidden lines and freedom. But Nell had to think carefully about the simplest tasks, questioning everything, trusting nothing.

Just as there was a way to move through a field or into a burrow so other rabbits noticed him, Nell found there were ways of behaving so he'd be ignored. Keeping his face – and nose – down as he hopped. Changing his voice, speaking faster or slower, letting others talk first or have the last word. He knew his disguise was good when he got within a few bounds of Maisy, and she didn't recognise him. It took a lot of willpower to not skip over and lick her face. Nell was learning not to be hasty. He rotated his ears and sniffed all the likely dangers, worrying more about clips than carns. After assuring himself it was safe, he still held back, to watch his mother, put himself in her paws, to think what she was going through.

It was an emotional reunion and, not surprisingly, after a brief catch-up, Maisy changed the conversation to what Nell was eating and her latest *discoveries*. On the lower slopes of the field, she'd found celandine for the liver, primrose roots for stubborn colds and arthritis, dead nettles for pregnant does, ground ivy for nose problems, and the occasional overlooked valerian roots which were in demand for anxiety and by rabbits having trouble sleeping. Nell started to tell her about rabbits getting high on valerian in the Common, when Maisy appeared to stupe.

'Hightail,' she whispered. 'For the alders.'

Nell reacted instantly, leaping into a ditch, then creeping in a direct line for the trees. As the ground rose again, he looked for cover. Tall clumps of meadowsweet swayed in the breeze. He hurried over and lay down among the stiff red stems, grateful for the sharp almond-like disguise of the grey leaves. He lifted one ear to pick the wind, smiling. His mother had sent him in the direction of the alders because they were downwind. From his hiding place, Nell watched as Levi and two other white bucks went up to Maisy. The prime towered over the tiny doe, nibbling calmly at a leaf. The breeze carried the voices.

'We're looking for your son, the varlet Nell.'

Maisy kept chewing.

'I asked you a question, varlet.'

Maisy stopped chewing.

'No, you didn't. You said you were looking for my son.'

Levi bristled.

'Don't argue with me, varlet. Where is Nell? Have you seen it?'

'My son is a rabbit, not an *it*. And yes, I have seen *him*.'

Nell grinned. His mother could never lie.

'When?'

'Just now. It's a shame you missed him. He went in that direction,' she said, pointing her nose to where he lay.

Nell's heart missed a beat, until Levi spoke.

'I'm not that stupid.'

He ordered his bruisers to fan out in the other directions. When they were gone, Maisy resumed her chewing, raising and flapping her ears in a way Nell understood meant *goodbye and good luck*.

36. Until my last moon

ACCOUNTS OF NELL'S SUCCESS evading capture, particularly his *disappearance* at Hilltop, swept through the warrens of the South Bank, reaching the ears of Fleet.

The news was about the only thing that put smiles on the faces of black rabbits in an otherwise dreary spell – like a slither of moonlight piercing clouds on a stormy night.

Nell was given the nickname *Black Robert,* after the flowers of the herb robert plant that cunningly close on the approach of rain to keep their pollen dry.

From rabbits who trusted the seer, Fleet was hearing stories of the Black Robert appearing unexpectedly among does grazing at the Point, at circle gatherings as far south as the Border and Low Warrens, and east to the burrows of the Row and High.

The seer marvelled at the organisation of the southern blacks. Servants on friendly terms with their white masters were chosen to give false reports about sightings of Nell, sending the eclipo on fruitless and time-wasting searches.

Rabbits too young to concern the eclipo, or bucks too old to be threats, were used to spread the news of what the Black Robert was really up to.

Each victory over the whites, however small, was celebrated by high-ups in the Cluster, though most were convinced it was a question of when – not if – they would all be made to suffer for them.

NELL HAD KEPT AWAY from Lexa. The risk of being chosen for a work gang, detected by a roving clip patrol, or spotted at one of the random checkpoints at the borders was too high. So, when he got a message to attend a Cluster gathering, he knew the matter to be discussed must be serious.

He also realised that, with the second flush of tim grass on the Upland keeping most white rabbits close to Toria, it was probably safe for a black rabbit to venture into the Common. The moon was low and setting, but the sky was ablaze with stars, so he kept to the shadows of the hedgerow all the way to Chest Tree Corner.

A black bolt hole – the only one still allowed in the Common – was positioned a few bounds from the overgrown barrier. From inside the hole, a tunnel ran under the thicket and joined another black bolt in the Narrows. Clips rarely entered black holes, but overweight rabbits known as stoppers were rostered to sit in front of the link holes, in case.

Nell hopped in, murmuring the password to the stopper, who didn't recognise him. He hopped along the joining passage and was annoyed to find no stopper concealing the exit into the Narrows bolt. The reason hit his nostrils as soon as he got above. A checkpoint. Three white clips and one black. Nell had heard that Vort was enticing black bucks by promising extra food and dry burrows.

Confident in his disguise, he stooped and limped to join the end of the queue of miserable rabbits waiting patiently to tell the clips who they were, where they'd come from, where they were going, and why. Nell cringed at the way they cowered for the arrogant whites. When he got to the front, he shut one eye tight and squinted through the other as if he were half-blind.

'Name?'

'David, master,' Nell rasped.

'Home warren?'

'Lexa, master.'

The clip yawned.

'Going to?'

'Home, master. Been visit cousin down the Point, master.'

'Pass.'

Nell dropped his chin to the ground twice in the annoying way black rabbits were expected to show respect to their masters.

'Wait.'

It was the black clip.

'What did you say your name was, varlet?'

Nell couldn't believe a black rabbit would use that word.

'David. Sir.'

The black clip came towards him, his nose brimming with suspicion.

'Stand up varlet. I want to…'

Alarm stamps, two of them, made every rabbit freeze. A long quivering *e-wick* signalled a tawny on the hunt. Although the rabbits were safe enough hidden under the branches of the chestnut tree, all remained still so they wouldn't give the owl another target.

Nell scanned the ground for a clue to the hunter's prey, and saw a weasel pulling at the carcass of a vole. The eyes of all the rabbits around him – black and white – would be fixed on the carn as it descended silently and pounced. The owl scooped up the unsuspecting victim in its talons, and gained height on a course that would take it directly over the tree. The weasel had not passed into the field of silence, and was wriggling furiously. Before the tawny disappeared from sight, the animal arched up and bit the throat of the owl. The tawny squealed and dropped its prey.

Nell reacted first. With the eyes of the clips following the bumping fall of the weasel through the branches, Nell hightailed. As he felt the thud of the weasel hitting the ground, he was nearing full speed, and by the time the clips remembered what they were doing before the distraction, the Black Robert had vanished into the night.

He arrived at the Cluster burrow, via a series of secret connecting passages and tunnels to fool the clips and nosy informers, and smelt the tension immediately. He apologised for taking so long, though soon realised the anxious faces and scents had nothing to do with him being late.

A host of new colour rules had been announced.

Black rabbits were banned from talking to white rabbits from the North Bank, which presumably included seers like Fleet. When a black rabbit went into the field of silence, his or her burrow could no longer be passed on to other members of the family, as was the custom. Clips would decide who would get the burrow, and preference would be given to rabbits who did as they were told. Black and crosser rabbits could no longer have more than one litter in twelve moons. There were no limits on white does, who were encouraged to have as many kittens as they could.

The showy buck listing the new rules waited for the cries of outrage to subside.

'I'm afraid there's more. Movement through the Narrows, which the former head rabbit allowed, is to be banned for all black rabbits from dayspring. The ban on blacks feeding in the Common is to become permanent, and I understand a new checkpoint will be...'

'It's already in place,' said Nell. 'I was stopped on my way here, and have a tawny to thank for distracting the clips.'

'That's unacceptable.'

'Disgraceful.'

'Ominous.'

'We've invited you tonight, Nell,' the buck continued, 'because some of us believe this news requires a rethink about where the Cluster goes from here.'

Nell had been wondering the same thing for days. He recalled the Patri's advice about giving ownership of ideas to others.

'I'd like to hear what the rest of you think?'

The showy buck went first.

'Some rabbits here want the Cluster to give up on being peaceful, Nell. To fight back. I for one disagree. Two wrongs never equal a right.'

'Our peaceful ways have failed us,' said Walter, the buck whose role in the Cluster was to find burrows for blacks kicked out of their homes. 'The whites are getting more brutal, their hearts more cruel.'

'Which is why talk of fighting them is crazy,' said another. 'It would end in disaster. They would send us all into the field silence.'

Walter was shaking his head. 'The attacks of a rabid carn cannot be fended off with paws alone.'

A buck still favouring a hind leg injured during the Point massacre limped to the centre of the burrow.

'I say that ever since Nell took over as leader of the Cluster, we've been outsmarted, crippled and broken by Levi and Vort and all they represent. And, having been led to this place of misery and hopelessness, some of you dare speak of rebellion and fighting, going against what makes black rabbits better than white rabbits. I say we must remain peaceful. Use our heads, not our claws, as Dingha did. If we give up on peace, we will be putting not only our lives at risk, but the lives of all black does and kittens on the South Bank.'

It was an open challenge to Nell's position as leader, and he sensed ears and noses pointing at him.

'In my wanderings over the past moon,' he began, 'I have been inspired by the courage of our brothers and sisters, and their patience. Patience, though, cannot last forever. It will not fill their stomachs, block the blows of the clips, or put an end to the humiliation we feel night after night.'

Henry's words came back to Nell. *The whites get away with what they do because we choose to let them. They take our silence as acceptance.*

'Friends,' he said, 'we are at a stage in our struggle where our choices have become simple. There are only two. Submit or fight.'

From the reaction he got, Nell sensed the Cluster was divided. He stamped to get their attention.

'As I said, I was late getting here tonight because I was stopped at the new checkpoint, and only got away because a hunting tawny distracted the clips. I didn't say what happened to the tawny's prey. A weasel. It was scooped up in the owl's talons and carried off to certain silence. Now, that weasel could have taken the path of submission some here tonight suggest. If it had, it would now be a long grey pellet of fur and bone. Instead, it chose to resist. Fight back. Not seeking to match the tawny for strength. By using its head, attacking when the owl didn't expect it. The result is that the tawny will be the one nursing a wound tonight, and will think twice about pouncing on a weasel again.'

There were more murmurings, and Nell detected a shift in the mood of the gathering.

'Friends, I believe a new moon is rising for us. If Levi and Vort's reaction to our peaceful protests is to attack and maim and make our lives more miserable, the time has come to rethink our… approach.'

The injured buck scowled, rising in a threatening pose.

'That's easy for you to say, Nell. Or should I say, *Black Robert*. Black Skulker more like it. You who are free to traipse the South Bank enjoying the good life, eating what you want, where you want. And whose friend and deputy lives it up in the Oakwood, while we are left here to feel the claws of Levi and his clips, and the confines of their keeps.'

Nell was more concerned with the gripe about Ollie, who couldn't defend herself, than the challenge to his leadership.

'Say what you want about me. How dare you suggest that Ollie has it easy? She had no choice but to uproot from the bank of her birth, from all she knew and cared about. Ollie has been working day after night after day, without the support and guidance of friends like we have around us tonight, to carry the word of our struggle to the warrens over the Torrent. At much loss to her health.'

Nell paused to judge the feeling of the burrow. It was still divided, could go either way.

'Friends, the clips have been hunting me for many nights now. As leader of this Cluster, I will not give myself up to Levi or Vort or any rabbit who rules based on the colour of a rabbit's fur. I can assure you this path I have chosen is more painful and risky than lying for a few days in Levi's keep. I have had to live apart from you, my friends, and the rabbits I love. To grovel as an outcast in my own land – our land, existing paw to mouth as many of our rabbits must do. I shall fight the whites, side by side with you, burrow by burrow, warren by warren, field by field, until we are free.'

Nods were now outnumbering grunts.

'My question is, will you join me? Or will you sit back and watch Levi and Vort succeed in their supremacist drive to crush the rights and dreams of the rabbits we claim to speak for?

'I have made my decision. I will never leave the South Bank. Nor will I give in to injustice and rules based on the colour of fur. I will keep fighting for our freedom until my last moon.'

The words silenced them. Including the injured buck, who was nosing at the ground.

Walter hopped forward.

'The Cluster's with you, Nell. What do you want us to do?'

On Nell's suggestion, it was agreed that the whites would be told that the Cluster remained committed to peaceful protest, and the showy buck had taken over as leader.

What they wouldn't be told was that a break-away group, to be called Claw and led by Nell, would plan how to fight back.

*****

LEVI WANTED to get out on an eclipo patrol, to have some *sport* and remind the varlets who was in charge. But Vort had convinced him to sit in on a meeting with Thatch's trade steward, who was visiting from the Oakwood.

Levi hopped into Vort's meeting chamber, yawning at the South Bank stewards in charge of the juniper diamond, the hazelnuts and chestnuts and the storage burrows.

The northern visitor was a skinny buck with a large brow and patches of thick silver fur hanging over his eyes.

'There you are, Levi. We've been discussing the coming mast.'

'Mast?'

'A bumper crop,' said Vort. 'From time to time, oak trees produce a mountain of acorns, far more than usual. It's about to happen in the Oakwood, first time in more than fifty moons.'

'Good to hear,' said Levi, licking his lips. 'Is that all?'

'It's not as simple as that, son. A mast raises issues. Problems.'

'Like?'

'Allow me to explain, Vort.'

The lanky Oakwooder talked as if he had a nut stuck in his throat.

'In normal seasons, most, if not all of the acorns are eaten or collected for trade, leaving few to sprout. We believe oak trees have masts to flood the ground with more acorns than can possibly be consumed, so some will be left on the ground to grow into new trees.'

Levi yawned.

'Then what's the problem?'

'A bumper crop of acorns means more food for all creatures that eat them. Rabbits, yes. Also squirrels, mice, voles, rats. And *others*.'

'So?'

Vort answered.

'More rabbits, squirrels, mice and the like mean more carns. In the last mast, the Oakwood was crawling with them. Foxes, stoats, weasels, badgers, tawny and barn owls, buzzards. The Torrent was no barrier. We had large numbers of carns invade the South Bank.'

Levi didn't see this as a problem. Sounded like a good way to get rid of more varlets.

Vort asked the southern stewards for their reports on the nut crop. The buck in charge of hazels was expecting a poorer season because of the hailstorm in the peacock moon that destroyed a lot of blossom. He predicted a third fewer nuts during the harvest season in the berry and ivy moons. Chestnuts were more promising.

'The trees weren't so badly damaged by the hail,' reported the steward. 'And we had a cold spring leading into this hot, damp summer, which means we could be in for a good harvest. And early. There are signs the first nuts could fall a whole moon earlier than usual.'

'That's good news,' said the northerner. 'We'll have far more acorns than we can possibly harvest for ourselves or send south. Most will be left to rot on the ground, I'm afraid. We want to get rid of as many as we can, so Thatch has instructed me to offer two acorns for a chestnut or hazel, three for a juniper. Only for this mast season, mind.'

'Which is why,' said Vort, 'we've been discussing a plan to send several of our var… rabbits of colour to the North to help with the acorn harvest. We should also bump up the number of carriers, who will have to be trained. If you agree, of course, prime.'

Levi pretended to take his time considering the suggestion.

'Do it.'

'Excellent. I'm sure you've got more important things to do, so you can leave us to work out the details, if you like.'

Levi couldn't get out fast enough.

37. Brambles, I'm sniffing

SETTING UP and leading Claw was a challenge for a rabbit whose natural instincts were peaceful. The only times Nell had used force – against another rabbit or carn – were when defending himself.

White rabbits had not been welcome in the Cluster, but Nell did not feel restrained by those rules when considering who should join him in Claw. Moons of servitude had left few blacks on the South Bank with the know-how needed to take on the whites. He recalled what Joseph had said about a relative involved in an uprising against a dom, so Nell asked the white rabbit to help.

Joseph agreed, and invited Nell to share his home at Brambleleaf, a community of white burrows between the chestnut and blackthorn trees. The only black rabbits allowed in the vicinity were servants. Nell became Joseph's guard. Above ground, he did the jobs of a servant – watching for carns and other threats as the white does fed, making trips to the storage burrows to collect nuts for Joseph's family, keeping an eye, nose, and ear on the kittens as they played around the blackberry bushes giving Brambleleaf its name.

Joseph's son was particularly inquisitive, although like the other rabbits at Brambleleaf, had no idea of the real identity of the family's newest guard.

During the day, when Nell was off duty, he used a servant's den beside the main entrance to the burrow. A tunnel was eventually dug linking the den to the chamber Joseph used for talking to visitors.

As a white rabbit, Joseph was free to go where he wanted, so was able to visit his relative in the warren beyond the Oakwood to seek advice. He returned to Brambleleaf one night at the end of the web moon, and invited Nell into his meeting chamber.

'The advice I've had is that you have four options for Claw. One, cause chaos by messing up or destroying symbols of Vort and Levi's power. Two, form teams of attackers to carry out hit-and-hightail raids on white burrows. Three, target vulnerable whites and attack them to unsettle and dishearten the enemy. Or four, all-out attack, using your overwhelming numbers to force the whites out.'

Nell thought about the rabbits he'd been living amongst since moving to Brambleleaf. Most were decent animals, whose minds had been poisoned into believing they were superior to blacks. Although white rabbits were better off, ate better and slept in better burrows, they were all rabbits who had the same habits, feared the same carns, shared the same beliefs about the sacredness of the burrow. The only difference was the colour of their fur. Nell had nothing against individual rabbits – white or black. His quarrel was with the system Vort and Levi used to control black rabbits and restrict their freedom.

'Let's forget about all-out attack,' he said. 'It's not possible. Claw has one member – who has never bitten another rabbit in anger – and you're staring at him.'

'Two, comrade, if you count me.'

Nell smiled. 'I welcome your support, Joseph, but let's be realistic. It would take moons upon moons to train enough bucks to tackle the whites in an all-in fight. We can also forget about targeting individual rabbits. Most are not to blame for the Parting and other warped ideas of Vort and Levi. How would you feel if someone decided your mate or your son were suitable *targets*? And attacking individuals, particularly if they're vulnerable, innocent, would outrage every other white rabbit, turning them against us and our cause.'

'Fair point,' said Joseph. 'What about hit-and-hightail?'

'It's a possibility. Though since the Cluster was reluctant to agree to fighting at all, actions that cause the least harm to individual rabbits might be more sensible to begin with.'

'Which leaves… causing chaos.'

'Hopefully without hurting anyone,' said Nell. 'Which will be important for those of us who want rabbits of all colours to live together peacefully in moons to rise. The last thing we want is everlasting hatred between black and white.'

'You're probably right, Nell. And it won't take large numbers of rabbits to cause chaos, if we're smart.'

'What do you suggest?'

'Have you heard the phrase, *the way to a buck's heart is through his stomach?*'

'No, but it sounds like something my mother would say.'

'Let's hit the supremacists where it hurts the most. In their stomachs. If we can find a way to disrupt the storage of acorns, nuts, and juniper berries, we'll frighten the whites of the South Bank who support Levi and Vort, and those in the Oakwood whose support helps them stay in power.'

Nell agreed. And if causing chaos did not bring about the change they wanted, he was prepared to consider Joseph's other – harsher – options.

Warm, moist air common early in the berry moon was ideal for plant growth, and Nell enjoyed the coarse stems, leaves, and seed-heads of forbidden tim grass that Joseph arranged to be taken below for his new guard. He gained weight, his fur thickened and became softer, and he was able to chew without pain for the first time in his life. It was a reminder of what his fellow blacks were missing out on. Teeth of rabbits forced to eat foxtail on the flats and beside the rindle often became so sharp they cut into cheeks and gums, and spikes from foxtail seed-heads found their way into eyes, noses, mouths. Constant blisters and sores were a part of life for rabbits who knew no different.

Nell felt guilty benefiting from food reserved for white rabbits, but realised the changes it was making to his appearance would help his disguise. It also made him more determined to fight the unfair colour rules.

He was thinking about his next moves, as he returned to Joseph's burrow one morning to find a black rabbit he had never seen.

Joseph introduced the newcomer as Merce, a third cousin from a warren on the eastern side of the Oakwood. Merce had a scent unlike anything Nell had experienced, delicate and sweet, and a voice to match. His words slid one into the other like a swift-flowing bourne. He was a good size, and the scars on his shoulder and flanks showed him as a buck who had been in many scraps and survived. He said he'd entered the South Bank through the Chilling Wood, because the usual entry points were now blocked to all black rabbits except nut and juniper carriers.

Nell was uncomfortable discussing their plans in front of a stranger, but Joseph assured him Merce could be trusted. The exotic visitor explained burrow collapsing techniques used in the uprising against the former rulers of his warren. At first Nell was horrified, because it went against a rabbit's natural view that a burrow was sacred. A sanctuary. The one place on Earth a rabbit should feel safe. It was Joseph who convinced him.

'Levi and Vort have violated the sanctity of the burrow by telling black rabbits where they can and cannot dig, the size of the holes, the depth, the number of entrances, who and how many rabbits can live in each. If we choose carefully which burrows to damage, we'll cause chaos to the whites' system without hurting individual rabbits.'

*****

OLLIE WASN'T SURE whether to laugh or cry at the sight in front of her. She'd spent most of the night trying to persuade rabbits to support their southern cousins, but there was only one subject Oakwooders wanted to talk about. The acorn mast.

There had been a whirlwind of activity since early in the berry moon, as the warren prepared for what most expected to be a difficult time. Horror stories about the last mast were on all rabbit's lips, and rumours – of two-headed foxes, stoats the size of badgers and giant owls hunting for sport – grew legs.

New bolt holes were being dug along both sides of the glade, which had been a hot spot for owl attacks during the last mast. What made Ollie wonder if she should be happy or sad was the sight of white and black does burrowing side by side, under the direction of a black buck who was telling them where to dig.

IN HIS DISGUISE as a guard, stooping like a frail rabbit and with his forehead smeared, Nell had become familiar to white rabbits living at Brambleleaf, to clips patrolling the trail to the blackthorn, and guards outside storage burrows he visited to collect nuts for Joseph's family. From the crossway, he was able to sidle up to black rabbits returning from work under the chestnut or hazel trees, and follow them back across the forbidden line onto the flats.

Bees were still humming a while after dayfall – a sure sign rain was coming – as Nell made for the burrow chosen for a trial collapse. None of the rabbits he passed showed any hint of recognising the Black Robert, which suited Nell as he neared the hill. Four black bucks were lingering near the entrance he wanted to use – ruffians from their swagger and rough language. The largest jumped into Nell's path.

'What we got here, boys? Smells like chestnut and… *bramble*.'

Nell crouched down.

'Please, I've had a hard work shift. I'm worn out, so I'd appreciate it if…'

'Work, my backside. Brambles, I'm sniffing.'

'Reckon she's a bloody sap,' jeered one of the other bucks, spitting and moving closer. *Sap* was the name given black rabbits working as informers for Toria. Nell could have ended the hassle by rubbing off the charcoal. Now was not the time.

The swipe to his head knocked him to the ground. A second bully jumped on him, snapping at his neck. He took two more thumps to his flanks before the onslaught stopped suddenly, and the attackers retreated. Nell dragged himself upright, flexing his hind leg. Sore, but nothing broken. He hadn't felt an alarm stamp, so scanned to see why the ruffians had withdrawn. A clip patrol – six bucks in formation like flying geese – was approaching. The ruffians scattered, leaving Nell to face the white rabbits.

'What's going on here?' the sergeant bellowed from several bounds away.

'Nothing master,' said Nell in a high voice. 'Misunderstanding is all. Those bucks confused me for someone else.'

'Typical,' sneered the clip. 'You varlets wouldn't know your dewlap from your pellet-hole.'

They snorted at the stale joke, and left Nell smiling at the irony of being rescued by clips.

Once through the hole, he hurried to where two does were working. One was scraping at the roof, which lay just under the surface where a swale had formed between two knolls. Water often ponded there during heavy rain. The second doe had dug through the floor to the vacant burrow beneath, and was scraping a channel to take water from the swale to the hole. Even below, the rabbits noticed the syrupy zing of the looming rain getting stronger, and soon sensed the first drops hitting the ground above.

'How far are you from the surface?' Nell asked the doe working on the roof.

'Almost there. Shall I punch it through?'

Nell could see that the other doe had finished the channel. He had to shout to be heard over the downpour. She drove her nose into the crack, then ducked away as muddy water poured through. Nell herded the does along the passage and yelled for them to leave. He peered over his shoulder to see the floor collapsing as the water cascaded into the hole.

38. A gush and a scream

THE EXPERIMENT at Lexa taught Nell two things. The technique could work, but the timing would need to be improved to ensure the safety of the burrowers. He was still uneasy about collapsing burrows, and wondered what Maisy would say if she found out what he was planning.

He'd spent the following nights shadowing Joseph, ten hops behind – the distance expected of black servants – as they searched for burrows to collapse.

Nell wanted Claw's first act to send a strong message to Levi and Vort, so they decided on one of the storage chambers at Toria holding the early season's collection of hazelnuts and some of last season's acorns. Walter, who had volunteered to join Nell in Claw, was given the job of persuading does who worked in burrows near the storage chamber to help out.

Late one afternoon, Nell went above with Joseph's son, who wanted to explore the field around Brambleleaf. With one eye, Nell watched the kitten sniffing at honeysuckle flowers growing amongst the brambles. The other eye tracked a heath butterfly flitting around a pile of soil. He watched the insect going in and out of a small cave, and accidently knocked the soil, trapping the insect inside. He looked up to see the young rabbit staring at him.

'Why did you send that butterfly to the field of silence? Its mother will be sad.'

Nell was ashamed. A white kitten had shown more sympathy for another living creature than he had.

*****

MAISY WAS NOSING for food around a small dell, where she often met another widow for a catch-up. The topic being discussed that night was a new rule: black bucks could now be ordered to work in the Golden Field from the age of nine moons. The rule used to be twelve. Maisy thought nine too young, though was more worried about what was – or wasn't yet – between a buck's ears than whether a nine mooner was strong enough.

'They say it's because of the acorn mast,' said her friend.

'But there's no oak trees on the South Bank.'

'No, I guess not.'

The daystar was beginning to suck the life out of the white giant Venus, which had been giving a brief but dazzling display in the sky to the east, so they started edging towards the warren.

'I remember now,' said the other doe. 'They say the white rabbits need more of our bucks to collect hazels and chestnuts, because the bucks who were collecting them are now needed to carry acorns.'

'Doesn't make sense to me,' said Maisy. 'And who are *they*?'

'They?'

'You keep saying *they say*. Who is saying these things?'

'I haven't the faintest idea.'

Maisy winked her nose at her friend, who was gazing off into the distance. Perhaps age had little to do with what was between a rabbit's ears.

*****

THE STORAGE CHAMBER chosen for Claw's first collapse was on the upper level of Toria. Does had worked on undermining the roof for five days. Now all that was needed was a downpour. Although Nell had chosen the target for the biggest impact, the risk of the plot being discovered was far higher than the trial collapse at Lexa, as was the risk of someone being hurt in a place used by more rabbits.

He was wondering if the choice was right as he nibbled at a dandelion leaf in the area for servants near Joseph's burrow. Other whites had got used to seeing him – in disguise – guarding the burrow, and he'd become popular among the kittens who played there. His hosts would have been horrified to learn that the most wanted rabbit on the South Bank was calmly feeding in their midst.

Nell smelt workers being marched behind Brambleleaf on the way to Chest Tree Corner. As he usually did at such times, he faced away from the approaching rabbits, more worried that a black worker would recognise him than a white supervisor. Today was not to be his day.

'You. Come.'

There was never a *Please*, or *Could you help us out?* Just two blunt words, and every black rabbit was expected to jump. Nell, hoping his charcoal disguise would hold, moved towards the line of workers.

'Stop. What's going on here?'

It was Joseph. The supervisor huffed.

'I'm borrowing your varlet for work duty. We're one short.'

'He… has jobs to do. Here.'

'Work duty always takes priority.'

'But…'

'If you've got a problem with the rules, go tell the prime rabbit.'

'It's alright,' said Nell, as he joined the line. 'I'll catch up on my duties when I'm finished. Master.'

'Shame all the varlets aren't as obedient as yours,' said the supervisor. 'On the bright side, you and your family can relax today. The Black Robert's been spotted scattering fleas around a varlet warren far off to the south.'

'That's… comforting,' said Joseph. 'Thank you.'

The work gang had the usual eight bucks, and Nell recognised one of them. A decent, if rather simple rabbit, and strong, which was why he was often chosen for work duties. Nell tried to keep his distance from the buck during the shift. The workers operated in pairs. Two spotters to watch for nuts falling or squirrels hiding them, two retrievers to collect the nuts, and four leafers, who had the most mindless job. They spent the entire time moving passed leaves from under the trees so nuts could be more easily spotted. The amount of work depended almost entirely on the wind. On a calm day there was little to do. When the wind loosened the nuts and sent leaves showering, everyone was busy.

Nell was assigned leaf duty alongside another buck with the odd habit of keeping one ear up and the other down. The rabbit not only enjoyed the work, he reckoned black rabbits should be grateful for the opportunity to serve the whites. Nell kept his mouth shut.

A light breeze during the morning dislodged leaves, and kept Nell on his paws. The retrievers had collected a small pile, when they were allowed a break. As they lay in the shade of the tree, the rabbits sensed the moisture rising from the ground around them. The change was delicate, and when the leaves stopped rustling and the birds went silent, they knew rain was coming. Nell tested the air. Would there be enough to trigger the burrow collapse?

They had been back at work only a short while when it began drizzling, and the clips harried them over to the pile to pick up the nuts. The rain intensified. Nell noticed the simple buck staring at him at the same time he tasted the bitter tang of charcoal. His disguise was washing off. He dropped the chestnut, then used his front paws to smear mud over his head.

'Hey, you, pick up that bloody nut.'

The supervisor was coming closer.

'What you think you're up to, varlet? This is no time to groom.'

The curious buck, last in line, winked his nose at Nell. It was as good as saying *your secret is safe with me.*

Rain swept over the field in waves and Nell kept his nose down. As they made the partial shelter of the blackthorn tree, water was pooling in the swales, and the floor of the dale was running with bubbling brown sludge. The mud on Nell's head was holding, though he wondered for how long. He could see the entrance to the main storage burrow, and willed the other workers to speed up.

The front of the line stopped. A stout rabbit Nell recognised as the burrow forebuck said something to the supervisor, who pointed his nose at Toria. Thunder rolled off the downs, sending white rabbits grazing nearby charging for their burrows as the work gang was led along the ridge. Nell wanted to drop his chestnut to ask where they were going. He couldn't take the risk. A few bounds before the main entrance to Toria, the black bucks were directed up a trail between a rock and the trunk of the rowan, and Nell realised they were being sent to the storage chamber that had been undermined.

The rain was now falling steadily, splashing off the rock and waterfalling down the trail. The bucks scrambled up, struggling for paw-holds.

The supervisor stopped them outside the entrance, and the workers were sent into the chamber one by one to drop their nuts. The roof could collapse at any time. It was agonising waiting for each rabbit. Buck number three came out and was dismissed, then buck number four. Then five. As the one with the splayed ears entered, a boom shook the ground, and the rain pounded Nell's flanks. The supervisor had backed into the lee of the rock for shelter, fortunately, because Nell was sure his forehead mark would be visible. The black buck jumped out of the hole, one ear pointing ridiculously skyward. He bowed to the supervisor and loped off. Nell was next. The voice of a white doe spat at him from the darkness.

'Over here, varlet, carefully, then piss off.'

Nell placed the nut where he was told. It was too dark to see the roof. As he hurried to the surface, a drop hit his head. The simple buck was waiting outside, holding two chestnuts.

'Get in and out as quickly as you can,' Nell whispered.

Water was streaming down both sides of the hole and merging into a channel.

'Piss off, varlet,' the supervisor yelled. 'You're done here.'

Nell moved off slowly, one ear facing behind, willing the last rabbit to follow him. He made it to the base of the rowan, when he heard a gush. Then a scream.

39. The head of the snake

'I DON'T GET the attraction. Why would a rabbit choose to swallow these things?'

Ollie had tried her first acorn. The powdery flesh was bitter and dry. She spat it out. Fleet grinned.

'Can't say I'm fond of them either, but the taste grows on some rabbits. The more you have, the more you get used to the flavour, and if you keep eating them, you get hooked.'

Ollie chewed on a leaf of ragwort to get rid of the horrid taste.

'Levi and Vort are welcome to them, as far as I'm concerned.'

'Rumour is they're both hopelessly addicted,' said Fleet, 'like many rabbits on the Golden Field. White ones, that is.'

Ollie and the seer had met to observe Oakwood rabbits being trained in carn detection. The acorn mast had begun, and the bucks and does had volunteered as temporary sentinels for the expected explosion of hunters over the coming moons. A crosser buck, dark face and light body, was explaining to the volunteers the *flimflam* technique used sometimes by hunting foxes. Ollie rotated her good ear to listen.

'The carn will stalk brazenly into the heart of a warren. Sentinels stamp and rabbits rush below. The fox then trots off, *appearing* to lose interest. After a while, the sentinels return to the surface, see no sign of the carn, so stamp the all-clear. What they don't know is that the fox is lying downwind, in a thicket or behind a rock, waiting to pounce.

That, my dear rabbits, is the flimflam.'

'How do you guard against it?' asked a black doe.

'That's where you mast sentinels come in. You don't go below. You stamp the alarm, and keep watching the fox.'

'Won't that put us in danger?'

'It would if you were stupid enough to sit in the middle of the field, twitching your nose and whirling your ears. During the mast, you'll be assigned special watching posts. The locations have been chosen for their view and cover, and distance to bolt holes.'

'Shrewd,' said Ollie.

'They need to be,' said Fleet. 'Things got shocking last time.'

The two rabbits wandered off. The rain had eased, and the fattening crescent moon was breaking through the clouds.

'What was the mast like, Fleet? I've heard ridiculous stories.'

'Depends who you ask. As far as I can tell, from *reliable* sources, there were five times as many acorns produced than a normal season. Which resulted in five times the number of animals feeding on them. We rabbits understood what was going on, so tried to restrict extra births. Even so, there were twice as many kittens in the Oakwood.'

'And the carns?'

'Didn't take them long to sense what was happening. They came from all directions, like bees to a foxglove. And it was the foxes that caused the most chaos. They went on hunting frenzies, sending rabbits to the field of silence for the sake of it, long after their stomachs were full.'

Ollie shuddered.

'When was this?'

'Shortly before Thatch took over as prime rabbit. She vowed that the warren would be better prepared for another mast, which is why you're seeing all this activity.'

'How did a doe become prime? I've only ever known bucks to lead warrens.'

Fleet scratched his nose with his paw.

'It is rare, but not unheard of. Mates of doms have been known to take over warrens when their bucks go to the field of silence. Thatch is the first doe I know of to become leader purely on merit.'

'I'm intrigued. Why her?'

'It was the last mast we've been talking about. In the moons leading up to it, Thatch was warning every rabbit who would listen that the Oakwood would be over-run with carns, telling them how to prepare. The old prime and all his high-ups took no notice. Many of them were taken by carns, and the old prime lost the confidence of the warren. Thatch was the logical replacement.'

'Weren't there stronger bucks to…'

'Takes more than strength to be a good leader, Ollie. Thatch is one of the smartest rabbits I know.'

As they went below, Fleet told Ollie he'd be crossing to the South Bank the following day. Thatch had asked for an update on the juniper harvest.

'I'd like to see Nell, get his views on how things are going with Levi as prime.'

'Good idea,' said Ollie.

'Problem is, I have no idea how to find *the Black Robert*.'

Ollie suggested the seer visit a rabbit called Joseph at Brambleleaf.

*****

THE RAIN that flooded the nut storage burrow, trapping the simple buck inside, had stopped when Nell got to the flats, but the scream was still ringing in his ears whiles later. Though there was always a chance black rabbits might end up in the field of silence because of Claw, this first passing cut deep.

The buck's fate would be an even bigger tragedy if the whites didn't realise the collapse had been caused deliberately. Nell waited until the next dayfall, then met four other members of Claw, all hefty bucks, and set off for the log to the juniper diamond. Black rabbits were searching for fresh leaves among the dried spikes of foxtail, and a barn owl was sharpening its claws in the high branches of one of the willows. They could tell from the carn's behaviour, it was not a threat.

The plan was to intercept a white rabbit – any rabbit as long as he or she was alone – coming down the dale to the log. Nell told the smartest buck what to say. They didn't have to wait long to see the limping frame of a large buck. It was Vort. Nell's companions were reluctant to confront such an important rabbit, but Nell persuaded them. He stayed behind the last tree so he could observe the encounter. The four bucks hopped into the trail and stopped.

'Out of my way, varlets.'

'Not till we've finished with you,' one of the bucks said, a tremor in his voice.

'What insolence,' huffed Vort. He tried to bluster his way through. The four bucks closed in around him.

'We got a message for you and your lot.'

Nell was close enough to see the veins in Vort's neck pulse. The white rabbit turned to face down each buck. When they stood their ground, his shoulders relaxed as he sensed he was alone and outnumbered.

'About the collapse of your nut storage burrow.'

Vort's ears twitched. Nell could tell the bucks had his attention.

'It was collapsed on purpose. By a new group. Claw.'

'This is an outrageous…'

'I haven't finished.' The buck was getting more confident, Nell was pleased to see. Vort snorted and tried again to force his way forward. His path was blocked.

'Black rabbits of the South Bank will never give in to your evil Parting. You and your lot have left us no choice but to strike back to defend our warrens, our freedom, our moons to rise. We rabbits of Claw – like the Cluster – want freedom without violence. Hopefully the burrow collapse will make you and Levi and all rabbits – white, black, or otherwise – see the disaster your colour rules are leading to. That first act was a warning. End the rules based on colour now, or face the consequences.'

The bucks hopped aside to let Vort pass, then melted into the night.

*****

THESE BRIEFINGS Vort insisted Levi attend were the part of the night he hated most. The deliberate collapse of the nut storage burrow had overshadowed the last three, and Levi was over the talk. He took little part, other than grunting his agreement, in a discussion about a new rule banning black does working in white burrows if their mate or brother was sent to a keep. He dozed through most of a report on how South Bank sages had been reassuring white warrens that the collapse was a one-off cowardly act by clumsy drifters, and everything was under control.

'Tell me something I don't know,' Levi smirked.

'I wouldn't be so sure about that,' said Vort. 'Have you spoken to the does of Poshia and Brambleleaf, or the outer parts of Toria? Because I have, and several of them don't believe things are under control. They're shocked, worrying if *their* burrows will be targeted next.'

Levi laughed, looking to the sergeant of the eclipo for support. He had been Vort's choice, too soft for Levi's liking.

'The danger as I see it,' the sergeant said, 'is that the collapse has given some of the varlets a lift. My squads are reporting a rise in cheeky behaviour. Whatever our sages are saying, there's no doubt the varlets know the truth. They're full of it. And they're not using words like *clumsy* and *one-off*. Our informers tell us the varlets' message is clear: there's a new force alongside the toothless Cluster, prepared to bring their fight to the heart of our power. We need to be careful.'

Vort nodded.

'I agree. We need to nip this little rebellion in the bud.'

'Talk, talk, talk,' said Levi, spitting out an acorn shell. 'What we need do is bite off the head of the snake.'

He turned to his father.

'Was Nell one of the varlets that ambushed you?'

'I don't believe so. I think I would have recognised it.'

'Not necessarily,' said the eclipo sergeant. 'We understand Nell uses disguises, sometimes different ones over a single night. The prime's right though. This outfit, Claw, the idea of collapsing burrows, has the Black Robert's paw prints all over it.'

Levi had heard enough.

'Black Robert my backside,' he sneered. 'It's nothing but a black weasel.'

He went to the brink and peered down over the sprawling flats of

Lexa. Light from the fattening moon pierced the clouds, revealing mobs of varlets scraping in the dirt, scattering their fleas and poxes. The varlets needed to be put in their place. He noticed a lone buck nibbling at something in a ditch. One of its ears stuck straight up like a startled dandelion leaf. He shouted for Thaden.

'Sir?'

'See that varlet with the dandelion ear? Bring it here.'

As Levi waited in the chamber, he tucked into a pile of early-season acorns. When the varlet was brought in, one ear was still sticking up and it was smiling, as if Thaden had done it a favour.

'It's an honour to…'

'Shut up, varlet. Answer the questions.'

'Yes, master. A pleasure, master.'

'Where is the varlet, Nell?'

'Thank you for asking, master. No idea, master.'

'You lying varlet,' hissed Levi, lashing out.

'Please, master. I'm telling the truth. I know a Neil, and a Noel, a Bell – though she's a doe, but no…'

Thaden's hind-leg strike sent the varlet flying into the wall, knocking over a pile of hazelnuts. It lay whimpering like a kitten, one ear still upright, like a taunt.

'Bring it to the brink,' yelled Levi.

Thaden grabbed the varlet by the ear and dragged it, bleating, across the floor of the chamber and flung it through to the ledge. Levi pushed it right to the lip.

'Tell me where to find Nell, the Black Robert, or you're carn turd.'

The varlet wet itself, and Levi skipped away from the vile puddle.

'Last chance, varlet. One, two…

'The robert, yes. I know where to find it, master. It likes the damp master, and the shadows. You'll find the robert in the hedgerows master, though its mostly finished now. It doesn't come out in the ivy moon.'

'It's talking about the bloody plant,' said Thaden.

Levi spun, kicked, and sent the varlet off the cliff.

*****

FLEET HAD ENTERED the South Bank over the stone bridge and was crossing the flats of Lexa, when he felt a flurry of distress stamps ending in a piercing shriek. He looked up to see a dark shape falling from the cliff. He rushed towards a crowd of rabbits gathering around the body of a buck, arriving at the same time as eclipo officers, who barged their way through, shouting 'Grab that varlet, it's trying to escape'.

Fleet could see that the buck couldn't get up, let alone escape. Both his legs appeared to be broken.

After getting directions to Joseph's burrow at Brambleleaf, the seer arrived to find a scruffy black rabbit who hadn't groomed for days guarding the entrance.

'Is this the burrow of Joseph?'

'It is completely and utterly. Your Highness.'

'I'd like to see him, please.'

'Is Joseph the one and only rabbit you're wishing to be seeing today then?'

'That's none of your business really, is it? May I enter please?'

'Be my guest, Your Highness. You'll be finding the master in his chamber, two holes to the right.'

Fleet thanked the cocky guard and hopped below. He found Joseph munching on a blackberry.

After introducing himself, and accepting one of the buck's berries, Fleet spoke.

'Forgive me, Joseph, I've come here hoping to see another rabbit. A black buck called Nell.'

'Thought so.'

Joseph yelled down the passage.

'David, there's someone here to see you.'

Fleet wondered if Joseph was going deaf, though didn't want to appear rude. Perhaps this David would take him to find Nell. He felt paws approaching, and the cocky guard appeared.

'Ah, there you are, David. You have a visitor.'

The guard licked his front paws and rubbed his forehead.

'There's no need to…' Fleet was about to say *groom* when he recognised the light patch.

'Nell! I don't believe it. How did you…? You certainly had me fooled.'

The two rabbits greeted warmly, and began chatting away. Joseph left them to it, as Nell asked Fleet question after question about Ollie, taking the seer back to their first meeting by the rindle.

'What brings you to the South this time, Fleet?'

'Thatch asked me to come over to check on the juniper harvest, and see what your new prime rabbit's up to. Which is why I've come seeking the *Black Robert*.'

Fleet told him what he'd seen down on the flats. Nell was shocked.

'Any idea who the poor buck was?'

'Hadn't seen him before. I'm told he had a curious habit of holding one ear up and the other down.'

Nell let out a long sigh.

'That's terrible. I met that buck only a few days ago. He had no idea who I was. And nothing to do with the Cluster. Or Claw. A complete innocent. Worse than that, he was happy about what Levi and Vort were doing. Sending a rabbit like him to the field of silence is unbelievably heartless. Shows you what we're up against here, my friend.'

They smelt Joseph returning. He'd just heard the latest plan to catch the Black Robert.

All white rabbits on the South Bank, including kittens getting lessons from roving sages, were being given descriptions of Nell's various disguises.

'Your kittens don't go to those lessons, do they?' asked Nell.

'Course not. They're nothing more than supremacist nonsense. But they play with kittens who do.'

Fleet studied Nell.

Disguise or not, he smelt tired and stressed. In need of a break.

'If what I've just witnessed is the way your new prime rabbit deals with innocent black rabbits who support him, I'd hate to think what he'd do if he got his claws on you, Nell.'

'He's got a point,' said Joseph. 'Wouldn't hurt to keep out of sight for a moon or so.'

Nell was shaking his head.

'Why not come to the North Bank?' said Fleet. 'See Ollie, regain your strength.'

'No. My place is on the South Bank. What sort of message would me running scared over the Torrent send to the black rabbits of the South?'

'What message would your passing into the field of silence send them, Nell?'

'I appreciate your concern, my friends. I have no intention of passing, however, or being caught. If *you* couldn't recognise me, Fleet, I'll take my chances with Levi and his bruisers.'

Before Fleet had the opportunity to warn Nell about the dangers of believing his own Black Robert legend, the buck had changed the subject, asking him about goings-on in the Oakwood.

*****

NELL AND THE SEER were in Joseph's meeting chamber two days later, discussing the similarities and differences between the two banks of the Torrent. Fleet had gathered the information he needed for his report to Thatch, and planned to leave at dayfall. Nell turned to see Joseph's son staring at them.

'You're the Black Robert, aren't you David?'

Nell didn't know what to say.

'My friend said the Black Robert has a light tuft over his eyes, and covers it over. Like you do.'

Joseph came into the chamber, and must have noticed the shock on Nell's face.

'Whatever has happened?'

Fleet answered.

'Your delightful son here has outed the Black Robert.'

Joseph's jaw sunk.

'Have you told anyone else, son?'

'No father. I figured it out. All by myself.'

Joseph sent for his mate to take the kitten away, and to keep him below for the night.

'Surely this changes things,' said Fleet.

Nell realised it did. If his identity could be detected by a kitten, his chances of evading the clips much longer were virtually nil.

'Is that offer of a few days in the North still open?'

'Absolutely.'

'And there's no time to lose,' said Joseph. 'If my son worked it out, there are plenty of other kittens around here who will soon.'

The challenge was how to get out. As Fleet had noted, all the usual exits were blocked to black rabbits and heavily patrolled on the South side.

'There's only one realistic route,' said Fleet. 'Through the Chilling Wood.'

That name brought back horror stories from Nell's early moons. Kittens were told about the wild, unnatural creatures roaming the wood. The White Stalker, winged beasts with talons as long as a bulrush head, black and white-faced demons, giant water-dwelling carns that hunted in packs. Worst of all was the Terrier. The ferocious monster chased rabbits deep into their burrows, dragging them out and tearing them to pieces. Kittens were warned that if they misbehaved, the Terrier would come for them in their sleep. Nell knew now the stories were about badgers, owls, and otters. The White Stalker was an albino fox, and the Terrier was a hound that lived moons ago when the wood and fields were haunted by man.

Fleet was describing a swinging bridge over the Torrent at the far end of the wood.

'It's not always guarded because, correct me if I'm wrong, Nell, black rabbits of the South Bank have some unearthly fear of the Chilling Wood.'

'Correct.'

'That could work in our favour,' said the seer. 'On the downside though, carriers use the bridge to bring in acorns from the western reaches of the Oakwood. In a mast, the route will be busier than usual. We'll have to be careful.'

They decided it was best to split up, because Fleet tended to attract attention. The plan was to meet at a hornet nest by the Narrows.

Nell stayed below until dayfall. The moon, rising over the Common, was almost full, so he took time with his disguise, applying extra layers of charcoal and rolling in vole droppings. When he set off for the meeting place, he darted here and there like a jittery doe.

He heard the hornets before he saw the nest, which was in the hollow trunk of a lime. The air around the tree vibrated to the rapidly beating wings of hundreds of the large striped insects. There was no sign of Fleet. Nell waited, unease growing, as close as he dared to the nest. When a second clip patrol passed near where he was pretending to nibble on the remains of a groundsel root, he reluctantly crept into the wood.

The moon and stars that had lit the field disappeared behind the canopy of trees unwilling to surrender their leaves to the fall. Nell recognised some from their bark – spindle, alder, hawthorn, blackthorn. Others were foreign to him. As he went further in, the gloom deepened, making him rely more on sound and smell. The hum of the hornets had been replaced with the crackling of leaves and creaking of branches, the clicking of passing bats, overlaid with the rose and citrus aroma of damp moss. No Fleet.

The trail swung south, and the canopy opened a whisker to let the night's lights cast shadows over the bowing fronds of ferns. Nell nosed at the splayed toe-tracks of a water vole. There was no indication a rabbit had passed for whiles. The fur-raising call of a fox sent him scurrying under a fallen log, where he stuped, heart thumping, until he was sure the sound had come from the other side of the rindle. As he ventured out from his hiding place, he caught a flash of white. He reversed, hoping the fishy burst of a rotting fungus would smother him. The shape of a large rabbit loomed in the darkness. Nell waited until the buck passed to make sure it was the seer, then hopped out. Fleet apologised for being late.

'I was being watched, so went a roundabout way to lose the tail.'

As Nell followed Fleet along the trail beside the rindle, his heart rate settled and, with the seer to guide him, began to relax and take more notice of the alien place. Signs of badger were unmistakable as they neared the sett – musky marks at the base of trees and on rocks, paw prints of five toes and rear pads, soft brown droppings in pits showing the carn had been eating mostly worms.

The rindle narrowed into a gorge, and Fleet took Nell over the fallen trunk of an alder to the other side. As they got deeper into the wood, the seer pointed out the strange trees. Aspen, silver birch, beech. After crossing an unnatural structure spanning the bourne, they passed beneath maples that sent pairs of seeds twirling to the ground around them. They met no other rabbits, and although they heard the distant hoots of male tawny owls and the *kuvitt-kuvitt* replies of their mates, saw no carns. Eventually the canopy thinned, and the sky lightened. Fleet crawled through a tunnel in a holly bush. A cave had been dug out of the bank, heavy with reminders of the seer.

'I use this place as a half-way burrow between the Oakwood and Golden Field. Gives a good view of the swinging bridge. See for yourself.'

Nell clambered up and nosed carefully through the spiny leaves. The Torrent flowed beneath a solid arch, like a crescent moon on its side with long vines floating above.

'Is it safe?'

'Absolutely. Man must have made it. They don't use it though. Haven't been seen around these parts for moons.'

Fleet suggested that Nell stay in the cave until he checked the crossing was unguarded.

After a while, the seer appeared at the near end of the swinging bridge, and Nell watched him cross, stopping to sniff every few hops. At the far end, he swivelled his ears, then returned to report that rabbits were approaching from the North Bank. From their hiding place, they watched as several white bucks, carrying acorns, crossed the bridge and bounded along another trail that took them beneath the cave. Once they'd passed, Fleet explained how the trail went all the way to the back of the juniper diamond.

'There's an eclipo post downstream, where the carriers will drop the nuts, so we better hightail.'

The surface of the bridge was made of pieces of wood as smooth as ice and too straight to be natural, laid one after the other all the way to the other side. It swayed under their paws and reeked a confusion of scents from hundreds of animals. Nell and Fleet were three-quarters of the way over when more white bucks appeared on the far side.

40. Freedom is a moving feast

'MY ADVICE is to keep your nose down, mouth shut, ten hops behind me, and start scratching,' said Fleet.

The white bucks reached the north end of the bridge and stopped.

Nell did as Fleet suggested. Head down, he could only hear the conversation. The carriers were led by a brusque clip, who did all the talking.

'Hop to it. Haven't got all night.'

'Sorry officer,' replied Fleet. 'My captive's got fleas, so I'm keeping my distance.'

Nell lifted his hind leg to scratch behind his ear. He sensed the carriers moving away, but not the clip.

'Why you taking him to the North? Varlets aren't allowed.'

'It's one of ours, I'm afraid officer,' said Fleet. 'Caught it stealing from one of Thatch's circle bucks. It skulked over to your side of the Torrent. Probably got the fleas from one of your… varlet warrens.'

Nell changed legs and scratched the other ear.

'No surprises there,' said the clip. 'Every last one of our thieving varlets is crawling with them.'

'So I've heard, officer. If it was up to me, I'd leave this one on the South Bank to rot. Thatch, though, insists he face… justice.'

'That doesn't sound like…'

'Can we get going please, sir?,' whined one of the carriers. 'These acorns won't carry themselves.'

'Okay, okay. Back off further then, and let them through. I don't want to catch the varlet's fleas.'

Fleet thanked the officer, and Nell limped past him and off the bridge, laying paw on the North Bank for the first time. He had mixed feelings. Relief they'd outwitted the clip. Guilt for breaking his promise to the Cluster not to leave the South until freedom was won. And excitement about exploring new fields, seeing Ollie again. He cleaned the charcoal from his forehead, then looked around, sucking in the delights of oak moss and wood blewit mushrooms. Fleet was smiling at him.

'Welcome to the North Bank, Nell. Out of curiosity, what are you sniffing?'

'Freedom. Safety.'

'I see. You'll find freedom is a moving feast, my friend. And though you're probably safe from the claws of Levi on this side of the Torrent, there are still dangers for rabbits of any colour. Especially now, during the mast. Stay alert. We've got a way to go to the warren.'

The oakwood, Fleet explained, was larger than the Chilling Wood. It stretched from where they stood in an arc all the way to a stone bridge. The main warren was in a large clearing, between a lake and a wide glade running south through the trees.

'Is there only the one warren for such a large area?'

'No, there's four. The main Oakwood Warren ruled by Thatch, and three smaller warrens – all currently led by bucks with fur the same colour as yours.'

Nell was confused.

'I had no idea blacks and whites lived separately on the North Bank.'

'They don't. Rabbits can live where they want. All four warrens have rabbits of all colours.'

The trail snaked up from the bridge and disappeared between the twisted trunks of trees Fleet identified as hornbeams. The two rabbits were soon swallowed in darkness, as the night lights were blocked by the crowns of ancient oaks whose leaves were still a moon from falling. Once the adrenalin rush from making it over the Torrent wore off, Nell tired. After a rest to snack on fresh shoots of primroses, they left the cover of the oaks and followed a trail that wound in and out of trunks on the fringe of the wood.

The first glimmers of daystar were nuzzling the treetops, drawing breath from the blazing Venus, as they arrived at the eastern side of a large field and re-entered the oakwood for the last leg of their journey. They had not met a single rabbit since the swinging bridge. Nell was about to ask Fleet why, when he saw a white doe and three kittens. He jumped aside to let them pass. The doe stopped.

'What's the matter with your friend, Fleet? Does he think we smell rotten or something?'

'Not at all, Valerie. He's visiting from the South Bank, where black rabbits are expected to move aside for white rabbits.'

'What on Earth for?'

'It's the rules.'

'How absurd,' she said, hurrying her kittens past the bucks.

As they pressed on through the wood, they saw bucks collecting acorns, does nosing, others deep in conservation, kittens playing, mixtures of black, white and shades between. There were no forbidden lines. For the first time in Nell's life, he felt like a free rabbit. It was eye-popping. They passed the last tree and entered a large circular clearing in which the Oakwood Warren was centred. Some rabbits welcomed Nell by name. Then he saw her.

*****

OLLIE HAD SPENT THE NIGHT as she had all the others – talking to as many rabbits as she could about the plight of their black cousins on the South Bank. Once the shadows from the daystar had retreated into the trees, and most inhabitants of the Oakwood Warren had drifted below for the day, she'd gone to her favourite grazing area on the western rim of the clearing.

Leaf-fall had sagged into its middle moon, and Ollie felt the nights cooling. She dreaded the coming winter. Plants were still reasonably plentiful, even for a rabbit who spent most of the nights talking rather than eating. She found the remains of a henbit, and was chewing a notched leaf when she detected a familiar scent. She winked her nose.

The memory had gone. Must have been imagining. She pawed at the soil to get at the roots.

'I wouldn't have believed a rabbit could do such a thing if I hadn't seen it with my own eyes.'

The voice, from downwind behind a clump of fescue, could belong to only one rabbit. Ollie spat out the root, and hopped up to Nell. They licked and necked like the long-lost friends they were.

'I'm glad *you* recognised me after all these moons, Ollie, because other rabbits I've never met somehow knew who I was.'

'Ah, you're a legend over here, thanks to Fleet.'

'That's stretching the truth more than a whisker,' said the seer, smiling. 'Ollie hasn't stopped talking since arriving here, about the outrage you rabbits face on the South Bank. I must, however, leave you to your reunion. I'm sure you have plenty to talk about, and Thatch will be awaiting my report. A word of warning though, Nell. Don't assume everyone who recognises you is friendly.'

Ollie could see that Nell was tired from the journey, so after allowing him to feed, showed him below to sleep for the day.

The pair spent the next few nights touring the North Bank, Ollie showing Nell around the clearing, the lake, the glade, the shared passages, and the guarded entrances to the homes of Thatch and her circle. Leaves on the mighty trees that gave the Oakwood its name were beginning to surrender their green hues to twinkles of orange and yellow, and the second flush of growth in the fescue that dominated the clearing was almost over. For Ollie, it was like a return to the magical, carefree days at Hilltop, reminiscing about the stories from Aunt Mina and Old Chief, the raid on the blackberry patch, the taunting of Vort and pissing on his plant. For a time, she forgot how stiff her legs felt on cold nights, how lonely she was in a foreign place away from her friends.

She asked Nell about events in the South, his life as the Black Robert, about Claw. And updated him on what she'd been doing to get support in the North, careful not to exaggerate or brag, because whatever difficulties she'd encountered at the Oakwood couldn't possibly be as bad as life in the South.

'You're being too modest,' said Nell. 'I've also had my ears flapping since coming across the Torrent, and I'm constantly hearing what a wonderful job you're doing representing us over here.'

Ollie brushed off the compliment, not letting on that her insides were glowing. They were resting at the Bowl – a place where any rabbit was free to speak, and others could listen, agree, argue. It was not far from one of the entrances to Thatch's burrow. The moon was high over the trees to the south-east, above the red star, Betelgeuse. Ollie explained how speakers ranged from sages to wits.

'Dom William would have been right at home here.'

Ollie had brought Nell to listen to a rabbit she wanted him to meet. A crosser was telling a story about the last mast, and getting laughs from a few white does.

'I'm finding this all so strange, Ollie. Rabbits of different colours mixing like this.'

'It does take some getting used to. Then you realise it's natural, as it should be. It's what happens on the South Bank that's unnatural.'

The black buck they'd come to hear talked about white privilege, how as a rabbit of colour his life was like *always hopping uphill into a headwind.*

'Should try living over the Torrent,' said Nell. 'He has no idea how lucky he is to live here.'

When the buck finished, Ollie offered to introduce Nell to him. As she turned, Nell stuped, as if he'd seen the White Stalker.

*****

NELL HAD BEEN FACING the entrance to Thatch's burrow and reacted the way he did because of the two rabbits he saw emerge. One was Vort. The other was a gigantic buck. Nell turned quickly back to Ollie, hiding his face from the white rabbits.

'Did Vort see me, recognise me?'

Ollie peeked over Nell's shoulder. 'Don't think so. He's too busy talking to Thatch's head sentinel. And they're coming this way.'

The two friends hopped off as casually as they could, Nell keeping his back to the white rabbits. The close escape jolted him. Seeing Vort was, as always, a reminder of his father, of Maisy struggling at home because of his actions. Here he was, romping around like a kitten while rabbits all over the South Bank were being smothered, living in hovels, eating where they were told, passing pellets where they were ordered, facing not the occasional headwind, but a never-ending whirlwind of injustice. Vort's cosy relationship with Thatch's right-paw rabbit also showed that the claws of Levi's power stretched deep into the North Bank.

'I've been a fool, Ollie,' he said, once they made the safety of his friend's burrow. 'Worse than careless. I've been reckless.'

'I'm sure Vort didn't recognise you, Nell.'

'It's more than that. I've let myself be blinded by the buzz of being recognised so far from home as some sort of hero. Put my own enjoyment – and big head – ahead of the rabbits I'm supposed to represent.'

'You're being a bit hard on yourself, Nell. Surely a rabbit in your position can take a break once in a moon.'

'I don't see it that way, my friend. How do you think black rabbits of the South Bank would feel if they knew their leader was prancing around the Oakwood when they can't pass wind without asking permission?'

'They'd…'

'Think badly of me, I'm sure. And that will weaken the support we've worked so hard to build up.'

'I guess you're right. So, what are you going to do?'

'I've got to resume my disguise.'

Ollie looked troubled.

'Have you got a problem with that?'

'Of course not,' she said. 'But there is one more thing I'd like you to do as *Nell* before you turn back into the Black Robert. There's a gathering at the Meadow Warren tomorrow. You should go. It could help our cause.'

41. Give it to the eejits again

THE MEADOW WARREN was a rambling collection of burrows on the south side of the thicket, reached through tunnels at the end of the glade. Rabbits were free to go between Meadow and the Oakwood, to live in either warren, and though bucks and does occasionally changed homes, the populations of both warrens remained relatively stable.

Ollie and Nell had spent the early evening in the wood to the east of the glade, observing the acorn harvest and watching from a safe distance the storing of nuts and their collection by carriers from the South. During the night, they wandered towards the tunnels. No-one recognised the rabbit too lazy to clean the mud from his forehead. The gathering was not until dayspring, so once through into the meadow, Ollie showed her friend where to find food. They grazed beside a black buck and his white mate. Ollie was enjoying an out-of-season comfrey confused by the warmth and length of days into thinking it was spring, when she felt the one-three stamp. Nell quickly tested the air and listened for the danger.

'It's alright, Nell,' said Ollie. 'That stamp means a carn's been detected, and the sentinels have things in control.'

She could smell Nell's confusion.

'Follow me. I'll show you.'

She took Nell to where a black rabbit, a sentinel, was sitting under fronds of bracken. From there they could see a large sweep of the meadow glowing from the thinning moon. A fox was closing in on a pair of black rabbits who kept their noses to the ground, unconcerned about the danger.

'Why don't they hightail?' Nell asked. 'They must have felt the stamps.'

'Watch and you'll see,' said the sentinel.

The fox was almost within striking distance of the rabbits, who kept feeding. Suddenly four bucks – three black and one white – appeared from nowhere and charged across the fox's path. The carn's eyes swept from one to another. The white buck turned and skipped up to the fox, which pounced, but got its angle wrong. The buck dodged clear and hightailed in the opposite direction, away from the warren, with the carn in pursuit.

*****

NELL WAS IMPRESSED, even more when Ollie explained how the rabbits had worked together to outsmart the fox. The carn would have been detected by sentinels on duty on the outskirts of the warren. They would have alerted the flusters – the four rabbits whose job was to distract the carn.

'What about the one at the end,' asked Nell, 'the brazen white buck who practically jumped in the face of the fox?'

'He was the lure. His job was to draw the carn off. Lures are specially chosen for their courage and speed.'

'But he was… white. Risking his life to draw a fox away from black rabbits. That would never happen in the South.'

With the danger gone, and the daystar glimmering over the oaks to the east, Nell and Ollie headed for the gathering place. As they passed rabbits feeding or talking, Nell was intrigued at the accents and mannerisms. Rabbits greeted by touching cheeks three times, first on the left, then the right, then the left again. Several spoke through rounded lips that softened the sound of their words. There were exotic fragrances Ollie identified as sage and mallow and chickweed, others she hadn't learnt yet. The way these rabbits sat – upright and proud and confident – was so unlike the restless flinching common among black rabbits of the South Bank. It was inspiring for Nell to see how rabbits from different places, with different backgrounds and stories, and different fur, had come together to create something unique, a new *place.*

The Meadow Warren was centred on a sprawling yew tree, and the gathering was to be held in a basin on the south side. Flat berms had been dug out of the three sloping sides so rabbits could watch and listen. They were filling up when Nell and Ollie arrived. She helped Nell lick away his disguise.

'We're among friends here.'

Ollie was pointing out the doms of the Cocksfoot and Drop Warrens, lying on a rock in the shadow of the yew, when Nell felt a regular stamping, and sensed the approach of many paws. From the far end of the basin appeared the largest black buck Nell had seen. Behind him marched lines of bucks in ranks of four. The buck in front, who Ollie said was the sergeant of the Meadow sentinels, raised one ear, then the other, and the marching lines stopped as one.

Nell watched in amazement as the sentinels fanned out to positions around the top of the basin, from where they faced outwards, presumably watching for carns. It was the first time Nell had seen black sentinels under the command of a black rabbit. The sergeant hadn't moved a whisker. He did now, revealing another buck who had been waiting behind him.

'That's the dom of Meadow,' said Ollie.

He was slightly smaller than his sergeant, with a rounder stomach and double chin. His black coat gleamed in the rising daystar. He lifted his right paw, and the crowd went silent. Then, to Nell's surprise, he came over.

'Ollie, me wee friend, glad yer could…'

He stopped, and stared at Nell.

'The Black Robert is indeed magic. Not only can he disappear from a yew on the South Bank, he can reappear under another on the North. All lured to see yer, Nell. Welcome to our humble warren.'

'Thank you, Dom. I'm looking forward to hearing… to the gathering.'

'Aye so am I, so am I, now we have a new speaker. Please, come with me.'

He took Nell over to the weathered and cracked stump of an oak tree, jumped up, and introduced him to the gathering, repeating his line about the Black Robert and the yews. He then asked Nell to join him on the stump. Nell was unprepared for this.

'What exactly do they want to know?'

'Everything. Aye, from the beginning. Always find that's a grand place to start.'

Nell told them how the life of a black rabbit on the South Bank compared to what he'd seen in the North, how the Cluster had tried for moons to get the white rabbits to relax the rules, including the does' work stoppage and the Resistance – without success, and how restrictions had got worse since Levi took over as prime. There were mutterings of *unnatural* and *how dare they*, although it wasn't until Nell mentioned the manner of Stephen's passing and how white clips deliberately lured foxes to attack defenceless does at Poshia, that he felt ears truly opened. By the time he'd described the massacre at the Point, he had to shout to be heard over the cries of *brutal* and *unforgivable* and *fekers*.

'Each peaceful act we've tried,' Nell went on, 'has either failed or made life worse for us.'

He scanned the basin. All ears and eyes were on him.

'I feel privileged that black rabbits of the South Bank chose me as their leader, and you're right to feel outrage about the tyranny we face. However, I say this, my friends: a leader also commits an outrage against the rabbits he represents if, having tried peaceful methods, he hesitates to sharpen his claws in the fight against injustice. That is why a nut storage burrow, an important symbol of white rule in the South, was deliberately destroyed. The whole of the South Bank shuddered from the first strike of a new group – Claw.'

'Give it to the eejits again,' shouted the dom of the Cocksfoot Warren. The crowd chanted *Again, again, again*, and the ground shuddered.

Nell held up his right paw for quiet.

'A few nights ago, I crossed the Torrent, having for the last six moons lived in my own fields as an outcast. When I was forced to lead this sort of life, I promised I would never abandon the South Bank, would keep working in the shadows. I meant it. Which is why, my friends, I will go back to resume the struggle.'

The pledge was greeted with nods and shouts of approval, and as soon as Nell hopped down from the stump, he was mobbed by rabbits eager to lick and shower him in words of encouragement.

*****

LEVI YAWNED through the briefing, taking little notice of reports on harvesting and storage, the number of nuts crossing to and from the North Bank, the location of carn attacks. *Blah blah blah.*

His good ear pricked up when an eclipo sergeant was asked to report on his recent visit to the Oakwood. The buck had spent a night with Thatch's head sentinel, touring the clearing and glade to see how the northerners were preparing for the expected explosion in carns after the acorn mast.

'Talk talk talk,' barked Levi. 'Who cares what the featherheads in the Oakwood are doing about a few extra carns. Did you learn anything useful from the northerners, or was it simply another *holiday*?'

'Matter of fact I did hear something you might be interested in, sir. Rumours that Nell has been seen in the Oakwood. Thatch's sentinel couldn't confirm it but, as they say, *where there's a stench, someone's passed wind.* Sir.'

42. Eyes staring, searching

SPEAKING to the Meadow rabbits about the struggle on the South Bank stirred a longing in Nell for home. Though it would mean exchanging this place of freedom and peace for fields of restriction and fear, he felt he should return quickly. He and Ollie were settling down for the day as guests at the Meadow, when they were visited by the dom of the Cocksfoot Warren. Nell recalled him as the buck who shouted *Give it to the eejits again* when he mentioned the burrow collapse.

He had come to give his support to the black rabbits of the South Bank, and offered to show Nell – and any members of Claw he could get over the Torrent – techniques they could use to cause more chaos than collapsing burrows. Nell accepted. He'd felt uncomfortable asking rabbits to attack the symbols of white rule in ways he himself was not prepared to do. He also remembered the gathering in the Cluster burrow, when he had been called the Black Skulker and was accused of enjoying the good life while others were left to feel the claws of Levi and his clips.

'Count me in too,' said Ollie.

Nell smiled at his brave friend. The doe whose body had once charged and dodged a swooping tawny had been battered and weakened through the moons of brutality and hunger and poor health. Yet here she was, unselfishly volunteering to take the fight to the supremacists.

'No, Ollie. You have more important things to do for us in this struggle. The wisdom in that head of yours, and gift for spreading our message, are too valuable to risk in a fight with seed-brained bucks like Levi and his half-wit yes-rabbits.'

It was decided that Ollie would arrange to get messages to the South Bank for selected members of Claw to come north for training, and she would meet Nell at the Cocksfoot Warren in a few nights.

Nell's instructor, a muscular buck known as the Captain, had led squads of warrior bucks in a battle against a burrow-grabbing warren to the west of the Oakwood, repeatedly repelling raids by rabbits trying to make them slaves. Nell was a fit rabbit from his roaming as the Black Robert and his earlier time as an errand runner. He was ignorant though, about different methods of fighting, of attack and defence, when to advance or retreat, how to cause maximum chaos using small numbers of trained rabbits. Over several nights, Nell learnt fighting and self-defence techniques, how to organise teams of rabbits to lure carns, confuse alarm signals to weaken a warren's defences, place carn droppings or mimic their smells to disrupt grazing or nut harvesting, and other ways to damage burrows.

On the final night, after a training session where a relay of rabbits fooled a pair of fox vixens into attacking an empty burrow, Nell and the Captain were hopping back to the warren. There was no moon, and a gathering fog had devoured every light except three stubborn stars. The rabbits had stopped on a bluff between the trunks of poplar trees to eat young leaves of cocksfoot grass, when a series of rasping squeals spiked the dark. The sound seemed to come from out on the Torrent.

'Don't worry yourself about that, Nell. There are plenty of past-moon does' tales about the creature or creatures behind that noise. Some say it's a fox gone blind and crazy with the mange, others that it's the ghost of rabbits sent there to pass into the field of silence.'

'Sent where?'

'The island. Can't see it through this fog, but the Torrent splits in two upstream from here. There's a large chunk of land cut off on both sides by rapids, powerful currents. Whatever it is, can't hurt us here.'

As a kitten, Nell had heard horror stories about an island of misery. He assumed they were myths, though remembered Aunt Mina saying that supporters of Dingha were sent to an island. Now, as he peered through the murk, the squeals grew louder, and he sensed eyes staring, searching for him.

His concentration was broken by the sound and scent of a rabbit hurrying along the trail. It was Merce, Joseph's friend who had given him the idea of collapsing the nut storage burrow. His message was alarming. He said Joseph had learnt of a plan to send the entire leadership of the Cluster to the field of silence, and urged Nell, as leader of Claw, to return immediately.

*****

OLLIE WAS WAITING for Nell when he got back to Cocksfoot. Her friend was in such a hurry to get home, he was prepared to risk travelling under the daystar. Ollie insisted on accompanying him to the swinging bridge.

'There's one more rabbit I'd like you to meet. The dom of the Drop Warren has asked for a word before you cross to the South.'

'We haven't time, Ollie.'

'The Drop's on the way. We could hop in for a quick chat. The dom's a wily no-nonsense buck, and if he has something to tell you, it's sure to be worth hearing.'

Patches of fog were still clinging to the ground, shielding them from the daystar, as they dipped into a dale that during storms channeled rain down to the Torrent. On the far side, near where the water dropped over a wide shelf extending from bank to bank, were the entrances to several burrows. Once below, the dom got straight to the point.

'Collapsing burrows and using other fancy techniques you might have learnt at Cocksfoot will get you only so far, Nell. Never forget that the purpose of creating chaos is to let loose other powers to bring down the enemy.'

'Like what?'

'Like planting doubt. Like making ordinary white rabbits of the South question their leaders and the direction they're taking them. Like giving confidence to others who might challenge the bad leaders. Like making alternative ways of doing things appear attractive. And don't focus all your efforts on the enemies you can see and sniff and hear in front of you. Every dom or prime depends on other rabbits, and special circumstances, to keep him or her in power. Find ways to undermine that support, change the circumstances propping up the evil.

'What I'm saying, Nell, is that collapsing burrows and fighting is not the only way to let loose these powers. Never underestimate the sharp power of the voice over the blunt power of violence.'

Ollie took Nell above.

The fog had lifted, and puffy white clouds were floating to surround the slither of moon defying the daystar.

On their way to the bridge, Nell thanked Ollie for talking him into seeing the last dom.

'What did you think of him?'

'Impressive. I liked that his burrows were simple, and he was humble. Don't get me wrong. The Cocksfoot Warren was also impressive. Its dom was… colourful… and his warren well organised, almost too organised. I found the last dom more *real*. A rabbit's rabbit.'

'You agreed with his advice?'

'He did talk a lot of sense, Ollie. Though I'm beginning to think like a fighter, I'm still unhappy with the idea of using claws against another rabbit. You know as well as I that two can take the path of violence, and violence by black rabbits will invite a more ruthless response from the whites. Violence alone will never convince Levi and Vort to give up power.'

The friends reached the trail zigzagging from the hornbeams down to the bridge, ahead of a line of nut carriers. They darted into the wood and waited until the bucks passed.

'Levi and his yes-rabbits are welcome to as many of those acorns as they want, if you ask me,' said Ollie. 'Have you tried one? They're disgusting.'

'No, though it gives me an idea. The dom was right about prime rabbits relying on others, and special circumstances, to stay in power. Levi and Vort and their circle have become addicted to acorns. What if we could find a way stop the flow of nuts from the North?'

'Won't be easy. The strongest bucks are chosen as carriers, and don't forget that the trade goes both ways. Thatch and her circle are just as fond of junipers.'

'I'll leave solving that problem for that oversized brain of yours, Ollie. There must be a way, and if there is, I'm sure you'll sniff it out.'

They dropped down to the bridge and were saying their farewells when four black bucks burst from the wood on the southern side and charged across towards them. Ollie and Nell were so stunned they stuped. The bucks stopped in front of Nell. All four did a rapid double *thu-thump* stamp.

'Great to see you again, Nell,' said the leader. 'And you, Ollie. What did you think of the salute?'

'I'm afraid I don't understand,' said Nell. 'Why would you want to salute?'

'To show support for Claw. Secretly. And not break Levi's latest insane rule. You might not have heard. We're no longer allowed to even utter the word *Claw*. The salute is our way of saying *the power is ours.*'

The buck explained that he and his friends were the first fighters to cross the Torrent for training with the Captain. Ollie noticed a hint of moisture in Nell's eyes. She was thinking the same. Until now, fighting the whites had been little more than an idea. These bucks were volunteering to risk their lives for that idea. For a chance at freedom. For Nell. This was real, and dangerous, particularly for the first recruits.

Nell thanked them and wished them luck, urging them to never lose sight of *the big field*. That the struggle was about more than collapsing a burrow or causing chaos. It was about creating a fair and free place for rabbits of all colours. The bucks repeated the Claw salute. Ollie and Nell saluted them back, then watched them climb up the trail.

*****

AS SOON AS THE RECRUITS disappeared between the hornbeams, Nell smeared mud over his forehead. Ollie teased him about how things had changed from when he used to groom repeatedly.

'Many things have changed since those moons, my friend, most for the worse. Seeing those bucks, though, gives me hope the change we seek could be round the corner.'

They wished each other safe fields, and Nell hopped onto the bridge. A forked tree branch rushed beneath him, the current carrying it close to the North, then yanking it to the South and the shade of an overhanging bluff. It reappeared briefly, then vanished round the bend where the island lay. Nell shivered at the thought. He jumped off the bridge and, feeling suddenly vulnerable, dashed into the Chilling Wood. How much had changed indeed. Not so many days ago, he would have been terrified entering the wood alone. Training from the Captain, particularly the time he'd spent learning how to sniff out danger, creep silently over fallen leaves, and how different carns hunted in a wood, gave him more confidence.

Fleet had once claimed that the aromas of his home warren smelt more fragrant after he'd been away. Nell paused to breathe in the familiar scents of watermint and cress. Although his visit to the North had given him his first taste of freedom, and he was returning to the South as a hunted rabbit, he was pleased to be back on the bank where he'd been born, where his destiny lay.

In the time Nell had been away from the South Bank, more leaves had fallen in the Chilling Wood, particularly from beeches and maples, allowing extra light to reach the ground. Shafts of daystar singled out bracken fronds turning reddish-brown and the funnel webs of labyrinth spiders waiting patiently within. Instead of feeling exposed, Nell felt energised, eager to pass on the lessons he'd learnt in the North, to take the struggle to the next level.

His excitement grew as he crossed the alder trunk over the rindle. Not even the badger, grooming noisily outside its sett, slowed him down. He veered south through the hawthorns and spindles to the clearing around the Erfeti stump. Nell stopped to sniff the breeze and listen. Leaves rustling, a field vole scurrying, chiffchaffs flitting between branches, grey wagtails doing what they're named after, but no rabbits. He went over to examine the strange markings on the stump. It occurred to him that such a powerful symbol of white rule should be added to the list of targets for Claw.

Wafts of mint lured him to the rindle, where he nibbled at the leaves and sipped the cool water. Far to the south-east, over the tops of the browning leaves of the spindles, he could see the reassuring ever-green crown of the Hilltop yew, and wondered if late ripening blackberries had survived the raids of the Patri's sons. He looked up to where the Point Warren lay, imagining Maisy sleeping in her burrow, dreaming up new uses for old herbs.

A gust scooped up a pile of fallen alder leaves, still defiantly green, spinning them in circles of air that muddled his senses of smell and hearing. Through the swirl came a whisper of hazelnut, and in the heartbeat before teeth closed roughly around his neck, Nell knew his life as the Black Robert was over.

PART THREE

THE RECKONING

43. Voices from moons past

POWERFUL LEGS pinned Nell to the ground. He considered trying a self-defence technique he'd learnt from the Captain, though could tell that even if he managed to break free and dash for the wood, he'd be quickly overrun and almost certainly flung into the field of silence. A new scent – acorn – filled his nostrils as the menacing face of Thaden, Levi's chief bruiser, blocked out the light.

'Well, well, well, well, well. What do you suppose we have here?'

'David. Master. My name's David. What's this about, officer? I'm a guard for… an important white rabbit at…'

Nell stopped. He could see how ridiculous he sounded. Thaden grinned.

'Course you are. And I'm the Black Rabbit of Inle,' he said, tossing his head and laughing. 'Welcome home, Nell. We've been expecting you.'

The colossal buck ordered the clips to form a tight circle around *the varlet*. It was the first time Nell had heard the despised word for whiles, and it added to his misery.

He'd always known there was a chance he'd be captured. Distracted by the excitement of standing once more on the bank of his birth, he'd foolishly dropped his guard. The ring of clips steered him alongside the wood to the Narrows, where the size of the escort doubled. The ambush had been carefully planned.

Someone must have alerted the clips.

As he was taken up the ridge between Chest Tree Corner and Brambleleaf, then through the whites-only area of the Golden Field, Nell tried to think who or what had been his undoing, until he realised guessing was pointless.

He had no-one but himself to blame. Too many rabbits knew he had been in the Oakwood and was coming home.

As they neared the rowan, the escort had doubled in size again. The clips were taking no chances. Nell's last vision before being ushered through a hole into Toria was of a rowan leaf, blood red and serrated like the teeth of a stoat, being trampled by the clip in front of him.

He was forced up and up, through the bowels of the warren, until the ground levelled off and they rounded a corner. Light seeped into the passage through a hole. Nell was shoved through, into a large chamber, and the victorious face of Levi.

The white rabbit scraped his chin roughly against the floor in a deliberate act of dominance, then began circling, nostrils flaring, his face contorted in demented fury.

Nell was transported to the rindle, to the disagreement between his father and Vort all those moons ago. Vort had talked of black parasites infesting *his* fields, and Henry had tried to reason with him. It made no difference then, and would make no difference now.

Nell was no match for a buck rabbit of Levi's size and strength. And malice. Resistance would be as pointless as words. His only weapon was his dignity. He would deny Levi the satisfaction the white buck craved so much.

The first strike, a loutish swipe to the face, opened a stinging cut on Nell's cheek. He stood his ground and looked at his attacker, recalling the advice of a rabbit who had survived nights of brutal bashing by keeping eye-contact with his attacker. *Make it personal.*

A vicious blow lifted Nell off the ground.

He hauled himself up again and faced Levi, expressionless. The white rabbit kicked hard, sending Nell thumping into the wall of the chamber. Though his lungs burned, he forced himself up to face the onslaught.

*****

LEVI HAD SO MANY REASONS to make the varlet suffer. Every obstacle, every humiliation, everything wrong in his life was caused by Nell.

The varlet's stinking father had mangled Vort's leg. Levi leaped into the air and came down with all his weight on Nell's hind leg.

The varlet and his snivelling friend had the nerve to mock Vort and piss on a plant he'd told them to leave. Levi raised his leg and aimed a stream of urine into Nell's face.

The varlet had embarrassed him in front of his kins at the border crossing, helped by that varlet-loving Crown. Levi bit into the fur around Nell's neck, tearing off a chunk and spitting it in the varlet's face.

For each embarrassing put-down, Levi thought up another way for Nell to feel pain.

For the varlet's manipulating friendship with the seer, Fleet. For filling the simple heads of varlets with disrespect and rebellion. For lurking in the shadows as the Black Robert. For organising the collapse of the storage burrow. For having a mother who stood up to stoats…

*****

NELL WAS HOVERING beyond agony. As he absorbed blow after blow and steadied himself for the next, he inhaled inner strength from flashes of memory.

The crinkling of his father's brow. His mother winking her nose at a sow thistle. Ollie side-stepping an owl. The cunning of the lacewing he was watching when he met Fleet. Soothing vapours of honeysuckle behind Hilltop. Wisps of silver fur dangling from one side of Aunt Mina's face as she told the story of Dingha. Purple juice dripping from the tusk of Old Chief as he spat the words: *You won't find what you're looking for in the soil. You should be aiming for the sky.*

*****

LEVI WAS ALSO HEARING VOICES. Of Erfeti and the other Mistle heroes who fought for and protected the South Bank from the varlet hordes. Urging him on. Every kick and bite and slash was for the memory of those heroes and the glory of white.

Attack!

Crush!

Mutilate!

Humiliate!

Field of…

'Enough!'

The last command was shouted from the other side of the chamber, as Levi raised his hind leg for the final, field-of-silence blow. He held the leg aloft, over the pathetic, lifeless body of the varlet. Then collapsed to the ground, panting. Through the fuzziness, Levi recognised not the shape of Erfeti, but the limping outline of his father, lumbering over to the varlet and putting an ear to its mouth.

'Fool,' Vort hissed. 'You hot-headed fool.'

Levi was confused. He dragged himself to his paws. Vort was still fussing over the varlet.

'Might not be too late. I can detect a faint breath.'

'What are you talking about?'

'Sending *this* rabbit to the field of silence, like this, will turn it into an even bigger hero to the varlets than it is now.'

Levi couldn't believe what he was hearing. Vort groaned.

'Better to make an example of the varlet, like they do in the North, and show all rabbits – blacks, whites, meddlers from the Oakwood – that Nell is nothing more than a murderer and spreader of terror.'

'But…'

'Can't you see, son? The evidence is so overwhelming, any fair-minded rabbit with half a brain would agree. *Then* you can send it to the field of silence and end this varlet rebellion forever.'

44. The brightest light of all

SINCE NEWS of Nell's capture reached the Oakwood, Ollie had hardly slept or eaten, which gnawed away at her already weak defences against the chilling of the privet moon and fast-approaching winter. Nothing had been heard of Nell's fate, and as time passed, hope faded. Most rabbits assumed Nell had passed into the field of silence. Ollie refused to give up.

Then news arrived about the hearing. Messengers and invitations had been sent far and wide by Levi and Vort. Ollie, of course, was not invited. She looked up at the sky and noticed the Follower, the bright red star that reminded her of the dreams she and Nell once shared. Of how they'd vowed not to bring kittens into the world until the South Bank was free.

*****

FLEET SCURRIED over the stone bridge and through the tunnel in the hedgerow. The South Bank guards ignored him, as they usually did. They were interested only in harassing rabbits of black or mixed fur. The seer had farewelled Ollie, promising to do what he could for Nell. He could tell from Ollie's reaction that nothing was expected.

Fleet was astonished at the number – and importance – of other rabbits from the North Bank also on their way to the hearing. Since leaving the Oakwood, he'd passed members of Thatch's circle, as well as the doms of the Meadow, Cocksfoot and Drop Warrens. It was one of the clearest nights of the winter. A massed gathering of stars and fattening privet moon illuminated the Golden Field all the way to Chest Tree Corner. The brightest light of all came from the Follower.

Fleet considered the red star as he descended into the gully, then stopped to rest for the climb to the Upland and Toria. Was he a follower or a leader? Observer or influencer? Not for the first time, he wondered if he'd done the right thing following the expected ways of a seer – watching and not becoming involved.

*****

THE SAME STAR lit the path for Maisy who, like many of the black rabbits of the South Bank, was entering the Upland for the first time. The prime rabbit of Toria had kindly relaxed the forbidden lines, so rabbits from the country warrens and Lexa could attend the hearing.

Maisy had mixed feelings. On one paw she felt special, accompanied by the Patri and the doms from the Willow, Platform and Hilltop field. Proud that such distinguished rabbits were here because of her son.

On the other was dread, and she could tell from the troubled scents of her companions that her fear was shared.

*****

LEVI WAS RECLINING on the prime rabbit's terrace beside the main entrance of Toria, the sheen from the star highlighting his fabulously healthy coat. At a signal from Thaden, he jumped down, and the two bucks strutted through the cheering crowd of white rabbits gathered around the rowan.

'Finally,' Levi barked. 'It ends now.'

*****

THE STAR glaring off Levi's flanks, shadowing the memories of Ollie and lighting the path for Fleet and Maisy was invisible to Nell. He'd been dragged to the deepest keep, where light never reached.

For the first few days and nights after his capture, he'd lapsed in and out of consciousness, bewildered and bruised from ear to paw. Assuming he'd been left to pass into the field of silence, he despaired that the connections he'd made in the North, the advice that could help the cause, would rot with him. That the ways of resistance he learnt from the Captain would never be used. He lost grip of time. Days passed like moons. With no rabbit to talk to, his thoughts twisted inward, burrowing for the dark fields of his mind. He became so desperate for company, he caught himself talking to a worm.

Some time after the beating – it could have been five nights or five moons – he was brought limp groundsel, roots of St John's Wort, and chunks of iced mud. He devoured the leaves, the moisture, and the acrid sap of the roots so greedily that his stomach hurt. The guard uttered no more words than the worm, though returned over the next few days to bring food. On one visit, the buck brought a stick to poke a hole through to an adjoining burrow to let a shiver of less rancid air challenge the foul stench of the keep.

Eat, drink, sleep, worry, panic, sleep, think. Eat, drink, sleep, worry, panic, sleep, think. The routine was finally interrupted when the frowzy aroma of hazelnut whistled down to the keep. It came from another guard, a larger buck tailed by two does carrying fresh dandelion leaves and frozen nettle.

'Enjoy it, varlet. It'll be your last meal.'

The words, the first Nell had heard since the beating, landed like drops of rain in a heat wave. Instead of frightening him, they quenched him with optimism. *A rabbit is only a rabbit because of other rabbits.* He was being kept alive for a purpose.

Eat, drink. Hope.

Passages above the keep were soon vibrating to the voices and paws of many rabbits. Nell sniffed Thaden before Levi's minder arrived.

'Move, varlet. Your time's up.'

Two clips in front and two behind, Nell was taken up to the surface. His heart pounded and his hind legs ached after being confined for so long, and when he limped above, his eyes screamed at the blinding of the starlight. A short blast of crisp, reviving air was swept away in the clamour of sweaty arrogance steaming from a squad of clips enclosing Nell in tight formation. They crossed grass flattened by the fresh prints of a multitude of rabbits, then he was hustled down another hole and dumped into another keep.

Through the walls swirled the boisterous rumble of many excited rabbits talking at once. Nell pressed one ear to the roof. He couldn't pick out individual voices. Thaden reappeared.

'Come, varlet.'

'Where to? What's going on?'

'You'll see.'

Nell was taken up another passage that ended in a ramp rising into a cavern. The hyperactive chatter he'd heard stopped immediately, overtaken by gasps. As he looked around the cavern, lit by starbeams flooding through dayholes between the rowan's surface roots, Nell realised the gasps were for his appearance. He licked at his chest and legs. The fur was a mess of dirt and dried mud and blood.

Two rapid stamps shattered the silence. Thu-thump. The Claw salute was quickly taken up by a host of paws. Black paws. Fearsome clips shuffled to form a line between Nell and the stamping rabbits. Rising on his hind legs to see over the clips' shoulders, he noticed the faces of the Patri and the doms of the southern warrens. Behind them were the doms from the North and other high-up rabbits Nell didn't recognise. To their left sat Fleet and two seers he'd met in the North. And up the very back, sitting proudly defiant, was Maisy. Small, frail, but smiling.

Their eyes met for an instant. Then a roar of *Quiet!* turned all heads in the cavern to a raised shelf framed by a gnarled arch of rowan roots.

45. In the cavern of the tyrant

NELL REALISED what was happening as soon as he saw the craggy buck pouting down from the shelf, which had been adorned in white mistletoe berries.

He'd heard of such gatherings being used in warrens on the North Bank to decide whether rabbits accused of serious rule-breaking were guilty or innocent. *Hearings*, they called them. The buck towering over the crowd was a judge – a supposedly fair rabbit whose task was to hear evidence and decide the fate of the accused.

Clever idea. Far too conniving for Levi. Behind and slightly to the side of the judge sat Vort. Beaming.

The cavern was enormous, and filled with more white rabbits than black.

Because the rowan was on high ground, exposed to wind, the horizontal roots, slope runners and sinkers spread over a vast area, and the exposed tap and heart roots reached deep into the soil to keep the tree anchored.

Nell was thinking it was a strange time for a hearing – Claw had carried out only one burrow collapse – when the judge shouted again for quiet.

The cavern hushed, as Levi mounted a coiled root.

'We are here to decide the fate of the varlet, Nell, who is the leader of the murderous Claw mob, which on purpose collapsed the nut storage burrow, ruining… lots of nuts, perfectly good nuts, disrupting trade, important trade to and from the North, and… caused lots of other…'

There was an awkward moment, as Levi appeared to forget where he was.

'… problems. And… yes, Nell sent a varlet worker to the field of silence when the burrow caved in.'

Howls of shock streamed from the white section of the cavern, overwhelming the *thu-thump thu-thump* stamping of the blacks. The judge waited for calm, then glowered at Levi.

'Is that all?'

'What? No. There's lots more.'

Levi leered at Nell.

'As the leader, the dreamer-upper of Claw, the varlet Nell also planned multinous acts of chaos, a violent uprising, an invasion from over the Torrent, to overthrow… the rightful ruler of the South Bank.'

'Prove it, yer dosser.'

Nell recognised the brave voice of the dom of the Cocksfoot Warren. Cries of *Prove it, prove it, prove it* boomed out from the black ranks, soon drowned by louder shouts of outrage from the whites. The judge struggled to be heard, and only regained control when clips split off from the line behind Nell and growled at both the black and white sections.

Interesting, thought Nell. He looked at Maisy, still defiant. When the cavern calmed, the judge again gazed down at Levi.

'These allegations by the prime rabbit are serious. Does he have proof?'

Levi looked distracted, raising Nell's hopes. The judge frowned.

'Is that all?'

Levi stomped over to stand in Nell's face.

'No. Far, far from it. Let's hear from the varlet, Merce.'

This time the loudest shouts and groans came from the black ranks, as Joseph's heavily scarred cousin was nudged forward. Nell caught a whiff of Merce's scent, but could not catch his eye. Levi was smirking.

'Tell the judge what you told me, varlet.'

The crowd hushed, as Merce began in his delicate voice.

'I wahs aht a meeteeng aht ze Brahmbleleaf burrows, een ze 'oles of ze rahbeet Jahseph. Nell wahs zere ahlso, pretendeeng to be Jahseph's guard.'

'And what happened at this *meeting*?'

'Nell ahnd Jahseph tahlked ahbout ze four stahges of zeir revhalution.'

'And they were?'

'First zey would create chaos by cahllahpseeng burrows. Stahge two wahs to fahrm teams of ahttahckers fahr heet-ahnd-hightail ahssaults on white burrows. Next zey plahnned to tahrget vulnerahble rahbbeets ahnd ahttahck zem to… unsettle ze enemy.'

Levi bared his teeth.

'You mentioned four stages to the Claw plan, varlet. What was number four?'

'Ahll-out ahttahck, useeng ze overwhelmeeng numbair of blahck rahbbeets to chase ze whites eento ze Tahrrent.'

Shrieks from the white section were answered with a thundering of *thu-thump* stamps. The judge waited for the noise to subside.

'Thank you Merce for your… honesty,' he said.

'Zat ees naht ahll, seer. I wahs ahlso present aht othair meeteengs aht Jahseph's burrow, where mahre sings were plahnned.'

'Go on.'

'I wahs zere when a request – ahn ordair – cahme frahm Nell's friend, Ollie, who ees Clahw's orgahneesair on ze Nahrth Bahnk. She ahsked – demahnded – Clahw recruits be sent to Cahcksfoot Wahrren fahr traineeng een fighteeng ahnd… othair meeschief.'

'We are here to decide the fate of Nell, not Ollie,' said the judge. 'Was Nell at this other meeting you speak of?'

'No seer. Nell wahs een ze Nahrth, traineeng ahnd plahnneeng mahre ahcts of chaos.'

Roars of indignation erupted from the whites. Merce wasn't finished, and Nell could see that his words, spoken in the buck's delicate tumbling-together fashion, were convincing. He mentioned another meeting at Brambleleaf a few nights ago, involving Joseph and high-ups of Claw.

'Zey deescussed plahns fahr a violent upreeseeng ahgainst white rule. Wahrrior rahbbeets frahm wahrrens on ze Nahrth Bahnk were to eenfeeltrahte ze South to ahttack chahsen tahrgets. Clahw orgahnisers were to recruit rahbbeets to fight ahlahngside ze Nahrtherners. *Shahmelessly ahttack ze weak* wahs mentioned mahre zan wance. Ahs zese ahcts of chaos were hahppeneeng, zere would ahlso be mahssed ahction – violent ahnd nahn-violent – ahll ovair ze South Bahnk.'

'And what were they hoping to achieve?

Merce looked up at the judge.

'*Operahtion Tahke Bahck Cahntrol* wahs whaht zey nahmed eet. Zee clear eentention wahs to create chaos ahnd cahnfusion ahmahng ze white wahrrens ahnd give cahnfidence to ze blahcks zat Clahw wahs cahpable of leadeeng zem to veectahry. Smahll teams of bucks were to strike outlying tahrgets such ahs Ecleepo burrows near ze Point ahnd elsewhere, ahhead of ze main ahttahcks, to divert Ecleepo officers ahway frahm ze prime rahbbeet's burrow. One of ze bucks aht ze meeteeng hahd been eenstructed to identeefy plahces where ze Nahrthern rahbbeets could entair ze South. Ahnahthair wahs given ze tahsk of wahtcheeng ze Ecleepo, where zey went, where zey burrowed, zeir pahtrahl pahtterns, to wahrk out zeir strengths ahnd weaknesses.'

The cavern was shocked into silence.

As was Nell.

Almost all of this was news to him, and must have been hatched while he was in the North. Most of it was unrealistic, fanciful. He also knew, though, there were enough strands through Merce's web of words to link him to the plan.

*****

LEVI JUMPED onto the root as soon as Merce finished.

He peered triumphantly around the cavern, grinning at all the pathetic varlets whimpering in the shadows, then chinned and looked up at the judge.

'The treachery and dishonesty of the varlet Nell is unbelievable. This is a clear case not only of murder, but of calculated terror. And the penalty for that shall be the field of silence.'

*****

THE REACTION was thunderous. Nell's eyes never left the judge. From what he'd heard about similar hearings in the North, it was the judge – not Levi nor the noisy crowd – who would decide his fate.

The judge appeared uncomfortable and would not look at him. Nell followed the line of the judge's eyes to where Fleet and the other seers from the North Bank were shaking their heads.

In a way that had never occurred to Nell until that moment, with the roars of *field of silence* competing against the vibrating *thu-thump thu-thump thu-thumps*, he saw the part he could play in this ridiculous sham. As a symbol of rightness in the cavern of the tyrant, a lightning bolt for the simple ideas of freedom and fairness in a place that abused those most basic of rabbit rights.

Rather than try to defend himself, Nell would tip the hearing upside down – directing a light onto the Cluster and Claw's opposition to rules based on the colour of fur – exposing Levi and Vort and the evil they stood for.

The judge finally restored order, and asked Nell if he had anything to say.

He limped to the coiled root and clambered up to face the cavern.

'I admit I was one of the rabbits who helped form Claw, and was chosen as its leader. My actions have always been driven by what I have witnessed and endured as a black rabbit on the South Bank – not by the words or wishes of any rabbit beyond the Torrent.

'I do not deny that I planned the collapse of the nut storage burrow. I was not guided by any passion for violence, but by careful consideration of the place black rabbits of the South Bank find themselves after moons of terror and Parting by Levi and Vort and rabbits like them.

'We have always opposed rules based on the colour of a rabbit's fur, and chose not to do anything that would widen the gap that already exists between white and black rabbits. Moons upon moons of peaceful protest, however, have resulted in ever harsher rules, and a continual shrinking of freedoms.'

Nell faced the judge.

'For some time, many black rabbits have been hungering for violence – dreaming of the time they would challenge the white rabbits and reclaim their fields. But we, the leaders of the Cluster, persuaded them to remain peaceful.'

'Lies, varlet lies,' shouted Levi. 'What about the training at Cocksfoot?'

'Let him finish,' said the judge. 'No more interruptions.'

Nell nodded his thanks.

'I admit I had training on the North Bank, because *if* there was to be an all-out fight, I wanted to be able to stand shoulder to shoulder with my friends and comrades. I did not believe, however, that we'd got to that stage. I believed we should keep searching for opportunities for chaos by attacking symbols of white rule, like the nut storage burrow, rather than individual rabbits.'

'You, judge, will never hear me utter the words *Chase the white rabbit into the Torrent*. What I stand for, what the Cluster stands for, what Claw is trying to achieve, is nothing more than the freedom of black rabbits in their own fields.

'White superiority, sir, can mean only black inferiority. Unpleasant tasks on the South Bank are left to rabbits with black fur. When anything has to be carried or cleaned, a burrow dug, carns distracted, nuts harvested, the white rabbit expects a black rabbit to do it for him or her. Black kittens wander the flats of Lexa hungry, unattended, and vulnerable to carns because both parents are harried to work – bucks harvesting nuts or juniper berries, does cleaning and digging burrows or nursing white kittens.

'When I was a young buck, I listened to the sages telling stories about the past-moons before white rabbits came to the South Bank. Back then, our ancestors were at peace, able to move about as they wished. The fields belonged to the whole warren. There were no forbidden lines. All were free and equal. We worked together against the common enemy: carns. It is that history my friends and I draw strength from.'

Nell looked around him, from the judge to the seers, to the fidgeting rows of plump white rabbits, the scarred, bone-and-fur bodies of the black rabbits, then up to the frail form of his mother. But it was his father he was thinking of.

'Each breath of black rabbits of the South Bank, sir, is a contest. A life and field of silence contest between either obeying rules based on colour, or listening to his or her conscience.

'Rules based on colour are not just, they are not natural, and they cannot be tolerated. Our consciences, sir, tell us we must not accept them, we must challenge them, do all we can to change them.

'I was forced, through the unnatural rules of Levi and Vort, to become an outcast. Not because of anything I had done, but because of what I believed – my conscience. And the colour of my fur. If any rabbit should be standing at this hearing answering the charge of violence, it is Levi. He and his father are the ones responsible for the violence – by using it to crush our peaceful requests for freedom.'

Nell noticed the cavern had become quiet. He directed his final words at the judge.

'I have always stood against white supremacy, just as I stand against black supremacy. I have dreamed of a free place where all rabbits live together in peace. It is a goal I hope to see reached in my lifetime. But if necessary, it is a goal for which I am prepared to pass into the field of silence.'

46. Welcome the worst

THE STARTLED, mouths-open reaction to Nell's dramatic final words lasted only heartbeats before the cavern ruptured into arguing and jostling and a babble of scents from anger and aggression to disbelief. And fear.

Fleet rotated his ears. The rabbits from Toria were howling for blood, black rabbits for justice. Both were soon overwhelmed by paws furiously pounding the Cluster salute. Eclipo officers moved swiftly to keep the sides apart. The judge appeared uncertain what to do. Vort limped the short distance to the shelf and muttered something to him. The judge nodded, then announced that he needed time to consider his decision.

'Take the captive to the keep.'

Nell was led away, and the judge disappeared through an opening behind the shelf, his hind leg dislodging some of the mistle berries. Officers herded rabbits out of the cavern, pushing the reluctant ones and breaking up scuffles. Soon Fleet was the only one left. Or so he believed. He heard a scraping of paws, and spotted Maisy. He felt jammed in by her stare, as if *he* was the rabbit being accused.

The frail doe padded down to the floor of the cavern. Fleet, the experienced seer who prided himself on his mastery of language and ability to explain things simply, could think of not a single word to say to the mother of a rabbit facing the field of silence. Maisy though, when she came close enough for Fleet to see the lines on her face, radiated tranquility. Dignity.

'I feel… terrible… Maisy. How can you be so calm when Nell… practically asked for…?'

His words trailed off.

'I am content, Fleet, because my son is following his conscience, doing what he believes, knows is right.'

The seer looked into Maisy's eyes, recalling that occasion long ago when he saw his reflection in the rindle after hiding in a clump of campions and doing nothing to stop the fight between Vort and Henry.

That single, needless act of violence, like dropping a pebble into water, had rippled and surged and overwhelmed all the way to this cavern, this abyss, this insanity. The image Fleet had seen reflecting at him that day from the rindle was the face of shame.

He also remembered one of the last things Henry had said.

It's time to face a truth I've been avoiding for too long.

*****

NELL WAS LED down the passage to the keep, and made to stand. When he complained that he was exhausted and needed to rest, the guard laughed.

'Rest should be the last thing on your mind right now, varlet. You're going to sleep for a long, long time.'

Nell shut out the cocky bluster and coarse smells of the clips clogging the passage, and thought of the words of his father:

'There are moments when a dom must listen to the voice inside his head and hop out in front of the warren. Lead it to a different, hopefully better place, even if it means he can't take the journey with them.'

Nell now understood the meaning of those words, uttered when his father knew he was about to go to the field of silence.

His passing had inspired Nell to take the journey that brought him to this place, this moment.

Henry also talked of *welcoming the worst, because any outcome would then be satisfying.*

Nell took a deep breath.

He too was prepared for the worst, realising that his passing could become a rallying cry for black rabbits to continue the fight for freedom. That a legacy can find its power in the silence left behind.

*****

FLEET CLIMBED up to the shelf, sending a few more mistle berries rolling to the floor of the cavern. He found a guard sitting outside the entrance to a burrow, and said he had an urgent message for the judge. He was allowed in.

Alone and chewing an acorn, the judge appeared smaller, brittle, an ordinary rabbit compared to the all-powerful image he'd projected from the shelf. Fleet, realising he was crossing a forbidden line for a seer who was supposed to report the facts rather than give his opinion, explained to the judge how rabbits on the North Bank and further afield would react if Nell was sent to the field of silence.

'All the warrens of the North Bank, sir, and those to the east and west, have eyes and ears on this hearing. The flow of nuts from the Oakwood – like that acorn you're enjoying – will be reduced to a trickle, and soon dry up completely. Sure, Levi and Vort might manage to smuggle a few nuts from the North for a moon or two, but the supply to the prime's circle and to privileged rabbits like you, will stop.

'That, however, will be the least of *your* worries. As the judge who decides Nell should pass into the field of silence, *you* will be the rabbit held responsible. Not Levi, not Vort. You, judge, are being set up to take the blame for what reasonable rabbits everywhere will consider a gross injustice.'

The judge had stopped chewing. He didn't reply, but the seer sensed he was at least considering the words. As he left, he smelt Vort approaching down another passage. Fleet ducked around a corner and waited long enough to hear snatches of the conversation.

'... *power of the words... riot... Oakwooders... distance decision from words...*' And finally, as Fleet had to leave or be caught listening, '*too good for it*'.

47. Wooden skeletons beckoning the damned

THERE WERE FEWER black rabbits in the cavern when Nell was pushed back in, and twice as many clips. The judge appeared, with Vort behind him. Ominously. The judge's eyes were fixed on the ledge where the seers sat. His shoulders were slouched, and he was twitching nervously, which Nell took to mean the decision was the field of silence. The judge hopped forward.

'The purpose of this gathering is to decide two things. First, did the rabbit Nell do the things the prime rabbit accuses him of? And second, if he did, what punishment does he deserve?

'On the first matter, there is little doubt. Nell has admitted he created Claw, was its leader, and planned the collapse of the nut storage burrow. The evidence of Merce, who struck me as an honest and reliable rabbit, was equally damning. It is also obvious that Claw – with Nell as its leader – was planning a violent uprising against the rulers of the South Bank.'

Calls of *field of silence, field of silence* radiated from the white section of the cavern. Levi started circling. The judge demanded quiet.

'Nell talked of injustices experienced by black rabbits on the South Bank, saying that what he did was inspired by no reason other than to lessen or remove those so-called injustices. I have my doubts that Nell's intentions were as pure as he claims. Bucks who plan uprisings usually take over the warrens of the dom or prime, becoming rulers themselves.'

The judge chinned the rowan root, then looked down.

'The prime rabbit has described what Nell has done as *calculated terror*. I am inclined to agree. As to the other matter on which I must decide, the punishment. The prime has asked for Nell… to be sent to the field of silence, which would be the normal punishment for what he has done.'

Levi circled, saliva dripping from his teeth. Nell followed the judge's eyes, past the seers to the section where representatives of Thatch were sitting.

'I, however, am a fair rabbit. I have decided to spare Nell's life. His punishment shall be to spend the rest of his moons… on the island.'

*****

FLEET HAD KEPT WATCHING Levi, who was seething. Froth oozed from his puckered lips. There was no doubt the idea of the island had been Vort's, and the snatches of words Fleet heard from the judge's chamber now made sense. They had been worried that the power of Nell's words, the effect they'd had on the black rabbits in the cavern, could have caused a riot if the judge let Levi take Nell immediately to the field of silence. Which was what was meant by *distancing the decision from the words*.

Delaying the announcement of the punishment eased some of the tension and gave the eclipo time to regain control in the cavern. Vort was also smart enough to realise that ending Nell's life would inspire a whole new generation of rabbits to join the struggle. The field of silence, they must have concluded, would be *too good for him*.

As Nell was dragged away, to cries of *shame, shame* and *thu-thump* stamps, Fleet felt a great weight had been lifted from his shoulders.

*****

NELL WAS KEPT BELOW, deep beneath the rowan, for days. He was heartened by the earthy scents of black rabbits seeping through from other pads, and the occasional *thu-thump* stamp. On the fifth day, before most rabbits went above for the late afternoon feed, a squad of clips arrived to take him away. He was hurried out of Toria and down towards the Torrent. The sky hung low and heavy, though a strip of daystar lit up the skerry. A white swan took to the air, the shadow of its effortless flight crossing the rabbits as they skirted the bank.

Nell's escort of clips slowed to cross the log to the diamond one-by-one, then surrounded him again as they swept past the mass of juniper bushes and through a tunnel near the end of the thicket. A well-trodden trail flanked the Torrent between towering reeds and sedge and the jutting limbs of alders and spindles. Nell guessed that the legions of paw-prints belonged to carrier bucks transporting berries and nuts to and from the Oakwood.

He saw no other rabbits, white or black, though the route was bustling with life. Squirrels spiralling down tree trunks, tail-jerking moorhens, fuzzy-eared water voles marking outside burrows. As dayfall gathered, woodmice hung upside down from branches and a little owl hovered brazenly over them. A pink-faced bat – normally hibernating so late in the privet moon – was foraging for flies.

They entered a grove of soaring aspen trees. Black knots on smooth grey-white trunks looked down like disapproving eyes, branches creaked and grumbled, and spoiled leaves clinging lonely to the memories of summer sparkled golden in the dimming daystar.

The rabbits came to a fork. The main trail continued in the direction of the swinging bridge, but Nell was herded onto a less-pawed path that soon mounted a steep bank. He scampered up, slipping as his throbbing left hind leg lost grip in the soft soil. From the top, he got his first view of the place where he would spend the rest of his moons, and the question of how he would get onto the island was answered.

The trunk of a once-mighty aspen lay across the chasm, and the slope he'd climbed must have been formed moons earlier after the tree toppled. The far end of the trunk had landed between two black poplar trees, wedging it in place. Three rats darted from the wood and squabbled over.

Sheer cliffs of brown sandstone jutted up on both sides of the divide, cloven by the swift-flowing Torrent that frothed and bickered over rocks piercing the surface like the teeth of some unworldly carn. A line of black poplars ranged along the top of the far cliff, wooden skeletons beckoning the damned. Nell shivered. Two rough white bucks appeared at the other end of the span. The leader of the clip escort nudged Nell forward.

'Over you go varlet. Shake that smart black backside.'

Nell concentrated on a raised knob near the middle of the span. He stopped beside it and looked down. The outline of a monstrous eel moved below the surface, between bristling rapids of white foam. He thought of the past-moon stories of rabbits banished to the island, who threw away their lives trying to swim to freedom. Nell had almost drowned when he and Ollie jumped into the rindle – a far smaller body of water – after fleeing from Hilltop. The Torrent could be dismissed as an escape route. He looked at the South Bank for the last time, then hopped the rest of the way.

'Welcome to my island, varlet,' barked the larger of the two bucks.

'Here you will pass into the field of silence.'

48. Like shattering rainbows

NELL WAS HUSTLED through a bleak heath of spent grass and fox sedge, then down a wide rutted slope into a crater enclosed by near-vertical faces of limestone. A third of the way down, he got the answer to another question that had been bothering him since the final night of his training on the North Bank. The rasping squeals he'd heard came from a hideous tangle of rats trapped in a pit to the side of the ramp. Twenty or more of the rodents – it was impossible to tell the number from the writhing knot of turmoil – were bound together by their tails at the bottom. Free rats clinging to crags were watching the wretched creatures, getting warped satisfaction from their captivity.

As Nell's guards stopped at the rim of the pit, he saw a free rat slide down the wall and rush in to bite the exposed flank of one of the trapped animals. The blindsided victim screeched, setting off a rolling howl that bounced off the walls and splintered the binding dayfall.

The sulphury reek of limestone deepened as they got to the floor of the crater, and Nell was prodded along the side of a broad pond. The slithering outline of an eel pierced the surface, which was swarming with gnats. Spent leaves rained down from above like shattering rainbows.

At the western end of the crater, Nell was pushed into a cavity at the foot of the cliff. He could tell from the acidy smell of the limestone that the hole had been scraped out recently. There were two chambers to his keep. The outer was exposed to wind and rain and carns.

The inner, reached by squeezing through a neck, was smaller but offered at least a blade of shelter.

'No burrowing, digging, scraping, tunnelling or enlarging,' barked one of the guards.

'How about eating? I'm starving.'

'You'll eat when we tell you to eat, varlet. You'll breathe, speak, fart, crap when we tell you.'

'I…'

'And you'll refer to me, and all of your guards, as *sir*.'

Nell looked back at him silently, smiling. And went hungry.

*****

ANY RELIEF Ollie felt at the news that her friend's life had been spared came and went like the last browning leaf on an oak. One day clinging desperately to hope, the next lying sodden, trampled in the decaying undergrowth. Winter sunk its bitter claws into the Oakwood, shrouding the clearing in gloom.

Joseph had escaped to the North Bank, where he faced a life separated from his family and friends, after it became known that his burrow at Brambleleaf was used for planning the uprising. Ollie accepted the white rabbit's assurances that he had nothing to do with Merce's betrayal, that he had been as shocked as other rabbits. Joseph asked how he could help. Ollie suggested he go to Cocksfoot to organise the training of Claw fighters.

Adding insult to suffering was the realisation that Thatch's burrow was now firmly blocked to Ollie. Stewards and high-ups she'd spent moons sidling up to shunned her. Those who would talk said the prime rabbit of the Oakwood would never agree to meet the friend of a rabbit accused, found guilty, and punished for what Nell had supposedly planned.

*****

NELL HAD LITTLE TIME to think about his own predicament, let alone the plight of black rabbits in other places, during his first moon on the island. Conditions were so bleak, he used every droplet of energy staying alive.

He was the only black rabbit on the island. The guards let him move around parts of the crater – though only under the daystar.

Venturing outside his keep was perilous. A buzzard often roosted in one of the poplars overhanging the cliff, and stoats and weasels were enticed to the cavern by the ceaseless uproar from the rats.

Unless it rained, and moisture clutched to shallow basins and rock clefts, the pond was the only source of water. Its murky depths were also home to the eel, which Nell had seen snatch and devour three bank voles that lingered too long. He feared each precious sip could be his last.

There was little food to be had in the crater. The guards brought wilting leaves and limp, tasteless grass Nell wouldn't have given a second lick on the flats of Lexa. He was losing weight, at a time a rabbit should be piling on fat to survive the coming winter.

He watched enviously as snails sealed their shells with mucus to prepare for hibernation in crevices in the limestone walls.

Worse than the hunger, confinement, and loneliness was the constant harassment from of the guards who, like the free rats in the cavern, got their laughs from tormenting their captive. The crassest of them rained streams of urine down from the cliff, laughing when Nell wasn't quick enough to dodge the spray. Their behavior added another layer to the despair overwhelming the crater like an oppressive white murk.

Then, at the thinning of the sleeping moon, a white peril of another kind arrived. The harshest storm in Nell's memory smothered the crater in an impassable barrier of snow, silencing even the rats. For the three days it took a pair of reluctant guards to reach Nell's keep, he survived by eating his own pellets.

*****

LEVI YAWNED and rolled over in the soft grass. The mouth-watering aroma of wood ear meant the varlet servants had delivered his favourite mushrooms, as ordered.

He stood, belched, then passed pellets. Another varlet would come to clean them up. He ambled through to his eating chamber.

There were two frozen masses of the crinkly mushrooms between piles of acorns and hazels. He nosed at the fungi, savouring the grassy fragrance, then devoured them.

49. From rapture to blind panic

MOST OF NELL'S GUARDS made it clear they would have lost not one wink of sleep if he'd passed into the field of silence during the snowstorm. Lots of varlets, they said, had perished throughout the South Bank. One more on the island wouldn't have been noticed.

Even easier to explain would have been an attack by a carn. As the snow flurries retreated and Nell was able to move around parts of the crater, he saw the large, webbed tracks and tail signs of otters, and the five splayed toes of weasels and stoats. Most alarming, though, were the tracks of a fox. The brightening skies also brought the rats hollering to life, a sound Nell found reassuring after his isolation, like the humming of bees after a summer downpour.

The next day, he was kept away from the eastern end of the crater, where he could see guards heckling black does to dig holes in the bank behind the pond. Nell was intrigued, but the guard who brought his meal refused to answer questions. The following morning, guards crouched outside his keep, preventing him from getting his daily exercise. He started to protest, then saw three black bucks being marched down the ramp. One he recognised as Walter, who was among the first rabbits he recruited to Claw. Nell tried to call out, and was kicked.

'Shut it, varlet. No talking to other captives. Not one word.'

The three bucks were goaded into the new holes. Nell was… elated. He knew he shouldn't be happy to see other freedom fighters brought to the island, but had missed good company for so long, he couldn't help himself.

He was kept away from the new captives, who were soon joined by others. Although he could see them mingling in the distance, make out individual scents when the breeze carried them from the east, he was blocked from communicating with them by burly guards who shadowed him wherever he went. After days of this torment, the new captives were escorted to the northern side of the crater and ordered to pick up stones from a pile of limestone scree below the cliff, and carry them to another pile near the pond. When Nell complained, he was pushed over to join the others in their senseless work.

'And if we hear you utter a single word to another varlet, it will be your last.'

Guards were assigned to stay among the captives to ensure no-one spoke. Nell's mouth and shoulders hurt at the end of shifts, but at least the work helped him keep warm. Towards the end of the owl moon, the black rabbits had shifted all the stones to the pile by the pond, and started a new pile further along the cliff near the mouth of a cave – the one place in the crater off-limits to captives. Guards were often seen entering or coming out of the cave, adding to its mystique. One day, Nell got close enough to the entrance to see hibernating bats lying on their sides in crevices in the rock.

The owl moon gave way to the snow moon, though none of the tiny white snowdrops that gave it its name graced the crater. Nor were there changes to the captives' routines or the rule forbidding talking. Male adders, pale grey with black zigzag markings, appeared sluggishly from their winter hideaways to bask in the weak daystar, and inquisitive rats scampered freely among the captives, grooming, chattering. With few leaves in the Chilling Wood to muffle sound, nights in the crater were interrupted constantly by the mating barks and screams of foxes.

Early one morning, Nell woke to a sky covered in a layer of pale white cloud so thin, the daystar remained visible, ringed by a halo. Snow was coming. He ate only half what he was given after work, saving the rest. By dayspring, the crater was powdered in drifts up to his shoulders. The captives were still expected to work, and by late afternoon when they were dismissed, Nell was starving, and his paws so numb he could hardly feel them. Fox prints, and a hint of musk from the carn hiding in wait behind a large rock not far from his keep, added to his misery.

'Guess I'll have to sleep somewhere else tonight,' he said to the guard escorting him.

'Not a chance, varlet. You'll have to use some of that Black Robert disappearing bollocks.'

Nell sniffed towards the rock, calculating the distance between it and the keep. He could see the white tip of the fox's tail twitching in anticipation.

He dashed for the entrance, aware of the carn rearing on its hind legs, bending its knees, then a surge of red-brown as it pounced. Nell adjusted his line slightly, feeling the claws skim his flank. Then he was through the opening and squeezing into his inner chamber.

His front paws were raw from scraping limestone, so he'd decided front-first was his best hope. He heard the fox wheeze, smelt it creeping towards him, and girded himself for the attack. When it came, Nell kicked hard, hitting something soft and wet. The nose perhaps. The fox hissed.

He heard the guard urge the carn to try again, not that it needed encouragement. He sensed the animal closing, felt the stabbing bite on his rump. He kicked out more violently this time, striking bone. The skull. The fox howled, and backed off.

Nell waited, tensed, for the next charge.

It never came.

When the last whiff of musk faded, he reversed out. The carn was lying in front of the rock, shivering, and scratching vigorously. Patches of fur hung like catkins on a scrawny body crusted with cracked skin and weeping scabs. Nell had heard of the condition. Mange, it was called. Parasites burrowed into the skin, making the fur fall out, sucking the strength and life from an animal half-insane from never-ending itching.

Nell could see that the fox was barely alive. The guard grunted and left. Nell, exhausted, could only shake his head.

*****

'LOOK MAISY, a peacock. This early in the moon. Surely it's a sign.'

'A sign of what, dear?'

'Luck, of course. Surely you've heard the saying, *Peacock on the wing, bumper spring*.'

'It's a butterfly. How can a butterfly possibly tell us what the weather's going to be in two moons? Or how plants will grow?'

Maisy and her widow friend had met for their regular catch-up, this time concealed in a jumble of pink vanilla-scented heliotropes hugging the bank of the rindle. The peacock butterfly, probably on its first outing after slumbering through winter, was sucking nectar from an early bluebell.

'That's another sign, surely Maisy. A bluebell in the peacock. That must be as rare as a snowdrop in the privet moon.'

'Depends on where you live, my dear. I saw snowdrops sprouting on the Golden Field in the last privet when I was there for Nell's… hearing. You wouldn't believe what grows up there. A doe who works for a family in Toria insisted she'd seen dead nettles showing as early as the blue moon, and corn marigolds as late as the sleeping.'

Her friend grimaced.

'The white rabbits are welcome to it, I say. Our stomachs couldn't handle most of the plants they eat.'

'Whatever do you mean?'

'Come now, Maisy, everyone knows the stomach of the black rabbit is simpler than the white, our brains less… complicated. I often think it would be sad if we were free to graze in places like the Golden Field. We'd get horribly sick on all that tim grass and… make fools of ourselves.'

'What nonsense, dear. Your stomach behaves the same way as a white doe's. It has nothing to do with the colour of…'

Maisy stuped. She'd picked up an unwelcome smell. Chestnut. It could mean only one thing. A rabbit from the Golden Field. The ground shook and the leaves of the heliotrope parted, as a clip blundered through.

'What mischief are you varlets up to in there?'

Maisy smiled at the clip.

'Just talking, officer.'

'You varlets never *just talk*. You lie and steal and stink and… plot.'

He hopped towards Maisy, twitching his nose.

'You're the mother of the varlet, Nell, aren't you?'

'Indeed, I am, officer. How can I help you this morning?'

'Shut your face, varlet. You're breaking the new rule, both of you.'

'What rule is that, officer?'

'Loitering.'

'What does that mean?'

'Being idle. Wasting time. Plotting. Doing anything other than working.'

'Oh dear, we're terribly sorry, officer. We weren't aware of that rule.'

'Ignorance is no excuse. I catch you varlets doing it again, you'll be for it. Now piss off.'

Maisy led her friend out of the heliotropes and up the bank. The peacock butterfly hovered, landing on the slender leaf of a willow and closing its wings so only the dark side showed, mimicking the leaf. Suddenly the insect rubbed its wings together, making a faint wheezing sound, and the colourful spots at the tips beamed like blinking eyes. In a blaze of yellow and blue, a tit swooped, plucking the peacock in its beak without missing a beat.

*****

THE STONE-SHIFTING routine on the island was interrupted briefly one day when a pair of stock doves appeared over the crater, wheeling and gliding and *coo-whooping* in a mating display. Nell was delighted when the birds chose for their nest a cranny over the place the rabbits worked.

He knew why he and his comrades had been sent to the island, made to sleep during the night and toil unnaturally under the daystar, and not talk to each other. It was to shatter their spirit and stamp out hope of rebellion. There had been times, particularly during his first moons on the island when he was the lone captive, that Nell almost gave up. On his own, resistance had been almost impossible. *A rabbit is only a rabbit because of other rabbits.*

Letting other captives on the island, whether Nell could talk to them or not, changed everything. The rabbits guzzled strength from being together, sharing heartbreaks and defeats as well as the occasional small victory. A surprising number of messages could be passed on – and burdens unloaded – in the twitch of a nose, toss of a head. Eventually the guards, bored and worn down by the hassle of watching them all day, relaxed the rules on talking. And Nell was allowed into a more comfortable hole beside the other captives. He finally got to hear what was happening on the South Bank, including the outraged reaction among the black warrens to his hearing and banishment. As more captives arrived bringing news from outside, Nell learnt that although he'd been flung to the shadows, he had not been forgotten.

There were no sweet violet splashes of bluebells to mark the arrival of the blue moon in the crater, but the warming temperatures, lengthening days and antics of the stock doves sharing incubation of their eggs tantalised the black rabbits with the optimistic evidence of spring. They were let off work early one afternoon, and as they tucked into the plants laid outside their keeps, noticed a new white face beside the guards. He was a Mistle sage.

'We have brought him here to educate you darkies on… manners.'

Good luck, thought Nell, as he chewed on a shriveled sorrel leaf. The warden was undeterred.

'The sage has kindly agreed to come to the island every other day, after your meal. You varlets have the choice. Go immediately to your keeps, or stay outside to… be educated.'

The *talks* were, like the sage's opinions on the place of black and white rabbits, so one-sided that most of the captives refused to listen and went to their keeps in protest. But as the days got longer and the wind lost its sting, the chance to bask in the warmth of the stubborn daystar after a hard shift on the stone piles became too tempting. And though the black rabbits could *hear* the supremacist sage, the guards couldn't force them to *listen*. Most tried to shut out his voice by dozing, snoring, or concentrating on the sounds of the rats or birds or the wind stirring the leaves in the poplars up on the heath.

Nell, eager to find out why white rabbits thought the way they did, usually listened. The *talks* helped relieve the monotony of the crater, as the stock doves helped break the drudgery of the work routine. Nell couldn't help noticing the contrast in fortunes. As he moved stones pointlessly from one pile to another, the birds replaced or rearranged twigs to improve their nest. As he forced down the same wilted plants for days in a row, the doves took turns to look for food, returning with beaks full of a bewildering variety of leaves, seeds, buds, berries, fruit. And as Nell squinted at the white glint of the cliffs, the birds soared over the crater, showing off the black edges of their wings.

*****

OLLIE'S HEALTH had improved with the weather. Milder nights and days brought the tart aroma of unfurling oak leaves and the promise of warmth, but she missed the bouquet of honeysuckle in the hedgerow at Hilltop, the musk of windflowers by the rindle, even the dry tang of the junipers that used to wash over the flats of Lexa.

Each day away from the South Bank, and Nell, was harder to bear than the last, and there were times Ollie wished she'd been banished to the island as well.

The leaf moon, as the hedge moon was called in the North, also gifted an abundance of woodruff and weasel-snout in the shade of oaks.

Ollie was nibbling on tasty shoots one night when she got talking to an intriguing white buck who had been born at Toria.

He introduced himself as Hugh, and freely admitted to Ollie that, growing up, he'd believed all he was fed about the differences between rabbits of white and black fur.

To him, forbidden lines, black servant does and black nut harvesters were as natural as the moon and the stars.

When he became a carrier, and visited the Oakwood to deliver chestnuts and collect acorns, he assumed that the way whites and blacks mixed in the North was odd rather than normal.

Over time, he grew to hate the taste of acorn. Then on one of his trips north, he met a doe.

'I gave up my job as a carrier, rushed to the Oakwood, and my mate and I have had many happy moons and twelve adorable kittens together.'

Hugh also had his eyes opened. To the absurdity of the South's colour rules.

'And to the teachings of The Divine. I've become a diviner.'

'Seriously?'

Ollie had heard of diviners; bucks or does who believed the fields, the Earth, sky, moons, the daystar – all living creatures and plants – were created by one rabbit-like *thing*, The Divine. They were vague about whether The Divine was a real rabbit or something magical. That wasn't the point. Enough bucks and does believed in The Divine, and that he, she or it laid out certain directions rabbits should follow to have full lives. Hugh did not seem to Ollie a rabbit who would believe in such things. The buck screwed up his face.

'To be honest, my mate's the true believer. And wouldn't have shown interest in a buck who didn't share her beliefs.'

'But to become a diviner?'

Hugh smiled.

'It's a lot easier than carrying foul acorns all the way to Toria, believe me.'

*****

BREEZES FROM THE SOUTH carried smells from as far as the Chilling Wood to the island, and through the hedge moon were leavened by the spicy almond of the hawthorns and balsamic mumbling of poplar leaves. When the wind dropped, it was the sickly stench of early blooming henbane that slithered down from the heath to invade the rabbits' nostrils.

Until now, all the other captives had been members of Claw or the Cluster, banished to the island for daring to challenge the colour rules. As Levi's keeps began filling, black rabbits caught stealing or fighting amongst themselves, or not working hard enough, arrived in the crater. These rabbits – known to Nell and his comrades as bumbles, after the short-tongued bees that bite holes in the base of flowers to steal nectar – were kept separate from the other captives, and at nights were let out of the crater to graze on the heath.

The bumbles had to bring plants down for Nell and his comrades. Most kept the best for themselves. Some gave their tastiest discoveries, like the fresh leaves of cow parsley or corn mint, to the guards in exchange for special favours. One exception was a timid buck, who was always respectful to Nell and occasionally brought him stems of ramson.

The guards were deliberately lenient to the bumbles, particularly if Nell or the comrades were nearby, to remind them they were considered the lowest of the low. Claw and Cluster bucks had to drop their noses to the ground whenever a guard approached. If they didn't, they were punished – with harsher work duties, missed meals or confinement in their keeps, sometimes for days. The bumbles were given only light tasks and plenty of time off. The comrades were pestered to move stones from pile to pile from dayspring to dayfall. If they slackened, guards would yell at them to work harder.

Nell had to be constantly alert. A small number of guards considered him a special captive, realising how bad it would look if he passed into the field of silence. Most, though, hated him so much, they wouldn't have hesitated to lead a carn to him. They blamed Nell for having to be on the island in the first place, away from their mates, so he often went hungry and spent days alone in his keep.

One morning early in the elder moon, the comrades were marched up the ramp, out of the crater. Their reactions covered the entire rainbow of emotions from rapture to blind panic. No two rabbits felt the same. There were those so overjoyed to escape the cling of the crater, they wet themselves. Others, lulled into a stupor through the sameness of their routine, had to be dragged up the ramp by their ears.

Nell was more concerned about where they were being taken, and why.

From the top of the ramp, he got his first decent view of the rest of the island. To the east, the heath rose gently to a wall of briar. Behind that, he could see the tops of what appeared to be hazel trees. The entire eastern end of the island was enclosed in a craggy barrier of rock blocking the Torrent or the South and North Banks from sight. The thick foliage of the poplars obscured the log span he'd crossed to get to the island, and all but the tallest beeches and sycamores of the Chilling Wood.

A section of the Torrent was visible to the west, though soon disappeared round a point, and the willows on the far side shielded what he guessed was the field of the Cocksfoot and Drop Warrens. The distant dark green hues of the oakwood ruled the northern sky.

As the rabbits were taken up the sloping heath, Nell's senses were overwhelmed with memories. Of purple spikes of loosestrife, towering sprays of hogweed, the pungency of marsh marigolds, lifting him back to his early days, to the rindle, to Maisy. The captives were halted before the briar. Their new job was to clear a path, so hazelnuts from the far side could be collected by the bumbles. Nell looked at the solid wall of intertwined branches, arching canes and menacing thorns.

'How do you suggest we…?'

'I couldn't give a rat's pellet-hole, varlet. Find a way. Quick smart.'

Nell organised the rabbits into teams. One to use their teeth to attack the briar, one to watch for carns, and the remainder to rest. He joined the first team on the briar. The work was tougher than he expected, and his gums and forepaws were bleeding when he signaled the resting team to take over. By late afternoon, the rabbits had got less than a quarter of the way through the thicket. They weren't allowed food until they returned to the crater, and Nell was so sore and exhausted, he fell asleep, his meal untouched.

If letting the captives see and nose but not taste the plants on the heath was intended to further trample their morale, it failed. Despite the blistered gums, scratched shoulders and splintered paws, most of the bucks felt invigorated. Nell preferred being in a place where he could see trees and birds, sniff the blossom, instead of trapped in the crater.

The next day, they were woken early, taken to the briar and ordered to work past dayfall. It had been a long time since many of the rabbits had seen such an array of stars at once. As they were hurried down the ramp, past the mayhem of the rat pit, the bumbles were coming up after delivering the comrades' meals. Nell stopped to thank the timid buck, who looked away, ignoring him, which Nell found strange. He was last down the ramp, and when he reached his keep, the faces of his friends were already buried in the small piles of leaves and roots laid outside their holes.

Nell was so hungry, and distracted by the stars, he took a mouthful of leaves with purple-spotted stems and chewed eagerly, ignoring the unusual taste. He was about to swallow when he remembered the musty smell on the carcass of a shrew Maisy said must have swallowed hemlock. He spat out the leaves and stumbled into the keep.

His throat burned through the night and his heart raced, keeping him awake. By dayspring, he'd recovered enough to crawl to the pond for a drink. The poisoning attempt had failed.

50. Our patch of paradise

NELL HAD BEEN ON THE ISLAND more than eight moons, long enough for a white doe at Toria to mate, give birth and nurse a litter of kittens – three times. He had been free to think about this, because his teams had finally finished the path through the briar and, as a reward, the guards let them graze part of the heath. The unexpected offer made Nell cautious, though didn't stop him enjoying a knobby root of a figwort.

The warden was waiting outside the keeps when they got back, chatting to a plump white buck with a triple chin. He was introduced as Jones, a diviner.

Nell had always been suspicious of diviners – particularly white ones – who roamed the fields trying to convince rabbits that their interpretation of The Divine's directions was the one true path to an afterlife of bliss in The Divine's warren. But Nell knew that a number of rabbits were believers, including a few of the other captives, so he kept quiet. If belief in The Divine explained the meaning of life and helped a rabbit survive on the island or face the field of silence, so be it. Some diviners used their positions to push their views on subjects other than The Divine. Nell was hearing good things about a southern black diviner named Desmond.

Not surprisingly, Jones' interpretation of The Divine's directions matched the Mistle view of life. They believed that because The Divine had deliberately given some rabbits white fur and others black, they were different animals, and it was perfectly natural for them to live separately. Apart.

Most of the captives, seduced by new voices, listened politely at first, until Jones mentioned the need for compromise, and it became plain he thought black rabbits needed to do all the compromising. The warden, sensing he was about to lose his audience, came over.

'Thank you, thank you, Jones. Most enlightening. All rabbits need to keep open minds, if they want to improve themselves. And speaking of open minds, next time we'll hear from an Oaker.'

Nell doubted that an Oaker diviner would be much better, though at least they didn't believe separating rabbits of black and white fur was ordered by some divine being. The warden surprised them again, letting the captives move freely around the crater. Nell went over to the cliff to check on the stock doves. One of the juveniles had spent the last few days on the ground, after fluttering down from the nest. Nell was pleased to see the bird had made it up, which meant it must have figured out how to fly.

The daystar had almost dipped behind the clifftop to the west, when Nell got to his keep. As he lifted his face to catch the last golden flickers, he noticed the silhouettes of three rabbits, and heard a familiar voice.

*****

FLEET'S REQUESTS to visit the island to see how the captives were being treated had been ignored, until Thatch got involved. Vort had assured the Oakwood prime that the captives were being properly cared for. In the end, Thatch asked if her seers could see for themselves, to stop them pestering her.

Fleet had been accompanied by his fellow seer, Donald, and arrived on the island as Nell and his comrades were feeding freely on the heath. The two Oakwood rabbits were kept away from the captives, who the guards warned were too dangerous. As they watched from the safety of the poplars, Fleet and Donald could see that the captives had plenty of food and appeared to be in good spirits, chatting contentedly among themselves or nibbling on cleavers and hogweed, mugwort, sorrel.

They'd joked with their guards as they went down a sloping trail into a large basin, where they lay under the late afternoon daystar listening to a talk by a diviner.

'As you can see, we're taking care of the minds as well as the bodies of our varlets,' the warden said.

'Where is the captive, Nell?', Fleet asked. 'I haven't seen him.'

'That's it under the cliff.'

No wonder Fleet hadn't recognised him. Nell had lost a lot of weight.

'We'd like to talk to the captives, please,' said Donald.

The warden started to say *no*, then changed his mind.

'A word or two then. Careful not to over-excite them. You mustn't stir them up, give the varlets false hope. Wouldn't be fair now, would it?'

The warden stayed beside Fleet as he went down the ramp. Up close, the seer could see Nell's backbone was sticking out, his ribs caved in, his claws chipped and fur dull. He was smiling, which was something. Fleet had plenty he wanted to say. Most of it would not be possible with the warden standing at his shoulder. He'd have to choose his words carefully.

'You must be Nell. I don't believe we've met. I'm Fleet, a seer from the North Bank.'

'Pleased to meet you,' said Nell, playing along. 'What brings you to our patch of paradise?'

'The warden here was kind enough to invite us to look around.'

'You're a long way from the North Bank. Don't you have a doe at home who'll be missing you?'

'As any doe misses her favourite mate. She's lucky she's got plenty of other friends to support her. Meets two, three or more new ones every single night, though not necessarily the ones that could help her the most.'

'So tell me… I'm sorry, I've forgotten your…'

'Fleet.'

'Yes, Fleet. Tell me, how are things on the North Bank?'

'Depends how you see things, where you live, whether you're standing in the shade or the daystar. Rabbits at the Meadow, Cocksfoot and Drop Warrens, for instance, have always been the most welcoming of new ideas, I've found.'

'And the Oakwood?'

'The prime is the same as always. As they say, *we are what we eat*. And as long as Thatch has got her junipers, she's not about to change.'

The warden was finally getting suspicious. Fleet decided he better pass on his most important message before it was too late.

'I was praising your warden on inviting diviners here to talk. I trust you'll be taking notice of what they say in moons to rise.'

Nell's eyes narrowed in confusion.

'Some diviners are more interesting than others, of course,' Fleet continued. 'Take my mate, for instance. She only takes notice of one particular diviner, a buck who has somehow convinced her our best days are yet to come.'

The warden jumped between the two rabbits.

'That's enough.'

*****

SEEING FLEET lifted Nell's spirits up the ramp, over the Torrent, through the Chilling Wood, up to the sky and the moon and the stars. He couldn't sleep, as he tried to figure out the messages hidden in the seer's carefully chosen words.

Some were clearer than others. Ollie was getting support from growing numbers of rabbits in the North, though *not from the ones that could help her the most*, which would mean Thatch and her circle. Black rabbits *standing in the shade* were more supportive than whites, and Thatch wasn't prepared to do anything to risk the trade in junipers. Nell was still trying to unravel the final riddle, as wisps of daystar tickled the ridgeline at the far end of the crater.

It had also dawned on Nell why the guards had been unusually kind to the captives the previous day. So they'd be in good moods and appear content when the seers visited. It worked, and Nell didn't care. He skipped out of the keep in time to see the juvenile dove take off from the ledge, swoop over the pond, then fly, up, up and away.

51. Wandering in the badlands

LEVI WAS AT THE PEAK of his powers, undisputed prime of the South Bank, an intimidating rabbit whose mere scent kept bucks and does out of his way. He had four mates, who have given him many kittens. One from the most recent litter, a buck called Drekkel, was nosing dandelion docks close to the terrace, where Levi was relaxing.

Other rabbits were enjoying the late web moon warmth, nibbling at leaves and seed heads of tim grass or purple stems of mugwort. The breeze that had been fanning varlet wind up from the flats swung to the west, ruffling the leaves and bringing a flurry of new smells, including the scent of a doe. An attractive rabbit with bright red eyes was chewing the small round fruits of cleavers, beside a buck who was probably her mate.

Levi slunk off the terrace, rubbing his chin on stones and clumps of grass to make his intentions clear. The doe's mate moved forward, preparing to defend her, which got Levi more excited. He raised his tail and clawed at the ground. The buck retreated. Levi attacked anyway. Unbelievably, he hit nothing but air. Worse, the buck kicked back, striking Levi flush in the stomach. Thaden appeared from nowhere to flatten the buck with a savage blow. As he moved in to finish him off, the buck sprang to his paws and hightailed. Levi strutted up to the doe, who was crouching flat to the ground, shaking.

'Your insolent mate needs to be taught who is master around here.'

She answered with a rapid scrape of soil that tore into Levi's eyes, stinging him and shutting out the light. When he regained his vision, the doe had disappeared. Levi noticed Thaden staring at him. He was mortified.

'That bitch will suffer for this,' he croaked, then stormed back to the terrace.

*****

AN OAKER DIVINER was waiting outside the keeps when the captives finished work a few days after Fleet's visit. It was a pleasant enough evening, though there were signs of a change in the weather. Birds were flying lower, the chirping of the wood crickets was slowing, and midges swarmed over the pond. So, after their meal, most of the rabbits stayed outside to enjoy the dry warmth.

Nell was lying on his side, only half-listening to the diviner, who was rambling on about how rabbits should spend less time worrying about the field of silence and more time channeling the energy of their births. His ears pricked up when the white buck that said all rabbits were launched from birth into rising moons as curious, questioning animals. Then came the phrase Fleet had mentioned: 'When we accept that what lies ahead of us is more important than what went before, we realise *our best days are yet to come.*'

Nell opened one eye. The diviner was looking straight at him. The guards, sitting on a rock, were chatting amongst themselves, showing little interest.

'The Divine teaches us to live our lives not as mortal animals awaiting the field of silence, but as breathing, adventurous, curious rabbits empowered by our birth.'

Nell stretched closer. One of the guards noticed.

'Keep your distance, varlet.'

'I only want to hear better, sir. What the diviner is saying is… fascinating.'

The guard's eyes widened.

'That may be so, varlet, but rules are rules. That'll be enough for today, thanks Hugh. Perhaps you *will* be able to talk some sense into these varlets after all.'

The Oaker diviner didn't return for days, and when he did, the message in his talk was depressing. Hugh spoke of rabbits *wandering in the badlands, lacking direction,* whose courage was *melting away,* and how belief in The Divine would *deliver them from their distress.* Nell felt frustrated that he was powerless to do anything about it.

*****

MISTS LINGERING in the basins and gullies of the Oakwood beckoned the cooler moons, when Ollie's joints swelled and the aches grew with the stretching of the nights. Thatch's burrow remained firmly out of reach to a friend of a spreader of terror, more impassable than any forbidden line in the South.

Fleet and the other seer who visited the island had been outfoxed by the guards, who convinced them that Nell and his comrades were being treated like high-ups. Ollie knew from reports she was getting from the occasional captive released from the island that this was not true.

The latest report from Joseph – on Claw recruits making it to the North for training – added to the bleakness. The numbers had dwindled to a trickle, and most were in poor health.

*****

THE IVY MOON brought the first heavy frost of leaf-fall to the island. Adult crickets that had mated and laid eggs succumbed in their hundreds to the abrupt drop in temperature. The captives had spent the last few days shifting stones in the crater, so were thrilled when the guards marched them up the ramp and through the heath to the brambles. Their task was to collect the last of the season's blackberries – fruit too far inside the thicket for the guards and bumbles to reach without scratching themselves.

Nell was given the job of retrieving two plump berries waving tantalisingly out of reach at the end of a cane hovering over a swale where the guards were resting, talking amongst themselves. He quickly worked out that the best way to get to the berries was to chew through the thick canc. He squirmed on his stomach to the base, out of view of the guards. They must have forgotten he was nearby, because they were discussing a planned attack at the Hilltop yew. Levi was mentioned, and the timing of the attack was to be the night after the next sighting of the Square of Erfeti. There was also something about *an eye for an eye* and *varlets from the east.*

Nell felt terrible, as he and the other captives were taken down to the crater, hoping Hugh would be there so he could somehow get a message to the Patri, though he realised it was the Mistle diviner's turn.

Rain thrashed the island for days. Nell heard from a guard that part of the rats' cavern had flooded. Most of the animals survived by wedging themselves into the ends of tunnels. The Mistle diviner visited during a lull in the storm, but the rain soon resumed, overflowing the basins with acidy water. The foul weather was like two sides of a leaf. The clouds hanging like a coat of sodden fur over the crater would prevent Levi's plotters seeing the Square of Erfeti. The rain, though, was also stopping Hugh visiting the island.

As it got heavier, so did the tension. Nell drifted in and out of sleep, and was eventually woken by moonlight seeping into his outer chamber. He looked out. The entire skyline was twinkling. Work that day was galling, and Nell's eyes were wandering up the ramp from the moment the shadows began their stretch across the crater. Would Hugh come? And would there be time?

The answers were *yes*, and *maybe*. The diviner appeared as the captives were being dismissed. Nell gulped through the unappetising stems of hawkweed laid outside his keep, then hopped over to Hugh.

'I had a question from your last visit, sir?'

Without warning, a guard thumped him.

'You insolent varlet. You will speak only when we tell you to speak.'

Nell was so livid, he snapped, striking the guard. The outburst cost him five days' confinement in his keep, and any chance of getting word to the Patri.

52. Fathers separated from sons

THE RAIN had made little difference to Levi. His burrow was the driest on the South Bank, stocked with a never-ending supply of acorns, haws, blackberries, hazelnuts, chestnuts, junipers. The one snag was having to listen to the ramblings of a visiting doe from the North – Thatch's personal diviner – who became trapped by the storm. He pretended to tolerate the blow-hard, to the point of making some of his minders wonder if he was going crazy.

When the storm ended, Levi managed to delay the diviner's departure, insisting that she visit the burrow of a promising Mistle diviner and listen to one of his talks. The doe agreed reluctantly, and Levi arranged for a buck to escort her to the burrow. As soon as they'd gone, Levi beckoned Thaden.

'Is everything ready?'

'Everything. The first lot will wait until the northern diviner's inside, and the others will get into position outside the burrow to wait for her to come out.'

'And is *she* there?

'She will be. And don't worry, she doesn't suspect a thing.'

*****

FLEET HAD SPENT most of the last two moons on a special assignment for Thatch. A distant cousin of the prime had been meddling in the affairs of warrens to the far east of the Oakwood, and badgering Thatch to send rabbits to help him. Fleet's task was to see what was really going on. He discovered that Thatch's cousin, who was supporting one warren in a dispute with a neighbouring warren, had sent a lot of rabbits to the field of silence for a hopeless cause. Fleet's conclusion was that the same fate would await Oakwood rabbits if Thatch got sucked into the quarrel.

Eager to get back to check developments on the South Bank, the seer had rested out the storm in his home burrow, then set off after midnight. He crossed the stone-bridge whiles before dayspring, and came across Thatch's diviner, panting. It took the doe some time to calm down enough to explain what happened. The prime rabbit of the South Bank had invited her to attend a talk by a Mistle diviner.

'Thirteen does, all white, were listening obediently, when four brutish black rabbits burst in, rounded up the does and the diviner and chased them out. All except one.

'Were you hurt?'

'No. They didn't touch me, or the diviner. All they were interested in was that one doe. She had the most unusual eyes, Fleet. Bright red like a pair of rowan berries.'

'Then what happened?'

'It was horrible. They… I couldn't watch. All I could do was hope The Divine would show mercy to that poor doe.'

The diviner sobbed, and Fleet waited for her to continue.

'When the four bucks left, I went to see if I could help the doe, but she had… passed.'

'What did you do?'

'I was shaking… I'm still shaking. I had to get out, into fresh air. A patrol of southern eclipo officers was nearby when I came up. I was able to tell them what I'd witnessed. They took off immediately to the south in pursuit of the… violators.'

*****

BOUNDING IN A SIMILAR DIRECTION, alone and via a less noticeable route, was Levi. He cut through the Common to the hedgerow Vort had allowed to be infested by the Row Warren of the crossers. He was appalled to see that the filthy half-breeds had extended their holes further into the field. Levi could never understand why Vort was so soft on the mongrels, and cringed at the idea of white blood mixing with whatever gunk ran through the cruddy veins of varlets.

He kept to the shade until the corner of the field, found a hiding place under whiffy honeysuckle, and waited for the show. He would have liked to take part himself, but Thaden had talked him out of it. From his position, with the moon close to full, Levi could see the barren mound the varlets called Hilltop. Decrepit bucks jabbered in the shadow of the rotting yew, as scraggy does and their feeble kittens poked at roots and jumped at the wind. Your typical varlet flea-fest. Lazy, worthless – and unsuspecting.

Levi didn't have to wait long. Four eclipo officers, led by Thaden, broke through the briar at the top of the chute, and made directly for the yew. The varlet does scurried off in fear, dragging their nipple-suckers below. Their good-for-nothing bucks stuped. Thaden stomped up to the Patri, said a few words, then pushed it aside. He chose four of the varlet bucks and hounded them into the yew.

The first scream, muffled through the spent-wood of the tree, got Levi's heart pounding in anticipation. The second – and third and fourth and fifth and sixth and seventh and eighth and ninth until he stopped counting – echoed around the varlet hillock like lightning in the hopping moon. Cracking, splintering, cleansing.

*****

NELL JUMPED onto the log separating the island from the South Bank, and scanned. The sky was a riot of light. Even normally dim stars were pulsing. There was no sound, nor smell of danger. No guards, no carns. Half-way over, he stopped and looked over his shoulder. No-one was coming after him. He was free.

He dashed to the end. There was no-one to meet him. No black rabbits, no white rabbits, no creatures of any kind. The branches of the aspens on the edge of the Chilling Wood were bare. He went along the trail beside the Torrent and through the unguarded tunnel to the juniper diamond. Bushes that should have been laden with berries were barren, stripped of their needles, silent like the wind.

He crossed the log over the bourne to the flats in front of Lexa. The soil was scorched. Nothing grew. On and on he went, through the Narrows and the empty field up the slope from the Point to the hedgerow by the rindle. The tunnel was overgrown, the border post abandoned. He was able to wriggle through the labyrinth of hawthorn seedlings and make it to the foot of the chute. He climbed up, ducking through toothed coils of briar and dodging patches of thistle cluttering the tunnel.

And so Nell arrived at Hilltop, to find no sign rabbits had ever lived there. He went over to the yew. Where there had once been a cleft to the circle chamber, flaky brown bark twisted in the shape of a tightened mouth, as if the ancient tree was trying to speak.

Nell reeled, and bumped his head on rock. He was in his keep in the crater. It had been a nightmare, similar to ones he'd had on each of the agonising days and nights he'd been forced to stay there since striking the guard.

Prolonged confinement in such a small space muddled a rabbit's head. Parted from his comrades, his meals cut in half, and not let out of the keep even to pass pellets, Nell craved the pointless toil of shifting stones. The first days were the worst. His body had become accustomed to daily exercise and regular meals, and the sudden change was agonising. By the fifth day, the pain and yearning to stretch his legs had faded, as had the pain in his stomach. Black rabbits on the South Bank were used to going hungry.

It was the mental challenge that pushed Nell to the brink of madness, unsure how long the confinement would last, when or if he would be able to speak to his friends again.

The guards who brought his miserable rations of bark and twigs had been instructed not to talk to him. His mind needled him constantly, jeering, scorning. What was dream, what was real? What happened at Hilltop, or was what he overheard the guards discussing also part of a dream? Had he been right to follow his conscience? Was his sacrifice worth this torment? Confined in his keep, there was no distraction from the haunting questions.

When Nell was finally let out to join his comrades, he was still in the dark about what, if anything, had happened at Hilltop. So were the other captives. There had been no visitors to the island, no new captives had arrived with news from outside. Hugh, they were advised, had become ill during the rains, and might not return. The guards gave nothing away, although behaved more puffed-up, getting crude pleasure from piling on the abuse and put-downs. They singled out different captives at random and for no reason. All of which made Nell appreciate how much he missed news from off the island. Messages had become like the first warm rays of daystar in spring, the most cherished prize in the crater, more yearned-for than the tastiest plant.

The guards understood it as well, and refused to answer questions, to hint at anything that might lift the captives' spirits or give them a slither of belief that rabbits on the South Bank hadn't forgotten them.

The fattening ivy moon surrendered to the new privet, the daystar hightailed between rising and setting in an indecent rush to winter, but to Nell, time had been frozen.

Then one morning, the mood of the guards flipped. The captives were allowed to stop work, and let up the ramp to feed on the heath. They discovered forgotten delicacies like groundsel and heliotrope, gorged on the leaves and stalks, and when they got to the crater for the evening, they found piles of watercress outside their keeps. The guards joked with them, and when Nell asked where the long stems and delicious dark green leaves had come from, he got a straight answer.

'From the other side of the bat cave.'

'How do you get there?'

'Through the cave. There's a hole at the other end that opens onto a shelf. You can reach the cress floating on the surface. Behave yourselves, and maybe one day we'll let you through.'

The following morning, the same thing happened.

They were free to explore the heath, shown where to find mushrooms – chanterelles and puffballs and trompettes, and there was more watercress when they returned to the crater. Nell didn't hear the word *varlet* all day.

Something was wrong. Nothing happened at random on the island.

Everything had a purpose.

The next day was a repeat, and the captives were left to sleep longer than usual. Then the reason for the kindness came hopping carefully down the ramp. Old bucks – and a doe – from the North Bank had arrived for an inspection.

Unlike the last time, when the guards stayed so close to Fleet and the visiting seers that it was impossible to talk freely, Nell was told the visitors wanted to speak to him alone.

'Who are you and why are you here?' he asked as soon as the guards were far enough away. The leader, a self-important buck, smiled.

'We're known as the Red Haws, and we've come to see how you and your friends are being looked after.'

Nell was wary.

'Red Haws?'

'Our group was named after the scarlet fruit of the hawthorn, a symbol of hope. Our goal, our duty, Nell, is to protect the lives and dignity of victims of violence and disaster. The Red Haws have been around for moons.'

'Did Thatch send you?'

'No. The Red Haws don't take sides. If you must know, it was your friend Ollie who asked us to visit. More than once. She's rather persistent.'

Though Nell wasn't sure whether to trust these strange rabbits, he decided he had little to lose.

'So, what is it you want?'

'As I said, how are you and the other captives being looked after? We've heard stories, rumours if you like, good and bad, and wanted to see for ourselves.'

Nell left nothing out. From the meaningless work they were ordered to do, in the most horrendous weather and sometimes when carns were about and hunting, to the feeble amount and quality of food they were given, and the constant insults and punishments they had to endure.

'Don't be fooled by what you saw when you arrived. This is the first time in ages we've been able to relax and eat like this, and it was all provided for *your* benefit.'

The white rabbits listened politely, then asked Nell if he had questions.

'We've had no news from outside for moons.'

The Red Haws were surprised that Nell hadn't heard of the unprovoked attack by black rabbits on the burrow of a diviner in the Golden Field, and the murder of a white doe.

'Thatch's own diviner witnessed it. Her reliability is unquestioned.'

Everything became obvious to Nell.

'That would explain whatever happened at Hilltop.'

This time, the visitors were surprised. Nell told them what he'd overheard, and how he was unable to get a message to warn the Patri. The leader of the Red Haws was shocked. He told Nell how the prime rabbit of the South Bank sent eclipo officers to Hilltop to investigate the atrocity, how they found the four black bucks hiding in the sacred yew and sent them to the field of silence.

An eye for an eye, thought Nell. The doe sitting behind the leader of the Haws spoke for the first time.

'This explains why the descriptions of the bucks seen leaving the diviner's burrow differed from those found in the yew.'

'Those bucks were brought in from a warren to the east,' said Nell. 'It was all part of the plan I overheard. Levi's plan. The black bucks murdered in the yew… had nothing to do with it.'

His words hung in the air, as their meaning was digested. After a while, the leader thanked Nell for his time.

'We shall do what we can.'

*****

MAISY'S CIRCLE of widows had grown to seven – a sad outcome of the journey to the silent field of so many black bucks. It meant, however, that one of the does could be spared to watch for clips, as the others had their regular catch-up. Maisy's ability to find ways to conceal a rabbit's scent also helped, and allowed the widows to *loiter* in confidence. Tonight's disguise was her cleverest yet. Last moon's fox droppings dipped in water from the rindle to refresh the musky smell. Repulsive hunks of droppings with undigested feathers and fur and hawthorn berries were left at three places around them.

After complimenting Maisy on her shrewdness, the widows got down to the topic for the night's discussion: the attack on the white doe in the burrow of a diviner, and the retaliation at Hilltop. The rulers of Toria had ensured the news travelled swiftly.

'What those black bucks did was unforgivable,' said a rabbit of fifty moons who lost her mate and two kittens in the attack on the Point Warren. 'They deserved what they got.'

'The Hilltop yew is sacred,' said another. 'Taking the lives of rabbits in such a place was equally unforgiveable.'

'So was the burrow of the diviner.'

'They say the four black bucks sent to the field of silence were innocent, nowhere near the diviner's burrow when the doe was attacked,' said a widow whose mate never recovered after a beating for looking at a white doe.

'Who are *they*?' asked Maisy.

'I'm not sure exactly. I've heard it from more than one rabbit.'

'I heard the bucks who attacked the doe were from a warren way to the east,' said another.

'I've heard they talked a foreign tongue.'

'And I heard they dropped from the sky.'

The other widows giggled.

Maisy wasn't sure what to believe any more.

*****

CONDITIONS ON THE ISLAND improved soon after the visit by the Red Haws. The food got a little better – leaves and the occasional new shoots of marsh thistle instead of tasteless bark and twigs – and after every five days of stone-shifting in the crater, the captives were given a day off to graze on the heath. Although most of the guards remained single-minded brutes, others at least tried to be polite. One or two began treating them like rabbits. Other than the one outburst for which he was cruelly punished, Nell had always tried to be friendly to the guards. Not all of them were monsters, and bitterness got a captive nowhere.

341

The easing in tension helped Nell and his comrades endure the worst of winter and come through spring feeling at least a flicker of hope, if not optimism. New captives arrived with news from the outside – almost always bad – and Hugh came whenever he could to pass on coded messages from Ollie. The stock dove boar and hen reappeared on the cliff, carrying mouthfuls of leaves and twigs, delighting the captives with their jerking antics and endless *coo-whoops*. One afternoon, after a rare feed of plantain discovered by one of the comrades between two poplars on the south side of the heath, they found Hugh waiting for them in the crater. Nell could tell from his face that he had dramatic news.

The diviner talked in his usual riddles – *fathers separated from sons in their prime… resting in supreme peace in the burrow of The Divine*. Nell had become so good at figuring out Hugh's messages, he knew instantly that Vort had been sent to the field of silence. Remarkably, the guards didn't seem to know. They were chatting amongst themselves – small talk about quarrelsome mates and annoying kittens. Nell slipped over to Walter and a couple of the older captives who were basking on a knoll outside their keeps. He whispered the news.

'Best thing I've heard in moons,' said one.

'About time,' said another.

'What will it mean?' asked Walter.

Nell was thinking the same thing. Vort and his perverse belief that black rabbits were beneath rats had caused misery. No rabbit, however, deserved to pass for what he or she believed.

'Careful, comrades. Taking another rabbit's life is not the way to overcome an enemy. The day we welcome or tolerate sending another rabbit to the field of silence is the day we become no better than the Vorts and the Levis. This is no time to celebrate. Vort might no longer be our concern. We must prepare ourselves for the wrath of his son.'

53. A kernel of goodness

THE FURY came in the deepness of the night. Nell and the other captives were dragged from their keeps and into a semi-circle. Parts of the crater were smothered in patches of thick mist, and through the gloom, Nell made out the shapes of the warden and most of his assistants disappearing up the ramp.

The captives shuffled nervously, uncertain what to do. The rat cavern went berserk. Then Nell smelt the arrogant, overbearing fetor of Thaden, as Levi's chief bruiser bounded into the crater with a mob of the meanest rabbits Nell had seen. Thaden came right up to Nell's face.

'Listen up, you pathetic excuses for rabbits. I am your new warden, and I'm here to tell you your soft, lazy life is over. History. Get to work.'

'It's not dayspring yet. How will we…'

A brutal thump to Nell's ribs from one of Thaden's yes-rabbits winded him. The captives were harassed to the base of the limestone cliff. There was no let-up, through dayspring, through the rising heat of morning and the searing afternoon.

It was as if Nell and his comrades were being held personally responsible for Vort's passing. The stars were out when they were finally shoved, exhausted, bruised and starving, into their keeps. Nell's meal rations had been cut in half, and the withered leaves of figwort were snatched away before he finished.

The captives were woken earlier than usual the next day, and Thaden was back in Nell's face to announce that work duties were being extended further, the number of stones to be moved increased, and the varlets banned from talking. Every rule was enforced to the maximum. Captives were kicked for no reason, and abused continually by Thaden's foul assistants. The worst was a vile buck the captives nicknamed Four-eyes, because of two spots of silver fur on his forehead. All complaints were ignored, the answer to every request was *no*, meals were cancelled without explanation, and rabbits were often confined to their keeps.

Nell, singled out for the harshest treatment, could see what was happening. Levi had sent Thaden to the island to not only avenge Vort, but to reassert control, and he was making an example of the rabbit considered responsible for the breakdown in discipline. Remembering Aunt Mina's story about Dingha vowing never to give in to violence, or ever use violence himself to make a point, Nell kept calm, refusing to react. Until the day Thaden crossed a line.

It was late on a blistering afternoon, and the captives had been working since before dayspring without a break. Weakened by hunger, Nell slipped as he stretched to reach a stone near the top of a pile of spoil. He landed heavily, and took a while to catch his breath. In an instant, Thaden was towering over him.

'You must pull your paw out of your pellet-hole, you varlet son of a drifter.'

Nell spat a sliver of spit and fragments of lime dust into the white buck's face. Thaden's massive frame shuddered with rage. Nell clenched his muscles.

Agonising heartbeats passed. Nothing happened. When Nell opened his eyes, Thaden was sneering down at him. All the captives were lined up, including the bumbles and rabbits too ill to work, who were pulled from their keeps.

'Because of Nell's insolence,' hissed Thaden, 'every one of you varlets will lose all privileges.'

Nell got the beating he'd expected, from Four-eyes, and was sealed in his keep for ten days – twice as long as any rabbit had been confined. The isolation, deep bruising, ripped claws and festering cuts were less painful to Nell than the shame and guilt over the grief his actions loaded onto his comrades. The guards, sensing they were close to breaking the spirit of their most troublesome captive, started leaving henbane outside his keep. The large sickly leaves gave Nell rolling headaches, making sleep almost impossible. But instead of finishing him off, which Nell realised was the aim of his tormentors, it made him more determined to survive.

He lost count of the days and nights, and only learned that Thaden had extended his confinement to twelve days when he was finally released to join his comrades. The muscles in his legs were so wasted from inactivity, he could hardly move, and his eyes staggered under the glare of the daystar. Clouds brought little relief. He longed for the dark solitude of his keep.

The captives were heckled to work past dayfall, and when they were dismissed, Nell had to be helped to his keep, where he collapsed, exhausted. He had just dozed off, when he was woken by Four-eyes and dragged out into the crater. All along the cliff base, bleary captives were being yanked from their keeps. The odour of valerian thickened the air, and Nell could tell from the slurred voices that most of the guards were high as buzzards. Four-eyes' drunken rant that the varlets were hiding valerian was absurd. The captives could do nothing, though, other than shake their heads, as the guards searched the keeps, making a show of pissing and passing pellets in them.

Fuming that no valerian had been unearthed, Four-eyes took his frustration out on one of the captives, kicking him so hard in the stomach, the buck yelped in pain.

When Nell went to his comrade's aid, Four-eyes switched his attack on him, flailing violently with his claws. Nell refused to defend himself, taking blow after blow until he was numb. He closed his eyes, shutting out the vision of hate.

The beating went on and on, and from the recesses of his mind, Nell remembered the lacewing. The delicate pattern of green veins as the insect searched for aphids on the bulrush at the Platform Warren. The black and yellow buzzing alarm of the wasp, hunting. The lacewing falling to the ground, lying still. Silent. The wasp hovering, then losing interest and flying off. Fooled.

The beating had stopped. Nell looked up, expecting to see Fleet. But it was not the Oakwood seer. It was the leering face of Thaden, who hadn't lifted a paw to control his drunken guard.

*****

OLLIE HAD ARRANGED to meet Fleet in a dell by the trail through the oakwood to the Cocksfoot Field. The seer had spent the last few days scouring the South Bank for news, and had agreed to update Ollie before giving his report to Thatch and the prime's circle.

Anxiety gnawed as the agreed meeting time came and went. Whenever Ollie shifted her weight, leaves of the ransoms matting the dell released snuffs of stale garlic, making it difficult to tell whether other smells were friend, enemy or carn.

Twice she gave up and bolted. Back in the dell, embarrassed for being so spineless and selfish, she forced herself to lie still long enough for the ransom stench to fade, her heart to stop darting and, finally, for her good ear to detect the approach of the seer.

Fleet's report, the first since Vort's passing, pointed to a South Bank in mounting chaos.

Levi, mad rather than sad at his father's passing, had reacted with brutality and new rules aimed not only at further restricting the freedom of black and crosser rabbits, but dousing the faintest glimmers of resistance.

Country warrens like the Platform, Willow and Hilltop were being stripped of their strong bucks, rooted out to replace workers who had been banished to keeps, become too sick or weak to harvest nuts and junipers, or passed into the field of silence.

The loss of young bucks – future family leaders and natural defenders of the warrens – meant the does, kittens and old rabbits left behind were vulnerable to carns.

Levi's eclipo was becoming more savage. Black rabbits were put away in keeps for the most piddling reasons, and rumours of cruel forms of punishment were mushrooming, as were reports of rabbits falling from Levi's brink *as they tried to escape.*

Fleet said that some of the new rules were so spiteful, they'd be laughable if their intentions and impact weren't so serious.

'Black and crosser rabbits, for instance, are now banned from having certain ideas.'

'Like what?'

'Like believing all rabbits are born equal, that a black rabbit's brain is the same size as a white's. Oh, and it's now against the rules to *think*, let alone *say*, a rabbit is a rabbit because of other rabbits.'

'Only a buck with a brain the size of Levi's could dream up stuff like this. What do the other rabbits at Toria make of it?'

'From what I saw last night, there are plenty who believe all their prime rabbit tells them, and they're expecting things to get worse. I came across eclipo officers teaching a group of white does how to defend themselves against attacks by black rabbits.'

*****

NELL TOOK DAYS to get over the latest beating, and on the morning he'd recovered enough to leave his keep, Hugh showed up. The guards were either so stupid, over-confident or distracted with hate, they still didn't suspect the white buck of being anything other than a harmless diviner. When Hugh started talking about how belief in The Divine promised a rabbit hope and meaning rather than a comfortable life, they loped off to chat among themselves or climb up to the rat pit for their morbid fix of entertainment. Left alone near Hugh, Nell was able give the diviner a full account of what had happened to his comrades since Thaden had taken over as warden.

Within days, the captives were alarmed to see the judge from Nell's hearing – the buck who sent him to the island – tottering carefully down the ramp. The judge wanted to speak to Nell on his own. Nell could see that Thaden was suspicious. He was also aware of a rumour that the judge was a friend of a buck in Thatch's circle. Perhaps this was an opportunity to use Thaden's temper to his advantage.

'I'd be happy to talk to you, judge,' said Nell, 'though it might be wise if the warden stays too. For *your* safety.'

Thaden could hardly refuse. Nell calmly explained to the judge how life had changed on the island since Thaden had taken over.

The outrageous amount of time the captives had to work, unnaturally under the daystar, the slashing of rations, cancelling of meals, the ban on talking, the constant abuse, violent and unprovoked attacks, the long confinements, the henbane torment. With each new complaint, Nell sensed Thaden's patience burning up like dew under the daystar. When Nell started describing the valerian incident, Thaden could take no more.

'Be careful, varlet. Too much talk will get you in trouble.'

Nell, who noticed the judge wince, seized his chance.

'You can see the type of rabbit we have in charge here, judge. If this is how the warden acts when you're here, imagine what he does when you're not.'

The departing judge had hardly cleared the top of the ramp, before Thaden got his vengeance. Nell was tossed into his keep, after another savage beating from Four-eyes.

A few mornings later, Thaden himself arrived to let Nell out of confinement.

'The judge reported your complaints not only to Levi. He also threatened that unless something was done, he would also report them to the Oakwood. So, I'm being transferred off the island. I wanted to wish you and your friends all the best.'

Nell was so astounded, he could think of nothing to say in reply.

That day as he worked, he thought about Thaden's words. Although the buck had been one of the most brutal guards on the island, he had shown another face to his character, one that had been clouded behind a white coat of ignorance. Even a rabbit like Thaden had a kernel of goodness. It was not the rabbit that was brutal, Nell decided. The brutality had been forced on him by a brutal system.

*****

LEVI WAS BECOMING increasingly frustrated. Life had been tolerable in the first moons after Vort's passing. No more tedious meetings, no more brown-nosing to meddlers from the North. Levi had been free to range over the South Bank, reminding *his* rabbits who was in charge.

He had brought in long-overdue rules his father had blocked, and got rid of the insane ones. Crossers were now treated like the disgusting half-breed vermin they were, and special advantages they had over the black varlets were scrapped. Levi banished them forever from the Golden Field. The mere sniff of them made his blood foam. Gone too were the untrustworthy black eclipo officers Vort had convinced him to take on. White bucks had been recruited in their place. Most were unsuitable for the work, or unwilling to do what was required – the ungrateful sons of shrews.

Levi also had to deal with ridiculous rumours from over the Torrent, spread by interfering seers and creaky Red Haws making up fake stories about life in the South. His sources assured him that Thatch remained firm, though some of those around the Oakwood prime were becoming flaky.

Levi blamed Nell. He should have dealt with the troublesome varlet when he had the chance, rather than letting his father talk him out of it. The hearing had been Vort's idea. Levi went along with it at the time, but the punishment was plainly wrong and he had suffered for it ever since. Now Vort was out of the way, it was time to eliminate the varlet.

Even Levi accepted that he couldn't simply have Nell tossed into the field of silence. The conniving varlet had infected the heads of rabbits in high places. And low places. Soon after Vort passed, varlet-lovers from the Oakwood, claiming to be acting on Thatch's instructions, let it be known they'd entered the Chilling Wood and had eyes and ears on the log spanning the Torrent to ensure he – Levi – didn't go to the island. The bloody nerve. They might be bluffing. He couldn't be sure. Nor could he turf white rabbits out of the wood simply for watching. It might tip Thatch over the edge. He had to find a way for it to look like he had no choice to send Nell to the field of silence. The problem had given him headaches for the last few moons, and he still didn't have an answer.

He was stretched out on his terrace with Thaden, watching Drekkel playing. The young buck was helping three friends herd a fourth into an ambush.

'I see your son's inherited some of his grandfather's smarts. And he's getting some size to him.'

'He needs to toughen up though, get more ruthless.'

The unsuspecting buck hopped straight into the trap Drekkel had laid.

'Whether he's tough or not, Levi, what he's done gives me an idea. We could plant a guard on the island, one who could friendly-up to Nell and gain its confidence, then tell the varlet he's working with friends off the island who will help it escape. If the meddlers from the North see the varlet making a dash for freedom, they'll have to tell Thatch it was silenced trying to escape.'

Levi liked the idea.

'Nell's not stupid, though,' said Thaden. 'For this to work, the varlet will have to be convinced the escape plan is real. To soften it up, we'll need someone Nell will trust.'

54. Not a breath too soon

NELL PAUSED at the elm stump to savour the familiar territorial marking overpowering the sweetness of the flag iris and remnants of the mayflowers carried on the breeze from the rindle. Further up the hill, kittens were playing in the long grass. Black and white kittens. Together.

He reached the burrow and nosed at the entrance. Along the passages fluttered the scents of Maisy and his sisters, and the voices of Henry and the Patri. And Ollie.

Then he woke up.

*****

THOUGH MAISY hadn't seen Nell for a full cycle of moons, not one night went by without thinking about her son. After the hearing, she'd tried to get to the island. The clips ignored her. Despite the rebuff, when she noticed one of the officers limping, she'd quietly mentioned that roots of the mugwort plant would help the pain in his paw.

The only news she'd received about Nell had come from Fleet, after he'd been allowed onto the island. Although the seer assured her Nell was doing fine, a mother could not be fooled. Listening behind the words, she could tell that her son wasn't eating properly, and his health was suffering.

To take her mind off Nell's bind, she spent more time digging into which parts of which plants worked best for this complaint or that illness. As for her own aches, she was making pleasing progress in her experiments using different parts of the hawthorn.

Maisy had tried to visit the island a second time, and after a long and gruelling journey, made it as far as the clip post at the juniper diamond. Her timing couldn't have been worse, arriving a few nights after the attack on that poor white doe in the diviner's burrow. Maisy assumed that outrage about the attack – and the tension around Lexa – was why her request to see her son was refused again. That time, though, the officers didn't ignore her. The clip with the limp had taken her advice about mugwort, and it worked. She was told politely that a visit to the island wasn't appropriate.

Then had come news of the passing of Vort. Maisy had every right to hate the buck responsible for sending her mate to the field of silence. All she felt, though, was sadness for Vort's family. Her widow friends were baffled how she could be so forgiving and trusting. Maisy, however, was not a rabbit to hold a grudge. What happened, happened.

As far as she was concerned, there was good in all rabbits. Which explained why she was delighted rather than cautious when a well-groomed and healthy-smelling black rabbit from the Cluster came to tell her about a plan to help Nell escape. Nor did Maisy sense anything other than happy coincidence when an important buck from Toria arrived soon after to tell her she could finally visit the island.

*****

THE MOONS of Nell's banishment to the island had been a bitter strain on Ollie. Since the hearing, her life had been tossed like a fickle wind, howling from times of absolute desolation, when giving up was the only realistic option, to breezes of optimism, gentler than the gales, but reason to hope.

As a distraction from the depressing setbacks, helplessness and loneliness, Ollie was spending even more time persuading, convincing, pestering the ears of any rabbit in the North willing to listen. There was a sprouting of support for the struggle. Ollie managed to convince a few Oakwooders to stop eating junipers as a protest, though never enough to have an impact on the South.

For each hop Ollie took forward with ordinary rabbits, the actions and attitudes of the prime and her circle of high-ups chased her two hops back.

Thatch's stubborn refusal to meet the friend of a *spreader of terror* – a ludicrous excuse, given the terror rabbits of the South Bank faced night and day from Levi – drove Ollie to work harder. She sought out rabbits on the fringes of Thatch's circle, her mates, friends, enemies, anyone who might have influence over her.

There had been breakthroughs. Persuading the Red Haw rabbits to visit the island, organising the diviner Hugh to pass messages, Fleet getting to see Nell – even if the seer had been fooled by the guards.

Thatch's eagerness to accept false assurances from the South that all was daisies was more than frustrating. Ollie felt like she was trying to burrow through rock. The distances she covered to find new ears, the long nights on the hop, were wearing her down. If her moods were flapping up and down like the wings of a bird, the state of her health was going in one steady direction, like an acorn tumbling from a tree. Her right ear had become so useless, she rarely bothered lifting it off her back.

She got most of her news of the South from Fleet, and updates about Nell and the island from the diviner Hugh. Occasionally, she was visited by black rabbits from Lexa and the Point who managed to cross the Torrent. Some were members of Claw, which was still active, carrying out random acts of chaos, though without direction.

A group of southern blacks was visiting Ollie now, in the glade, and not for the first time she was being asked to take over leadership of the Cluster and Claw. In the past, Ollie had laughed off such suggestions. Tonight though, feeling exhausted and frustrated after whiles and whiles of fruitless talk, she agreed to at least think about it. She asked the rabbits to return the following night for her decision.

*****

'ARE YOU in there, Fleet?'

The voice outside the burrow belonged to the seer, Donald, who

Fleet hadn't talked with for some time.

'I am indeed. Come in, please.'

Donald hopped through the entrance, dragging a strange aroma.

'What's that smell?'

'You must be the tenth rabbit to ask me. It's sage. Surely you tasted it when you were out east?'

'So that's where you've been. How's that cousin of Thatch's? Still poking his nose where it doesn't belong?'

'That's what I've come to see you about, Fleet. Something Thatch said after I gave her my report has got me wondering.'

'About what?'

'You've been covering the South Bank longer than any seer. What do you think this Cluster really wants? Is there some hidden plan?'

'That's a curious…'

'I'll tell you why I'm asking, Fleet. As you would have seen out east, Thatch's cousin is supporting one warren in their disagreement with their neighbours, because he's concerned if the other lot get the upper paw, their extreme ideas about all rabbits being equal and sharing everything will swell like a swarm of starlings, threatening his own warren. Thatch is also worried about that happening here, infecting the Oakwood, because she believes that's the Cluster's hidden plan.'

'That's ridiculous.'

'How can you be so sure?'

'Because I've known Nell and Ollie – the brains behind the Cluster – since they were kittens. Yes, they believe all rabbits are born equal. As do I. It's hardly an extreme view. They *don't* believe, though, all rabbits are the same and should share *everything*. If you and I lived under that sort of arrangement, this burrow wouldn't belong to me, but to the whole warren. You or any other rabbit could presumably move in any time you wanted. There'd be no prime rabbit or circles of high-ups, and a drifter would have the same say on how the warren should be run as a smart rabbit like Thatch. One moon we'd be seers, the next we'd be thinning brambles or raising kittens or patrolling for carns. Nell and Ollie understand that rabbits have different strengths, and the best-run warrens make the best use of all of them.'

'Hope you're right, Fleet.'

'I am. I only wish Thatch would get down off her high perch and talk to Ollie, and Nell. Then she'd see she has nothing to worry about.'

*****

BEING ASKED to take over leadership of the Cluster and Claw got Ollie thinking. In the dark and safe quietness of her burrow, she pondered the qualities of a leader, and why she had always said *no*. It wasn't a question of loyalty to Nell. It was loyalty to the struggle. So, what was it that made Nell a better leader?

Intelligence? Both rabbits were smart. If anything, Ollie considered herself the better thinker.

Strength was important in the natural world. Though not all-important. Thatch cleverly chose stronger, trustworthy rabbits as minders and sentinels. As did the Patri. Even Levi. He was a powerful rabbit, but surrounded himself with brutish yes-rabbits, some of whom could beat him in a one-on-one fight. And though Levi had been the *leader* sitting on the prime rabbit's terrace, Vort's paws were all over the big decisions. When he was alive. And comparing Nell and Ollie, strength was hardly a factor with her friend trapped on the island.

Experience was important. Nell, though, had spent so much of his adult moons banished from the South Bank, experiencing little of the ups and downs of the rabbits who considered him their leader.

No-one could question Nell's commitment. He'd been prepared to go to the field of silence for the cause. Some would say he was suffering an even greater punishment for a rabbit – giving up his freedom. Yet Ollie felt just as committed. How often had she thought she'd gladly swap places with her friend? And she had worked tirelessly for the cause since Nell was sent to the island.

A *good* leader needed all these qualities. A *great* leader, though, needed more. Humility. And the ability to inspire. Nell was the most humble rabbit Ollie knew, always putting the interests of others ahead of himself.

She reflected on the times he had stirred other rabbits to act, or to think outside the tight passages of their own lives, to dream of better moons. There had been many.

The showdown at the border near the Point Warren, when Nell and Ollie were on their way to the Golden Field all those moons ago. It was as if Nell had put the white governor, Crown, under some sort of spell, persuading him to let them through the border over the objections of Levi.

The time they saw black and white rabbits arguing over valerian. The way Nell convinced the clip, who would normally have sided with the whites. Ollie remembered the officer's wide-open mouth like it was last night.

The first protest against the ban on black rabbits grazing in the Common. The way Nell – new to the Golden Field and virtually unknown – was propelled to the front of the marchers.

The night Nell took over from Alfred as leader of the Cluster. How everyone was waiting for him to speak.

His first act as leader, organising and explaining the Resistance. How, despite the menacing threat of the clips, most rabbits clung to Nell's words like hazel catkins in an ivy moon gale.

During Nell's visit to the North, the way the rabbits who heard him speak at the Meadow Warren reacted to his passionate plea for support.

And those were just the examples of inspiration Ollie had *witnessed*. Rabbits of all colours, including those like Ollie who were not at the hearing, were still talking about Nell's speech, how he'd been willing to give up his life for the freedom of others.

Ollie began questioning the way she'd been trying to convince North Bankers to support the struggle. She'd concentrated on the unfairness of the colour rules, the ruthlessness of the rabbits in charge, the unnaturalness of the forbidden lines, the unjustness of Vort's grand plan of Parting. All of it was big-field stuff which, if she was being honest, had gone in one ear of most of the rabbits she was trying to convince, and wafted out the other. The times ears pricked up, eyes opened in wonder, were the times she'd talked about Nell.

Ollie sensed rabbits moving above for the evening. She'd made her decision. Rather than turning her back on Nell, she needed to bring him front and centre. Take the focus away from fuzzy ideas about equality and fairness, and direct it to the plight of a single, inspirational rabbit. Instead of wearing her claws out trying to remove the rock blocking Thatch's burrow, she would appeal directly to ordinary rabbits.

*****

THE DEPARTURE of Thaden from the island was like that moment when a heavy fog scatters, welcoming the first twinkles of daystar to tickle the grass. Four-eyes and the other aggressive guards disappeared with Thaden, replaced by more moderate bucks. The new warden was a no-nonsense rabbit, but not a closed-minded supremacist.

Nell and his comrades were given more free time, and the food improved, including watercress and mint collected by bumbles from the ledge through the bat cave. Although they were still required to shift stones in the crater, they could at least talk among themselves. Some of the new guards chatted to the captives as if they were rabbits instead of rats. One or two let them rest when they should be working, and told them if the warden was approaching.

It happened one warm afternoon when Nell was stretched out beside a rock, patiently answering questions from an inquisitive guard named Gregory. The white rabbit couldn't understand why Nell and the other captives were causing trouble, when they had dry burrows and meals brought to them. Nell enjoyed talking to rabbits like Gregory, who were at least prepared to consider new ideas. The guard suddenly stopped talking, leant forward, and whispered that the warden was coming. Nell picked up a stone and carried it to the next pile. The warden beckoned him over, and he prepared for a tongue-lashing or worse. The last thing he expected was to be told to finish work early because he had a special visitor.

Maisy.

Nell's heart was racing past the warden to the ramp. He was so worried how he would appear to his mother, what she would think of him, he hardly noticed the shrieking as they passed the rat pit. He was guided through the heath to the poplars, and up to the end of the log over the Torrent.

The black eye-knots on the trunks of the aspens patrolling the

Chilling Wood were only just visible behind their summer foliage of bright green.

Then he saw her. Frail and vulnerable at the far end of the span, dwarfed between a pair of huge, brash clips. Nell grimaced as Maisy bowed in the belittling way of South Bank black rabbits in the presence of whites. At her age, with her knowledge and wisdom and dignity, Maisy should be respected by all rabbits.

Nell's frown softened as he watched his mother nose the flank of one of her escorts and start chatting to him. He imagined she'd detected some ailment, and was telling the buck which plants to use to fix the problem. *You are what you eat.*

Maisy padded along the span, and son and mother greeted with the licks of a lifetime of lost embraces. They were left alone, in the shade of one of the poplars, and showered questions on each other about their health, Nell's sisters and their families, friends and shared acquaintances. Maisy soon steered the conversation to plants, and Nell was happy to let his mother ramble. She had become reliant, she explained, on hawthorn to ease the late-moon pain in her legs and shoulders.

'The leaves and flowers are best, the berries if you can get them soon after they go red. Helps the blood flow through your body and chases away blights that clog up your joints.'

'How easy is hawthorn to get?'

'Depends on the season, Nell. The hedge moon is best for the leaves and flowers, and they dry well if you get them below quickly to keep the colour. The berries are at their most potent in the web. If you collect them when they're firm and keep them dry, they can last all the way to the peacock.'

'Are you finding enough to see you through?'

'Most of the time. There's a good supply in the thicket not far from my burrow.'

Nell asked Maisy what life was like now that Levi was prime.

'It is what it is,' she said, before pointing out how poorly Nell smelt. How he should try stems of cleavers and roots of nettles for his chafed skin and patchy fur, rub chewed elder petals into his cracked paws, and marigold on the cuts on his ears. She mistook his tears of joy as a runny eye needing a good smearing with meadowsweet. Nell, who felt the healthiest he'd been for moons, was about to tell her he had no choice over his diet. He kept quiet. Why worry her?

The warden shouted that their time was up.

'How silly of me, Nell. I almost forgot. I've got a message from one of your friends in Paw.'

'You mean Claw?'

'Yes. I suppose that was it. Your friends have a plan to get you out of here. They've been talking to a white rabbit, Boarbuck, who will come to the island soon, to help you escape. Isn't that wonderful, Nell? And not a breath too soon, from the smell of you.'

Nell had a thousand questions, but was prevented from asking them when a guard came to escort Maisy over the Torrent. They managed a quick farewell lick. Maisy climbed up to the span, stopping at the top.

'Henry would have been proud of you, son,' she said, and disappeared.

Nell heard her telling the guard to chew dandelion leaves for his gout. Then her voice trailed off, lost to the babbling of the Torrent.

55. In the pawprints of the bully

BOARBUCK ARRIVED on the island soon after, but spent his first few days patrolling the top of the ramp, so Nell was unable to talk to him. The chance came when Boarbuck was given the job of checking the captives were in their keeps during the night.

Guards took turns at the various jobs on the island – patrolling the crater, the ramp, the span crossing the Torrent, supervising work gangs, escorting captives, passing on messages from the warden. The plan, Boarbuck explained, was to wait until he was a messenger, so he could move freely around the island without raising suspicion.

'When the time's right, I will come and get you from work duty, making up a story that the warden wants to see you.'

'What about the span guards?'

'Your friends from Claw will be waiting in the Chilling Wood for my signal. They've been taught the alarm stamp the guards use when a hunting fox is approaching. Trust me, the guards will hightail below immediately. And to be sure, a white rabbit your friends have chosen will run onto the bridge as if he's being chased by the carn.'

It sounded to Nell like a good plan. He was confused, though, about one thing.

'Who are these *friends*?'

'Their leader is Matthan, the son of Stephen. They will meet you on the other side to take you to safety.'

Nell thought of Stephen's words at the burrow at Lexa. *My fur is black, my son Matthan's fur is black, his kittens' fur will be black, and it is beautiful.* Stephen had been sent to the field of silence for his beliefs. Although Nell never met Matthan, he had little doubt he could be relied on. Boarbuck left, saying he would let Nell know when the time was right.

'Be patient. Comrade.'

Nell was so excited, he couldn't sleep. The fattening web moon flushed through the entrance to the keep, warming his entire body and sending his thoughts bounding. Over the span, through the Chilling Wood, all the way to Maisy's burrow. He must eventually have nodded off, because the moon was still shining when Boarbuck woke him. All was in readiness for that day.

'So soon?'

'The messenger had to deal with a family matter at Toria. The warden's asked me to take his place today.'

'You're sure about this?'

'Absolutely. And there's another reason today's perfect. I happen to know the two guards who will be patrolling the span have spent most of the night munching on valerian. They'll have no idea what's going on.'

*****

FLEET COULDN'T BELIEVE what he was seeing. A golden glow from the bulging web moon at the peak of its arc lit up the curious faces of a large number of rabbits crowded in front of the speaking mound by the Oakwood lake.

The *Free Nell* gathering had been Ollie's idea, a new way to bring attention to the injustices black rabbits faced in the South. She'd made up a Free Nell signal – a variation on the Claw salute, which she was demonstrating to the rabbits at the mound. After a few stop-start attempts, most managed the double stamp and nose jerk.

Ollie then sprung another surprise. She'd somehow managed to smuggle Desmond, an impressive black diviner, across from the South Bank to speak. The short, stocky rabbit with popping eyes was an instant hit, even though he spent most of his time chewing out

Oakwooders for ignoring what was happening to their cousins over the Torrent.

'A rabbit who chooses not to speak up against injustice is hopping in the pawprints of the bully,' he shouted. 'If a squirrel has its paw on the tail of a shrew, and you refuse to intervene, the shrew will not appreciate your refusal to take sides.'

Desmond got the biggest reaction when he talked about Nell, explaining what the rabbit had gone through, and what he was having to endure for standing up for what he believed. The diviner's final message – that Nell was shoulders and ears higher than all other leaders on the South Bank, and only his influence could bring peace to the other side of the Torrent – was greeted with rowdy stamping and Free Nell signals.

The next speaker was the leader of the Red Haws, who talked of his visit to the island, how much Nell impressed him.

Fleet scanned the faces of the crowd. There were rabbits of all ages, white, black, crosser. Off to one side, watching and listening, were a few minor rabbits from Thatch's outer circle. They stared at the ground when the Red Haw buck's comment that Thatch was not doing enough to put pressure on the South prompted a rousing Free Nell signal. Fleet overheard a doe telling her friend that she'd *like to meet this Freenell.*

'The rabbit's name is Nell. He's been banished on the island for twenty moons.'

'That's like… so wrong.'

Fleet studied the doe. White, free, privileged in ways outside the imagination of a black rabbit on the South Bank.

'How old are you, if you don't mind me asking?'

'Twelve moons.'

Fleet was intrigued. Nell had not been seen off the island for so long, yet he was able to inspire rabbits born moons after his hearing. The gathering broke up to enthusiastic stamps of *Free Nell.*

Surely it would be only a matter of time before the message in the signal became reality.

*****

NELL DECIDED to tell only his closest comrade of his impending escape, when the captives got their first break from shifting stones that morning. He didn't want to risk loose lips dashing the plan. Walter urged him to go for it.

'I've met Matthan. A fine rabbit. A yearning for freedom just like Stephen. Looks like his father too. Has the same fur hanging from his chin.'

Boarbuck showed up soon after, telling the work duty guards that the warden wanted to see the varlet Nell immediately. All went smoothly as they crossed the crater and climbed the ramp. The guard at the top let them past when Boarbuck mentioned that the warden was in a foul mood.

'Better not keep him waiting then.'

They crossed the heath to the entrance to the warden's burrow, hidden between the roots of one of the poplars, out of view of the guards. Boarbuck steered Nell past the tree and onto a trail heavy with the scent of white rabbits, snaking between rocks along the top of the cliff. All the guards not on duty would be below at that time of the morning.

They reached the deeply furrowed stump of a poplar concealed from the log span by its leafy neighbour, then crawled through a channel dug between the sandstone of the cliff and a wall of limestone. Boarbuck motioned for Nell to lie flat beside him. Nell could see the start of the span. Two guards were lying on their backs, legs wide apart, warming their bellies.

'What now?'

'We give the signal.'

Boarbuck went through the channel and onto the stump. He rose on his hind legs and flapped his ears. A black rabbit appeared in the aspens on the far bank, too far away to recognise. He flapped his ears in reply, and disappeared into the wood. Then Nell felt a series of strange stamps. The guards stirred, stumbled to their paws, ears spinning and noses winking furiously. Nell detected movement at the far end of the bridge. A white rabbit was charging across, shouting *Carns! Carns! Hightail for your lives!*

The guards bolted.

'Now, Nell,' said Boarbuck. 'Quickly.'

They raced down to the abandoned guard post. Boarbuck leapt onto the log. A black rabbit appeared at the far end. Nell stuped. Something wasn't right. The rabbit had no fur hanging from his chin. Boarbuck urged Nell on.

'Quickly, comrade. Matthew there will take you to safety.'

Matthew? Stephen's son was called Matthan. Boarbuck and the black rabbit were pleading with him to keep going. Nell sniffed towards the Chilling Wood, the South Bank, freedom. He was thinking of Maisy, Ollie. His heart yelled *go*. His head said *no*. That he'd been a fool, putting his own interests ahead of his comrades and all other black rabbits on the South Bank.

He shuffled backwards along the log, and the reactions of Boarbuck and the black rabbit, whoever he was, confirmed his suspicions. He hurried across the heath, past the astonished guard at the top of the ramp, and down to join his workmates in the crater.

*****

LEVI WAS FURIOUS. He'd been waiting at the juniper diamond for news that Nell was finally rotting in the field of silence.

When he'd heard nothing, he sent Thaden to find out what was going on. He returned to report that the plot had failed and Boarbuck had vanished.

Levi was tempted to go to the island and finish the varlet off himself, until Thaden reminded him of the spies in the wood.

On the way to his burrow, he brushed through whimpering clutters of varlets, most cringing away in fright. One dim-wit greeted him with a ludicrous double stamp and jerked its nose in the air. Along the top of the ridge, white rabbits murmuring amongst themselves went quiet as he approached. What was going on? They couldn't possibly know what happened on the island.

The answer was waiting in his meeting chamber, helping himself to an acorn. The rabbit – one of Levi's spies in the North – had journeyed over the Torrent, and his news turned a bad night into a nightmare. A huge gathering of rabbits, organised by the varlet Ollie, had taken place in the Oakwood clearing – demanding Nell be freed.

'Who cares?' scoffed Levi.

The spy hesitated.

'I believe *you*... *we all* should, sir. Some of Thatch's circle were at the gathering, and there was a lot of... agreeing. I could hear what they were saying. That if Nell is harmed...'

'How dare the varlet-lovers try to tell *me* what to do on *my* bank.'

The spy said that news of the gathering had beaten him to the Golden Field, thanks to mischievous seers, and was leaching through the South like a bane.

'I saw a white kitten giving the varlet salute on my way down here. Sir.'

'What varlet salute?'

When the spy explained the stamp-and-toss and what it meant, Levi realised the varlet he'd passed on the flats was mocking him. To his face. In a rage, he yelled for the sergeant of the eclipo. The buck was out on patrol, so his deputy hopped into the chamber, nervously.

Levi spat out orders for new rules.

'The varlet salute is banned.

'Gatherings of more than two varlets are banned.

'Varlets can only move about in single file.

'All varlets are to lie flat to the ground in the presence of white rabbits.

'No varlet is to stand higher than a white rabbit.

Levi thought of Nell's mother, who must have tipped off the varlet about the escape plot.

'Varlets are banned from eating hawthorn. All parts, even the roots.

'And all varlets must pledge their obedience and devotion to... to... the prime rabbit. And repeat it every full moon.'

'And how exactly, sir, will we...'

They were the deputy's last words. Levi, shouting that he would send every last varlet and crosser to the field of silence with his own claws if that's what it took, attacked the buck so violently, Thaden looked away.

56. Turning eyes and ears

AFTER DODGING the escape plot, Nell prepared for retaliation. The opposite happened. Boarbuck had disappeared. A few mornings later, instead of being ordered to the stone piles, Nell and Walter were shown into the bat cave. Heaps of guano and urine reeked beneath clusters of the bizarre animals hanging from cracks in the ceiling. Nell held his breath, until they rounded a corner and saw light spilling through a tall slit rising from the floor of the cave like the floating trunk of an aspen. The guard beckoned them through, onto a wide shelf of rock sloping down one end to a sheltered, pebbly beach.

In front of Nell, the Torrent sparkled in the blaze of the daystar. On the far side, behind the rushes, the thick waving grass of the Cocksfoot field flowed up to meet the towering greens and browns fringing the oakwood.

The North Bank.

So close, it hurt.

The guard showed Nell and Walter how to collect water crowfoot. Mats of white-petalled flowers floated on the rippling surface, their green tooth-like leaves straggling behind. Though it was tiring work, Nell would not have swapped places for anything. He was thrilled by the view, the caress of the breeze on his face, the soothing buzz of young bees, the chuckling of the current, the scarlet and gold of the minnows, swifts swooping to snatch insects hovering near the surface.

He was allowed through to the shelf often after that. He could have gone each day if he wanted. Instead, Nell insisted on sharing the privilege with his comrades. Friendly guards like Gregory let them have some of the fresh crowfoot they collected and relax in the sun before carrying their harvest through the cave to the crater.

Late one afternoon, Nell found Hugh waiting outside the keeps. The guards had grown tired of listening to the Oaker diviner, so wandered off to watch the rats. Hugh updated Nell on the growing push in the North to have him and his comrades freed from the island, and how Ollie had changed tactics – focusing on Nell rather than the plight of every black rabbit.

'Don't like the sound of that,' said Nell. 'This is not about me. I'm only one rabbit. We're all in this together.'

Hugh disagreed.

'I think Ollie might be onto something. I've spoken to rabbits – North Bank bucks and does – who went to a gathering she organised in the Oakwood clearing. There were so many. Rabbits of all colours. Ollie somehow got Desmond to speak to the crowd, and the leader of the Red Haws, the one who came to see you here on the island. Both talked about you, Nell, as the only rabbit capable of bringing peace to the South Bank.'

'That's ridiculous. Surely…'

'Not if it works, Nell. Ollie's tried everything under the moon since you were sent here. None have made a difference. This latest gathering made a lot of rabbits take notice. I've heard it pricked the ears of Thatch's circle. Some are talking about cutting the flow of acorns to the South.'

'What about Thatch?'

Hugh shrugged.

'I'm afraid she still thinks you and your comrades are violent spreaders of terror. That if you take over the South Bank, all the whites will leave Toria and overrun the Oakwood. If you want my opinion, Thatch's biggest fear is losing her supply of juniper berries. She's addicted to them.'

After Hugh left, the captives discussed the diviner's message. Some were indignant at Ollie's change of tactics, saying her efforts to free one rabbit went against what the Cluster and Claw were fighting for.

'How often have you told us, Nell, that a rabbit is only a rabbit because of other rabbits?'

Nell couldn't argue with that. To his dismay though, most of his comrades disagreed.

'I can see what Ollie's trying to do,' said Walter. 'If turning eyes and ears and thoughts to Nell outrages and stirs enough rabbits to support us, we and all black rabbits benefit.'

News of the success of Ollie's tactic began filtering through over the coming days, as new captives arrived on the island. The Free Nell salute was being seen at Lexa, the Point and black warrens to the south and east.

After moons when Nell's name had been hardly mentioned, it was now on the lips of rabbits all over the South Bank. Other reports came from members of Claw sent to the island for collapsing burrows, refusing to work, or for merely saying the word *Nell*. Though never thrilled to see rabbits banished, he was always keen to hear their stories.

Some new captives, particularly rabbits who had been on the North Bank for training, were hot-tempered, impatient for change. They objected to shifting stones in the crater, and spent days and nights confined to their keeps.

There were also growing rumours of anger and restlessness among Claw recruits, and a lack of direction and leadership.

Then came news that saddened the long-serving captives. Levi had ordered clips to make random checks on black kittens to make sure they were being told the correct Mistle version of history, and not *poisoned with varlet nonsense*. Bucks and does at Hilltop, including kittens little more than three moons, had protested and were attacked. One passed into the field of silence. Nell was shocked.

But instead of the attack ending the protests, as Levi would have hoped, it sparked similar acts of defiance at the Border and Low Warrens, which quickly spread as far as the Willow to the south and Lexa to the north.

The crater was soon echoing to the energetic chatter of black rebels banished for challenging the colour rules. Some were happy to be on the island – feeling protected by Nell's growing fame – rather than wasting away in Levi's keeps.

Then, as the hopping moon thinned and clouds tinged with purple and green rolled in, forewarning of the first serious storm of summer, new captives descended on the crater with ominous news.

Levi's cliff keep was being emptied – temporarily – so it could be doubled in size.

*****

LEVI WAS ALONE in the chamber behind the brink when the thunderstorm swept in. The rain got heavier, and he was about to leave when he noticed a drip in one corner of the ceiling. Curious, he went over to investigate, and found a hole had been gouged out. He cursed the devious varlets.

The drip quickly became a flow, which ran along a channel in the floor to another hole that had been scratched in the opposite corner. As he watched, the hole mushroomed in size until its rim collapsed, sending the water cascading into the chamber on the next level. He hollered for help, but his cries were lost in the downpour. He clawed soil from the wall, and tried to drag it to the hole in the floor. There was a honeycomb of keeps below him, most with no external exits. Vort, when he was alive, had halted work on extensions. Something about advice from burrowing does that more keeps would weaken the hillside.

Levi grinned, thinking of all the varlets about to slide into the field of silence, what the reckless seed-brains were doing to their own. Then he remembered that the keep had been emptied. The only rabbits in the deeper levels were white does digging out new keeps because varlets couldn't be trusted.

He had to get out. To save himself.

There was an almighty gush and the floor collapsed, sucking him through the hole. Dazed, covered in thick black slime and overwhelmed with the stench of varlet wind, he scrambled through the mud for the hole to the access passage. He reached it a heartbeat before the floor caved in behind him. When he got to the surface, he stood and stretched so the rain washed away the filth, as the storm muffled the cries of the white does trapped and unable to escape.

FLEET DIDN'T REALISE IT, but the place he was sitting in the hedgerow between the Willow and Hilltop fields was the Hide from where Levi once watched Nell and his friends playing Patch. The place where Vort had explained the difference between white and black rabbits, how the most harmless-looking black rabbit would, at the first whisper of pressure, revert to savagery.

From where he sat, Fleet could see plenty and not be seen by others, which suited the rabbit the seer had come to meet. The buck who'd taken over as governor at the rowan after Vort and Levi went to the Golden Field had agreed to talk to the seer. Secretly.

'No-one can know I'm here,' he whispered. 'I've been to a gathering of country governors ordered to Toria for *instructions*. As punishment for the collapse at his keep, Levi's spewed up a mouthful of new rules tasting more of spite than sense, that will return to bite him on the backside.'

'Like what?'

'Bucks and does too weak or idle to work are to be banished from Lexa to country warrens. And black rabbits must get permission from white governors to go from one field to another. Can you imagine how much time that will take?'

'Did you, or the other country governors, complain?'

'You must be joking, Fleet. Levi would set his beasts on any governor who dared challenge him. I did hear, though, a couple of brave rabbits in the prime's inner circle advised him against it, including his son.'

Fleet had not met Drekkel, though had heard interesting reports about the buck.

'One thing's for sure,' said the governor, 'with these eyes and ears all over the South Bank, watching and listening, even Levi realises he can't go around beating up varl... rabbits of colour for no reason.'

'Eyes and ears?'

'Seers like you, Fleet. And other observers. From the Oakwood, of course. There's also talk that warrens further north and out west have eyes and ears, prying. Ever since these Free Nell gatherings began. They even had one in Creamia the other night, if the rumours are correct.'

Fleet knew of the gathering in the distant warren of Thatch's cousin. It had been organised by Ollie. He also knew there were only three seers from the Oakwood, including himself, watching the South, and one from a warren to the west through the Chilling Wood. Levi had tried hard to keep seers out, and limit the movement of the ones who did get in. His clips, though, couldn't be everywhere. Fleet suspected his own web of informers and sources was better than Levi's, especially since Vort's passing. Levi talked only to yes-rabbits who told him what he wanted to hear. Vort had kept his ears open to broader advice.

'What's got the rabbits of Toria worked up though,' continued the governor, 'is fear that the Oakwood will stop sending acorns. Some are so worried, they're starting to question if it's worth keeping old Nell on the island.'

Fleet thanked the buck for the information, and reassured him the conversation would stay private. The breeze strengthened, tossing the zing of herb robert, the thick fruit smell of honeysuckle and the nose-tingling of tansy into a mishmash of odours mimicking the seer's thoughts.

If Nell was *old*, Fleet was ancient. Ten moons older, to be precise, and he was feeling it. In his bones, in the legs struggling to cover the ground of his youth, the teeth and claws that had lost their sharpness, the eyes that blurred distances. Each time he crossed the Torrent, he wondered if it would be the last. He'd devoted most of his adult moons to covering the South Bank, and would miss the intriguing rabbits and friends he'd met. Hopping aside, though, would be easier now that there were other seers interested enough in the affairs of the bank to take his place.

A flock of geese honked overhead, crossing the rindle and disappearing above the towering greenness of the Chilling Wood. Seeing the rindle took the seer back yet again to that fateful day when he chose to stay silent rather than warn Nell's father of the approaching danger. Fleet's mind and attitudes, like his body, had changed with the moons. If he understood then what he understood now, that all rabbits – seers included – were involved in the lives of other rabbits, things could have turned out differently.

Scrawny does nibbling on tasteless foxtail grass at the edge of the Point Warren's ridiculously small grazing area scattered when they smelt Fleet coming. To these poor creatures, any white rabbit was as dangerous as a fox. And yet it wasn't seeing rabbits forced to survive on scraps at the height of the hopping moon, when plants in *white* areas were plentiful, that depressed the seer. A lifetime spent observing and reporting on misery dulled the senses. A rabbit who had seen thirty rabbits pass into the field of silence was not so shocked by number thirty-one.

No, Fleet felt depressed because he had been unable to do anything to prevent what he was seeing all around him. He considered the southern governor's final words. Some rabbits in Toria were questioning the sense of keeping Nell on the island. Perhaps things were finally changing. He shook his ears to expel the sad thoughts, then ambled over to the rindle for a drink. At least things couldn't get worse. Surely there was only one way from here. Up. He caught a whiff of sweat and rotten food. Then noticed a small dark shape sprawled in the shadow of spiking brown seed heads of bulrushes. It was Maisy, barely breathing.

*****

NEWS OF THE COLLAPSE of the cliff keep lifted the morale of captives on the island. Nell dared believe it might force change. When times had been grim and he'd wondered if he could go on, he'd always grasped for the slightest murmur of change. There had been many such moments, all of them dashed. Perhaps this time...

Messages about the spreading popularity of the Free Nell push, which he'd reluctantly accepted was worth trying, had given him hope he might not pass into the field of silence from the island. That one day he might be free. Free to be with Ollie, and Maisy. That although he'd been stuck in one place for so long, rabbits off the island might finally be creeping *towards* his position rather than hightailing away from it.

Gregory and a few of the other guards believed Nell should be freed, and did what they could to make life as easy as possible for him.

They willingly shared information about what was happening off the island. Most news was welcomed, but this latest message – passed on from Fleet to a guard at the log span, then to Gregory – drove a thorn into Nell's heart. Maisy was so unwell, she was unlikely to live more than a night or so. Nell begged to be allowed to visit her, giving his word he'd return immediately to the island. Gregory said he'd speak to the warden, try to persuade him.

Nell – bereft and alone in his keep – brooded over his failures as a son.

Maisy's life had been incredibly tough, and when Nell was sent to the island, he'd been unable to help her. Worse, his actions made her life more wretched because she was harassed and penalised simply for being the mother of the most despised rabbit on the South Bank.

Had he done the right thing, putting the wider interests of black rabbits ahead of his own mother? Did Maisy really understand his devotion to the struggle for freedom? There had been hints that she did. Her *one piece of advice from an old country doe* the day she visited. *Follow your conscience. Knowing that wherever your conscience takes you, you have the support and love of your mother. And, I believe, your father.*

For an old country doe, Maisy realised long before Nell that it was the system of colour hate rather than the actions of individual white rabbits that was the problem. It had taken the words of Thaden to reveal that truth to Nell.

Only now, he appreciated what Maisy meant when she defended Levi after he left the body of a shrew in her burrow.

It was not Levi's fault, she had said. *A rabbit who would do such a thing must have a sickness of the head. You mustn't be annoyed at someone who is ill.* If his mother was right about that, was she right about other things? When Nell had asked her what life was like under Levi as prime, she'd summed it up in five words. *It is what it is.*

Perhaps it was as simple as that. Accept your place in life and get on with it. Then there was her parting message: *Henry would have been proud of you, son.*

'What about you, mother?', Nell shouted at the wall of the keep.

Gripped by a sudden desperation to know the answer, to see Maisy one last time, he bolted into the crater, past the dozing guards. At the bottom of the ramp, he slid to a halt as if blindsided by a fox. Gregory was coming down. Nell could tell from his slumped shoulders that the answer was *no*.

'I'm sorry Nell. *I* realise you're a rabbit of your word and would not try to flee. The warden says he cannot trust your own friends, who he thinks will try to help you escape.'

*****

LEVI WAS MUNCHING on thrush-haws, the small fleshy berries of hawthorn that had passed through the bodies of thrushes – one of his favourite delicacies of the web moon. He was waiting for his inner circle of stewards to assemble for their talkfest. Levi had reluctantly agreed to Drekkel's suggestion that he start holding regular briefings again, *so the right paw knows what the left paw is up to.*

Drekkel was the last to arrive, and Levi noticed the way the others greeted him as he entered. There was more to their grovelling than the respect rabbits would normally show to the son of a prime. Drekkel was gaining in size, and if it came to a one-on-one fight, he would be a threat to any of these stewards. Levi sensed there was another reason for his son's growing status, though he couldn't put his claw on it. He chinned repeatedly to remind them who was in charge, and munched loudly as the circle babbled away.

The food supply steward predicted that the coming juniper harvest would be smaller than usual because the bushes hadn't been maintained as well as in previous seasons.

'Get rid of whoever's responsible,' barked Levi.

'*That* was the problem, father. The black rabbit who used to tend the junipers for us, was *got rid of* when you banned black rabbits from being supervisors. We've tried three white rabbits since then. None of them understand the bushes like the old buck.'

'Then find someone who does, you idiots. Can't be that difficult if a dim-witted varlet could do it.'

'We're trying, father,' said Drekkel in a voice so calm, it was becoming irritating. He asked the steward if he had more to report.

The buck looked at Drekkel as he replied.

'Yes, sir. About the thrush-haws requested by the prime. They're extremely hard to find this early in the season. We've had to take a lot of black does off burrow duties to watch for… thrushes.'

'So what?' yelled Levi.

'Sir, it's… I've been getting complaints from the rabbits whose servants have been… reassigned.'

'How dare they? Which rabbits? I'll teach them to question a command from their prime.'

'I'm sure that won't be necessary, father. I'll have a word to them… about priorities.'

Drekkel moved on quickly to another steward. Reports on black workers, and the coming and going of carns, were predictably boring.

Levi yawned through a moaning summary from the sergeant of the eclipo about how difficult it was to enforce some of the prime's latest rules. He stopped eating when the rabbit in charge of the varlet and crosser warrens mentioned that the doe Maisy had passed into the field of silence.

'Best news I've heard all day.'

Drekkel asked how she passed.

'As I understand it, sir, the doe had grown to rely on the hawthorn plant, which the prime rabbit declared off-limits to… rabbits of colour.'

'Next,' hollered Levi, ignoring the glances between Drekkel and the other stewards.

The buck in charge of keeps outlined plans for redigging the ones destroyed during the recent storm. Levi cut him short.

'All I want to know is which varlets caused the collapse.'

Thaden, who had been quiet until now, rose.

'We're not sure of the varlets involved. However, we've heard from our informers where they got the idea and where they were trained. At a warren on the North Bank. And that's where the cowards almost certainly squirmed back to, straight after the storm.'

'Which warren?' Levi demanded.

'Either the Cocksfoot or Drop. The varlets use both as training bases for their… uprising.'

Levi had heard enough: 'Out. All of you. Now.'

'We haven't heard from the steward on trade,' said Drekkel. 'I asked for his opinion on the likelihood of the Oakwood imposing… restrictions.'

Levi grimaced.

'Thatch will never agree to it. Out! I *said* the meeting is over.'

The stewards wavered, leaving only when Drekkel nodded. Levi waited till they'd gone.

'Never, ever question me in front of other rabbits again.'

Drekkel didn't blink. For a heartbeat, Levi thought of a rat-hole in an alder tree by the rindle, another pair of eyes that showed no fear. The memory passed. He ordered Thaden to assemble two squads of eclipo.

'What are you doing?,' asked Drekkel, the first sign of concern in his voice.

'What I should have done a long time ago.'

'You'll be making a serious mistake, father, if you're thinking of causing trouble over the Torrent… without getting agreement from the circle.'

'Out of my way.'

57. At the front of the queue

LEVI MET the eclipo squads at the juniper diamond.

Thaden's choices were good. Hardened scrappers who would obey orders and never ask questions. The rabbits bounded along the trail between the Torrent and Chilling Wood, Levi hoping the varlet-loving Oakwood watchers would try to stop him. As they got to the fork, one of the officers suggested they dash over the log and finish Nell.

'It can wait', snapped Levi, hardly breaking stride. 'That varlet's not going anywhere.'

Officers guarding the swinging bridge jumped out to block their path, then moved aside quickly when they recognised the rabbit in front. Levi, who had never laid paw outside the South Bank, leapt onto the bridge. He stopped on the far side to chin and let Thaden catch up.

'Which way?'

'Both warrens are through there, in the field to the east. We should wait for our informer, though. He'll know the best way to do this. Speak of the Terrier. There he is now.'

Levi looked up the winding trail to the fringe of the oakwood, lit by a third-quarter moon. A crosser, its white flanks and the tips of its ears infested with hideous black patches, slithered out from behind the gnarled trunk of a tree.

'I'm not taking instructions from one of… those.'

'He's… it's shoulders and ears above all our other informers.'

'I don't care if it's the Prince With A Thousand Enemies, I don't want it – or its perverted mind – near me.'

'As you wish. At least let me ask it for the latest intelligence. It might help us.'

'The day I need help from a half-breed will be the day I take my last lungful of air. Go if you must. Quickly. And don't get too close.'

Thaden did as he was instructed, and they were soon skirting the shadows of the oakwood, aiming for the cracked brown trunk of a service tree mid-way between the two northern warrens. The daystar was nudging over a line of oaks to the east, and rabbits were grazing down the slope towards the Torrent. Levi waited until he saw the last varlets disappear below for the day. He ordered Thaden to take one group to the Drop. He would lead the attack on the larger Cocksfoot Warren.

'Special instructions, sir?'

'Biggest impact in the shortest time. Then meet back at the swinging bridge. And I want one buck from each squad to ensure a clear message is left: this is punishment for the collapse of my… our keep.'

'Special targets, sir?'

'Soft ones – does, kittens, any old bucks that stand in your way.'

*****

IT HAD BEEN a summer of plenty in the Oakwood. Plenty to eat, plenty of balmy nights, plenty of new-born kittens. And plenty of rabbits attending gathering after gathering throughout the North Bank after the success of the first Free Nell event late in the elder moon.

Pressure for change was growing, like a hovering cloud sucking up more and more moisture, ready to burst. Some of Thatch's inner circle were calling for a halt in the flow of acorns to the South, and there were signs the prime rabbit's stance was softening.

Thatch still hadn't agreed to meet Ollie. The Oakwood prime had, however, sent a message to Toria asking if some of her stewards could visit the South Bank and the island, to see for themselves what was going on. Unlike the previous group to visit the island, the Red Haws, this one would have real influence. It was to include Thatch's deputy, the rabbit whose opinion the prime trusted over all others.

The messenger returned with the news that Levi had refused to let the stewards enter the South. Ollie was initially disheartened. She desperately wanted them to see the conditions black rabbits had to endure. When Fleet mentioned how Levi's refusal had been greeted by the stewards, who took it to mean the southern prime had something to hide, Ollie saw an opportunity.

She invited them to visit Cocksfoot, to hear from black rabbits who had recently escaped from the South. They agreed, and had spent the evening listening to horrendous tales of beatings and rabbits being flung from Levi's brink. The youngsters had made an impression, though Thatch's deputy would take more convincing. The buck couldn't believe that a prime rabbit could behave in the way the southerners described.

When the meeting ended and the stewards went below to the large guest sleeping chamber, Ollie was dejected. It seemed that Levi's refusal to let the Oakwood rabbits cross the Torrent would defeat the blacks of the South yet again. She lingered in the swale, then padded over to the main entrance. As a frequent visitor to Cocksfoot, Ollie was familiar to the sentinels squatting on either side of the hole, watching for carns.

The sentinels would later report thinking nothing unusual when five white bucks arrived soon after, asking for a burrow to rest in for the day, as visiting rabbits did from time to time. The sentinels would report they were curious though, that once below, the visitors went the wrong way – down the passage to the single does' quarters.

Ollie was at the Junction, a star-shaped intersection at the heart of the warren, when she heard cries for help. She hurried towards the sound. The cries became screams.

She sniffed through the entrance. Defenceless does were being attacked by five enormous white bucks. Ollie yelled for them to stop. As they whirled to face her, she recognised the blood-covered features of Levi. He flung aside the doe he'd grabbed by the neck, and charged at Ollie, who spun and tore up the passage.

She felt Levi gaining on her, smelt the revolting mash of blood and sweat, but made the Junction a bound in front. A small rabbit can get around a tight corner easier than a large one, and Ollie used her size and knowledge of the passages to increase the distance between them. Not for long. Levi snapped at her rump as she burst through the entrance to the guest chamber and collapsed at the paws of Thatch's deputy.

Ollie could tell from the astonished faces that Levi had come through behind her. He was panting, his nose smeared with blood, black fur hanging from his lips. His demented gaze jerked from Ollie to take in the faces of the Oakwood rabbits, sizing them up. When he realised he was outnumbered, he collapsed to the ground.

'It is my pleasure,' Ollie announced, 'to introduce the prime rabbit of the South Bank.'

*****

FLEET HAD LEFT Hilltop soon after dayfall, and spent the night visiting the High and Row Warrens to complete his tour of the South. He'd decided the order of the subjects to report to Thatch. Now, as he scampered over the stone-bridge, he was thinking how to break the news of Maisy's passing to Ollie.

The daystar was stirring as he left the gloom of the trees and made for the tunnel. Meadow rabbits above ground were abuzz with news of attacks on the Cocksfoot and Drop Warrens. It was on every rabbit's lips, including a rumour that the prime rabbit of the South had hightailed back over the swinging bridge, chased by black clips.

Fleet had missed something big. Huge. He headed as fast as his tired legs would take him through the glade to the Oakwood clearing, where one of Thatch's circle bucks intercepted him and told him to report to the prime immediately. This was unusual. He sometimes had to wait days to give his report.

The passages to Thatch's burrow were busier than usual, and in side chambers Fleet noticed important rabbits deep in conversation. The words *Levi* and *the South*, and occasionally *Nell* flickered below like rain-cooled air rushing outward before a storm. Thatch's deputy met Fleet and escorted him past a line of other rabbits the prime had summoned. At the front of the queue was Ollie. Another first, and surely a sign of something momentous.

58. Spoken like a true friend

OLLIE HAD BEEN WAITING for whiles outside the prime rabbit's inner sanctum, called the White Hall, as members of her circle came and went in a bustle of activity. Some went out of their way to smile or wink their noses at her.

She'd rehearsed many times what she'd say if she finally got to see Thatch. Now she'd been summoned, in such dramatic circumstances, she was nervous. She understood how important the meeting could be to the South Bank in moons to rise, and wished Nell was here. He'd know exactly what to say.

A familiar scent brushed Ollie's nose, as Fleet entered the chamber. The seer smiled with his mouth, not his eyes. Ollie could tell something was wrong. She was about to ask, when she felt heavy paws on the ground behind her. She turned to see a magnificent white doe, the distinctive fur on her head swept back like the cap of a pennybun mushroom. Thatch. Her deputy came over to Ollie.

'Thank you for taking time out of your busy schedule to see us, Olivia. Allow me to introduce Thatch, the prime rabbit of the Oakwood.'

'It is an honour,' said Ollie.

Thatch noticed the seer sitting in the corner.

'Good of you to come, Fleet. Join us, please.'

The White Hall was an airy cavern walled in chalk. Dayholes spilt soft light onto tiered shelves piled with enough nuts and leaves to feed half of Lexa. Thatch asked Ollie if she'd recovered from her ordeal at Cocksfoot.

'Yes. I'm fine thank you.'

She started telling Thatch what happened. The prime listened politely for a while, then raised her paw.

'I'm aware of what happened, Olivia. I have been briefed.'

She turned to the seer.

'What can you tell us, Fleet, to give context to this… event?'

Fleet outlined what he'd seen in the South Bank after the collapse of Levi's keep – the rules imposed in response. Thatch listened intently, asking questions here and there. Fleet ended his report with the shocking news that Maisy had passed into the field of silence. Thatch, noticing Ollie was crying, thanked the seer and asked him to wait outside. She offered Ollie food, and they chewed quietly for a while.

'Feeling better?'

Ollie wiped her eyes.

'Yes, thank you.'

'Tell me about Nell. I believe the two of you are close.'

Ollie talked of their common roots by the rindle, how their friendship blossomed at Hilltop, their move to the Golden Field and their awakening to the unfairness of the colour rules and the Parting. She described Nell's intelligence, honesty, selflessness. She ended by summarising her friend's now-famous final words at the hearing.

'Nell has always stood against white supremacy, as well as black supremacy, dreaming of a free place where all rabbits live together in peace, like here in the Oakwood. It is a goal he hopes to see reached in his life…'

'Spoken like a true friend, I'm sure,' said Thatch. 'Experience has taught me, Olivia, to be wary of the flattery of friends. Which is why I have sought the views of other rabbits, including those with less reason to exaggerate, to disregard shortcomings. From what they tell me, it seems I have misjudged Nell. And you. I admit I have been prepared to hang something of a deaf ear to goings-on in the South, not wanting to interfere in the concerns of other warrens. Levi's reckless decision to launch an attack on the North Bank… changes things.

'I have never been a rabbit for the rather barbaric custom of an eye for an eye, so will not order an attack on Toria. Two frowns do not make a smile. So, tell me, Olivia, what would you have me do?'

'Stop sending acorns to the Golden Field. Hit Levi where it hurts. And free Nell.'

'Interesting,' said Thatch, rising. The meeting was over.

'Thank you, Olivia, for your time and counsel. Please wait outside, if you will.'

Ollie went out to crouch beside Fleet. A lanky rabbit with tufts of grey fur over his eyes arrived soon after and was ushered into the White Hall.

'That's Thatch's trade steward,' said the seer.

Ollie's stomach felt like a knot as they waited. And waited. Three more rabbits were summoned, all members of the prime rabbit's inner circle. The tension in the chamber was becoming suffocating. Finally, the face of Thatch's deputy appeared through the hole.

'Olivia, Fleet, please join us.'

Thatch was sitting on one of the raised shelves, flanked by her most trusted stewards. She waited for Ollie and Fleet to take their places.

'An attack on any rabbit of the North Bank from outside our warrens is an attack on us all. And cannot go unchallenged. We also believe rules based on the colour of a rabbit's fur are an offence against the rules of nature. In response, we have decided that all trade in nuts and berries between the North Bank and South Bank will cease immediately. Trade will only resume once we are satisfied the leaders of the South Bank have removed all rules based on the colour of a rabbit's fur. Messengers will be sent to Toria to advise the prime rabbit of the South Bank of our decision.'

Ollie stuped, for a heartbeat. After refusing to see her for so many moons, after one short meeting, Thatch had flipped completely, agreeing to everything Ollie had asked for. Except one.

'Thank you, Prime. What you have done today, all black rabbits on the South Bank will welcome. We also believe an injustice against one rabbit on the basis of the colour of his or her fur is an injustice against us all. Which is why I also asked you to free Nell.'

Thatch rubbed her chin.

'Well said, Olivia. I'm afraid, however, that is beyond my control. It was not me who banished Nell to the island.'

*****

IN THE DAYS since Maisy's passing and the attacks on the Cocksfoot and Drop Warrens, time loitered on the island. Signs of the changing season were glaring in the dew-drenched threads of spiders' webs suspended over the entrance to the keeps, the spotted flycatchers heading south. The daily routines of the captives, though, stayed the same.

From the constant flow of information from new captives, the guards and Hugh, it became clear that Thatch's decision to stop sending acorns to the South was biting. Levi was maddened by the restrictions, and had vowed to never surrender. His first response had been to hoard all the remaining nuts. Supplies were taken to new stores at his private chambers in Toria, and clips ordered to guard them. Most complained, if not to Levi's face, to any other rabbit who would listen. White does had to carry the nuts – Levi didn't trust a single black – and they complained louder.

White rabbits with relations in the Oakwood moved their families to the North Bank, and others unable to go became increasingly irate. Some pleaded for Drekkel to do something. When Levi heard of the traitorous talk, he declared that if a white rabbit spent more than a single moon away from the South Bank, he would be considered an alien, and his burrow taken over.

By the ivy moon, when hazelnuts began falling in the trees of the Golden Field, Levi insisted they be stored until Thatch saw sense, which he was convinced would be only a matter of time. Black bucks were still forced to harvest the juniper berries, but instead of releasing them for South Bank whites, Levi demanded they be left to rot on the ground. Clips carrying out these instructions gossiped that Levi was losing his mind. Jokes were being whispered behind the prime rabbit's back, something that would never have happened only moons earlier.

Another problem was the white carriers who had nothing to do. They had been chosen for their strength, and kept in line with the promise of extra acorns. With the supply dried up, they grew bitter and restless. They formed into bands of ruffians, taking out their frustrations on not only black rabbits. More whites prepared to leave for the North.

Thatch's restrictions and the pain they were causing the whites were a boost for the long-suffering black rabbits. The Cluster was rejuvenated and, with frustrated clips being used to guard acorn stores rather than keep black rabbits in their place, protest gatherings in the South were held for the first time in moons. The theme of all the gatherings was Free Nell, in bold defiance of the rule forbidding mention of the captive's name. Nell was also on the lips of rabbits in the comfortable burrows of Toria, and some particularly brave whites went to the gatherings, where they were welcomed by their black cousins. Claw was overrun with rabbits of all moons wanting to join, with daring plans for creating chaos. More white rabbits fled to the North.

Then, as the ivy moon thinned and massed clouds of starlings twisted and dipped to form sinister shapes over the crater at dayfall, rumours about Levi intensified. He hadn't been seen outside his burrow for nights. Depending on who Nell listened to, the South Bank prime was either ill, in the field of silence or had gone mad. The only constant rumour was that he was becoming increasingly isolated. It was as if all rabbits – black, white and crosser – were holding their breath, waiting to see what would happen next.

*****

WITH EACH SETBACK, Levi retreated further into the dark places in his head. He spent days on his own in the repaired chamber behind the brink, moaning at the treacherous walls and floor and ceiling. Every scratch or creak was an unseen varlet jeering, undermining him. Food was brought by eclipo officers, always in pairs. Does – black and white – were too frightened to be alone in the same burrow as their prime.

Levi ignored pleas from his stewards to attend circle meetings and give leadership. Disorder wormed through the warren and seeped into the fields of the South Bank. Burrow digging and cleaning stopped, and plant scraps, nut shells and pellets cluttered the passages of Toria. Guard rosters were mixed up and stores raided. Carn attacks claimed the lives of white rabbits, including one of Levi's mates. More whites crossed to the North Bank. Levi's nightmares were filled with double stamps, gushing mud. And wailing.

He stretched to peek through the hole and out over the flats. Varlet kittens were playing Patch, *practising to lie and murder and crap in their burrows*. To the west, a rabbit sped towards the juniper diamond, his white coat highlighted by the third-quarter moon. It was Thaden, trailed by five eclipo officers. Levi sensed someone in the chamber behind him. He turned to see Drekkel.

'Where's Thaden going? I haven't given orders?'

'He's leaving the South Bank. Leaving you, father. It's over.'

'Says who? What rabbit dares challenge me?'

'I do, father. The circle has asked me to take over. To save what's left of the warren.'

Levi's mouth dropped.

'You? My own son?'

He raised his tail, clenched his shoulders and scowled at the pretender. Drekkel remained crouched, not even bracing to defend himself.

'I've come to ask you to give up peacefully, father. Though if it's a fight you want, a fight you will get.'

Levi continued circling.

'This is *my* warren. I built it up from nothing.'

'It was burrowed from soil that was unstable, father, on foundations and ideas and rules that could never last. It is *you* who has torn down the warren.'

Levi couldn't believe the foul words oozing from his own son, Vort's grandson, a direct blood descendant from the line of Erfeti.

'Where is the loyalty, the respect of a son for his father?'

'I am doing this, father, because I want my own sons and daughters to have decent lives. Respect must be earnt, not taken for granted like a pile of thrush-haws. You speak of loyalty. A prime must be loyal to the rabbits he represents. All of them. White, black and crosser.'

'Never,' cried Levi, swiping at the face, the insolence, the insanity.

Drekkel leaned out of the way like he was dodging a dragonfly. Levi lost his balance and toppled. His head thumped into something hard, and his world went black.

*****

OLLIE'S POSITION in the pecking order of the Oakwood had changed in the three moons since meeting Thatch. She was now being consulted by members of the prime rabbit's circle on matters concerning the South, and had been given a choice of burrows off a passage from the White Hall. She chose the smallest for herself, making the rest available to visiting black rabbits from the South who, because of the growing indifference of the border guards, were finding it easier to cross the Torrent.

The visitors reported that since Drekkel ousted his father, violence on the South Bank had worsened. Marauding packs of enraged former carriers had been creating mayhem, and retaliation from black rabbits had become bolder. To reduce the chances of white and black rabbits getting into arguments or fighting, Drekkel had tried to limit the times rabbits of different coloured fur could go above ground. It failed. Black does had to finish their work in the burrows of Toria early to get to Lexa ahead of the curfew, infuriating their masters who were left with half-cleaned chambers and unexercised kittens demanding attention.

By far the biggest inconvenience to the rabbits of Toria, though, was the trade ban. They had become so used to an endless supply of acorns, having them suddenly removed from their diets caused unexpected reactions.

Black servant does came down from Toria with stories of their masters complaining of headaches, stomach aches, dizziness, sweating, and of moods swinging from sadness to madness. Drekkel, they said, was struggling to keep control.

A messenger from Toria had shown up at the White Hall two nights earlier to tell Thatch of Drekkel's latest give-backs, which the southern prime hoped would end the restrictions. The curfews were being dropped, and there was a new rule: *no rabbit of any colour was to say anything that might lead to arguments between rabbits of different colours.* Thatch, who asked Ollie's opinion before giving her reply, agreed that Drekkel's give-backs were a joke.

Ollie was used to being visited by the black doms of the Cocksfoot and Meadow Warrens, and was in her meeting burrow discussing carn management with the dom from the Drop when her assistant interrupted to say that important-looking white bucks from the South Bank were waiting outside to see her.

'This is a first,' said Ollie. 'Who are they, and why are they here?'

'They say they've come on behalf of rabbits from Toria. And will speak only to you, Ollie.'

Levi's attack on the northern warrens was still fresh in Ollie's memory.

'Do they appear… dangerous? Should we ask Thatch to send guards as a precaution?'

'I wouldn't think so,' said the assistant. 'They don't smell aggressive in the least. More nervous.'

Ollie was intrigued.

'Tell them I'll be there shortly.'

The Drop dom was grinning. Ollie asked what was so funny.

'You mentioned *firsts*. I imagine this is the first time white rabbits from the South Bank have been asked… *told* to wait for a black rabbit. Because she's busy talking to another black rabbit. It's about time, I say.'

'What could they possibly want with me?'

'You better find out,' said the dom, hopping to the entrance. 'And don't forget, Ollie my friend, *you* speak on behalf of far more rabbits than your *nervous* visitors.'

The white rabbits, led by an ancient but proud buck, came into the chamber looking as uncomfortable as Ollie imagined she would in a burrow in Toria. He assured her that the group had not been sent by Drekkel or Levi, and that the southern prime would probably have them banished to the island if he found out they were here.

'Frankly, Olivia…'

'Please, call me Ollie.'

'As you wish… Ollie. We've journeyed here because we're worried about what's happening in the South, and for our kittens and their kittens in moons to rise. We, all of us, suspect the prime rabbit and his father, and his grandfather, have fed us a constant diet of fake news, exaggerations and outright lies. We've come to find out for ourselves what exactly this Cluster of yours wants.'

Ollie studied the rabbits, deciding whether to trust them. All held eye contact, looking back respectfully.

They appeared genuinely interested, as she explained how rules based on the colour of fur were not only at the root of the South's problems, they were preventing rabbits of every colour reaching their potential. How she hated violence so much, she hopped around ladybirds.

How the senseless and unnatural brutality of the white rulers had left black rabbits two choices: resist or pass into the field of silence.

'You ask what we want. It's simple. For rabbits of all colours to live together in peace, with equal opportunities, in a free South Bank.'

The white buck, who had been nodding as Ollie talked, smiled.

'Vort and Levi have been telling us that you and all your colleagues in the Cluster are a rabid mob of violent half-wits intent on driving us into the Torrent. And what do we find? An intelligent rabbit who wouldn't hurt a ladybird. On behalf of my friends, I want to thank you Ollie, for your time, for agreeing to see us, for opening our eyes and ears.'

'You're welcome.'

'I have one more question. What needs to be done to stop the madness? How do we get to this place you talk of, where rabbits of all colours live together in peace?'

'Free Nell,' said Ollie. 'It's the only way.'

*****

NELL KEPT GETTING UPDATES on what was happening off the island. Chaos was billowing like thunderclouds throughout the South Bank. Drekkel offered more give-backs, including removing some of the forbidden lines, in the hope that Thatch would end the acorn ban. She didn't.

It would take something significant to make her budge.

One of the give-backs was to make Nell's captivity more comfortable. Through the friendly warder, Gregory, Nell learnt that Drekkel didn't share his father's obsession with the bank's most famous captive. Although he considered Nell a dangerous and violent spreader of terror, he did not see why the black rabbit should suffer unnecessarily. He was also smart enough to understand that if anything happened to Nell, whatever control he had over the South would disappear, and he would be blamed.

Instructions were sent to the island for Nell to be offered a larger burrow, better food, easier work. And he was allowed to sleep during the day and work and roam at night. Nell said *no* to the change of burrow. He'd become attached to his keep. He would, however, accept the improved food and work, only if the comrades who had been on the island almost as long as him were given the same deal. He was astonished how easily his requests were granted. He and a few others no longer had to shift stones in the crater. They were let up to the heath for extended whiles during the night. Nell marvelled at the rare sight of Venus dragging the thinning crescent moon over the poplars, and wondered what he was being prepared for.

A few nights later, Hugh arrived, and when he asked to speak to Nell on his own, the guards agreed immediately. The diviner waited until they were out of hearing.

'I have a message from Drekkel,' said Hugh, grinning like a kitten.

'He's prepared to free you from the island. On two conditions. You are to order the Cluster and Claw to stop their violence, and return quietly to your birth warren by the rindle.'

59. In the way of freedom

NELL HAD BEEN THINKING a lot lately about relaxing beside the rindle. It was a place of happy memories. The sweet murmur of campion on warm spring nights, the honey tones of flag iris. The joys of adventure, of making sense of the natural world of a rabbit. Of playing Patch, outwitting weasels. The rindle, though, was also a place of violence, of painful discovery and the loss of innocence. The crunching of bone against the trunk of a willow, the chilling tap of a deathwatch beetle, finding out that the natural world could be turned upside-down because of the colour of a rabbit's fur.

Hugh winked his nose.

'What shall I tell Drekkel?'

Nell knew he could trust the diviner.

'Tell me, Hugh, who else knows about this offer?'

'Very few. Drekkel swore me to secrecy. Said I should tell you, and you only.'

'Can we trust him?'

'Not completely. Though he's more reliable than Levi ever was.'

'That's what I'm hearing too.'

'Thatch will know soon enough. As I was leaving, I overheard Drekkel telling one of his stewards to take a message to the Oakwood prime.'

Clever, thought Nell.

'I see what Drekkel's up to. By insisting that *I* speak out against violence, he's putting responsibility for the chaos on black rabbits rather than white. Telling Thatch about the conditions for my release makes it appear it's me, not Drekkel, standing in the way of my freedom.'

'You're probably right,' said Hugh. 'He's trying to split you away from your supporters. Classic Vort technique, that. Divide and rule. I'm told Drekkel spent a lot of time with his grandfather. What, then, will you do? Drekkel will expect an answer.'

'And he shall have one, Hugh. First though, I have a special favour to ask. You know the black diviner, Desmond?'

'I do.'

'On your way to Toria to give my answer to Drekkel, I want you to explain it to Desmond, and ask him to tell as many rabbits as he can.'

'Of course.'

Nell gave Hugh his response to Drekkel's offer. The diviner listened, tears forming in his eyes.

'I have one more favour, my friend. As soon as you've delivered the messages to Desmond and Drekkel, I want you to cross the Torrent to see Ollie, tell her what I've done.'

*****

NEWS SPED through the black warrens of the South Bank that an important gathering was taking place at the Mound of Mark, named after the brave Cluster buck sent to the field of silence after encouraging does to stop working in the burrows of Toria forty moons earlier.

Fleet joined rabbits from as far away as Hilltop, who'd started gathering ahead of the appointed time. The mood matched the grim grey of the clouds, the heavy air stinging lungs, sharpening senses. Nervous whispers thanked The Divine for the coming storm that should keep the eclipo dozing in the warm burrows of Toria. Fleet wasn't sure what to expect. He was surprised when the black diviner Desmond appeared on the mound.

'I have a message for you all from our leader, Nell.'

The crowd went so quiet, the rabbits would have been able to hear the wingbeat of a winter moth.

'Drekkel has offered Nell his freedom – if he agrees to speak against violence and return peacefully to the Willow Warren.'

Cheers and shouts of joy sounded all around Fleet, then a series of thu-thumps as the rabbits gave their banished leader a massed salute that shook the ground, sending shards of frost into the air. Fleet watched Desmond, who waited patiently, one paw raised.

'Nell's message is this,' he shouted. 'He is puzzled by the conditions of Drekkel's offer. Nell says he is not, and never has been, a violent rabbit. It was only when black rabbits of the South Bank had tried all peaceful forms of protest – unsuccessfully – that the Cluster was forced to meet claw with claw.'

Desmond had to wait through another barrage of thu-thump salutes.

'Nell says Drekkel needs to show that he is a different rabbit to Levi and Vort. Let *him* say no to violence.'

The ground shook once more. Desmond waited patiently.

'Nell says Drekkel must end all rules based on the colour of a rabbit's fur. Let Drekkel free all rabbits who have been put in his keeps or banished to the island, or chased away from the South Bank for their opposition to the colour rules.'

The salutes resumed, but stopped as soon as Desmond raised his paw.

'Nell says he longs for his own freedom, but not as much as he longs for *your* freedom. Too many rabbits have passed into the field of silence since he was sent to the island, or suffered for the simple and natural craving to be free.

'Nell asks, what freedom will he enjoy if he may be attacked and punished the instant he hops over another forbidden line?

'Nell says this: Only rabbits who are truly free can discuss the way forward. Captives cannot. Nell will give no promise to Drekkel, as long as he, and you, all the rabbits of the South Bank, are not free. Because *his* freedom and *your* freedom cannot be parted, Nell says he will remain on the island.'

60. Time to talk

NELL WAS FEELING HIS AGE. The passing moons, shifting stones, breathing lime dust and poor eating had battered his lungs, blunted and chipped his teeth, and reduced his body's ability to fight ailments common in late-moon rabbits. Working in the crater under the daystar had weakened his eyesight. Though his mind remained sharp, it took little to drag him back on his hindquarters. Stiffening in his joints was making the journey up and down the ramp difficult, and he couldn't groom as he used to. He'd lost most of the fur on his hind paws and the parts of his legs that touched the ground when he sat.

That night at work, he got a splinter in his right hind paw, which was causing him grief. At the end of the shift, Nell and his inner circle of comrades were discussing the latest reports from incoming captives. Curfews were being defied, black does were refusing to clean white burrows, bucks refusing to harvest nuts and berries. They were being marched off to keeps, and when those became full, they were beaten. With each black *victory*, the wrath and brutality of the clips hardened.

Nell listened to the discussion around him. From what most of his comrades were saying, they believed freedom would only be won by violence, that they were stronger, more numerous than the whites, and it would be foolish for the Cluster to talk peace now that black rabbits held the upper paw. Nell was not so sure. He remembered what his father said after hearing of Maisy's rosy version of why their ancestors came to the South Bank. *There are two sides to every story. At least two. And the truth usually lives somewhere in the middle.*

From Gregory and Hugh and other guards who had little reason to flavour their information with their own desires, Nell was hearing of disturbing happenings off the island. Black rabbits being cruel to whites. Black rabbits attacking other blacks suspected of being informers. Some had been kicked out of their burrows and were living rough above ground, at the mercy of carns.

As he'd been listening to his friends, Walter had been trying to get the splinter out of his paw. Unsuccessfully. It had gone in too deep and snapped off under the surface. Nell had a sleepless day. When he was woken at dayfall, he could hardly move. The splinter had burrowed deeper, the whole paw was inflamed, and pain shot up his leg when he tried to put weight on it. He was given the night off work and moved to one of the guards' bolt holes at the eastern end of the heath. The hole was four times the size of his keep in the crater, had three entrances, and was sheltered from the wind and rain. Soft grass and moss lined the floor.

'You'll find all the food you need close by,' said Gregory. 'Help yourself.'

'Thanks, but I won't be going far with this splinter. I wish Maisy was here. She'd know how to get it out.'

'That gives me an idea,' said Gregory. 'Your mother helped one of the guards at the span one time. I'm sure he had a splinter. I'll check.'

Gregory soon confirmed it had been a splinter, and Maisy's suggestion to draw it out using chewed elder berries had worked. The warden had been informed, and word had gone out for the South Bank to be scoured for berries. The next night, a white doe was brought to his hole on the heath, carrying plantain. After dropping it at Nell's paws, she apologised that no elder berries could be found that time of the year.

'This plant will be better for you anyway, sir.'

No white rabbit had ever referred to Nell as *sir.*

The doe, like a paler version of his mother, explained how the bitter sap from the leaves would remove swelling around the splinter, and suck out the toxins. She showed Nell how to chew the leaves and apply the sticky substance to his injured paw. It was another reminder that kindness had nothing to do with the colour of a rabbit's fur. Nell thanked the doe, who left, telling the guard escorting her where to find more rosettes of plantain.

'He'll need to apply them to the wound for three days, then the splinter will pop out.'

Nell used the time, on his own and away from the other captives, to think. The change of burrow, he decided, might not be so bad after all. It could be an opportunity. He sensed the time had come to talk to Drekkel, or risk both sides reaching the darkest places from which there could be no return. Henry's words echoed in Nell's ears. *There are moments, son, when a dom must listen to the voice inside his head and hop out in front of the warren.*

Being alone, Nell saw now, might give him the chance to take the first necessary hop along that path.

In the name of Claw – Nell's creation – black rabbits had been causing chaos for moons and had few positives to show for it. The negatives were piling up. Too many rabbits had passed into the field of silence. The enemy remained powerful. Yes, they were showing cracks, but the white rabbits were stronger, healthier, better organised. Despite what most of the captives in the crater might think, outmuscling the whites was a distant, if not impossible dream. It made no sense for more rabbits to pass in a struggle so unnecessary. Drekkel, he sensed, was coming to the same conclusion.

Yes, it was time to talk.

Nell would have to tread carefully.

Narrow-minded rabbits with rooted views – of both colours – would consider the mere suggestion of talking to the other side as betrayal. His comrades would ground the idea before it took flight. A decision to talk to Drekkel was so important, it should involve the high-ups of the Cluster, particularly Ollie. There was no way, however, nor time, to have the conversation. It was up to Nell to take the first hop, and it had to be in secret.

Telling no-one what he was doing would also give the Cluster an excuse if things went wrong. *The silly late-mooner was left on his own, removed from the advice of his comrades, and in so much pain, he wasn't thinking straight.*

Nell woke on the third night after the doe's visit.

A fattening crescent moon was being tugged through its low arc by Mars, glowing red in the sky to the south. The splinter had fallen out during the day, and Nell was greeted by Hugh as he fed near the burrow.

'Tell Drekkel I'm willing to talk.'

*****

AFTER BEING DISPLACED as prime of the South Bank, Levi had roamed the rabbit-free marshlands to the east, sleeping rough and eating rougher. Hunger in the end conquered shame, forcing him back to the rowan above the rindle. He challenged the new governor but, in his weakened condition, was chased off.

He found his way to his old Hide and dozed there through the days, shivering in the chill of the sleeping moon, sneaking out in the darkest parts of the nights to steal privet berries from the governor's patch. He stumbled back one night to find an unexpected visitor waiting for him.

Levi hadn't seen his mother since Vort passed. He'd heard she'd gone south, but had never been close enough to Helga to care. Now here she was, in his face, stinking of ivy.

'There's something I've been waiting a lifetime to tell you, Levi, something your father should have told you, something you need to know.'

Levi was too exhausted to object.

'I am not your mother.'

'What?'

'Vort, your father, mated with another doe. A black doe.'

'Don't be ridiculous. He would never...'

'He rescued you from your mother's nest during a storm.'

From the pit of his memory, Levi felt a rush of cold air, sharp teeth grabbing his neck, his hind legs thrashing as he was carried away.

'There's something else, Levi. You had a sister.'

Again, a flash of memory. A boom, a warm body shaking beside him. Sharing the terror of the storm.

'The black doe who took your sister in after your mother was... drowned... had named her Olivia. I believe she has become known throughout the South Bank, and the North, as Ollie.

'She… it's… a varlet?'

'By the colour of her fur, yes. But Ollie – and you Levi – coming from a white father and black mother, are actually…'

'Crossers.'

Levi bolted from the Hide, no longer caring who saw him. As he hurtled down to the rindle, he felt the fleas biting, gorging on his skin, his fur, laying their repulsive eggs, their evil crosser blood surging from his claws to his ears.

61. The summit of Ash Green

THE GUARD, Gregory, came to escort Nell off the island while the other captives were still in their keeps. White puffs spilled from their mouths as they crunched along the clifftop trail, past the deserted guard post, and crossed the frosted log span. All around him, Nell heard, saw and smelt beauty in the forgotten. The *tit-tit-tit* and *ke-zik* rattles of a wren. Glistening bark on trees invisible from the crater, their branches tipped with buds pointing to spring. The dug-soil smell of scarlet elf cups sprouting from spent twigs.

Gregory was Nell's only companion as they picked their way between the wood and the Torrent, unlike the journey to the island after the hearing, when he was surrounded by aggressive clips. Nell noticed white bucks crouched a few bounds into the wood, facing away from the trail. Gregory said they were sentinels.

'Really? Who would they be protecting out here?'

'You.'

They saw no other rabbits until they approached the guard post at the tunnel through to the juniper diamond. Gregory and his special captive were expected. The guards let them through. The juniper bushes were in a terrible state. There were passed patches near the trunks and overlapping branches suffocated new growth. Nell had heard that the black rabbit who tended the bushes had been chased off and replaced with a white supervisor.

He and Gregory were almost at the dale when they saw their first black rabbits. It was impossible not to notice the mangled ears, the festering sores, missing fur, the limps, stooped shoulders, eyes downcast in defeat. Tracts of dried mud where grass had been gnawed past the roots pocked the flats of Lexa. It was far worse than when Nell was banished to the island – outrageous in a place as naturally abundant as the South Bank.

Nell needn't have worried about being recognised. He'd been on the island so long, the pale tuft on his forehead was virtually lost in the grey flecks thrushing his fur. No rabbit gave him a second glance.

Climbing up from the flats onto the Golden Field was like moving from the bleakest winter to the extravagance of spring. The tim grass was inviting, even for the sleeping moon, and dotted not with mud but clumps of enticing nettles and wood blewit and early-flowering dandelions. Bunches of fruit hung low from the privets and hawthorns. Obscenely healthy white rabbits in thick unblemished winter coats grazed calmly and confidently in the field, never far from bolt holes, watched over by a ring of sentinels. It did not appear to Nell like a bank in chaos. He expected Gregory to take him to Toria. Instead, they veered south and through to the Common.

'Drekkel also wants the meeting to be away from prying eyes and ears,' said the guard. 'We're early. Would you like to meet my family, Nell?'

'You live *here*, in the Common?'

'Hasn't been called that for moons. We call it Ash Green now, after the tree up there on the hill. And yes. Families – white families – have come here to get away… too frightened to live so close to Lexa and… the troubles.'

'How often do you get to see your family?'

'I get two days off a moon.'

It hadn't occurred to Nell that his guards were also victims of the Parting.

Gregory's mate was friendly enough, though Nell noticed she scanned constantly, probably checking that none of her neighbours recognised her guest. Kittens from her latest litter were playing with friends outside the burrow.

Nell overheard one of the guard's sons boasting that their visitor was the Black Robert. The reactions of the youngsters dismayed Nell.

'That varlet's mad as an adder and crazy as a hare,' said one.

'It wants to send every white rabbit into the field of silence and colour the Torrent red with our blood,' said another.

Three of the kittens hightailed for their burrows, as if they'd heard that the Terrier was loose in the field. Nell was saddened, rather than angry. The kittens would be echoing the words of their parents. They were victims, too, brought up to hate rabbits purely because of the colour of their fur.

'We should get going, Nell.'

They made for the flat-topped hill protruding from the hedgerow at the eastern boundary of the field. The summit, marked by its lone ash tree, was reached via a snaking tunnel through briar similar to the thicket on the way to Hilltop. Nell, padding tenderly on the paw that had the splinter, soon fell behind the stronger, fitter guard. He stopped to rest. A pair of long-tailed tits chattering somewhere above went silent. Nell became aware that he was alone and not guarded for the first time in more than twenty-five moons. The tits resumed their *si-si-si* calls. As if they were urging Nell to *run-run-RUN*.

There was a gap at the base of the briar large enough for him to crawl through. Too tight for Gregory or a clip. On the other side, he could see a channel veering off diagonally to… freedom. Nell's heart was thumping. He squeezed his eyes shut. This could all be a trap, like the escape plot on the island. Running would be irresponsible. And dangerous. He heard paws shuffling above him, and thought of Levi, one of the few white rabbits other than the guard who *would* recognise him. He shivered, sweating, his hind legs rooted.

A white face appeared.

It was Gregory.

'You alright?'

Nell exhaled.

'I am now. Let's do this.'

They came out at the lip of the plateau. White rabbits were lying beside holes around the ash, which Nell could now see was infested with mistletoe. The white rabbits glanced at the newcomers, then resumed their grooming. The wide passage Gregory took Nell down had the smell of recently dug soil, and they passed side burrows being enlarged by white does. A giant of a rabbit was guarding the entrance to Drekkel's private chamber.

'The prime's expecting you,' he said.

Nell's heart thumped again as he entered. Shafts from the daystar spilled through holes in the roof, mingling with tiny fragments of dust to light the coat of Drekkel sitting on the far side of the chamber. The white rabbit smiled and hopped towards Nell, meeting him half-way. The son of Levi – and grandson of Vort – put Nell at ease by asking about the wound to his paw.

'Tender, though manageable. The journey was a little longer than I expected.'

'My apologies for that, Nell. I believe it is in both our interests to keep this meeting between ourselves, for now at least.'

Nell nodded.

'Forgive me, you must be tired, and hungry. Please, help yourself.'

There was the choice of hazel and chestnuts, dried tim grass and assorted fruits.

'Thanks, but I haven't come all this way to eat.'

'Of course. So…'

Drekkel seemed unsure where to start. Nell seized the moment.

'I am deeply worried about the way the South Bank is being torn apart. Black rabbits and white rabbits sending each other to the field of silence, sucking the breath out of *our* place.'

Drekkel scratched his chin.

'So am I, Nell. Which is why I asked you and your Cluster to say no to violence, commit to peace, before we can consider new *arrangements*. Violence is against the rules we live under in the South Bank, cannot be tolerated.'

'You speak of rules, Drekkel. It is the rabbits who claim to rule the South Bank who are responsible for the violence. If a leader uses violence to get his way, the rabbits he rules have no choice but to fight back, to defend themselves. If you tell your clips – eclipo officers – to use words rather than claws, we will do the same. It is up to you, not us, to say no to violence. Our refusal is not the problem. The problem Drekkel, is that you and the rabbits you speak for are not ready to share power with black rabbits.'

The white prime swallowed.

'You speak of *sharing* power. You know as well as I, Nell, that black rabbits outnumber white rabbits. We would be in the minority. At your mercy. How would you and this Cluster of yours protect the rights of the few over the many?'

Nell had expected the question.

'Contrary to what you may think, Drekkel, or have heard, we do not want to chase white rabbits into or over the Torrent. Your fear of the few being ruled by the many is simply a disguised attempt to keep control.'

Drekkel smiled.

'I'm told you became something of an expert at disguises.'

The quip punctured some of the tension, and showed Drekkel was indeed a different rabbit to Levi and Vort.

'The South Bank belongs to all rabbits who live on it,' said Nell, 'whatever the colour of their fur. White rabbits are South Bankers too. Black rabbits need white rabbits, as you need us. We have much to learn from the way you use sentinels to protect warrens from carns, how you manage grazing areas so there's enough food for everyone. And white rabbits could certainly benefit from our knowledge of healing plants. It's time to face reality, Drekkel. Rule by the many and peace are like two sides of the same leaf. You and your friends need to accept there will never be peace on the South Bank until the many are free to decide how they want to live.'

'What is it you expect, Nell? How do you suggest we move forward?'

'Get rid of the rules based on colour, end the restrictions on the Cluster and Claw, release our captives and let exiles return to the South Bank.'

Drekkel exhaled, sending speckles of dust whirling up to the roof of the chamber. Nell went on.

'When I came into this world, Drekkel, I had no longing to be free, because I was born free. Free to hop in the field at our warren by the rindle, free to play Patch with my friends, free to eat whatever plants I could find. As long as I lived according to the natural way of rabbits.

It was only when… our family… went to the Platform Warren, and I discovered my kitten freedoms were fantasies, that my freedom had been stolen because of the colour of my fur, that I began to long for it. At first I was thinking only of myself. I wanted the freedom to go where I wanted, eat what I wanted. Later, when I came to the Golden Field, I longed for the simple freedoms of being what I could be, finding a mate, fathering kittens.

'But when I became aware that it wasn't just my liberty being taken away, but the liberty of all rabbits who shared my fur colour, I joined the Cluster. It was that longing for all rabbits to have the freedom to live our lives in dignity and self-respect that changed a shy buck into a daring one, a rule-following rabbit into a rebel… and outcast.'

The white rabbit was listening intently.

'As to your offer, Drekkel, I have no more desire than the next rabbit to suffer. My conscience, though, would never let me accept the limited freedoms you are offering *me*, while other black rabbits are not free. Freedom, you see, is unbreakable. Restrictions on one rabbit are restrictions on us all. Black and white.'

The white prime opened his mouth to speak, but remained silent.

'Tell me something, Drekkel. Do you have kittens?'

'I have. What of it?'

'Do I appear threatening to you?'

'Not in the least.'

'Mad as an adder? Crazy as a hare?'

'On the contrary. You are one of the most intelligent, caring rabbits I have had the pleasure to meet.'

Nell mentioned what the white kitten friends of his guard's son had said.

'And I have little doubt, Drekkel, that if you were to visit the Willow Warren, black kittens there would describe you in a similar way. This is what it has come to.'

Drekkel shook his head.

Not in disagreement. In sadness.

Nell looked directly into the eyes of the son of Levi.

'A rabbit who takes away another rabbit's freedom is himself a captive. He – or she – is trapped behind a thicket of hate. The ruler and the ruled are robbed of the qualities that make them rabbits. Which is why both need to be free.'

The two rabbits held each other's gaze long enough to take Nell back to that fateful day as a kitten when he stared down Levi, deep into the heart of his eye, and saw hate. It was Drekkel who looked away first.

'Thank you for coming, Nell. You've given me plenty to consider. I cannot give you an answer today. I must talk to some in my circle.'

Nell was still trying to identify what he'd seen in Drekkel's face, as he and Gregory entered the briar on their journey back to the island. Anguish, for sure. Sympathy, perhaps. As they got to the bottom of the hill, it came to him. Compassion.

*****

THE MEETING between Drekkel and Nell had remained so secret that few, other than the two rabbits, the guard and Hugh, knew it had taken place. Even Fleet's vast web of sources on the South Bank were unaware.

So when a messenger from Toria arrived with invitations for Fleet and other North Bank high-ups to hear an announcement by Drekkel in the cavern where Nell's hearing had been held, the seer's first reaction was to not bother. He expected yet another minor give-back to the blacks of the South, which he was confident other seers would tell him about. When the messenger explained that Drekkel had asked for Fleet specifically, the seer became curious and agreed to go.

As he toiled up the slope to Toria, he was reminded of the buzz of activity outside the cavern before the hearing. The sleeping moon was full, but few stars shone brightly enough this time to pierce the clouds hanging in the gully like a patchy coat of fur between the Oakwood and the Golden Field.

The size of the gathering crammed into the cavern was similar, the rabbits equally important. The seer noticed the doms of the Cocksfoot and Drop and Meadow Warrens, rabbits from Thatch's circle, including her trusted deputy. Most of the southern warrens were represented by doms or their deputies. Fleet spotted Levi, lurking in a corner. The former prime stared back. Although he'd been stripped of his power and there were rumours he was losing his mind, he was still strong, the eyes penetrating. Menacing.

The crowd went quiet as Drekkel entered the cavern and mounted the shelf where the judge sat on that fateful day moons ago. There were no mistle berries this time. Drekkel rose.

'Thank you all for coming here today. Special thanks to our friends who have journeyed far, from the Oakwood and other warrens in the North to the Willow in the South.'

There were groans from some of the Toria rabbits. Drekkel ignored them.

'The moons of violence and Parting are over. The time for peace and togetherness has arrived. Hate has to be replaced with friendship, fighting with working together, injustice with justice. All rules based on the colour of a rabbit's fur are therefore gone. Rules separating rabbits based on the colour of their fur, such as forbidden lines, grazing areas, access to burrows, bolt holes and grass and plants of all types, are gone. Rules restricting the location and size of burrows, and preventing a burrow being improved… are gone. Rabbits of all colours are free to go wherever they want, between warrens, between fields, between the South and North Bank, and rules stating how a rabbit of one colour should stand or behave in the presence of a rabbit of another colour… are gone. Rabbits brought against their will to the Golden Field to work in nut and berry harvesting, or in the burrows of Toria, are free to return to their home warrens.'

Drekkel paused to take a breath. So, Fleet noticed, did every rabbit in the cavern, so stunned were they by what they were hearing. Drekkel looked up at his father.

'Squads of eclipo officers assigned to enforce rules relating to colour will be disbanded, and their members reassigned to patrolling for carns and expanding and maintaining bolt holes in *all* warrens of the South Bank. Keeps dug to hold rabbits caught breaking colour rules are to be sealed off or, if suitable, enlarged and given to black and crosser rabbits needing burrows. The Cluster and Claw are no longer banned, and rabbits of any colour born on the South Bank who left for whatever reason are welcome to come home.'

Fleet's eyes had stayed on Levi, whose body shuddered with each announcement. Finally, the crowd numb with shock, Drekkel ordered the release from the island of Nell and his fellow captives.

As the cavern erupted in shouting and stamping, Fleet noticed Levi storm out.

*****

HER BODY WAS WEARY, the joints in her legs throbbing, and her fur was knotted in the places her paws could no longer stretch to groom, but Ollie's heart was soaring with the kestrels far above the Oakwood. She'd spent the morning going from burrow to burrow, saying goodbye and thanking the friends she'd made over the moons of her exile. In the afternoon she rested, preparing her body for what lay ahead. Now, as the daystar dipped past the frosted silhouettes of the oaks at the western edge of the clearing, she set off down the glade on the first leg of her journey.

Though Ollie's paws were treading on the North Bank, her thoughts were bounding forward, to a happier time in the South. Memory after memory carried her closer to home. Kittens playing in a hollowed trunk reminded her of sheltering inside a willow, disguised by the smell of weasels. Seeing a doe talking to kittens at the Meadow Warren took Ollie back to the stories of Aunt Mina.

Each pleasant memory of the South was a shared experience with her dearest friend. The two rabbits were like the stalk and blade of a leaf, the beginning and end of an idea. The excitement of seeing Nell, of sitting side by side once again, joking, crying, catching up on all they'd missed together, nudged Ollie on.

62. As if no-one else existed

NELL WAS THINKING of Ollie as he took one last nose around the keep that had been not only a barrier to freedom for most of his adult moons, but a familiar home and sanctuary. He knew every curve, every crevice, the exact distance from the tip of his raised ears to the ceiling, the precise play of every draft, the subtle shifts from winter to spring to summer in the moisture of the soil and echo of the rock.

Ollie, Nell realised, had been a captive longer than him. She'd been forced to flee the South Bank, her home, and live away from her friends, her roots, everything dear to her. Nell was as pleased that Ollie's banishment was over as he was his own, and eager to return with her to the places of their happiest memories together. He hopped to the bottom of the ramp, where the other captives were waiting. The white giant Venus was shining brightly, as if competing with the moon. Nell could taste excitement in the air.

'Ready?' asked Gregory, smiling broadly.

'Ready.'

They went up the ramp, the other captives a few bounds behind. Nell wanted no special treatment. The others had insisted. They passed the rat pit, unusually silent.

'Strange thing,' said Gregory. 'All the rats left in the night.'

As Nell pondered its significance, an ancient male, its face twisted in a permanent snarl, scurried in front of them and leapt into the pit.

'There's always one.'

Gregory laughed. At the top of the ramp, Nell stopped to say goodbye to guards lined along the start of the trail through the heath. Most wished him luck. One used his name for the first time, instead of calling him *varlet*.

As they approached the log span, Nell sensed a flurry of activity on the far side. His vision had deteriorated, though he guessed there could be as many as ten rabbits waiting to see him and his comrades. Half-way over, he stopped at the raised knob, as he had the day he arrived on the island. He sniffed over the side. The Torrent that once spewed white foam now rippled gently black, the current steady, inevitable, unstoppable.

Stamps vibrated along the log from the other captives, impatient for freedom. Nell moved on. The crowd he now saw numbered at least thirty. He climbed off the log and, grinning, gave a *thu-thump* stamp. The ground trembled as the rabbits responded as one to the salute. Nell shivered with joy. And pride.

As he was swamped by greetings and questions and bucks and does wanting to lick and welcome him, he searched the faces and scents for one in particular. The crowd went quiet and parted. Two late-moon rabbits were making their way slowly towards him.

One black. One white.

Ollie and Fleet.

*****

OLLIE'S INFLAMED HIPS and knees were burning, despite the lingering chill of the sleeping moon. Having caught a glimpse of Nell though, nothing was going to stop her completing her journey. When the two friends came together, they cried, they licked and nuzzled as if no-one else existed. Words were lost in the emotion of the embrace. As rabbits gathered around them, stamping and cheering, it was obvious to Ollie that they would have to wait a little longer to be alone together.

'It's time, Nell my friend,' she shouted over the noise, 'for you to resume your rightful position as the leader of...'

'No, Ollie. You have led the rabbits of the South Bank, in exile, far better than I could ever have.'

'Still talking nonsense after all these moons, I see. My work is over, Nell. Now you are free, we… all… are free.'

'There is so much I want to say, Ollie, that we need to…'

His voice was swamped by the impatience of the swarm.

'There'll be plenty of time for talk later, my dear friend,' Ollie shouted. 'A big gathering is waiting for you at Lexa.'

'But…'

'And I need to rest a while. I will follow soon, and join you.'

Ollie watched as Nell was swept away on a flood of excitement.

*****

MORE WELLWISHERS joined the throng of rabbits on the trail between the Torrent and the Chilling Wood, each newcomer wanting to touch noses, or at least glimpse Nell as he made his way to Lexa. Despite the joy, Nell couldn't help notice the colour of the fur around him. Other than Gregory and Fleet, he'd seen no white rabbits since leaving the island. Unlike the last time he passed along this route to his meeting with Drekkel, there were no white bucks in the wood watching for carns. Nell wondered what had changed.

The moon was fading over the trees at their backs, its light replaced by the daystar trying to push through clouds gathering in the east, as the rabbits swarmed to the thicket behind the juniper diamond and found their way blocked by clips. There was a stand-off, until the sergeant in charge spoke.

'I'm sorry, Nell. The junipers are being fixed up. We can't have all these rabbits trudging through the diamond. You'll have to go through there.'

He motioned to a trail disappearing between the hedgerow and the trunk of a holly. Nell could sense the frustration rising behind him. A buck pranced up to the face of the sergeant, bristling.

'Out of our way, Mistle-face. This is *our* bank now. We go where we want.'

'Calm down,' said Nell. 'The sergeant's right. We could damage the junipers.'

Grumbles melted away as Nell ducked under a branch weighed down by bunches of bright red berries. The trail twisted through hollies and spindles, with stale markings suggesting it had been used as an alternate route by carriers. It ended abruptly, a few bounds from where the bourne spilled from deeper into the wood. An old white rabbit was sitting beside the fallen trunk of a silver birch. He pointed his nose at a hole beneath it.

'Through there, sir.'

The tunnel, wide enough for rabbits to pass comfortably both ways, came out on the corner of the diamond near the log bridge. Nell sensed a large gathering of black rabbits on the flats. He crossed the bridge and waited on the far side for the rest of his supporters to join him.

Up above, he could see white rabbits staring nervously at them. Three – a doe and two kittens – detached from the others and came down. They halted a short distance away, and the doe gave a rapid *thu-thump* stamp followed by a jerk. The salute of Claw.

Nell was so astonished, and inspired by the doe's bravery, he went over to thank her. Perhaps this South Bank *was* different to the one he grew up in.

*****

FLEET MOVED in behind Nell's shoulder, as he guided the rabbits to the Mound of Mark. Black bucks patrolled the outer edges, watching for carns. Nell appeared to be overwhelmed. He kept looking around, as if he was uncertain, or had lost something.

'Have you seen Ollie? She should be here, to join me, to... be part of this. She's the real hero.'

'Haven't seen her since you left the island,' said Fleet. 'She was tired after the long trip from the Oakwood, said she needed to rest. Don't worry, Nell. Ollie will be here soon. There's no way she'd miss this.'

The crowd, which had parted to let Nell through, was growing impatient.

'You better talk to them, Nell. These rabbits have been waiting moons upon moons for this moment.'

'Who are those in the front?'

Fleet pointed out Thatch's deputy and rabbits from her inner circle, the new leaders of the Meadow and Drop Warrens, new doms of South Bank warrens from the Point to the Willow, the new leader of the Red Haws, seers from the North Bank, Creamia and warrens to the west.

Nell hesitated.

'This isn't right, Fleet. I feel like an imposter. Ollie should be standing with me up there.'

The crowd stamped, chanting *Nell, Nell, Nell, Nell…*

He climbed reluctantly onto the mound. As he waited for the noise to thin, Fleet marvelled that, although the moons and banishment to the island had worn Nell down, the buck had lost none of the charm he remembered from their first meeting.

'Friends, I stand here as a servant of you, the rabbits of the South Bank. It is only because of *your* courage and selflessness that I am here tonight. I therefore place the remaining moons of my life in your paws.'

The ground vibrated in hysterical stamping, and the chill air melted in frenzied cries of *Nell, Nell, Nell, Nell.* Fleet could see that this troubled the buck, who was looking for Ollie.

'Friends, I thank you. Your praise, however, is misplaced. I am a simple rabbit chosen to lead because of the incredible challenges we faced. The real heroes are the bucks and does and kittens who gave their lives for the struggle, those of you who suffered for the cause, and rabbits like Ollie who organised the resistance during its darkest moons and never gave up. For all the moons I was trapped on the island, it was Ollie who kept up the struggle, spread the word, who finally got the support of the Oakwood.'

Nell pointed his nose at the northerners.

'I thank our friends from the North for the pressure you put on Levi and Drekkel to release my comrades and I, and the support you've given the oppressed rabbits of the South Bank.'

'Better late than never,' grunted the ancient dom of Cocksfoot, who Fleet hadn't recognised earlier. His comment touched off a burst of uncertain laughter and paw-shuffling. Nell smiled, then looked up the rise at the Golden Field.

'I also want to thank Drekkel.'

There were boos and hisses and angry shouts until Nell raised his paw. Fleet was amazed how quickly the rabbits went quiet.

'Friends, it took courage for Drekkel to admit the colour rules were wrong and recognise the suffering it has caused our warrens – black, white and crosser.'

There were cries of *Chase the Mistles into the Torrent, Give the whites a whiff of their own storm, Banish all of them to the island.* Again, Nell hushed the shouters with his paw.

'I do not hate white rabbits. What I hated, was the system of colour rules that made us enemies of one another. There is a shared path, my friends, between the fears of white rabbits and the hopes of black rabbits, and we – all of us, whatever the colour of our fur – must find it. I am opposed to white supremacists, as I am opposed to black supremacists. We must give the enemies of freedom, whether white or black, no opportunity to drag us back down the dark hole. I say that any rabbit who turns his or her back on rules and beliefs and anger based on colour is welcome in the new South Bank. They… are… us.'

The cheers and enthusiastic stamping made the ground rumble. Fleet relaxed. Nell had the crowd in his paw.

'Friends, we must do all we can to persuade our white brothers and sisters that the new South Bank will be a better place for *all* rabbits. It troubles me to hear that since Drekkel's announcement, black rabbits pretending to represent the Cluster have been hassling white rabbits, terrifying their kittens, chasing them from their burrows. Bullies like that have no place here and should be punished. If we – white and black – cannot live in peace, we will never truly be…'

Nell stopped talking, interrupted by a disturbance at the back.

A white doe, her nose, face and chest smeared with blood, hopped forward.

63. The power is ours

RABBITS MOVED ASIDE as the doe, who Nell recognised as the one who had bravely given him the Claw salute, came towards him. She reached the foot of the mound, stumbled, then uttered words that sunk a bramble thorn into Nell's heart.

'Ollie has gone to the field of silence.'

As the shocking news rippled through the gathering, the doe explained to Nell what happened.

'I was taking my kittens to see what was happening on the diamond, when I heard a choking sound from the tunnel. I went to see what it was, and found Ollie, covered in blood from a bad wound to her throat. She was gulping for air. I tried to lick away some of the blood blocking… preventing her speaking. There was nothing I could do for her, sir. I'm so sorry.'

'Did she… say anything… before she…?'

'No, sir. She couldn't. Her throat was… All she could do was stamp her hind leg. Twice. And try to lift her head.'

Nell shook – half in disbelief, half in wonder. Ollie's last act, last message, was to give the Claw salute.

The power is ours.

'I assumed from the wound that she must have been attacked by a fox,' said the doe.

'Then I heard a howl, a crazed howl, further into the tunnel. I hopped towards the sound. And saw the rump of a white rabbit disappear into the Chilling Wood.'

Nell thought of his dear friend, lying in the field of silence, cold, alone, discarded in some white rabbit's side-tunnel. A big part of him passed into the field of silence with her.

Ollie, Ollie. The ray of moonlight sweetening the bleakest night. There were moonbeams in her intelligence, her mischievous wit, in the way she finished Nell's sentences. Moonbeams in her friendship, devotion and loyalty, in her resilience and her countless sacrifices for the cause of freedom. She was so much more than the colour of her fur. Though Nell and Ollie had been apart for so long, he'd thought of his friend every night, every day. Now, just as they'd been reunited, she'd been yanked away. Not only from Nell. From all the rabbits she'd spent her life fighting for.

Nell felt suddenly drained. Like he'd been winded, his breath taken away not by the joy of freedom but the most unexpected, vicious kick to the stomach. He never got the chance to say goodbye.

Fury in the voices of hotheads hollering for revenge jolted him. Some were calling for the white doe to be sent to the field of silence, in the mistaken belief she was Ollie's murderer.

*****

FLEET COULD SMELL the anguish, the grief surging through the crowd, sense the outrage pulsing, jabbing, like a newborn chick chipping away at the inside of an eggshell, impatient to break free. He looked up at Nell, whose gaping mouth and eyes were still absorbing the news, and at the brave white doe, shaking at his paws.

Nell hopped between the doe and the advancing rabbits, protecting her. In that moment, Fleet saw the white doe as a symbol of how fragile the South Bank had become. He wondered if his friend would see Ollie's murder for what it was: an attempt by white supremacists to prevent the inevitable. Evil rabbits who would rather the South Bank collapse down a bottomless hole of hate than be ruled by the majority of rabbits whose fur happened to be a different colour.

Bucks behind Fleet were talking of going into the Chilling Wood to hunt the murderer, who they assumed was one of the embittered former carriers who'd been rampaging the bank, causing mayhem. Another was urging his friends to attack Toria.

Surely this was more pressure than any rabbit could bear, let alone one who'd spent the last twenty-five moons cooped in an island bolt hole, battling his own demons.

Yet there Nell was, facing the likelihood that Ollie's murder would unleash an unstoppable cascade of fury from bucks willing, eager, to pass into the field of silence for the memory of the rabbit Nell had just told them was the real hero of their struggle. And Nell's closest friend.

'Stop,' shouted Nell in a voice of unquestionable authority.

The hot-heads turned back.

'Now is the time,' said Nell, 'for all of us, black and white, to keep calm. To dignify the memory of our comrade, Ollie.'

Not for the first time that day, Fleet was astonished by Nell's self-control. And how ironic, he thought, that a black rabbit and supposed spreader of terror – rather than the white prime – was the one calling for calm. Nell appeared to grow in size in front of them.

'The trunk of a mighty tree that carried the heaviest of burdens has been toppled this night, my friends. A heart whose imagination gave belief to the enslaved has stopped beating. A remarkable rabbit whose gentle words blunted the claws of tyrants has been silenced. But I say, Ollie has not passed. Because the values she gave her life for can never be silenced. The tree has sprouted seedlings to take up the burden. In our hearts, we feel the beat of freedom, and our voices shout to the stars: Black lives matter!'

The crowd took up the call… *Black lives matter, Black lives matter, Black lives matter.*

Fleet was witnessing something remarkable, unlike anything he'd seen.

He glanced around at the other seers and could see they felt it too. Nell raised his paw.

'Friends, this is not the time to be misled by rabbits who want to trample over what is rightfully ours. Now is the time for all South Bankers to stand together against rabbits – of whatever colour – who want to destroy what Ollie gave her life for. Freedom.'

As the rabbits burst into another round of shouting and stamping,

Nell beckoned the white doe to stand beside him.

Fleet heard him ask her to take the last bounds with him.

*****

AS NELL LED THE CROWD towards the Golden Field, he wasn't sure what would happen. It felt right though. That Ollie would have approved. Was hopping beside him – in spirit, if not in body.

He stopped at the rut etched from the base of the blackthorn to the far side of the dale. The forbidden line.

Over his shoulder, he saw hundreds of patient bucks and does who'd waited their entire lives to lay paw on the Golden Field as free rabbits. As Nell jumped over the line, he was thinking of Ollie, Mark, Stephen, Maisy, Henry, Old Nell. All the heroes.

This was for them.

At the top, he peered out over the field. A few white rabbits were fleeing to the east. The rowan, stripped of its leaves, appeared less prominent and commanding in winter, so unlike the evergreen yew of Hilltop, the keeper of knowledge, wisdom, stories.

As the massed line moved on cautiously, the white doe's kittens hopped over to join them. It was like a signal. White rabbits who'd been watching the spectacle mingled in. Nell heard one saying how proud he was to live at last on a free bank.

The mood lightened as they passed the outer holes of Toria and neared the entrance to the prime rabbit's burrow, where they came up against a row of clips. The line stopped. It began to drizzle. Behind and above the barrier of clips sat Drekkel on the prime's terrace, sizing up the black throng. Although he must see that he was heavily outnumbered, Nell wondered if he was still reluctant to surrender power.

There was a standoff, neither side sure what to do. The drizzle strengthened, seeping just as uncomfortably into black fur as white, and loosening the soil under paw. No rabbit moved.

A commotion, starting as a twitching of ears on the fringe of the crowd, grew into a scraping of paws, then gasps as Gregory appeared over the crest, pushing a rabbit into the gap of uncertainty between the black rabbits and Drekkel's clips.

'Here,' announced the guard, 'is Ollie's murderer.'

Nell looked down at the bloodied face of Levi.

*****

MONSTROUS. Fleet could think of no other word for it. As Levi's name soaked through the rabbits in shocked whispers, it was met first with shock, then an anger that surged into rage, coming together in a deafening clamour: *Field of silence, silence, silence…*

Some of the loudest shouts came from white rabbits. The wind howled and the rain intensified, sweeping across the Golden Field in waves. No-one was leaving. To Fleet, it was as if the grey of the clouds was cascading from the sky to the soil, washing away the colour. Nature making a statement.

The wind dropped, the downpour eased. The eclipo sergeant asked the prime what he wanted done with Levi. Drekkel stretched on the terrace to his full height, clenching his claws. The officers shuffled forward. Fleet could see that Drekkel was torn between loyalty to his father and justice.

Nell hopped into the void separating the two sides and stood over Levi. Fleet felt a drawing of breath, as if every rabbit, every creature, every plant and tree, the entire world stood still.

'We say he should live,' said Nell. 'It is time for the madness to end.'

Drekkel, seeing that Nell had the heart to spare his father, came down from the ruler's terrace and motioned with a jerk of his head for the black rabbit to take his place.

Epilogue

CHEERFUL SNOWDROPS that gave their name to the last moon of winter were dotting the fields by the time Nell got the chance to return to the Willow Warren.

He and Fleet had journeyed south from the Golden Field, resting from the daystar as honoured guests at the Point, Hilltop and Platform Warrens, before arriving at the elm stump where Nell was born.

Black and white kittens were playing Patch above the warren's burrows.

Nell was gazing upstream at the willows, already showing masses of soft catkins. Spring was beckoning. He looked at Fleet, and noticed the seer looking in the same direction, worry lining his brow.

'What's troubling you, my friend?'

'Regrets.'

Nell thought back to the moment in the alder when he stared down Levi for the first time.

'Yes, we've all got regrets.'

Fleet, still facing upstream, sighed.

'I was there you know, on the other side of the rindle, hiding in the thicket. The day Vort attacked your father. There were more leaves and blossom in the hedge moon, as you southerners call it, but I saw… everything.'

Nell remembered hearing a cough that day. He sniffed at Fleet. The seer's eyes were moist, his lips quivering.

'There's nothing you could have done.'

'I could have warned Henry, and you.'

'Henry understood exactly what was coming, Fleet, what he was doing. In his own way, he was guiding the warren to a better place, and knew he wouldn't be taking the journey with us. If you'd stamped a warning, he would have ignored you.'

'I find that hard to believe, Nell. That mistake, my decision not to take the side of good over evil, has haunted me ever since.'

Nell looked at the seer.

'We've made more mistakes than most rabbits in our lifetime, Fleet. We all make them. The important thing is whether we learn from them. Change. Become better rabbits. That's exactly what you did, and we've never had the chance to thank you.'

'What do you mean?'

'We know what you did at the end of the hearing. The judge told us when he came to see us on the island.'

'But…'

'You saved our life, Fleet. By becoming involved. By changing.

'So, let's have no more talk of regrets. What's done, is done. The only history worth worrying about is the history being made as we breathe.'

Acknowledgements

This book was written in the shadow and light of Nelson Mandela, whose life reminds us what it means to walk through fire and emerge with grace.

It is also a tribute to those who walked beside him. To the brave souls who rose up against injustice, who endured, resisted, and hoped – in silence or song, in protest or quiet resolve – often at great cost.

To the journalists who bore witness when it was dangerous to do so, and helped the world to see. And to the writers, historians, and storytellers whose work has deepened our understanding of that time – especially Mandela's own words in *Long Walk to Freedom*, which offered not only clarity and insight, but helped shape the emotional heart of this story.

I owe a special debt to Richard Adams and *Watership Down*, which showed me how animals – when written with care, depth, and empathy – can carry the weight of the human spirit.

This novel is offered in that spirit: not as a history, but as a tribute – imagined, yes, but rooted in truth – to those who dreamed of a better world, and dared to make it real.

www.geoffreyrobert.com

AFTERWORDS

The history lesson

BETWEEN THEM, these three rabbits knew all one would ever need to know about the history of the South Bank. And Fleet had all three in one burrow. Bringing them together was easier than he'd expected. Although the sages had different views on the way things had happened, the moons had a way of wearing down hard edges of disagreement. Sworn enemies when they lived in the South, since moving to the North Bank, they'd become friends. A word in their ears from Thatch, the Oakwood prime rabbit, helped, though the bucks appeared genuinely excited by the request for a chat.

Fleet had been eager for the meeting too. He'd arranged for a doe to dig one of the day-holes that had become fashionable among the high-ups in the Oakwood. Day-holes worked best in chambers like this that were close to the surface. Light shone through small holes dug into the side wall of the bluff, illuminating the faces of the three sages.

Holmes, the Oaker, looked all his seventy-five moons. His brow was deeply wrinkled, his double chin rested on the ground, his face crimped in a permanent grimace. Sidney, the black sage, smelt almost as ancient, though he was seven moons younger. His body was shrunken and withered, but the face sparkled intelligence. At sixty-four moons, Fritz, the Mistle, was the youngest. His pure white coat glimmered over a powerful frame that made the gentle, almost doe-like features of his face appear out of place. All three had spent most of their adult lives in the South, though none, Fleet noted, shouldered the scars typical of rabbits so old. He wondered if he was expected to speak first, but was saved by Sidney.

'Black rabbits began arriving on the South Bank over one hundred and twenty moons ago. The first warren was set up at the tree now known as the Hilltop yew. There were no other rabbits on the South Bank at the time.'

'Not true,' said Fritz. 'The Mistles were the first there, and when they arrived there were nothing other than a few brown hares. Not a single black rabbit from the Torrent to the downs. Didn't take your lot long though. Soon as the sweet smell of white rabbit reached their nostrils, they rolled over from those downs like a dark mist.'

Sidney cleared his throat again.

'Through natural growth, and mature bucks moving out to find new territories, black rabbits had established warrens in the fields around Hilltop. Most are still there, roughly where the Border, Low, High and Row Warrens are today. Within another twenty moons, there were warrens as far as the Golden Field to the north and Platform to the south. Hilltop, based around the sacred yew, remained the largest. Most of the others were small, and had little contact with each other.'

'How long ago are we talking about?' Fleet asked, hesitantly.

'Eighty moons or so,' said Holmes. 'Not long before I was born. The first white rabbit to cross from the North to the South Bank did so a few moons after that. He was chased to the field of silence by black rabbits almost immediately, though we didn't know that at the time.'

'That's right,' said Sidney. 'It was the hedge moon, and the hawthorn stunk more than usual. The old does talked about a pale rabbit so sick, it was a blessing to be put out of its misery.'

'Could only have been an Oaker,' said Fritz.

Holmes and Sidney smiled, and Fleet relaxed a little.

'A few moons after that,' Fritz went on, 'some Mistles led by a rabbit called Jan crossed the Torrent and dug burrows on the high plateau beside the stone bridge.'

'Why did they leave the North?' asked Fleet.

'They were harassed for what they believed, banned from doing the simple rituals that were such an important part of the Mistle's life, who they were.'

'They were kicked out because their rituals offended the spirits of the Oakwood,' said Holmes. 'Treating the parasite mistletoe plant as more sacred than the oak was bad enough. Sacrificing does for a little white berry was barbaric.'

Fleet expected an angry reaction, but Fritz's face was calm.

'For the first moon or so, relations with the black warrens on the flat and on the Golden Field were friendly. There were only a few Mistles, so it wasn't in their interests to cause trouble.'

'Black rabbits ignored them,' said Sidney. 'It was only when the whites tried to graze on the Upland that things became... testy.'

'The blacks chose the wrong time to send a Mistle doe into the field of silence,' said Fritz. 'A second lot of Mistles had joined them after being banished from the North. They were spoiling for a fight. The blacks were attacked, and driven off.'

'They didn't stand a chance,' said Sidney. 'The whites were bigger, better organised. The black warrens were made up of small family groups that didn't think of working together. They hightailed for their lives. When another family of blacks living in burrows on the flats saw what was happening, they ran away too.'

There was a pause, then Fritz went on.

'The Mistles now had the entire Golden Field to themselves. They put a lot of effort into a new warren at the rowan, which they intended to become a shrine to their... kind. We Mistles have a fondness for the rowan, often seek out the trees when establishing new warrens. We named it Toria.

'In the winter of that year, the Mistles at the Golden Field brought in some small rabbits called Aidins to do the work – mainly burrow digging. They were given empty holes in an area on the flats. Then during the berry moon, disease hit Toria, wiping out many, including the dom, and both my parents.'

His voice tailed off. The clipped tone of Holmes filled the void.

'It was decided at the Oakwood that a son of the prime rabbit would take over Toria and run it as an outlier warren of the North.'

Fritz recovered his composure quickly, as if eager to give his version of the story.

'The Oakwooders took over the main Toria Warren at the rowan, kicking the Mistles out, although they were allowed to use burrows on the plateau by the stone bridge. So they remained in the Golden Field, able to feed on the plateau, through the Narrows and also along the flats. They had to accept, though were unhappy about it, and their resentment of the Oakwooders festered away.'

Holmes directed his words at Fleet.

'The new rulers of the field – who became known from about that time as Oakers – were not as concerned about the colour of a rabbit's fur as the Mistles, so let blacks live in the burrows on the flats.'

Sidney didn't want to be left out.

'About that time, an ambitious and powerful rabbit, Haska, took over as Patri of Hilltop. Through bullying, he gave the outlying warrens of the field, and the Row and High Warrens to the east, no choice but to accept his control. For the first time, the black warrens were united. There were still no warrens to the south of Hilltop, where the Platform and Willow Warrens are today.

'In the following moon, Haska was sent to the field of silence by one of his half-brothers, who kept control of the black warrens, though lacked his brother's ideas and… flair.'

Fleet shivered at the thought of a rabbit ending his brother's life.

'White rabbits flourished at Toria, and were joined by new arrivals from the Oakwood.'

Fritz butted in.

'As the number of Oakers grew, the Mistles were squeezed into smaller and smaller ranges, and the resentment deepened. Finally, in the early moons of that winter, the Mistles, led by an heroic buck, Erfeti, could stand it no longer. He took the Mistles away from the Golden Field to establish a new warren to the south-west.'

Fleet noticed Sidney tensing.

'Erfeti chose as the site for his new warren a rowan near the Point occupied by black rabbits. The burrows were half-completed when Erfeti was invited by the Patri to share a meal.'

Sidney took this as his cue to speak.

'The Patri genuinely sought peace, was prepared to let the whites stay, as long as they were peaceful and respected the customs of the black rabbits. He expected Erfeti to come alone. When he showed up surrounded by a group of huge bucks, who trampled over sacred ground on the way, then stalked round and round them, baring their teeth, the Patri became alarmed. He agreed to let the whites have their warren, and suggested they celebrate their arrival with some refreshments. The whites were given dry hops, and failed to notice the large number of black rabbits closing in on them throughout the night. At a signal from the Patri, they pounced. The Patri then had his bucks attack the half-completed warren, drive the intruders out, chase them over the rindle and into the Chilling Wood.'

Fleet cringed, thinking of the needless violence, the pain that must have been inflicted, the terror those rabbits must have felt during the attacks.

'You alright?'

'Sorry. I'm fine, please go on.'

It was Fritz who spoke next.

'I can't let my friend's version of events go unchallenged. Erfeti wanted peace, but was betrayed. He took a number of rabbits as a sign of respect, as was the Mistle custom. They assumed from the friendliness of the Patri that the blacks were impressed, especially when he said they could complete their warren, and organised a feast to celebrate. They didn't know they were being drugged with hops. As they prepared to leave, they were stormed by hundreds of bucks who rushed from the shadows. A survivor later reported that the Patri ordered his rabbits to *toss the outsiders into the field of silence*. The blacks then attacked the half-completed warren, ending the lives of innocent and defenceless does and kittens. A band of Mistles, led by Erfeti's son Tory, were off foraging at the time, so dodged the bloodbath. They returned and were attacked by the black hordes, but managed to flee and hide in the Chilling Wood. They were joined there by stragglers who also escaped the massacre. For most of that winter they survived in the wood on leaves and mushrooms. Tory organised, trained and inspired his supporters to prepare for revenge.'

The emphasis on *revenge* saddened Fleet. It was a word soaked in hate, at the root of so many problems. Most of them unnecessary, in his view. Could this have been the case here? Could it be that a small misunderstanding over different customs, over the meaning of Erfeti's rabbits circling the Patri, puffballed into something that got out of control, took on a life of its own? So many disagreements were based on ignorance, fear of the unknown, unwillingness to talk honestly. To ask questions and listen to the answers. Rather than using language as if it was teeth or claws. Like that disgusting Mistle phrase, *varlet*.

Fleet sniffed the sages. They smelt virtually identical. If only Vort and his kind could be here with their nostrils and minds open rather than clogged by ignorance, they'd see that scent came from the field a rabbit lived in, the plants he or she ate, not the colour of fur.

Those black rabbits being surrounded by circling whites would have been terrified. All it would have taken would have been one rabbit to ask one question, and the misunderstanding could have been cleared up. Instead, both sides leaped to conclusions, and that single act could have changed the passage of history. Fleet had always considered history something solid, definite. Was he wrong? Was it more like a leaf in fall, tossed this way and that by the breeze, something that could be changed by a single act?

'When food had become almost impossible to find,' continued Fritz, 'one of the old ones discovered mistletoe growing in a poplar. It was an omen.'

Holmes raised his eyes to the roof, though let his friend go on.

'Tory took them out into the field. This time they were prepared for an attack. They began feeding around a stump not far from a badger sett. The black rabbits took the bait, and reports came in that a large band of the Patri's bucks was approaching from the south. Tory had deliberately chosen a strong position. To one side, the rindle was too deep to cross, to the north a large ditch made attack from that direction difficult. The south was protected by the Chilling Wood, which Tory knew the blacks would not enter. This left only one channel for the attack – from the east, and they could do so only in small enough numbers at a time for the whites to handle. This time the blacks were the ones light in the head, for they expected another easy victory.'

Sidney rose to speak, and Fritz showed no objection.

'Word reached the Patri that the whites were back and taunting them. So the Patri sent wave upon wave of bucks in a series of attacks on the white position around the stump. The whites behaved like cowardly does, refusing to come out of their hole. There were a few losses of particularly brave black rabbits.'

'Nonsense,' said Fritz. 'Masses of black bucks swarmed over the field, heavily outnumbering the whites. Apart from a few cuts and bruises, there was not one white casualty. Many blacks, however, passed into the field of silence. Several fell into the rindle, colouring the water red. It was a fine example of the superiority of the brain over the claw. Not to mention Tory's astute use of the stump.'

Sidney was on his paws again.

'After the horror at the stump, the black warrens split. One of the Patri's brothers, who was dom of the Point Warren, agreed to let the whites develop their new warren at the rowan on higher ground to the east, not that he had a choice.'

'And what happened to the Patri?' asked Fleet.

'He went back to Hilltop, tail between his legs, and was soon overthrown by a more moderate rabbit – the father of the current Patri.'

'The Mistles,' said Fritz, 'settled around the rowan up the slope from the Point, and flourished. There was peace for a few moons, through the spring and summer, until the Oakwood prime tasted a juniper.'

'What's a berry got to do with history?' asked Fleet.

'Quite a lot, actually.'

It was Holmes.

'The Oakwood whites – Oakers as you call them – who had settled over the Torrent at Toria, enjoyed the hazels and junipers, though didn't harvest them efficiently. They claimed a sort of guardianship over the junipers, which wasn't challenged by the blacks because – correct me if I'm wrong Sidney – they weren't particularly interested in them.'

'You're not far off,' said the black sage. 'Our lot found the junipers pleasant enough to eat, if a bit peppery, but not worth the effort to harvest.'

Holmes went on.

'The whites feasted themselves sick and then struggled to last until the next season's crop. Then two smart brothers called Nicholas and Diederick came to the Oakwood and discovered there were no juniper bushes on this side of the Torrent. The Oakwood prime had never tasted one of the berries. The brothers tried the local delicacy, which as we all know are acorns. They didn't like them at first, as few rabbits do, because of the tanins. Eventually, the taste grew on them.

'They asked if they could take one of the acorns to show their friends in the South, promising to return with a juniper for the Oakwood prime to try. Their friends thought, as they suspected on their first tasting, the acorn was foul. The brothers had proved, though, it was possible for a rabbit to carry an acorn that far. With practice and bigger mouths, they could achieve it quite comfortably.

'For the plan they were dreaming up to work, they had to make sure it was also possible to carry juniper berries the other way. Their first attempt failed because they'd chosen berries too ripe. They tried again using firmer fruit, and made it all the way. The Oakwood prime loved them, and the great cross-Torrent trade was born.

'Such became the desire for junipers in the North, they gladly swapped them for acorns, which over time, became as sought-after by the whites of the South Bank. It also became known that there was demand on the North Bank for hazelnuts and chestnuts, so these were added to the trade.

'Everything was fine until the whites in the South got tired of all the work required to harvest the berries and nuts. Collecting junipers was a dirty, painful business. And waiting for squirrels to hoard hazelnuts, then raiding their cache, though suiting the white rabbits' liking for sitting round doing little, soon became rather tiresome. And carrying a chestnut can be plain hard work. That's where Rabon comes into it.'

'Rabon?' asked Fleet.

Sidney interrupted.

'May I?'

'Of course,' said Holmes, motioning for the black sage to take up the story.

'Rabon was a wily white rabbit. It was his idea to use black rabbits to do the dirty work, getting the junipers and harvesting the nuts. Strong – if not particularly smart – bucks were used. Some passed into the field of silence during the cold moons of winter. So, during the spring and summer, in preparation for the harvest, black rabbits from country warrens were lured to the Golden Field to replace them and prepare for the work.

'Going paw in paw with the use of black bucks to do the hard work were the countless black does used as servants in the burrows of Toria. Over the moons of softening, white does developed a hatred for burrowing, like bucks of any colour. Some of the more uppity ones, it was said, wouldn't have been able to dig a hole to save themselves.

'Quite right,' agreed Holmes.

'What most black rabbits didn't grasp,' said Sidney, 'was the tricks the whites were using to keep them in line and divided. Little more than slaves. They spread the word throughout the black warrens that life in the Golden Field was like permanent spring for rabbits of all colours. The whites also *rewarded* the occasional carefully-selected black rabbit a privileged lifestyle. Some of those yes-rabbits were paraded around the countryside as living proof of the advantages of moving to the Golden Field.

'Many rabbits were taken in by this deception. Me included. That's not something I'm proud of. I should have seen what was happening, done something about it.'

Fleet could feel Sidney's eyes on him as he nosed at the soil in front of his paws.

'One or two of the black yes-rabbits were *allowed* to live in retirement at the warrens of their birth, under the envious noses of their kins and the searching ears of the white governors.'

'Of course,' said Fritz, 'all this was controlled by the Oakers. So, you can imagine, during that summer, the resentment of the Mistles was at breaking point.'

'Quite true,' said Holmes. 'The harvest was due. The Oakwood prime, addicted to juniper, became worried about growing rumours that the Mistles were planning to take over Toria and the Golden Field. So he invaded the South Bank.'

Fritz chuckled.

'The Oakers expected an easy victory. The Mistles, though, had spent moons sharpening their claws against the blacks. They understood there was more than one way to fight, were used to spending long periods above, away from their warrens. The Oakwood rabbits from the North were soft. They stuck together like flocks of birds, only advancing after digging temporary burrows. Mistles were better suited to the needs of rabbits defending frontier warrens, and the Oakwooders were held back by outdated ideas about how to fight, and high-up leaders who refused to share the same burrows as their fighting bucks. The Mistles believed passionately in their cause, whereas the Oakwooders were away from home and had far less appetite for sacrifice.

'After the Mistles had repelled the first invasion from the North, they tried to stop Oakwooders who were hiding in the burrows of the rowan warren from leaving.'

'That,' said Holmes, 'was their big mistake. The rest of the Oakwooders, reinforced by recruits from the North, came to their rescue, sent the Mistle leader into the field of silence and chased his bucks away.'

Fleet expected Fritz to be downcast, but he was smiling.

'They thought that was the end of it. Then through that sleeping moon, the Mistles formed into bands of hit-and-hightail fighters. One particularly notorious band was led by Schickler.'

Fleet had heard of him, though couldn't remember when.

'He was the father of Governor Vort,' said Fritz. 'These bands of Mistles harassed the Oakwooders and were successful. Too successful. Frustrated the Oakwooders so much, they started fighting dirty themselves.'

'You could hardly blame them,' said Holmes.

Fritz frowned at him, and for the first time Fleet felt tension between the two sages.

'They will never, ever, be forgiven for what they did next.'

Holmes shook his head as Fritz continued quietly.

'They destroyed Mistle burrows. Blocked entrances. Dug chasms atop passages to let rain flood through. Innocent does and kittens, who until then had been left out of the fighting, were rounded up and driven over a log onto an island in the Torrent. Many never made it to the other side. They fell into the gorge and were swept away. Mothers jumped in to rescue their kittens and drowned with them. Of those that got to the island, half passed into the field of silence from disease. Mainly the kittens.'

Fleet was shocked. He thought of his own kittens, imagining them being chased over a slippery log, the terror as they lost their balance.

He thought of another time. Another stretch of water. The rindle. A pair of eyes staring up at him. Filled with shame. He was shaking, and glanced up quickly to see if anyone had noticed. Holmes was licking his paws. Sidney was looking away. Fritz was staring straight at him.

'You okay?'

'Fine,' he lied.

'These barbaric tactics by the Oakwooders gradually snuffed out the Mistle resistance. By that owl moon, gutted by the passings, captures and desertions, only five small bands of starving, exhausted and dispirited Mistles remained free. They decided four to one to surrender to the Oakwooders. The one voting against was Vort's father.

'The Oakwooders believed that was the end of the Mistles and what they stood for. The humiliation though, particularly the treatment of those kittens and does on the island, had achieved the opposite. It convinced Mistles like Schickler and Vort, who was one of a tiny number to escape from the island, that their cause was just.'

Sidney, who had been quiet for some time, took up the tale.

'No sooner had the fight between the whites finished, the bank was hit by the bane. Rabbits – mostly blacks – went down like leaves in fall.'

'It wasn't only the blacks,' said Holmes. 'No warrens were immune. The white rabbits of Toria suddenly had too few does to work in their burrows, and were worried about not having enough workers for the next harvest. The Oaker buck in charge of the South Bank at the time came up with an idea that blacks should be brought in from outlying warrens, and used to re-populate the bank, or more importantly, work on the bank.'

'That summer,' said Fritz, 'Schickler was persuaded to go over the downs to bring them in.'

'Why would he have agreed to that?' asked Fleet.

It was Sidney who answered.

'He was given control of the Hilltop fields. So he went and… got them and returned to dig burrows at a rowan in the Willow field. The blacks were uprooted from their burrows, and some passed on the way to the rindle. More would have perished, if it wasn't for the efforts of a wily rabbit who became known as Old Nell. The father of Henry, who I believe you… knew.'

'It's getting late,' said Fritz. 'Perhaps we should finish it there.'

'Quite,' said Holmes.

'Not till he's heard the end, up until now,' insisted Sidney. 'Schickler imposed rules based on the colour of a rabbit's fur. It was his idea to have forbidden lines at times of food shortages, which restricted black grazing, and reserved the best for the whites. And to keep the new black recruits in their place, some of the colour rules of Schickler were copied by other white doms and by the buck in charge at Toria, who began calling himself the head rabbit of the Golden Field.

'Schickler and Old Nell passed into the field of silence within a couple of moons of each other. Henry became dom of the warren at the rindle, and Vort took over as governor. He inherited all the worst traits of his father, and some.'

Joy's legacy

IF TREES COULD TALK, few would believe the Hilltop yew's story. It was seeded at the beginning of the sixth century, almost one hundred years before the hedge surrounding the field was laid. As the tree got higher, fresh shoots grew from its base. Those that survived thickened until they merged with the main trunk, which over centuries expanded into a colossus. But although the yew exuded strength and longevity to the outside world, its core slowly rotted away to create a void.

It was that void which hid a farm maid from marauding soldiers of the Viking king Swein, who swept through the area in 1006. More than two hundred years later, a family from Devon sheltered in the yew from a storm that delayed their pilgrimage to the shrine of St Thomas a'Becket.

On a hot afternoon in June 1381, the head of a poll tax collector swung from a noose tied to a branch inside the yew, cheered on by farm workers incensed at having to pay one shilling for each of their own heads. Another group of agricultural workers used the tree as a rendezvous point after a night out wrecking threshing machines in 1830. Between those times, the floor of the yew provided a mattress for a soldier from the army of Oliver Cromwell and the wife of the local lord.

The farm was bought by Robert McCarthy in 1946, and four years later the void in the yew was discovered by his daughter, Joy. It became her secret place. She was six, and already besotted by the creatures inhabiting the meadows and hedgerows and woods. It was a love affair she never grew out of, even after she left to live in London the day after her twenty-first birthday.

Robert continued to run the farm, rotating the fields between pasture and crops, keeping the hedges in order the old way with handsaws and billhooks. All over the countryside, farmers were cutting down hedges, hocking off their livestock, ploughing in chemicals and creating huge fields of potatoes or carrots or peas. Robert would have none of it, until he saw the magazine.

Ironically, the copy of *National Geographic* had been sent to him by Joy. She subscribed to more wildlife and environmental journals than some public libraries, and was kind enough to send the odd one to the farm, once she'd processed it. Robert wondered if she ever really read them. Whenever he visited the little flat in Wimbledon, her desk would be covered in a tablecloth of clippings, every one with scribbles in the margin and paragraphs daubed with highlighter pens.

Joy had formed a one-woman lobby group to save the country's hedgerows and the creatures that relied on them. She spent all her spare time, and much of her working hours, writing letters to the editors of newspapers all over Britain, to local councillors, members of Parliament, heads of farmers' groups, fertiliser companies, anyone she viewed as a likely enemy. Even the secretaries of fencing contractors and wire manufacturers tasted the venom from her typewriter.

It was in March 1996, on one of her too infrequent visits to see her father, when he dropped the bombshell. He was too old to maintain the hedgerows, and the bulldozer was booked for the first of April. Joy was in a state of shock. But as she looked across at Robert slumped in his chair, looking every one of his eighty years, she couldn't bring herself to be indignant. Until he mentioned the magazine.

'Cows'll have to go as well, to make way for the spuds.'

'Spuds?'

'Ones that won't wander 'cross the road,' he said with a wicked grin.

Senility is not a word one uses in the presence of one's elderly father. It was, however, at the tip of Joy's tongue as she watched Robert waddle to the sideboard and pick up the *National Geographic*.

'It's all in here,' he said, taking out the leather bookmark and placing the magazine in her lap. Three sentences had been underlined with a thick pencil.

Once you no longer have animals, you don't need field boundaries. Potatoes, after all, don't wander across the road. In such an environment, traditional features like hedges and small woods are not just unnecessary, but a positive nuisance.

'You can't be serious, father.'

'First of April. And the same firm bringing the bulldozer puts up the wire fence. It's a good deal. I've asked around.'

'What about the animals living in the hedgerows? Have you asked them? Look here,' she said, recalling a figure in the article, '*hedgerows are home to more than 800 kinds of plants and countless small animals*. Look at the picture. There are badgers living in those hedges. And foxes and rabbits and shrews and voles. And look, dormice and squirrels and moles, not to mention the birds. Oh, the birds. Think of the nuthatches, the tits, the jays, the warblers. The wrens. The tiny wrens. Please father, tell me you're not serious.'

But there was nothing to tell. The old man had fallen asleep in his chair. Joy fumed all the way back to London, trying to think of a way to stop the destruction of the hedgerows and the certain death of all those creatures.

The solution came in a way she neither expected nor would ever have wished. Robert was hit by a car while out measuring a hedgerow with a length of twine. The driver, a tourist from New Zealand, was too busy admiring the hedge to see the old man, who died in hospital before Joy could get to his side.

The irony of the accident was not lost on the grief-stricken daughter, but it was only when cards for the funeral service arrived that she realised the significance of the date, printed above her favourite photograph of Robert standing outside the farmhouse with his border terrier, Harvey. The first of April. Joy was now owner of the farm. After all those years coming off second best in her battle with deputy editors and ignorant secretaries who wouldn't know the difference between a hedgerow and a hedgehog, she was suddenly in a position of power. She acted immediately, cancelling the bulldozer.

As the last carload headed down the driveway after the wake, she pulled on a pair of her father's Wellingtons and, with Harvey on a tight leash, headed for the yew. It was there and then the idea was born. Why not let the farm revert to its wild state?

Once her mind was made up, Joy attacked the project with customary vengeance. Her enemies became the fences, the wires, the gates, the posts, the rusting wrecks of farm machinery lying in the fields. If it wasn't growing, it wasn't staying.

Every weekend, Joy drove to the farm and waged war. It took

longer than expected, but by the middle of December she was satisfied. The only obvious signs of humanity left on the farm were so overgrown, that to remove them would kill something with more right to be there. She decided, at the last minute, to leave the swing bridge, the logs across the rindle and bourne, and the aspen trunk to the old quarry on the island. She'd forgotten about the mesh fence across the rindle.

On Christmas Day, Joy held a party inside the yew with four kindred spirits, each of whom she'd stalked through *letters to the editor* columns. They opened a bottle of champagne to celebrate the giving back of the land, and no-one noticed that the cork didn't return to earth. Later that afternoon, when her friends had gone, Joy hugged the trunk of the yew, and left the fields to the animals.

Glossary

Aidin: A small black-furred rabbit from a warren far to the north of the Oakwood.

Bane: A viral disease known to humans as myxomatosis, which can spread quickly through wild warrens, killing many rabbits.

Bitch: A female weasel.

Black Rabbit of Inle: A character from Richard Adams' wonderful novel, *Watership Down*. The Black Rabbit of Inle represented death.

Boar: A male badger or stock dove.

Bourne: A medium-sized stream.

Bruiser: A tough rabbit, an enforcer.

Buck: A male rabbit.

Bumble: A rabbit caught stealing, fighting or slacking off at work, named after the short-tongued bees that bite holes in the base of flowers to steal nectar.

Carn: A natural enemy of rabbits, such as a fox, stoat, weasel, owl or other bird of prey. Short for carnivore, or meat-eater.

Carrier: A buck whose job is to carry nuts and juniper berries between the South and North Banks.

Chinning: Rabbits rub their chin on plants or objects, releasing scented fluid from glands under their jaw, to claim territory or show dominance.

Circle: A group or meeting of advisers to a dom, head or prime rabbit.

Clip: Short for eclipo (see below); a slang term used by black rabbits.

Combe: A narrow, usually dry, valley.

Creamia: A powerful warren to the west of the Oakwood.

Crosser: A rabbit whose father and mother had different-coloured fur.

Dale: A valley.

Dayfall: Dusk.

Dayspring: Dawn.

Daystar: The sun.

Dewlap: A fold of skin under the neck of a rabbit.

Doe: A female rabbit.

Divine: The creator of life, similar to a human God.

Diviner: A rabbit who spreads the word of The Divine; similar to a human priest or religious teacher.

Dom: The dominant rabbit, or leader, of a small warren.

Eclipo: Bucks who enforce the rules of a warren, similar to human police.

Falsie: A nut infested with weevil.

Field of silence: Death. When a rabbit dies, it passes into the field of silence.

Flim-flam: A hunting technique used by foxes.

Flower of silence: The tansy, which is rubbed on the corpse of a rabbit who has passed into the field of silence, to keep away flies and worms.

Foxtail: A bitter grass, named after its long seed heads which look like fox tails.

Hearing: A gathering to decide if a rabbit accused of serious rule-breaking is guilty or innocent, similar to a trial in a human court.

Hightail: To run quickly.

High-up: An important rabbit, such as a member of a head rabbit's circle.

Keep: A hole, or holes, in which rabbits are kept captive, like a human prison.

Kernel: The soft, edible part of a nut.

Kin: A half-brother or sister.

Kitten: A young rabbit, referred to as a kit for short.

Leaf-fall: Autumn.

Mast: A bumper crop of acorns. Some rabbits believe oak trees have masts to flood the ground with more acorns than can be eaten by animals, so some will be left on the ground to grow into new trees.

Minder: A rabbit whose job is to protect a high-up, similar to a human bodyguard.

Mistle: A descendant of rabbits from a warren far to the east, who consider the mistletoe sacred.

Mistletoe: A parasitic plant that grows on the branches of trees such as hawthorn, poplar and ash, producing clusters of white berries.

Moon names: Rabbits mark the passing of the year by the moons, and the names they give to each relate to the natural world around them. January is the **owl moon** because of barn owls hunting day and night. February is the **snow moon** for the snowdrops that bloom that time of the year. March is called the **peacock moon** for the peacock butterflies that overwinter in rabbit burrows and are considered lucky omens. April is the **blue moon** after the bluebells that flower in mid-spring. May is the **hedge moon** for the blooming of two common hedgerow plants, the hawthorn and mayflower. June is the **elder moon**, named after the plant of the same name. July is the **hopping moon**. Some rabbits believe it is so named because of the habit of many to hop-around during mid-summer, but the origin of the name relates to the hop plant, which flowers that time of the year. August is the **web moon** for the spiders' webs common on the ground. September is the **berry moon** after the ripening blackberries. October is the **ivy moon** for the plant flowering in mid-autumn (or leaf-fall, as rabbits call it). November is the **privet moon**, named for the ripening privet berries. December is the **sleeping moon** for the hibernating animals. Rabbits from the Oakwood Warren refer to October as the *acorn moon*.

Oaker: A descendant of rabbits who moved to the South Bank from the Oakwood.

Oakwood: The largest warren on the North Bank, named after the wood surrounding it.

Parting: The Mistle whites' master plan to keep white and black rabbits apart.

Pass: To die; to pass into the field of silence.

Patri: The traditional leader of black rabbits of the South Bank.

Prime rabbit: The leader of a group of warrens, similar to a human prime minister or president.

Prince With A Thousand Enemies: Another character from *Watership Down*; also known as El-Ahrairah, the legendary ruler of all rabbits.

Rindle: A small stream.

Ruffian: A rough, violent rabbit, often part of a pack of troublemakers.

Sage: A wise rabbit who passes on knowledge, similar to a human teacher.

Sap: A black rabbit working as an informer for the white rabbits of Toria.

Seer: A rabbit whose job is to observe happenings and report to the leader and other rabbits of their warren. Similar to a human journalist.

Sentinel: A rabbit responsible for protecting a warren from carns and attacks from outsiders.

Sergeant: The officer in charge.

Square of Erfeti: A group of four stars – Alpheratz, Scheat, Markab and Algenib – known to humans as the Great Square of Pegasus.

Steward: An adviser to a dom or head rabbit, usually specialising in an activity such as carn management, food storage, burrow improvements.

Stopper: A black rabbit, usually overweight, rostered to sit in front of a hole to conceal its entrance from clips.

Stupe: A rabbit stupes when it becomes so frightened, its muscles *freeze* and it is unable to move.

Supremacist: A rabbit who believes he or she and other rabbits of the same colour are superior to all other rabbits.

Tim: Short for timothy grass, the most nutritious for rabbits.

Toria: The largest warren on the South Bank.

Torrent: A wide, swift-flowing river.

Varlet: An offensive term for a rabbit with black fur.

Vixen: A female fox.

Warden: The rabbit, or head guard, in charge of a keep.

While: To rabbits, a *while* can be any length of time from about ten human minutes to several hours.

About the author

As a young journalist in the early 1980s, while colleagues and friends in New Zealand were settling onto career treadmills or heading for their OE (overseas experience) in Europe, Geoffrey quit his job, grabbed a backpack and flew to Africa on a one-way ticket with his wife, Sue.

Cape Town to Cairo in eight months, on less than NZ$10 a day, changed his outlook on life, leading to decades of adventure and a passion for backing the underdog, the vulnerable, the dispossessed.

Through travel and work as a journalist, political press secretary, news director and volunteer, Geoffrey has witnessed first-hand the swelling disparities in wealth and influence at the root of many of the world's problems. From the orderly streets of London to the chaotic bus stations of Kenya, the bountiful swagger of Sydney to the clogged alleys of India, the seductive dazzle of Times Square to the dirt floor poverty of Timor Leste.

His earlier novels, *The Alo Release*, *Finding Fabi*, and *The Ghost Shipment*, propel readers from armchairs and devices into hair-raising missions to exotic and unfamiliar places with everyday characters pitted against powerful vested interests. Each story is seasoned with values Aotearoa New Zealand and Kiwis are renowned for: independent, ethical, authentic, edgy. And fun.

Geoffrey and Sue live in Rangiora, New Zealand, with their feisty border terrier, Harvey.

www.geoffreyrobert.com

Nine days.
Three fugitives.
One momentous outcome.

Nine days before the global release of a genetically-modified seed coating set to make starvation history, the IT advisor for an environmental group receives a cryptic email from an old friend working for the seed corporation. The email triggers a frantic manhunt from the glass towers of Los Angeles to the towering rainforests of New Zealand as the corporation's security chief tries to track down and silence the English IT advisor and his colleagues – an American biologist and Kiwi eco-warrior, Jay Duggan.

As the clock ticks down to the much-anticipated and highly stage-managed release of the coated seeds, the trio are pitched against ruthless corporate thugs, law enforcement agencies, politicians, journalists and bloggers... and the overwhelming weight of world opinion as they race to unravel the truth behind the email.

For more details:
www.geoffreyrobert.com

An unexplained death.
A chilling conspiracy.
A daughter's search for answers.

When brilliant but emotionally-tortured New York journalist Bec Corelli learns her father has died mysteriously on vacation in India, she walks out on her job and heads to Delhi.

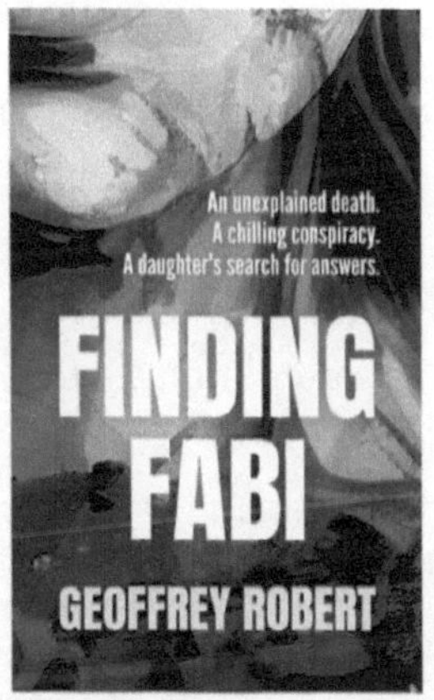

Pharmaceutical CEO Ernst Reiniger, facing ruin over a failed drug, has hatched a chilling plan to save his 300-year-old family company. With a lethal virus decimating the Mexican resort city of Cabo San Lucas and threatening a global pandemic more deadly than Covid, Reiniger has the inside running on producing a vaccine.

As Bec chases leads across India, supported by blogger Mike Duggan and New Zealand eco-warrior Jay Duggan, she is confronted by powerful forces determined to stop her discovering the truth about her father.

For more details:
www.geoffreyrobert.com

Drugs and political intrigue collide in a high stakes pursuit of power, justice and redemption

When a young American tourist dies in a surfing accident in Bali while high on cocaine, his billionaire father hires the investigative journalism team known as Aristotle to track down the drug kingpin ultimately responsible for his son's death.

Ped Garland, a maverick with a troubled past who is campaigning to become the Republican presidential candidate, captivates voters with his candid and unorthodox approach to politics, and bold plan to end the nation's drug nightmare.

With Garland's bid gaining momentum, the journalists' investigation leads them from the exotic resorts and nightclubs of Bali to the lawless backstreets of Colombia, seemingly tranquil neighborhoods of New Zealand and rarefied halls of Washington's elite as they battle powerful adversaries determined to protect their secrets.

For more details:

www.geoffreyrobert.com